The Secret Shopper's Revenge

The
Secret Shopper's
Revenge

Kate Harrison

W F HOWES LTD

This large print edition published in 2008 by
W F Howes Ltd
Unit 4, Rearsby Business Park, Gaddesby Lane,
Rearsby, Leicester LE7 4YH

1 3 5 7 9 10 8 6 4 2

First published in the United Kingdom in 2008
by Orion Books

A CIP catalogue record for this book is available
from the British Library

ISBN 978 140742 500 9

Typeset by Palimpsest Book Production Limited,
Grangemouth, Stirlingshire
Printed and bound in Great Britain
by MPG Books Ltd, Bodmin, Cornwall

FSC
Mixed Sources
Product group from well-managed
forests and other controlled sources
Cert no. SGS-COC-2953
www.fsc.org
© 1996 Forest Stewardship Council

To Jenny Eden and Geri Lewis,
the best shopping companions a girl could wish for.

CHRISTMAS SHOPPING

At Christmas, we need to seduce the shopper all over again, like a spouse trying to reignite the flame. The temptations elsewhere are multiple – we can't expect fidelity. So we must convince her that we are the only ones who can make her dream come true . . .

From *The Art and Science of Seducing Shoppers: a Seasonal Guide for Retailers*

CHAPTER 1

EMILY

Once upon a time, there was a country bumpkin who dreamed of moving to London.

(That's me, in case you hadn't guessed.)

From the attic bedroom she shared with her very ugly sister in their parents' hay barn (21 Haybarn Close, Rowminster, Somerset) the young bumpkin imagined the city in every detail. A world away from the cowpats and cornfields (and the tacky annual carnival and the swearing, scrumpy-drinking teenagers).

In London, there would be Swarovski crystal Christmas lanterns lighting up the night sky. There would be black chariots to sweep her from one enchanted store to the next. There would be elegant shop assistants inviting her to try on their designer goods or taste their gourmet foods. By association, she would become elegant herself: shopping would transform her.

In time, the dream faded, as dreams do. The bumpkin settled down to real life with a charmer called Duncan Prince, a job in the bank, and a little pink line which appeared on a magic wand

3

she weed on first thing one cider-crisp autumn morning. London was further away than ever.

Then one day, the fairy godmother recruitment consultant called up charming Mr Prince and offered him the job of his life-assurance fantasies.

In London.

And so – as if by magic – here I am.

Garnett's Department Store ('The Greatest Goods on Earth Brought to the Greatest Store on Earth') is the most gorgeous shop in the world. Back in April as we packed our belongings into orange crates for the big move, I imagined shopping here for our first Christmas. I'd order a black chariot . . . well, a cab, to take me to Oxford Street. I'd stock up on last-minute treats for a festive extravaganza chez me and Duncan, in our extensively refurbished Victorian cottage in West London. My shopping list would be as lavish as Nigella's: light-as-air panettone with chocolate chestnut filling, spicy German tree-shaped biscuits with silver balls in place of fairy lights, orchard fruit mince pies with all-butter shortbread pastry, a tub of pine-nut-and-clementine stuffing for our pre-ordered organic turkey, and the essential watermelon-sized truckle of red-waxed Cheddar cheese to remind me of home.

My Burberry-lined willow shopping basket (as modelled by Kate Moss) would be tucked under my arm, crammed with more goodies: a vintage lace angel to grace our twelve-foot spruce, a periwinkle-blue cashmere cardigan and an organic

4

fleecy rabbit for our new baby, a perfect white shirt and miniature Vespa cufflinks for Duncan. Assistants dressed in Garnett's crimson uniform would giftwrap each item so you could barely see the paper for bows.

At home, Duncan would be busy preparing a supper party for our new neighbours: city lawyers on one side, a theatrical agent and an award-winning documentary maker on the other. Canapés courtesy of Tesco (with the packaging hidden in the compost bin, so you might be fooled into thinking they're from Harrods). Wine from our new-found supplier (instead of that evil scrumpy from Duncan's dad's off-licence). Ripe French cheeses, rich as clotted cream, with charcoal crackers that stain your tongue black. On the CD player, an up-and-coming girl singer would be in mid-lament. Our real fire sizzles with sustainable smoke-free wood, topped with orange peel for festive aromas. Our baby stirs, watching Daddy with gurgling alertness, while in town, Mummy eyes up silk pyjamas that skim her Pilates-toned-virtually-untouched-by-childbirth body. She hesitates, trying to choose between the lavender and the aqua silk, before putting both in her basket, with gloriously guilty pleasure. A treat to herself for putting in place the ingredients for the *perfect* family celebration.

'Oi. Is the kid yours?'

'Eh?' I am in Garnett's, sure enough. But something's changed. I look at the purple face of the

5

woman standing next to me, and follow her gaze to the child in the pushchair.

Freddie. Freddie! *Shit.* 'Yes, yes, sorry, that's my son. Is everything OK?' Though even as I speak I know it's not OK. Not even remotely OK.

I feel a sharp elbow in my back as a frazzled businessman forces his way through, tugging half a dozen glossy Garnett's bags behind him. The purple-faced woman holds up a distinctly non-organic, not-fleecy-for-a-very-long-time rabbit in a deathly shade of grey. 'He dropped this.'

I take it from her, and wedge it into the nest of carrier bags in the Fredster's pushchair. *Pull yourself together, Emily.* You're turning into that pop-art poster – I LEFT THE BABY ON THE BUS.

As if sensing my appalling amnesia – it can only have lasted a millisecond, surely? – Freddie begins to bawl his adorable head off. The store PA system plays *In the Bleak Midwinter* and it's all I can do not to bawl along with my son.

Garnett's is pretty overwhelming for a thirty-year-old, so it must be terrifying for a six-month-old. The singing snowmen are aggressively camp, and the in-store Santa is being played by last year's X-Factor winner (and I thought it was just policemen who were getting younger).

This *is* the Christmas I'd dreamed about. I *am* stocking up on last-minute items for our first Christmas in our unconverted upper floor maisonette in the arse end of Shepherd's Bush, a place we bought because the estate agents randomly

6

added 'village' to the name of the main street and we thought Lime Village sounded lovely. Which presumably makes us the Lime Village Idiots.

In my plastic folding plaid holdall (as modelled by sheikhs' wives trying to buy up the entire contents of the Marble Arch branch of M&S), I have a *mini*-panettone, the German tree biscuits, and a Cheddar truckle the size of a Granny Smith. But no stuffing: my Turkey Breast for One comes pre-stuffed.

The newly purchased angel – a little large for our four-foot plastic tree – already looks the worse for wear. Freddie somehow got hold of her and gave her a damned good chew. Her lacy wings are now earthbound with carrot and spittle.

Last Christmas, just after the appearance of the little pink line, everything was blissful. 'Next year,' Duncan kept saying as he patted my still-flat stomach, 'next year we'll give Junior the best Christmas a kid can have. We'll pull out all the stops, Em.'

Duncan is, no doubt, pulling out all the stops at this very minute. Lighting candles, or preparing a supper party for the new neighbours.

Except his new neighbours are Swiss, because his new neighbourhood is Geneva. The gluhwein will be flowing and the Gruyere cheese will be bubbling away in the fondue pan. And new lover Heidi, who also happens to be his boss and 'intellectual equal', has probably let down her flaxen plaits in recognition of the holiday season. I've no proof that she plaits her hair, or that it's flaxen, but it's little things like that that get me up in the morning.

And I am holding up the size 14 silk pyjamas – which represent a third of this month's mortgage payment – trying to second-guess whether they have a hope of circumnavigating my thighs. And I'm wondering why I let myself be side-tracked from the Food Hall into this stupid Cinderella-themed Gift Grotto for Adults ('. . . *because it's not only the little ones who deserve the greatest gifts from the Greatest Store on Earth*').

Garnett's is, admittedly, the Greatest Store on Earth blah blah blah. It's just that, right now, that world-famous magic seems as hollow as a hand-blown tree bauble.

'Can I help you?'

I doubt it very much. The shop assistant is doll-sized and her skin is dewy and I'd spend the rest of this month's mortgage payment on whatever wonder serum she's been using if I thought it would change things. But her smile is forced, the upper half of her face paralysed by indifference. Or possibly Botox. 'Um . . . I'm browsing.'

She looks around her and raises one fine-tuned eyebrow (so it can't be Botox – her forehead is simply unravaged by life. I remember how that felt). No one in their right mind would browse in the week before Christmas. Then she resurrects her smile: after all, even if I am certifiable, I might still have a credit card.

'Aren't they beautiful?'

It's a killer question. No woman could honestly deny it. *Everything* about these jim-jams smacks of understated elegance. A woman wearing these will sneak down to steal the Sainsbury's *Taste the Difference* Amontillado sherry left for Father Christmas and his reindeers. She'll place stockings on the bedposts of her softly snoring children before donning stockings of her own for a bout of athletic, silk-pyjama-induced sex with her six-packed husband.

'And,' the assistant whispers, 'Selfridges are charging forty pounds more for exactly the same design.'

'Well . . .' I don't need them. I have pyjamas. Not silk ones, but who is going to know the ruddy difference? There's no one at home to stroke them, or tease them off.

'Like it says on the sign,' she says, pointing, 'we grown-ups deserve the greatest gifts too. And we can never rely on the men in our lives to get it right, can we?' She laughs, and her boobs wobble above the top button of her crimson waistcoat. Her badge tells me her name is Marsha: I bet Marsha and her breasts receive an endless array of perfect presents from small armies of Unwise Men.

'The thing is . . .' but my voice is quieter now and she sees weakness.

'You look like you deserve a treat. Not to mention a sit down. Why don't you try them on? The changing rooms are right here, and we're laying on complimentary hot white chocolate.

There's room for the little one, too,' she says, with a final faked smile in the Fredster's direction. He seems dazzled by her. Maybe it's her boobs.

Like father, like son.

But the hot chocolate clinches it: a tiny vestige of that fantasy London I'd pictured as we set off up the M4 in the removal van, hope in our hearts, bugger all in our joint account. OK, so I'd imagined sipping the hot chocolate after a bracing skate on the rink at Kew Gardens, me in pink-and-white fake fur like a chic marshmallow, Duncan dashing in soft greys, pulling our baby round in circles in a silver child-sized sleigh from Daisy and Tom.

I follow her into the themed changing rooms, a Garnett's speciality. This one is like Cinderella's carriage, with liveried mice stencilled round the edges, spiced pumpkin candles in storm lamps, and a purple velvet banquette. Freddie peers up from his pushchair, suspicious of all the girliness.

I begin to undress, avoiding my reflection in the curlicued mirror. As I pull my sweater off, I realise how musty it smells. The flat has always been damp anyway and since the dryer gave up tumbling, nothing ever quite dries out.

I leave my bra and pants on rather than risk a glimpse of my boobs or bottom. My English rose complexion has turned porridge grey, and no part of my body is unaffected by carrying Freddie for nine months. If I were a true high-maintenance West End girl, I'd have a weekly salon appointment to be detoxified and airbrushed Fake-Bake brown. But given that I can't even manage to dry my jumpers, I am a lost cause.

The lavender silk feels like the cool touch of soft hands as I pull the pyjama pants up my legs. I draw the tie-waist tight, then put on the top half: the tiny buttons are edged in silver, with opaque blue-grey glass in the centre the exact shade of Freddie's eyes. I begin at the bottom, and with each button, become more convinced that I *must* have this pyjama set, that somehow everything else will fall into place when I take it home: the dryer will tumble again, Freddie will have a perfect first Christmas, and Duncan will ditch horrible Heidi and fly home on the Santa Express to the bosom of his family.

But when I reach my bust, I realise it's hopeless. The button won't do up, the tumble dryer's fatally injured, and there's no reason on earth that Duncan would return to this particular bosom, when he can enjoy perfect Swiss peaks.

Freddie senses the change in my mood and begins to grizzle. Why did I let myself be seduced by a stupid shop and a stupid idea that a pair of pyjamas will make me feel better?

I hear the machine-gun rattle of approaching high heels, and Marsha pokes her head round the purple flock curtain. 'Oh that colour is so *you*,' she says, averting her eyes from my gaping cleavage.

'The top's too small,' I say. Freddie stares at Marsha and the grizzling turns to a howl.

'Hmmm . . .' She hands over the hot chocolate,

in a polar bear mug. 'These are great stocking fillers, by the way. Nineteen ninety-nine for this one and a matching penguin. I can get you size sixteen pyjamas if you like. Though when you're not wearing a bra it'll probably be less of a problem.'

'What do you mean?'

'Well,' she says, giving me a 'you asked for it' frown, 'frankly, most women who've had children will experience a little droop in the cleavage area, sans support. So your boobs will hang down . . . er, be more evenly distributed and *voila*, the top won't gape.'

'Thanks a bunch.' Freddie's cries are now of the outraged variety, daring to express what I can't. 'You know, I'm not sure about them. And they are expensive for what they are. Even if they are cheaper than Selfridges.'

'Oh, if that's what's worrying you,' she says, her face steely, 'and of course, we all find things tight at Christmas, the Garnett's Red Carpet Card gets you a fifteen per cent discount. And nothing to pay till February. I'll get you a form.'

'I really don't think—'

Freddie lets out a howl of sympathetic anguish.

'Do you think you can quieten him down?' Marsha asks. 'It sounds like he's being thrashed.' And she sounds like she'd love to do the thrashing herself.

I sigh and wish her five years of sleepless nights when she produces heirs for some wealthy banker.

I reach over and undo the buggy straps to release Freddie. He continues to howl as I hold him tight, trying to stop him shaking with rage. 'Ordinarily he's a very even-tempered child,' I find myself saying, though her sceptical expression makes me wish I hadn't bothered. And, to be fair, six months ago the same sound would have turned my stomach too.

Finally, the shaking stops and I hold my son's raging purple face up to mine. 'There's a good Freddie, there's a good boy—'

He opens his mouth for what I hope will be his final howl . . . but there's something ominous in his eyes as the remainder of his lunch is propelled from inside that tummy with the force of a mashed carrot tornado.

Why was I so keen to experiment with solids?

Within microseconds, Freddie's face returns to placid loveliness. I hesitate before daring to look down at the pyjama top.

'Ah.' The orangey stain stretches from the collar to the hem, and has even spattered the waist-ties and tops of my legs.

Stupid, *stupid* Emily for trying the bloody things on, stupid for believing they could make any difference, stupid, *stupid* for marrying Duncan and getting pregnant and coming to London and thinking a life of silk pyjamas and ice-skating could ever be in my grasp.

I remember I'm not alone, and look up. In the tiny moment before Marsha rearranges her face into *can I help you* blandness, I see disgust, and then satisfaction.

'So,' she says finally, 'how exactly would you like to pay?'

It all goes rather quickly after that. I just know that the price of the pyjamas will be the straw that breaks the back of my Mastercard, so I agree to apply for a Garnett's card, without realising that the form will add insult to injury: are you married? Technically. Number of adults in the household: one. Monthly income: as much as Duncan decides to send over from sodding Switzerland. Estimated monthly outgoings: *always* more than my monthly income.

It's no great surprise when Marsha comes back looking sour and announces that the card company has turned me down. When I explain I've no other means of paying, her manager appears, a tall black woman who looks younger than me, but wears the stern expression of a tough-but-fair headmistress. She introduces herself as Sandie Barrow, Section Head, and asks me how much cash I have on me.

I take out my purse and count notes and coins out onto the banquette in little piles, like a child playing shop with chocolate money. My humili-ation is now complete: the gap between my fantasy Christmas and the reality couldn't be wider.

'I need that for the bus home,' I explain, setting aside two pounds.

Marsha tuts. 'Only a fool pays cash. Haven't you heard of Oyster cards?'

'Thank you, Marsha,' Sandie says sharply. 'I'm sure you're needed back on the shop floor. I can handle this.'

Marsha flounces off, and Sandie watches as I continue to count. I used to pity women like me, the ones in the supermarket queue who had to hand back tins and packets till the total fell within budget. Except I can hardly ask Garnett's to sell me a sleeve, which is all my cash would buy me.

Sandie sits down on the banquette. Close up, she looks less stern: she'd actually be rather beautiful if she smiled and let her hair grow out of that severe crop. She's used so much spray that her hair looks ever so slightly like a helmet and her deep-brown eyes are bloodshot with tiredness. But she seems a hundred times more human than Marsha. 'Not been your day, then?' she says.

'Not been my year. I didn't *want* the bloody pyjamas. I mean, they're lovely, but I can't afford them and I knew that so I don't know why I tried them on when there's so much else I should be spending what little money—' I stop. The shame of describing my sorry domestic state is too much to bear: I wonder if there's an equivalent of restaurant dish-washing for customers who can't pay the bill? Clearing out the stockroom, maybe, or sweeping the floor.

But even though she doesn't know the full sob story, Sandie Barrow looks at me as if she

15

understands. Her face is softer, and I get this utterly irrational feeling that things are going to be OK. 'We can't sell these now anyway. Don't worry about it; I'll mark them down as shop-soiled.'

'But . . .'

'My gramma always swears by bicarbonate of soda. Tub costs under a quid from the supermarket. They'll be as good as new. If any of Garnett's thousands of customers today deserves a bit of a treat, I reckon it's probably you.' Her slight Brummie accent suddenly sounds like the sweetest thing I've ever heard.

She leaves the cubicle and waits while I get changed. When I emerge, she gives me another mug of hot chocolate and takes the pyjamas away and returns a few minutes later with them wrapped in tissue paper. 'I got rid of the worst of the debris,' she says.

It's only when I get home to Lime Village and open the crimson Garnett's carrier bag that I realise she's added a pair of lavender slippers. On a note, she's written: 'These have a slight pull in the silk, so we were going to return them to the manufacturer, but I thought you might like a matching set. Merry Christmas from all at Garnett's.'

I haven't believed in Father Christmas for years, but as I poke my cold toes into the softest slippers I've ever owned, like Cinders trying on her glass slipper, I let myself believe that angels might exist.

CHAPTER 2

SANDIE

Marsha drops a boxful of lilac feather boas on the shop floor and sighs loudly. 'I can't believe you let that woman get away with it. You'll be giving free samples to shoplifters next!'

'What should I have done, exactly? Called the cops and had her locked up with her baby till Boxing Day? I'm all for themed Christmases, but in case you hadn't noticed, Marsha, we're not doing *Scrooge* this year.'

She shrugs, as if a spell inside is exactly what she thinks that poor woman deserved. It's taken ninety-five painstaking years to build the reputation of Garnett's, but my deputy could destroy all that in a single nasty comment or uncharitable act. Though as she averages at least half a dozen super-bitch moments a day, it's a mystery to me how she's got this far.

Marsha passes a mirror and pouts, before responding to her reflection with a tiny flick of the hair. *That's* how she's got this far. She flirts compulsively, even with herself. And the all-male members of Garnett's board of management are suckers for a pretty face. She got where she is today by flashing teeth and tits, while I got where I am . . .

I got where I am by grafting for seven years. By working till four in the morning sewing stars onto ninety metres of netting for our Christmas grotto, because I couldn't find anything gorgeous enough amongst the ready-made ribbons and voiles in haberdashery.

I got where I am by driving to Felixstowe and back after closing time last month when the lorry drivers staged a blockade, to rescue a size twenty wedding dress bodice trapped in a container-load of lingerie from China. I'd promised the bride it would be there for her wedding that Saturday, and I managed it, though it did take all my charm and a boot-load of our Food Hall's gourmet sarnies to bribe the hungry guys on the picket line.

I got where I am by shampooing the last puppy in the window of our pet department, the poor cross-eyed mutt that no one ever wanted to buy. I'm not convinced we should stock live animals, but I could see he'd be happier romping through parks and muddy ponds than sitting in his cage, being tormented by the bored offspring of rich shoppers. I used Aveda Be Curly Shampoo, followed by a good coating of Elnett hairspray and, after my coiffure, he was snapped up by an equally cross-eyed widow to be her faithful companion on her generous Surrey estate.

It's all about magic. A shop like Garnett's is an

everyday slice of enchantment, a year-round pantomime of gorgeous things that you probably don't need but still covet beyond measure. And the conjurors are the hundreds of people grafting away behind the scenes: people like Felipe the head buyer, and Sara the merchandiser, and Luis on security, and Mason who dresses the best windows in London, and me, and – God help us – Marsha.

If I had my way, I'd stick Marsha permanently in menswear, where her simpering and hair-flicking might actually sell some goods. Surely it wouldn't take long for a man to pick her up, along with a new Armani suit.

'It *must* be time to go now,' Marsha says, kicking the box of boas towards an empty shelf. 'I'm running so late that I might have to miss my Piccadilly party and go straight to the Mayfair one.'

I stare meaningfully at the clock, but she doesn't take the hint. 'I suppose I could finish it off if you really need to go,' I say eventually. 'Only twenty boxes of stock to shift onto the shop floor.'

'Well, if you don't mind . . .' she says, not waiting for an answer. Her metal-tipped heels click-clack away and I breathe deeply. I have never lost it in front of anyone. I don't *do* angry. 'Rage is the opposite of ladylike,' my gramma says, and she's right.

At least with Marsha gone I can put my feet up, just for a few minutes. My legs are leaden and my well-worn court shoes pinch my swollen feet. The scarlet velvet chaise longue that I chose as the centrepiece of this year's grotto stretches out seductively, inviting me to take the weight off my size sixes. Thousands of shoppers have been tempted to park their posteriors here in the last few weeks. At least having a deputy as idle as Marsha means I know the success of my Christmas concession is all my own work.

She says I am ridiculously anal about the whole thing, and she's right, but I defy any female customer to pass the grotto without being drawn inside. It's partly why I let that woman take the pyjamas home: I almost feel guilty at the irresistibly seductive power of the display. Even though I do say it myself, I think my real moment of genius was the Cinderella theme – I brainstormed endless fairy stories to work out which heroine busy women would most identify with.

And don't I identify with Cinders now, as Marsha heads for the ball? Though, if I'm completely honest, I'd rather be here than at any party. Sometimes I'm here at midnight, when the shelf-stackers have gone home and there's no one in the store but me and Luis in his little security hatch (asleep, usually – he double-shifts here and at Madame Tussaud's). And then I go from the Food Hall in the basement all the way to Fine Art and Gadgets on the top floor, drinking it all in, working out what I'd do if I ever made it onto the board.

I was five when I first came here, barely tall enough to see over the counters, but the memories are sharp. The entrance, guarded by a doorman whose long woollen coat was flecked with snow, the intense wave of perfume, so potent it made me sneeze, and the assistants dashing about in their neat red waistcoats and matching skirts. The proud feeling as Gramma and I carried our crimson parcels home on the train, beribboned and finished with a sprinkling of gold stars, although they only contained Lily of the Valley bath salts and a jar of Garnett's Special Recipe English Marmalade.

My grandmother swears that if she'd known I was going to waste my grammar school education and my fancy degree and end up a *shop girl*, she'd never have brought me here at all, would have kept me in our dowdy Birmingham suburb, where the only retail temptations were the butcher, the post office and the corner shop. Then I'd have ended up a solicitor or an accountant like the other girls in my class, and everyone would have been happy.

Everyone except me.

'Sandie?'

Toby Garnett, great-great-grandson of the original Mr Garnett, is the only family member still on the board and I have *never* seen him in store after hours. He spends his spare time – and a good chunk of his ancestors' money – on hosting parties at the family's Gloucestershire estate, and hanging out with the aristo crowd at Bouji's. He's twenty-eight, like me, and a poster boy for the spoiled, stupid, blond-floppy-haired look that always seems to go with inherited wealth. Marsha's dream man, except actually, he's not stupid at all. He's just a tiny bit lazy. Usually I loathe laziness but in his case, it's accompanied by buckets of charm. Toby is a lounge lizard in Hunter's wellies. And he must earn his salary back in the free publicity generated by his party lifestyle.

We started in the same month, Toby and I. He'd come down from Oxford where he'd scraped a third and been press-ganged into the family firm: I'd got a first in politics from Warwick, and fought for my position as a fast-track trainee in ladies' accessories. He was as sophisticated as I was wide-eyed and . . . well, I'll admit, I did develop a crush on him, though perhaps it was more of a crush on everything he represented: glamour, good breeding, the whole Garnett's package.

He knew it, of course, and for a while, I actually thought it might be reciprocated. At first it was a business arrangement: Oxford hadn't equipped him to read spreadsheets or sales projections, so he used to treat me to lunch at a sandwich bar before board meetings. I'd explain what it all meant, he'd tease me for it – *Sandie Brains* – is his nickname for me – and then he'd wow the old duffers with his observations. *My* observations. It niggled that I couldn't present my ideas directly, but as Gramma always says, pride comes before a fall.

And then he began to treat me to dinners out: at his club off Sloane Street, or one of those wood-panelled places where they serve heavy English food to remind public schoolboys of their old refectories. Over toad-in-the-hole and syrup sponge, we'd discuss Garnett's and sometimes, even, our own lives. I'd listen to Toby's stories of skiing at Klosters and sipping Bollinger at the Royal Enclosure at Ascot, and deflect his questions about me: there was nothing to tell. I've always kept myself to myself, the way I was brought up.

Two months ago, something changed. At the end of our meal, he produced a little box wrapped in green silk, and gave it to me. I blushed, though thankfully the room was too dark for him to notice. Inside was a fine-chain gold necklace, with a large crimson pendant positioned in the centre of the navy velvet cushion.

'It's a garnet, Brains. Not a precious stone, but it's antique, and real gold. I wanted to thank you for all the advice. You're the only person there I can really trust. You see, they're making me a full partner. I know they wouldn't have done that until I was at least fifty if I hadn't had your support.'

Toby took back the box, and removed the necklace. He leaned across the table holding the two ends of the chain apart and I didn't quite know what to do when he reached over, his slender fingers grazing my skin. I darted backwards and he let go, and the necklace almost landed in my half-empty coffee cup before I caught it. I tried to fasten the clasp at the nape of my neck, my large hands struggling with the delicate jewellery. Finally, after what felt like hours, I managed it and the pendant rested against my chest, below the dip in my collarbone.

'That's exactly how I imagined it would look, Sandie. It glows against your skin, it's perfect—'

I interrupted him. 'I can't take it.'

'Of course you can. God knows, Garnett's bonuses aren't much to speak of. Think of it as a reward.'

'But I've got nothing for you.'

He waved his hand dismissively. 'Most of the women I buy trinkets for don't deserve it. You do. And I don't think I've ever seen you wear jewellery. You should. It suits you.'

I realised he wasn't going to relent, so I stood up, my napkin dropping to the floor. 'Thank you again. I really have to go. I said I'd go in early tomorrow.' And I raced out of the restaurant.

Things were a little awkward after that: he avoided me, and I avoided him. And then the next board meeting came and he asked me to lunch and we pretended it hadn't happened. No one else knows, of course. I keep the secret with my usual efficiency, and Toby is always cool with me in public.

'Sandie?' He's closer to me now, I can smell wine on his breath. He must be popping in between parties.

'Evening, Toby. Come to see if the peasants are revolting?'

'Um. Well. In a way,' he says, his confident voice stilted. It's only now that I spot Luis behind him. Oh, and the new hotshot woman from Human Resources, a sour-faced fortysomething in a cheap chainstore suit that I *know* she couldn't have bought at Garnett's. 'Sandie, I think we need to have a chat.'

'Certainly,' I say, sensing that this isn't about the record-breaking sales-per-square-metre performance of the grotto. Luis won't look at me, and Toby's face refuses to break into that trademark languid smile.

'We have some . . . concerns. About figures and things.' Toby blushes. So it is about sales after all. Perhaps this is an elaborate set-up, and he has a magnum of champagne concealed under his Barbour.

'The initial receipts *have* been really good, possibly better than last year, despite the credit crunch,' I say, my own voice suddenly high-pitched. 'I should have more accurate figures on Boxing Day. I always come in straight after Christmas, when it's quiet, to get them done.'

'Well, it's more to do with day-to-day receipts . . .' Toby looks to the HR woman for support.

'It's the suggestion box,' she says.

'Oh yes,' I say, smiling modestly. Another of my ideas, a way of opening up full communication between workers and management.

'There's been an anonymous note that we couldn't ignore,' she says. 'An accusation.'

'Ri-ight . . .'

'Miss Barrow, we search your locker,' Luis says.

I feel hot. Confused. This isn't happening. Any minute now, Luis will break into giggles at this practical joke, revealing his terrible teeth, eroded by the Dulce de Leche sandwiches his wife packs for him.

I breathe deeply. *Stay calm.* Perhaps they're doing this to everyone. Some kind of crazy crackdown after a scare report about 'retail shrinkage', the polite term for shoplifting and staff with their hands in the till.

'Right, well, obviously, if that's really necessary then I'll co-operate fully. I have nothing to hide.' I reach into my waistcoat pocket for the key but all my fingers close around is my emergency eyedrops (for reducing the effects of late-night working from November to January). 'I can't seem to find my key. I must have dropped it in the staffroom.'

Toby and Luis exchange glances, 'Is OK. Have skeleton key,' Luis says.

'This way.' Toby gestures towards the Staff Only door, and I follow him, trying to remember how to walk. As we pass through, I feel dozens of eyes on me: temps who're enjoying the spectacle, and colleagues who've known me years.

Would one of them send an anonymous note? I didn't think I had any real enemies at Garnett's, though I don't have any real friends either. If you want to get to the top, friendship can weaken you. The nearest I've got would be Toby.

I think what's worrying me most tonight is that he's not called me Brains.

You're being silly, Sandie.

We take the stairs: Toby ahead of me, Luis and Human Resources Woman behind, as if I might make a run for it. The smell of floor polish and Jeyes Fluid reminds me of the first time I went 'backstage', during my induction. The *Upstairs, Downstairs* contrast between the gloss of the store and the browns and greys of the staff areas only seemed to increase the feeling of awe, of being allowed access to a secret world.

Perhaps it's all a wind-up, and they're leading me to a surprise party to celebrate my achievements with the Grotto. But when we reach the door to the women's changing room, there's no mutter of excited voices from my surprise party guests. Toby knocks.

'Who is it?' Marsha pokes her powdered face round the door, and launches a dazzling smile when she sees who it is.

'Can we come in, Marsha?' Toby asks, and she opens the door wide. She's wearing a pink tutu dress that would look charming on a five-year-old – actually it would probably fit a five-year-old – but seems indecent clinging to her curves.

Luis won't look at her, either. He shares my loathing of Marsha. 'You want me send her away, Miss Barrow?'

'Oh, don't mind me,' Marsha says, sitting down on the bench to pull a fishnet stocking up her tanned, toned leg. 'I'm almost done.'

'This one yours, yes?' Luis says, approaching the grey steel locker.

I nod. I know what he'll find, and shudder with embarrassment. My grubby 'civvies' – jeans and jumper I haven't had time to wash because the launderette's always shut by the time I get home, and a copy of *Retail Week*. No ball gown for this Cinderella.

But as he places the key in the lock, and Human Resources Woman, Toby and Marsha all stare at the door, I have a horrible premonition. I imagine a locker packed with sparkly contraband: boas and crystal body scrubs and cut-glass perfume bottles and piles of those bloody silk pyjamas.

I blink the image away.

I hear the lock click and we all hold our breath as the door creaks open and I wait for my worst nightmare, for fur and feathers and fairy dust all over the floor.

Nothing.

I let go of my breath and feel light-headed with relief. Of course. There's nothing there but my jeans and my T-shirt and my magazine.

Luis finally meets my eye and gives me an embarrassed smile as he runs his hand along the top shelf of the locker. Going through the motions. In five minutes we'll be in his security hut, laughing about this over one of his disgusting sandwiches. Then he turns towards the locker, his hand seemingly stuck right at the back. 'Jesu!'

When he pulls his hand out, it contains a large brown envelope. How odd. It looks exactly like the envelope my council tax bill came in yesterday. He tips the envelope up and notes fly out, tens and twenties, wafting slowly onto the lino like the flakes in our best-selling range of snow-domes.

It can't be . . . I open my mouth to say something but my voice won't work. We all stare as a final note flutters onto the small pile on the floor.

Human Resources Woman races forward, producing a clear plastic bag like the ones the cops use for evidence on *CSI*. She turns it inside out, reaching for the envelope and the notes through the plastic barrier, avoiding direct contact. Then she seals it shut.

This isn't happening.

'You don't think . . . you *can't* think . . .' My voice sounds small and tight.

Toby stares at the bag and then back up at me, an unfathomable expression on his face.

Human Resources Woman tucks the evidence into her faux suede briefcase, before withdrawing a thick sheaf of papers bearing the Garnett's logo, embossed in red. She lifts the reading glasses chained around her neck up to her face and peers at the small print.

'Normally, Miss Barrow, a member of staff facing disciplinary action receives forty-eight hours notice of the hearing, and the chance to choose a representative from the staff association. The exception is where the charge could be construed as gross misconduct when a more . . . summary process can be enacted. If you'd like to follow me, I think we have matters to discuss.'

I look to Toby. 'But . . . Toby, you can't believe . . . I mean, you *know* me, you know what I've done here, how hard I've worked.'

He's shaking his head. 'Seven years. Seven years Garnett's has nurtured you, Sandie. Seven years we've trusted you, and this is how you repay us. I really hope it's all been worth it.'

NEW YEAR SALES

After many suffocating days with the in-laws, the shopper is desperate to spread her wings. A January sale should sweep the customer into a passionate, almost torrid frenzy of shopping. Look, touch, grab, buy. Make her feel like an explorer, panning for gold . . .

CHAPTER 3

EMILY

I'm not a moper by nature, but Christmas has tested me to my ruddy limits. Nine days of Freddie trying to munch pine needles. Nine days searching Channel 4 for something festive (it's the only channel our dodgy aerial picks up) and finding nothing but depressing documentaries about pagan rituals and *Where are they now?* programmes featuring Big Brother runners-up. Nine days of wondering if it's snowing in Geneva, because it's definitely raining in my heart.

The Boxing Day trip home to Somerset with Freddie was no better, because I'm only now realising the full implications of my failure to mention Duncan's Swiss flit to my folks. OK, so they know he's been working out there since October. What they don't know is that he's not planning to come home. The only times I stopped fibbing were when I was a) asleep, b) listening to the latest scandalous Rowminster gossip or c) scoffing mince pies. I must have told several thousand lies and I was only there for one night.

There were lies about our fabulous festive skiing trip near Mont Blanc (I did realise at the time that there was something not quite right about having a Black Belt in skiing, but fortunately Mum and Dad are equally ignorant) and lies about après-ski (my faked tan is patchy but they seemed convinced). Then there are lies that will breed thousands more: the extensive house refurbishment work which means they can't come to visit us for another three months (then what?). And then there are the lies about the visits I've made to Geneva with my jet-setting baby. I fear my *Holiday* programme facts about cuckoo clocks and the Alps won't sustain me much longer.

Of course, the biggest reason of all why I'm going to have to come clean soon is Freddie himself: he doesn't yet have the words to explain that *Mummy's turning into a compulsive liar, and actually we spent the festive season in front of the telly and the fan heater*, but it's only a matter of time. He's already begun chattering in Double Dutch, and if he's anything like his dad, the gift of the gab will come naturally.

But if I tell my parents the truth, my London dream is over. They'll just tow me, Freddie and all our belongings back to Somerset on the Carnival Club trailer. And while some evenings I dream of being rescued, and of girlie nights in with my old friends from the bank, I can't let that happen yet. If I go back, I'll never find the guts to leave again. The things I miss about small-town life are exactly the things I hated during the three decades I lived there: everyone knowing your business, and you knowing everyone else's; the fact that I will always be known in the village as the Little Mermaid who Wet Herself, after an embarrassing incident at the 1985 Carnival. The slavish devotion to cheese and shoes and local weather presenters.

No, as comforting as Cheddar and Clarks are, I can't go back. Not after all the fuss I made about leaving in the first place.

So, I have set myself three resolutions. Short and sweet:

1. Stop moping.
2. Make some London friends.
3. Get a job.

And that's where I begin to break into a cold sweat. A job will mean me and Freddie will be separated. The bond between me and my Little Londoner seems unbreakable, perhaps because it's always felt like the two of us against the world, from the moment our eyes first met in that sweltering delivery room.

It wasn't Duncan's fault I went into labour a fortnight early. *Everyone* says first babies arrive late, and he'd only gone to Switzerland for twenty-four hours, and anyway we knew travel to company HQ in Geneva would be part of his new job. But after the utter loneliness of my labour, with a midwife whose English was so heavily accented that I couldn't understand a word except 'Pouushh' and

'NO pouushh', meeting Freddie was the most joyful moment of my life.

Of course, I have left my baby with other people once or twice. I trust my parents and I trust Duncan, despite the fact that before he became a dad, I wouldn't have trusted him to nurse a pint. He only put in three months of parenting before he left me for Heidi, but it was long enough to convince me he'd never harm Freddie.

But childminders and nurseries and au pairs are an unknown quantity. The idea of leaving my precious partner in crime makes me feel sick, but I have to do it, don't I? I need the money and anyway, a job is key to the other two resolutions: I'll have no time to mope, and I'll make friends. Time to get tough with myself.

'Mummy needs to look the business, eh, Freddie?' I carry him into the bedroom and open the wardrobe. I already know what's in there: shelves full of tracksuit bottoms and sloppy T-shirts, plus a neat row of little suits from my days at the bank. I've never been a stick insect – before I was pregnant I was ten or twelve in the kinder shops (though always a large in Zara, of course). I used to read my older sister's romantic novels when I was growing up, and the heroines were all built like me: an un-showy hourglass, with tidy curves.

My curves are no longer tidy. They're positively chaotic. I knew things were bad when Duncan started calling me Chubster ('I mean it affectionately, though, Em!'). There's no point in trying to wrestle my way into one of my old suits: it'd be like trying to fit Posh Spice's bikini on a hippo.

I close the wardrobe door and wince at my reflection in the mirror. Even my wavy blond hair seems puffy and overblown. 'No one's going to employ your mummy looking like this, are they, mate?'

But I force myself to look again. This is what happens to every new mum – well, except for the A-list celebs who have a tummy tuck done at the same time as their caesarean. I don't have to look *sexy* to get myself a job. I just have to look capable, which means swapping my elasticated waists for something more structured.

There is no way round it. I have to go back into the lion's den. There are worse things in life than being a size fourteen. Aren't there?

I manoeuvre Freddie through the door of our first-floor maisonette, hanging onto the buggy to stop it toppling straight down the steep stairs to the communal front door. We actually own the downstairs flat as well: the outrageous mortgage pays for not one, but *two* bodged kitchenettes, *two* dodgy boilers, *two* unspeakable bathrooms, and a single west-facing junkyard . . . sorry, patio, piled high with motorbike parts and rusty barbecues full of cigarette butts. Our original masterplan was to convert the place back into a family house, but as I've barely had enough energy to get dressed in the morning or enough money to cover the gas bill, the plan's on hold.

On the mat, there's the usual pile of unpaid bills for the previous occupants, and a few glitzy interiors catalogues. When we first moved in, I signed up for every brochure in the back of *Living Etc*: Italian glass-topped furniture, Egyptian cotton bedding, German kitchens, American white goods. My circumstances were drastically reduced before I had time to order so much as a pillowcase.

'Onwards and upwards, eh, Freddie?'

The streets around Lime Village are frosty, and scattered with rubbish and skips. This part of town is truly a tale of two cities: some of my neighbours are lawyers, yes, and film-makers, exactly as I imagined. But the large house opposite is a hostel for former drug addicts, and one of the occupants spends his day sitting on the wall, whatever the weather. He waves his stick at me across the street. It's a sign of how lonely I get that I've tried to talk to him, but he replies in deepest gibberish.

I pass another mum with a buggy containing a baby whose tiny pink face pokes out of multiple layers of fleece. I smile at the woman, out of habit, but she looks down. It's the same at the swings. The brighter my grin, the more rapidly they back away. The cafes are full of braying groups of women, but mums on their own seem to prefer to keep up the pretence that their babies' burps are scintillating, rather than admit they might like an adult friend. Confessing to loneliness in London seems the greatest taboo.

I cross the main road towards Hammersmith. My sights are set lower than my last big shopping expedition in Oxford Street, with its seductive shops and staggering price tags. I enter the arcade, with its skiving teenagers and its fast-food stalls. I know my place.

Primark.

But what a place. Until my first trip here, I didn't believe nylon *had* a smell. But when you're confronted with enough to clothe an entire squadron of overweight mums, the scent is over-powering, like sniffing a Barbie doll. Best of all: there are no mirrors.

After Lime Village, where the posh mothers wear their arch boniness as a badge of honour to distin-guish themselves from poorer, fatter locals, this is a place where I can finally loosen my waistband, I know Primark's now supposed to be the hangout of fashionable young things, but they must come in their lunch hour, because right now, cellulite is the order of the day.

I push Freddie's buggy between the tables with their sky-scrapers of jeans and jumpers, and begin to fill my mesh bag: forgiving black and brown cords, two woolly cardigans, a handful of fleecy socks. I steer clear of the unidentifiable sparkly strappy things on hangers that might be party tops but might equally be harnesses for a Shetland pony. They probably stock them in my size, but frankly I think I *would* scare the horses.

I spy a suit that might work for interviews, in charcoal pin-stripes. Pin-stripes are probably *so* last season, but beggars can't be choosers. The check-out assistant doesn't look up as she throws my stuff into a bag. But I *like* indifference when I'm shopping. Give me her over that bitch in Garnett's anyway.

'Firty pounds.'

£30! Maybe with the money I've saved I can treat myself to a coffee in the little Spanish place by the Tube, where they sell those sugary straight doughnuts. There! I'm cosmopolitan now. Everyone in my home town thinks that doughnuts only come in rings.

Yes. Definitely treat time, after I've stocked up on nappies and Nurofen. Boots feels awfully glossy and glam after the pile-it-high rawness of Primark.

'Isn't he a poppet?'

Without looking up, I know from the woman's cloying voice that she must either be a lunatic, or a saleswoman.

'But his mummy looks in need of a bit of a boost.'

Sod off. I'm not going to get caught out again by the hard sell. Not after the pyjama incident. I brace myself to push past the woman, perhaps catching her legs with the buggy on the way, but when I glance up, she looks a bit like my mum, flushed and jowly.

She's standing next to the Charmant display. Now I'm no make-up guru. I've worn mascara a total of three times since Freddie appeared last June. But even I've seen the big posters for Charmant, the new kid on the block, featuring Scarlett or Keira or one of those other starlets with big eyes and a big future in Hollywood.

'Charmant is *the* brand of choice for the style-aware woman. All our products are made in the top Parisian cosmetics houses, but because that's a secret, you pay a third of the price.' Something about the way she waggles her eyebrows while reciting her script makes me warm to her. Then she adds. 'And I can give you lots of free samples!'

What have I got to lose? If I'm going to get back into the workplace, I'll need to upgrade my beauty regime, which currently consists of brushing teeth, brushing hair, cleaning face with flannel (this step is optional), and brushing teeth again at the end of the day if I don't fall asleep first.

I check the Fredster, who seems content staring at shoppers' legs, and then ease myself onto the stool.

'I'll give you a little cleanse first,' she says, reaching for a frosted bottle. 'This is our Honey Blossom Cleanser and Toner, with extracts of St John's Wort.' She runs the cold lotion over my cheeks. 'Oh!' She holds up the cotton wool ball, which is covered in what appears to be soot. 'Oh, we haven't been cleansing, have we, dear?'

I nod towards Freddie. 'You know how it is.'

41

She nods back, then, seamlessly, the nod turns into a sorrowful shake. 'But we can't neglect ourselves, dear. You'll have a moustache before you know it.'

And who would notice? I want to say. But then I realise that counts as moping so I just smile through very gritted teeth.

'Let's do a bit of a spot check, shall we? A skin MOT, so we know what we're dealing with.' She pulls a large mirror out of a drawer, and stands next to me, pointing at my reflection. It's not good: under the strip lights I look like I haven't slept for a hundred years. 'Oh dear. Natural childbirth was it, dear?'

In the mirror, my pupils dilate in terror. Twenty-two hours in labour. And they say you're meant to *forget* the bollocking pain. As if . . . 'How do you know?'

'Spider veins,' she says, pushing the mirror closer so I can see the tiny red lines that give my face its only colour. 'The facial equivalent of stretch marks. All that pushing! Say what you like about Caesareans, but I'd rather sacrifice my bikini line than my complexion. Bit late for you now, though, dear.'

I'm not convinced by the science, but there's no doubting the physical evidence: the closer I look, the more lines I can see, a network of wiggles the same shade of red as the Central Line.

'It's blood you can see there, under the skin,' she says. 'But our Spidered Out Cream contains laser technology that directly attacks the veins without damaging surrounding tissue.' She hands me a tiny silver pot.

'How much is it?'

'Oh, fifteen ninety-nine for that size. Lasts for months, though.'

I wince. 'Wouldn't concealer do the job?'

She frowns. 'Well, it's like doing up a derelict house, isn't it? You *can* paint over the damp and the cracks, but they'll only come back. Anyway, let's see what else we need . . . now, you see those freckles around the top of your lips? That's the first sign of colour seepage or loss caused by age. Very common in ladies as they approach forty.'

'I'm thirty,' I say, crossly.

She whistles. 'Oh! I'm normally spot on with ages. You do need to take positive action, now, or you'll have no lips to speak of by the time you're thirty-five.'

I try to stand up, but she holds onto my hand. 'It's always a shock after the first baby, dear. But don't worry. We can repair the damage. Well, perhaps that's a little optimistic. We can definitely stop it getting any worse.'

I think of Duncan, then, of how much I'd like to tell him about this over a glass of wine at home. His ability to laugh at my jokes and at life – even, occasionally, at himself – was always his most redeeming feature. But then I remember Heidi: I can't imagine a girl brought up on mountain air and chamber music has a single spider vein.

The make-up woman warbles on about more problems I never knew I had . . . discolouration of the eyelids, cappuccino cheeks, in-growing brow hair, greasy ears. I mean, greasy ears! After taking me to pieces, she begins to build me back up again, like the Six Million Dollar Man, or in my case, the £600 woman. I stop counting the products she's recommended when she gets to fourteen, and surrender instead to the surprisingly soft touch of her hands on my face, as she massages in some lotion that promises to prime my skin, heal my inner hurt and stave off bird flu.

Touch is what I miss. Freddie almost makes up for it, with that earthy neediness babies have, grabbing as much of me as he can with those determined fists. But sometimes I long for delicacy and tenderness. Even though I always knew it was a 'you rub my back, I'll rub yours' arrangement, Duncan made me feel special.

Words can lie, of course, but surely not his touch, the hearts and flowers he used to draw with his fingers on my spine? Or was he just playing to the gallery? Duncan always did have that way of spotting the fatal weakness in a person, turning it against them, all the while hiding behind that grin of his. I thought that because I knew his tricks, because I saw him charming other people, I was safe.

'This is my favourite. Magic. It's like Tipp-Ex for the face.'

I open my eyes as the woman dabs beige liquid

44

onto the countless flaws on the left hand side of my face, leaving the right side untouched. I thought maybe all that slap might have made me look more like the old me. Nope. It's just a mask.

I don't want to be here, another punter to be undermined, patronised, ripped off. I push away her blusher brush before she fakes me a rosy glow. 'I don't want to be rude, but I need to go. Now!'

'But you're looking so much better already.'

'That's debatable.'

'At least let me finish you off, dear; I've only done half your face!' she says, sounding desperate.

'There's really no ruddy point!' I'm shouting now, and people are staring, but I don't care. 'I've got no money, no husband, no one to impress, and no intention of wasting any more of your time or mine on this *farce*!'

I push myself off the stool, trying to ignore the wobbliness in my legs, and lean against Freddie's buggy for support. My son looks at me with curiosity: normally I can't bear raised voices, especially my own.

I race blindly for the door, and collide with a stack of metal baskets as I leave, tearing the sleeve of my jacket and making my eyes water with pain. As I storm through the arcade, I don't look back, but it takes less than ten seconds for the guilt to kick in. The poor woman was only doing her job, probably for the minimum wage plus a measly commission and, along the way, doing her best to bring some sparkle back into my life.

I spot a plastic bench and slump down on it, rummaging in my pocket for the cucumber sticks I brought for Freddie to snack on.

'Excuse me, may I have a moment of your time?'

I sigh loudly, before glaring upwards. The Italian accent has an Italian-looking owner, a woman who looks young at first glance, but is probably forty-five – there's something *preserved* looking about her high-gloss skin and wide-mascaraed eyes and deep scarlet lips (no sign of colour seepage on *her* face). Her black suit is perfectly cut, and the white blouse so crisp the collar could draw blood. Another make-up saleswoman. That's all I need.

'No, you can't. Not even a millisecond of my flipping time, thank you very much. Do I look like the kind of woman who wants pure silk pyjamas or silk extract foundation? Do I?'

My voice echoes off the marble floor and the plate glass windows of the arcade, but I don't care. Neither, irritatingly, does the Italian woman. If anything, she looks amused. 'No, you do not, but I was watching you in the shop and—'

'And WHAT? Don't tell me, you have a miracle diet that's guaranteed to shrink me to a size zero overnight? Or, I don't know, you run a model agency and you can't believe no one's ever approached me before and you're going to whisk me off to Milan to become the next Naomi Campbell?'

She's definitely laughing now, her black ringlets shaking against her shoulder pads. 'No, I cannot offer you Milano.'

I gather up my Primark bags, and what remains of my dignity. Will no one leave me in peace?

'But I did wonder if you might be interested in working for me.'

I stare at her. All that make-up . . . she couldn't be a *madam*, could she? There are a couple of massage parlours a few streets away from Lime Village.

I dismiss the thought. No one in their right mind would pay me for sexual favours. It must be pyramid selling, or running Tupperware parties, or gambling or . . .

'It is nothing perilous,' she says, that accent lending her sentences a sense of instant drama. 'Nothing illegal. I do not have the habit of stopping and offering strangers work, but you are what I am looking for.'

'Yeah, because I really look like the ideal employee, don't I?'

She smiles. 'For what I have in mind, maybe. I think here is not the best place for a business discussion. Can I buy you coffee?'

I begin to push the buggy away from her. 'Whatever it is, I don't think—'

She steps in line beside me, speeding up to keep pace. 'Pah! My friend, don't think. Do! What can be more appealing than free coffee? Or maybe you'd prefer hot chocolate and Spanish churros donuts, the perfect January food?'

It's the offer of churros that does it. That, and my suspicion that this woman will follow me home

47

and possibly abseil up the wall of the maisonette if I don't give in. 'All right. But if you're trying to sell me something, you're definitely barking up the wrong tree.'

'All I have to sell is a better life for you and the baby. You have my word.' She holds out her hand, which is weighed down by expensive-looking rings. 'My pleasure to meet you. I am Grazia.'

I shake the hand, and the rings are cold against my fingers. 'Emily. And this is Freddie.'

She crouches down. 'Hello, Freddie. I have plans that will involve you also. Top secret plans. Exciting plans. Come, all will be revealed!'

And she flounces across the marble floor for a meeting that she at least seems convinced will change my life.

CHAPTER 4

SANDIE

Life as a lady of leisure has never appealed to me. Student life drove me to distraction. While my flatmates sat glued to *Neighbours*, moaning if a lecture started before noon, it was all I could do not to repeat Gramma's mantras about the devil making work for idle hands. Instead, I got two part-time jobs in shops off-campus, and breathed a huge sigh of relief when I graduated.

So it's been a shock to join the world of the non-workers. I'm familiar with the West Enders who made up Garnett's clientele: the ladies who lunch, the secretaries buying for their bosses' mistresses, the mistresses themselves, and the rich Arabs with their black-clad wives, who'd descend into riotous giggles as soon as the changing room doors were closed and the hijabs came off.

But it's a different story in Zone Two. I've lived in the same N4 flat since I moved to London seven years ago, but only now do I realise I don't know my neighbourhood at all. The Women Merchants' Hostel is a museum piece: a grey 1930s mansion block, divided into thirty units which are only let to single women in the 'mercantile and distributive trades'. The flats are *technically* studios, with doll-sized kitchenettes and tiny bathrooms, but they're also beautiful. There's a grand tiled entrance hall (complete with a porter who must be almost as old as the building itself), high ceilings with ornate cornices, and a dignified fireplace in every bedroom. Mine has pink tulips rising from deep green foliage, and tiles the colour of a tropical lagoon.

The rents are low, because it's run by a trust set up by Lady Benedicta Sinclair, a notorious and wealthy shopaholic who died without offspring, but wanted to give something back to the impoverished spinster shopgirls who'd served her so well. Hence the block's alternative name: Dixie's Digs.

And now I have Dixie's Digs to thank for getting me up in the morning. It's not like me to want to hide from the world under my duvet, but in the days since my sacking, the temptation to retreat has been almost overwhelming. Except . . .

Except I have no choice. If the porter had an inkling that I'd lost my job, I'd lose my home too. It's in my lease: unemployment is grounds for eviction. So every day I dress in my spare uniform (Human Resources Woman insisted that Luis confiscated the one I was wearing, plus *everything* in my locker, except my handbag, and I was only allowed to take that after the contents were tipped upside down on the desk). Every day I spray my stubborn hair with lacquer for a full twenty seconds as I always did, to create a 'do' that stays rigid for twelve hours. Buff my shoes, run the lint remover across my clothes in case of fluff. Choose a perfume for the day from the two dozen bottles on my washstand (my only indulgence, inspired by that first ever visit to Garnett's, when the cosmetics department seemed like an Aladdin's cave). Then I stride purposefully out of the entrance hall as if everything is normal.

In the first week I was so traumatised that one morning I forgot I'd been sacked, getting as far as Oxford Street before I remembered. I skulked on the other side of the road, a copy of *Metro* held up in front of my face in case my colleagues saw me. I felt like a dirty old man in Soho, drawn to the place despite the risks. I sneaked into the cafe opposite, sat with my latte and watched Garnett's waking up – the lights coming on, floor by floor, followed by the ebb and flow of customers: the trickle of nannies needing urgent nursery supplies, the mothers and daughters up from the home counties to compile wedding lists, the stylists from the magazines off Bond Street, blagging freebies for a photo shoot. I saw Toby, cosy in his dark green Barbour, striding through the doors like he owns the place.

Which of course, he will do, one day.

How *could* he betray me? I really thought he had honour, that he'd look for an alternative reason why an envelope stuffed with cash would be found in my locker. I thought he might wonder why I'd

51

wait seven years to raid the tills and then store my stash on the premises. I thought he knew me better than that, after all the hours we'd spent together.

But he didn't say a word in my defence as I was marched up to HR on the top floor, and made to sign various forms before I was despatched from the premises for the last time. Luis escorted me onto Oxford Street, hailing me a taxi on account, under a false name. 'Don't think you make it home alone on the Tube, you so pale.'

I turned back as the taxi pulled away, and looked up towards the windows of the management suite on the top floor, wondering if Toby was watching me leave. But he was probably long gone, already sipping Bellinis at some Sloane's party. I felt the tears welling up and had to keep reminding myself of what Gramma used to tell me when I was bullied for being a swot at school: 'Remember you're better than them, Sandra. No one can make you feel inferior without your permission.'

No, but they can make you unemployed.

It was Marsha, of course. It had to be. I'd never describe myself as the most popular Section Head at Garnett's – I've been accused of being uptight and a stickler for detail, which I take as a back-handed compliment – but no one else there *hated* me. Or at least, I hope they didn't.

But Marsha always despised me, and what's more, she always wanted my job. It doesn't take Miss Marple to work out that she could easily have pocketed my locker key, and she knew I always opened my post during my lunch break. All it took was a discarded envelope to complete her plan.

At Christmas I was pathetically grateful that HR Woman offered me the chance to resign, rather than sacking me. It's only now, three weeks on, that I realise it makes no difference whether I jumped or was pushed. Garnett's won't give me a reference, and without a reference, I won't ever find another job in retail.

I'm not tearful any more. No, I'm filled with a big roaring rage that I have to keep tethered. Gramma always used to warn me that anger was the Barrow family's fatal weakness: 'Like a big black bear on a chain, Sandra. You need to keep it on that chain. If you let it go, it will be the ugliest thing you ever saw.'

I've forced myself to stay away from Oxford Street. Instead I take the bus to a local shopping centre, where I watch people buying and selling. It's all I can do not to march into the deserted shops, tell them how to make things better: different music, more flattering lighting, improved navigation to help customers find what they came for. But if they ask me what makes me such an expert, what would I say? So instead I keep quiet and make a latte last for two or three hours in the mall-land of dazed new mothers and grouchy pensioners.

Every day I give myself a budget of one pound

for sixty minutes on the Internet, searching for jobs. My heart isn't really in it, but what else do I do? I type combinations into Google: RETAIL JOBS + NO REFERENCE REQUIRED, or UK FREELANCE OPPORTUNITIES. The vacancies that pop up are the kind you'd see on *Watchdog* – dodgy franchises, or jobs on Tarot-reading chatlines. I've applied for a few of the more kosher-looking ones, but never heard back. Now every time I log onto my email, there seems to be more spam from Nigeria.

Today I am seriously considering Tarot lines: not to tell my future, but as a career option. How hard can it be to promise women with more money than sense that a handsome stranger is lurking around the next corner?

But actually, I'd only end up telling them the truth – that the handsome stranger is probably a mugger – and start sounding like Gramma, advising them to find something more productive to do with their time. Maybe sex lines would be more lucrative; at least you're offering a service, but then I've never been terribly good on the male psyche.

I sip my lukewarm coffee, rack my brains for another combination. STORE + VACANCY + CUSTOMER SERVICE.

I hit return and lots of jobs appear, all specifying three years of direct customer contact and good references.

Let's try SITS VAC + NO EXPERIENCE

NECESSARY. No, that brings up a whole load of links with £££ and $$$$ signs, followed by endless rows of !!!!!!. No point clicking on them.

What *am* I good at? Shops, plain and simple. What works, what doesn't. Making the customer feel like she's the only person that matters, that not only is she always right, but that she's special.

SHOPS + CUSTOMER SERVICE + BEST + JOBS.

1.3 million sites. Most of them offering me call centre jobs (and again, I'd need a reference). Then I see it:

Are you a super-consumer? Can you spot the very best – and the very worst – in customer service in Britain's high street shops?

I click on the link, expecting a gaudy scam site with a hundred pornographic pop-ups, but instead I get a white screen, with discreet black lettering.

We are a small, exclusive company which conducts mystery shopping missions for a range of key retailers across the UK.

Mystery shoppers. The scourge of lazy shop assistants and rude managers. I always used to think there was something sneaky about spying on your own staff, until Marsha got caught on camera trying to hard-sell a push-up bra to an elderly widow who only came in for support tights. I didn't stop smiling for a week.

I read on: *We're looking for completely reliable, tactful freelance operatives, ideally with experience of the retail industry, but at the very least a passion for good service and excellence in shops. Our hallmarks are quality, accuracy and reliability and we have pioneered the use of hidden cameras. Assignments will only be offered following a rigorous testing process and may not be regular, but for the right candidate, this could be a rewarding and exciting opportunity.*

Apply in confidence, with CV and a detailed review of a store recently visited, to Charlie@shoppingangels.net

I drain the last of my latte, not caring that it's cold and gritty. Me, a secret shopper? Poacher turned gamekeeper, stitching up people in the industry I used to be part of. Isn't that the ultimate betrayal?

But the more I think about it, the more excited I feel. I'd only be stitching up the assistants who deserve it – the Marshas of this world. For the first time in weeks, there's the tiniest possibility that I might still have a future in retailing.

Of course, it's almost certainly a scam. Shopping Angels? They're probably based in Lagos and will want my full bank details before proceeding. But it's got to be worth a shot.

It's not like I have any other options right now.

CHAPTER 5

GRAZIA

We live in a cottage in the country, just a stone's throw from London.

When I was fifteen, I taught myself English: it was the most important rung on my escape ladder. In the village where I grew up, our nearest neighbour was Edith, a widow from Clapham Common who had fallen in love with Italy and moved to Liguria upon retirement. I did errands in return for lessons. Hours and hours I spent listening to her stories, looking out of the window at the olive groves and scorched fields, dreaming of double-decker buses and Trafalgar Square.

After she died, I borrowed Conversational English LPs from the library, featuring actors repeating the same phrases to each other: I did not realise it then, but the recordings had been made in 1959, and when I met my husband he informed me that my English had a black-and-white, Noël Coward quality, thanks to those old LPs. *How do you do? It's such a pleasure to meet you. No, the pleasure's all mine. Where do you hail from?*

We live in a cottage in the country, just a stone's throw from London.

And now we do.

Except it isn't *we* any more. Now it is just me, walking from room to room, still expecting to glimpse the back of Leon's head, the little bald patch he has failed to notice, the one he would be mortified to notice, the horrible proof he is not immune to ageing.

God's little joke. My husband *is* immune to ageing now. For ever forty-four. The first of the Young British Artists to die of natural causes. The *Times* said it was 'a bittersweet, tragic end, yet a death redolent with the tattered irony of Leon's best work'.

Leon, who declared often that he wished to smoke and drink himself to death, simply ran out of breath. I returned from my morning run and found him, mouth frozen in a desperate gasp. An asthma attack. The doctor said it is often the things we encounter on a daily basis that suddenly become allergens. It might even have been triggered by paint.

Tattered irony, indeed. You would have liked that, no, Leon?

I have done nothing to the house since he died eighteen months ago. His studio is out of bounds. I locked it the day the coroner's officer told me they had completed their investigations, satisfied he died of natural causes. I am like the woman I saw on the TV news who left the bedroom of her missing son untouched for the day he came home. I am not so stupid to think that Leon will walk through the door, but if anyone deserves a shrine, it is Leon, and as his muse, what else have I to do but preserve his memory, keep his work space exactly as he left it?

The idea of strangers here – that overweight girl with her messy baby, and this woman Sandra whom I have not met – makes me want to lock myself inside for all eternity. But it is only through strangers that I can save this place, keep it as close as possible to what Leon intended.

Because without strangers I am stony broke.

'Welcome, welcome!'

A motley crew and no mistake.

The girl, Emily, and her baby boy both look damp, although it has not rained for four days. Perhaps they are followed around by their own raincloud. And the only other person on the platform is a tall black girl with the slumped shoulders of the recently disappointed. Her rigid tailoring is good quality, but the dark fabric and boxy shapes age her. She resembles a prison warder. Shame. In better clothes, and in a better mood, she could be striking.

'You must be Sandra?'

She nods sullenly. 'People call me Sandie.'

Sandie the Sour-Puss and Dishevelled Emily. My raw recruits. I try to think of a silver lining. Yes, I have found it. These downtrodden individuals are perfect for this job. They are the chainstore infantry, the customers no one notices, the ones most likely to be ignored, abused and ill-served.

The ideal agents provocateurs.

'It's not far to my home, so shall we all . . .'

It is only now that it occurs to me that my current vehicle – a new. Porsche Cayman S, with flawless olive green paintwork – will not accommodate three grown women, a wriggling child, and a buggy with more armour-plating than a Sherman tank.

'That's some car,' says Sandie.

We all stare at it. There *is* a back seat, but to fit the baby and his equipment into the space available would necessitate the removal of his legs.

'How far is not far?' says Emily, attempting to smile.

'Under a kilometre.' In fact, it is more like three, but I trust that like most Britons, these women will still not have grasped metric measurements.

We form a strange procession. This car is capable of two hundred and forty kilometres per hour in optimum conditions. I drive it at pushchair speed, crawling along at the same pace as Emily. It is a biting cold day, and in her situation I would move faster, but maybe she's too plump. And that is the way she will stay, judging from her determined consumption of churros the day we met. But this chubbiness is why I chose her from a dozen other specimens I spotted during my hunt in the shopping arcade, so I can hardly object now.

Next to her on the pavement is Sandie, who refused to sit in the passenger seat with me, and instead walks in gloomy solidarity with Emily. Despite the aura of negativity. I am surprised she is interested in a job like this. She looks far too employable.

I am sorry, Leon, for the imminent invasion of your sanctuary.

Just when it can get no worse, that nosy gossip from Beechford Stores comes outside for a cigarette break and gawps as we pass. This will be around the village before you can say *toffee-nosed newcomers with their Bohemian ways.*

I hate villages. I know them too well. Small places suit small minds. Moving to Beechford was the only thing Leon and I ever argued about. Of course, I let him win.

The car engine growls in frustration and I hunger to accelerate away and leave these strangers behind. Emily is panting and Freddie's complexion is a mottled red, white and blue. *So* patriotic. Well, it is his mother's fault. I did offer to take the boy in the front seat and promised not to brake sharply, but she looked at me as if I had suggested feeding him to the foxes.

Oh, Leon. I know, I know. But what else can I do?

My recruits have their heads in the sand. They don't notice the rabbits, watchful in the bushes. Or the bare trees that line our route, powerful branches grasping at the heavy sky. They're looking down. I must train them to look everywhere, to notice everything, as my husband trained me.

Finally, we turn the corner and the gravel crunches under the car wheels. *Now* they notice.

Rose Cottage. Leon's little joke.

There is nothing cottagey about our house. A concrete-and-glass wedge, deposited in the clearing like a slice of white light. The locals objected to the plans, of course, but the planners had no grounds to turn us down because our plot was hidden away from the virulently insipid thatched cottages that dot the rest of Beechford.

If I am honest, I do not hate the cottages: I merely hate the people inside them, their closed minds, their nosiness. It was Leon who came up with 'virulently insipid' (for a think-piece in the *Guardian Weekend* magazine on the politics of internal urban/rural migration) and it certainly did not help our integration into village life.

I click the remote control to open the electronic gates, and my bedraggled procession reaches the front of the house.

'Wow, Grazia, it's like something out of *Ideal Home*,' Emily says.

I don't tell her that we turned down the bourgeois *Ideal Home* in favour of a centre-spread in *Wallpaper*.

We continue up the path to the front door. Freddie strains to free himself of his buggy straps and I suppress my irritation until I realise . . . he's reaching for the wall, to trace the pattern of the black-and-white rambling rose that Leon painted around our door after deciding on the name *Rose Cottage*.

I feel an unexpected tightness in my throat as the little boy, like the child in the Emperor's New Clothes, sees what the adults do not: that even a wall painting has the mark of genius. But I do not cry. Have not cried once. Strength is one of the qualities Leon admired in me.

'Stop it, Freddie,' Emily shifts his buggy backwards so he can't touch, though he keeps trying, sticky hands splayed out.

'Who did that?' Sandie asks.

'My husband,' I say. 'He is dead.'

She opens her mouth to say something sympathetic but I turn my back. I unlock the door and disarm the Swiss-made alarm system before ushering my recruits through the hallway with its dozen doors, into the salon. First they look from side to side, a full 180-degree sweep across this room, which forms the entire back half of the house. Then, like every other visitor before them, they peer up at the triple-height ceiling and the wall of glass that lets in so much light, even on a grey January afternoon.

They gasp.

Then, inevitably, they turn round and see the painting suspended from the ceiling, five by five metres, a perfect square canvas. Leon's last work: *Muse 7*. I did not sit for this one, hence the strangeness of the image, an ethereal quality, almost

63

blurred. I always felt that Leon was unusual among the YBAs because he *could* actually paint, rather than simply ship his unmade bed to a gallery, or dunk the corpses of farmyard animals in formaldehyde. Perhaps it is why he never quite made it to the very top, why he never reached the heights – or the earnings – of Damien and Lucian and the rest. *Muse 7* is one of his more traditional pieces. It shows only my back and my neck, stopping short of the hairline, a tattoo in the shape of one of his rambling roses midway down the spine.

After he showed me the painting, I knew what I had to do. I secretly went to a tattoo parlour in Reading, with a photograph of the cottage roses. I nearly fainted at the pain, but it was worth it when I undressed in front of my husband. He said it was a remarkably good facsimile.

Sandie looks at me. 'Is that an original Leon?'

The girl goes up in my estimation. 'Yes it is. His last painting.' More people have seen my tattoo than the painting: it was one he chose to keep private. Money was never his priority, a fact that became much clearer after his death.

'But how . . . ?'

'I am his widow,' I say briskly. 'You must be parched after your journey. What can I get you to drink?'

Despite his mother's fear that it might provoke an attack of wind, Freddie takes to San Pellegrino like a duck to water, giggling every time a sharp bubble rises up his nose. Sandie opts for rocket-fuel espresso and downs it in one. Good girl. She confuses me: there is no trace of make-up on her skin, yet now we are inside I notice she is wearing perfume. Not just any perfume, but – incredibly – Opium, *the* scent all the ground crew wore back in the shoulder-padded 1980s when I worked at Malpensa airport. It seems Sandie wishes to seem in control.

Emily has cranberry juice but seems to have forgotten her drink. Her eyes are as large as Cerignola olives as we take our seats around the Apple Mac.

'What you must understand about secret shopping, first of all, is that we are not here only to catch the bad guys. OK? In some shops they call us the Gestapo, as though we're evil spies out to ruin the assistants' lives.

Sandie looks away. Her CV mentions 'direct customer experience at senior level' but is suspiciously vague about where or when. Still, all I care about is the money I will receive for training her, and my commission for every assignment she completes.

I continue my speech. 'Women spend eight years of their lives shopping. We deserve the best. If everyone was doing their job, if customer service in this country was always tip-top, then there would be no work for us.' I pause to let this sink in. 'Alas, this is not so.'

Emily nods. 'God, yes. I can't bear shopping in

London. I don't mind the shops, they're *fabulous*; it's the staff. I mean, either they try to press-gang you into buying or worse, they're so rude. I'm incapable of being rude to anyone, but these girls, and it is mainly girls, the way they look at you if you have the cheek to bring a buggy into *their* shop, or bring yourself, if you're over a size zero or if your make-up isn't perfect or if you don't have the wardrobe to match Posh Spice or you're carrying a fake handbag or . . .' She stops mid-sentence and stares at Sandie, as though she has not noticed her before. 'It was *you*, wasn't it?'

Sandie looks down. 'I don't know what you mean.'

'Yes, yes, I'm sure it was.' Emily turns to me. 'I was so *low*. I'm a cheerful person usually, well, I know I was a bit bad tempered when we met in the shopping centre, Grazia, but the last few months have been so bloody hard. And before Christmas, oh, I thought my world was ending. I went shopping in Oxford Street, on autopilot really, and I let some superior, spiteful shop assistant bully me into trying on these expensive pyjamas and then Freddie threw up all over them and I could have wept and then the manager turned up and I thought I was for the high jump and the manager . . .' she points at Sandie, 'I'd recognise you anywhere. You saved my life. She let me take the pyjamas, even threw in a pair of slippers, it was the nicest thing that had happened to me for months.'

Sandie frowns. 'Giving stock away? That sounds crazy. Not something I would ever do.'

Emily squints, uncertain now. 'Well, I was a bit flaky at the time but I'm sure . . .'

I hold up my hand. 'No matter. Because the story you tell is the story of shopping: the good, the bad and the ugly. Except that before, you had to suffer in silence at the hands of nasty assistants. Now you can strike back. You are the patron saints of the shop floor, the—'

I'm interrupted by the computer speakers ringing like an old-fashioned telephone.

'That,' I say, reaching for the mouse, 'will be Charlie.'

The Mac screen bursts into life: I move in front of the webcam and click ANSWER. A full-sized silhouette of a man's head appears, complete with Churchill-style cigar.

'Grazia. Good afternoon, darling.' His voice is hoarse and gangster-like.

'Hi, Charlie.' I do not know if his name is Charlie or whether it is all part of the joke. Like his TV alter ego, he is a shadowy figure, despatching his women on missions to the frontline while he takes the proceeds. I beckon Sandie and Emily to sit next to me. 'Wave into the camera, ladies, and say hello to the boss.'

They edge towards me, hesitant as fawns.

'Don't be shy, girls.' Charlie's voice reverberates through the speakers. It makes me feel shivery. 'That's right, darling. You must be Sandra.'

Sandie nods towards the motionless silhouette.

'So where's Emily? Come on, missy, we don't have all day. Give Charlie a big smile. That's better. I do like to get a look at the goods before I buy.'

Sandie moves her head out of the camera range, her face unreadable. I remember I too felt uncomfortable when I first made contact with Charlie. A friend, Rosa, gave me his number, discreetly, as though needing to work was something shameful, and this in a world where cocaine is displayed in proud pyramids on dinner tables, and where wanting to have sex only with your partner in bed at home is regarded as a freakish perversion.

Rosa could tell all was not hunky dory after Leon's death. Never before had I worn last season's clothes to an exhibition launch. I took the Tube to the gallery, getting out a stop early so no one would see that I could not afford a taxi. Inheritance planning had never been high on Leon's list.

Rosa took me aside. 'It's none of my business, Grazia, but . . . there's this guy. I know someone who did a bit of work for him. You get to do what you always do – shopping, eating out, hotels – but someone else picks up the tab. I'm sure you don't need the money, but I thought you might be looking for something to do, to fill your days. Now that Leon's not there to be looked after.'

I called Charlie and that voice informed me, in mocking Cockney tones, that he wasn't in the business of providing spoiled women with hobbies.

He has this way of weaselling out what he needs to know and so I had to tell him what I would not tell anyone else: that I needed the money.

This is no job for people with options.

'I will leave you in the capable hands of Grazia here,' he growls. 'If you pass the initial test, then I'll be seeing much more of you on Shopping Angels assignments. Good luck, girls.'

Emily opens her mouth to reply but the silhouette has already disappeared.

'Is he for real?' Sandie asks, still staring at the blank screen.

I shrug. 'He can be brusque. But he always pays. This is more important than manners, would you agree?' I stand up, and open one of the huge white lacquered cupboards that line the back walls to keep the space clutter-free. I pull out two large handbags, and a hard-sided silver flight case. 'Now, we must get down to business. To the untrained eye, these are simply cheap handbags of the kind carried by inelegant women. But, as you are about to discover, these are in fact the ultimate in designer accessories, costing more than a thousand pounds each. They also happen to be the tools of your trade.'

CHAPTER 6

EMILY

This is the strangest day of my life.

Actually, it's been a strange week. Duncan used to accuse me of living in a fantasy world, but I could never have imagined this. First of all I get ambushed by a Nancy Dell'Olio look-alike and offered Spanish doughnuts and a job. Then I'm invited to an all-white house more streamlined than a millionaire's yacht, feeling like a grubby intruder who'll be made to walk the plank at any moment. Next I'm talking to an invisible man who thinks he's Tony Soprano.

And now I'm walking into the Beechford Village Stores, clutching a grand's worth of hidden camera equipment in a brown crocodile handbag, to record the shopkeeper's reaction when I try to buy a pint of milk, a loaf of bread and . . . um, a tin of caviar.

I think Grazia's trying to test our embarrass-ment threshold, but since being prodded and poked during labour by half a dozen midwifery students, mine is non-existent.

A bell rings as I push open the door and manoeuvre Freddie's buggy inside. The store is cramped and dark, with a strong smell of cabbage. In the briefing I was told to try to commit every detail to memory. Right. Here goes. The woman behind the counter – fifty-ish, very fat, with weasel-brown eyes magnified by half-moon glasses – stares at me and Freddie, and I feel quite naked. I clutch the camera bag closer to my body and I'm sure I can feel the electronic purr of the recorder inside. And *hear* it, too. Surely if I can, so will the shopkeeper?

I smile at her, but I don't know what to do with my hands, how to walk normally, what to say. Grazia warned us we might feel like this, but I hadn't expected it to be so intense. My palms are sweaty and my face is hot. Now, what did she say about positioning the camera? It has to be held so that the lens, behind a tiny circular hole in the fake crocodile-skin, is level with the people or events I'm trying to capture. After a while this will be second nature, apparently.

But I may not have a while. Everything hinges on this ruddy test.

'All right?' says the woman and I twist myself around to angle the bag-cam towards her. Is it recording her face, or her spare tyre (which is mesmerising, but not strictly relevant)? I pull the strap backwards so the bag faces up.

But hang on, in that position, surely the lens is pointing directly at the fluorescent lights on the ceiling and . . . ugh, that rather nasty stain.

You certainly see the world in a very different way when you're recording it.

The woman's staring at me, expecting a reply. 'Yeah, all right,' I parrot back, my voice helium-high. 'I'm looking for . . .' I spin around, then stop sharply when I remember Grazia's advice to *move slowly while filming, like a tiger in the long grass, stalking your prey.* I turn back. '. . . for bread.'

She nods curtly, then peers over the top of her glasses. 'Friend, are you? Of the widow? Can't remember the last time she got a visitor. Let alone two on the same day.'

I freeze. News travels fast in villages – I should know – but this has to be a record. We've been here less than two hours. What if she knows about the camera, too? Perhaps that's part of the test. 'More of an acquaintance, really,' I say, deliberately vague.

She beckons towards the corner, where loaves of sliced bread sag and sweat in their plastic wrapping. I take one at random, pretending not to notice the circles of green mould, desperate to get out of the shop before this woman rumbles me.

'She doesn't seem to have many friends. Not like her late husband.'

She sounds like a snake hissing. *Go on,* she's saying, *take the bait: I'm not going to say more unless you ask me, but you know you want to.*

No, I don't! I need to get out of here. 'Next on my list is . . . milk.' I walk towards the fridge, and she follows me: I can hear her polyester-encased thighs whooshing against each other. *Observe,*

observe, observe, but never judge, Grazia said. *You are paid for observation, not opinion.*

'He had so many friends. *Female* friends.' The closer we get to the chiller cabinet, the louder the motor gets. She raises her voice to compensate. 'He never could seem to bear being on his own, even for a few hours when his missus went out. Funny though, those young ladies never came when she was at home.'

What a bitch. In the purple-tinted glow from the fridge light, she resembles a corpse. I wonder how she'll look in the video when we watch it back . . .

Shit. The video also picks up sound. What is it Grazia said? 'The microphone is very sensitive, so do not forget to switch off before using the lavatory. I do not want to hear you piddling.' I laughed at the time. She speaks such quaint English. Now it doesn't seem quite so funny.

I stare down at the bag, trying to work out how the hell I can stop it recording. There's no override button, but I can't let the shopkeeper gossip away on tape about the very person who'll be monitoring the video for quality control.

Especially as something tells me all this would be news to Grazia.

'I'll take this,' I say, grabbing the milk and heading back towards Freddie and the till. Concentrate, Emily. You need this job. What else was on the list? 'I am in a bit of a hurry, but I don't suppose you'd happen to have any caviar?'

She raises her eyebrows, then squeezes back behind her counter, and dips down behind it for an uncomfortably long time, before emerging triumphant with a rusty tin the size of a fifty pence coin. 'There. Knew I had some. Got expensive tastes then, like the artist? You know they did drugs, don't you? I mean, I'm not one to talk behind people's backs, but I'm just thinking of the kiddie – you wouldn't want him exposed to that kind of—'

'Don't worry about us,' I say, coldly. 'Like I said, I am in a rush.'

She tuts, disappointed, then throws the items into a stripy plastic bag, rings up a ridiculous price on the till, and bares her teeth when I ask for a receipt. *Without a receipt*, Grazia warned us, *Charlie will not reimburse you for your purchases, and you do not want to end up out of pocket.*

I push the buggy back outside: the icy wind feels refreshing after the stuffiness of the shop. Now I can think straight again. There's only one thing to be done.

I keep walking until I spot a tiny churchyard. There, perched on a gravestone, I try out the edit function on the video recorder with frozen fingers, to wipe out my recording and with it, my best chance of gainful employment.

Still, what's a job compared to destroying someone's memories?

Grazia frowns as she presses rewind and looks at the plasma screen.

74

'This is not logical. I have never seen a gap in the recording like this.'

I shrug apologetically. 'Trust me to mess it up. Those buttons were very fiddly.'

She sighs. 'I told you not to touch any buttons except stop and start. Still . . .' she reviews the earlier footage, 'the framing is not bad. You seem to have the position of the bag spot on, and the sound is good. I will recommend to Charlie that we give you a proper assignment, see if you can do better next time.'

'Really? That's brilliant, Grazia. Thanks so much.'

'Do not get too excited. Most of the assignments are not glamorous. And although the pay is fair, you will not get rich on this work.'

I think of the amazing car she drives and wonder why she does this. She's not exactly broke. But perhaps she's lonely. The natives don't seem very friendly.

Grazia ejects my miniature tape and places Sandie's in the machine.

Sandie's another odd one. I'm *sure* that was her in Garnett's at Christmas but she got so bloody defensive with me when I suggested it. And I can't see why she'd be doing this job, either. I recognise the signs of someone at the last chance saloon – takes one to know one, as my big sister Jane says – and she's not one of us. She isn't nearly chaotic enough: she's too groomed, down to that helmet hairdo and the perfume that makes my nose tickle.

'Now, this is not so good.' Grazia is shaking her head as Sandie's video plays. Well, I *think* it's playing: the footage resembles the bottom of the ocean, a kind of swirling darkness, and the sound . . . all we can hear is rustling.

Sandie stares at the screen in disbelief. 'You must be looking in the wrong place. I caught the woman in the post office on camera taking a drag from her cigarette under the counter. You could see the smoke rising from her ashtray. Think of the fire risk. That should definitely be sent to her employer.'

'Are you quite certain you were pointing the camera the right way?'

'Of course, I'm not a complete idiot.' She picks up her camera bag – another mock-croc, this time in a filthy shade of bottle green – and wedges it in position. 'There!'

I lean forward. 'Um . . . actually, I think you've got the lens tucked into your armpit.' And I point at the teeny-tiny gap in the faux-crocodile skin.

She blinks several times in disbelief. 'But . . . I don't make mistakes.'

There's something indignant yet plaintive about her voice, like my sister Jane's five-year-old whenever he tries to frame his imaginary friend for yet another misdemeanour. Grazia is unmoved.

'Some people do not have the knack. Simple as that.' She removes the tape with a dismissive wave of her hand.

Sandie's face falls. 'Give me another chance.

Please. Emily had whole bits missing, and you let her try again.'

Grazia scowls. 'Charlie's Shopping Angels is not a charity for the incompetent. I am sure you will find something more suitable.'

'No!' Sandie's voice is loud now, almost hysterical. 'Look, please. This matters so much to me. I promise I can do it: I've spent years working in shops, I know all the tricks. I will definitely get results.'

Grazia surveys her coolly. 'Years in shops? Shops like Garnett's of Oxford Street?'

Two near-perfect circles of blush appear on Sandie's dark cheeks. She nods. 'Emily, I'm sorry, I'm not in the habit of lying. I did work at Garnett's, yes, for years, and then . . .' She stops. 'I can't talk about it. But I need this job, Grazia. I'll practise and practise until I am shooting better movies than Tarantino.'

'You have placed me between a rock and a hard place,' Grazia says. 'I do not know which way to turn. This job is hard work, Sandie. It involves standing in queues, sore feet, paperwork, and the pay is average. I must ask myself why a woman like you would want it so badly.'

I notice she doesn't ask herself why *I* would want it, though.

'Because retail is my passion,' Sandie says, quieter now. 'Because, through no fault of my own, I can't work at Garnett's any more. And I miss it.'

Grazia closes her eyes for a moment, as though

she's seeking guidance from above, and when she opens them again she shakes her head slightly. 'Against my better judgement, I will recommend that you are both given a further assignment, on probationary terms. If you mess it up, you will not be paid, however.'

'Thank you,' Sandie whispers.

Grazia switches off the TV and begins to tidy away the secret cameras. 'Time for you to go home now. You must be dead upon your feet.' She nods towards Freddie, who is lying flat out on the white leather sofa, cupid's bow lips moving softly in his dream with words he can't yet speak.

I look out of the window: dusk is moving in swiftly, the January wind has picked up, and the trees seem menacing against the silver sky. I shiver.

Grazia notices. 'Too dark now to walk. I will order you a taxi. I am a hard taskmaster; I demand the highest standards, but if you look after me and Charlie, we will look after you too.'

Despite the trials and tribulations involved in getting Freddie and his buggy back from Buckinghamshire, and then through London in rush hour on the Pink Line of Hell (otherwise known as the Hammersmith and City line), I feel rather pleased with myself as I head for Lime Village.

I have *nearly* landed myself a paid job. Not only that, but I actually seem to be better at it than Sandie, a proper professional woman with not a hair out of place.

When you've been as low as I have for the last few months, even something so insignificant is a huge boost. I feel the eternal optimism of the old Emily beginning to bubble inside me again. So I live in a fantasy world, eh, Duncan? Well, it's so much nicer here. The hoodies on bicycles at the end of my road look cuddly rather than threatening. I have a paper bag of falafel from the market, freshly fried and still warm to the touch, tucked inside my coat. I'm looking forward to a quiet night in front of the telly; there's a Barbara Taylor Bradford adaptation on. Rags to riches. Just the job. I might risk being a terribly irresponsible mummy and see if I can get away with topping and tailing my grubby son rather than the rigmarole of a whole bath. Dirt is meant to be good for babies, isn't it?

This is what I love about winter: the cosy lights on inside houses, especially when people forget to draw the curtains so you can have a guilt-free nose. I walk slowly, singing to myself. *Want to live like common people* . . .

Common people like the bickering teenagers on the other side of that big bay window: the girl attacking the younger boy with a ruler. And the aproned woman at that kitchen window, dancing to her radio. And the four workmen sitting around a bare table surrounded by packing boxes in that basement maisonette.

Hang on.

That's *our* maisonette.

'Shit, Freddie, we're being burgled.'

By people who leave the lights on. And bring boxes with them?

Perhaps the boxes are for taking away the spoils. Thank God I got back in time.

But there are no spoils in our maisonette, except dodgy melamine kitchen units, a twin-tub washing machine that hasn't washed for decades, and a load of fireplaces. Oh no. Not the fireplaces. It was the fireplaces that convinced me we should buy this old wreck. I imagined logs burning in the hearth, an antique mirror above it reflecting the rosy, smiling faces of my gorgeous family, like something out of the Boden catalogue.

Duncan was more impressed by the growth potential.

The dire threat to our mantelpieces propels me into action. I keep walking, trying to look non-chalant, but at the last possible moment, I excute a handbrake-style turn with the buggy and career through the gap in the fence (thank God we hadn't replaced the gate that was stolen the week we moved in), towards the communal front door. It's ajar, no doubt ready for their quick getaway.

I sweep my son into my arms, abandoning the buggy in the porch, and launch myself at the maisonette door, shoulder first, clinging onto Freddie. I don't think about exactly what I'm going to do when I face these burglars, until microseconds before my body makes contact with the door . . .

Which offers no resistance whatsoever, as it's not locked. I go shooting into the flat at fifty miles an hour, my feet skating across the filthy lino, as I try to work out how to brake.

Finally I regain my balance, and my voice.

'Get out of my fucking house, you bollocking bastards! OUT! OUT! OUT!'

In the moments that follow, a few things occur to me. One, the four men sitting at the table look surprised, but not especially threatening. Two, they're eating fish and chips from newspapers, an audaciously blasé thing for burglars to do mid-blag.

Three, one of the burglars looks remarkably like my father-in-law.

'Well, if it isn't the Leaky Little Mermaid!'

'Steve?'

He gets up from the table and moves towards me, oilier than the chip paper. 'Bloody hell, sweetheart, I never realised you knew language like that.'

I back away. 'What do you think you're doing here, Steve?'

The men watch us with oddly passive expressions. Steve chuckles unconvincingly. 'Now, what kind of way is that to talk to Granddad, eh, young Freddie?'

'Either you tell me what you and the Blues Brothers are doing here, Steve, or I *am* calling the police. You scared the bloody life out of me. You've got two minutes.'

He pulls a face. 'I take it the son and heir hasn't mentioned anything?'

81

'I haven't spoken to Duncan since New Year's Day.' Oh, and what a festive discussion that was, auld lang syne followed by yet another argument about whether I'm taking advantage of his ignorance of the cost of baby goods by applying what he called 'wronged-woman inflation' to my maintenance demands.

'Little sod. Typical of him to leave me to explain. Thing is, Em, it's about cash flow. Come on, sit down.' He gestures to one of the men to give up his chair. 'That's it. Cash flow and, to be honest with you, your own personal security. I mean, I know things aren't too good between you and Dunc but that doesn't mean he doesn't worry—'

'Not too good? He's in sodding Switzerland. With his lover.'

'Do you have to swear, sweetheart? In front of the boy?' Steve leans forward and puts his hands over Freddie's ears. Until now, my boy's been too busy gazing around him to cry, but he begins to whimper and I know I have only seconds to get a convincing explanation out of my father-in-law before meltdown.

'Tell me what's going on. Fast.'

He smiles awkwardly. 'These boys – Big Janis,' a large man with a blond pornstar moustache nods at me, 'Little Janis,' a smaller man with a darker moustache does the same, 'and Kaspar,' clean-shaven and much older than the rest, looks away, 'are your new downstairs neighbours.'

Despite his bravado, Steve winces in anticipation of my reaction. That's how I know he's not joking.

'Neighbours? As in, they're going to *live* here?' Freddie's whimper moves up a notch.

He nods, once. 'They're from Latvia. They're here to work, as builders. Good boys, they are. Business associate of mine found them; I wouldn't let just anyone move in under the same roof as family, Em, you know that.'

Hmmm. Given Steve's shady past – he was a big cheese in the Bristol badlands, for God's sake, before he was forced to flee to Somerset to run Rowminster's off-licence – I don't find this reassuring.

I whisper the next bit. 'I'm sure they're delightful company but . . . No way. No, I won't have it, Steve.'

'Oh, don't worry about whispering. They're good as gold but they don't speak much English.'

'That's meant to make me feel better?' Freddie is wailing now, but I know I can't lose this argument so I stay put: besides, the wails could be a weapon. I am used to them. Steve is not.

'Sweetheart, if you want Duncan to keep paying your mortgage, there's no way round it. Now I agree the little toerag should have told you himself, but, well, let's face it, he's not the only one who's been chickening out of passing on news, is he?'

I stare at him. 'I don't know what you mean.' Except, of course, I do.

'You're gonna have to break it to your folks soon, aren't you? Before they hear it somewhere else. Not like London where you can run a brothel from your garden shed and no one bats an eyelid. Someone's bound to tell 'em.'

'Are you threatening me, Steve?'

'Em. Would I do a thing like that?'

This from the man who undercuts his own off-licence with moonshine. Who threatened to disinherit Duncan for getting together with a girl from the 'wrong side of the tracks' (just because my dad belongs to the Madcap Knights Carnival Club, rather than the Old Devils' Club run by Steve). Whenever I spend time with Steve Prince, I think it's a miracle that Duncan didn't turn out worse.

'Yes. You would do a thing like that.'

'Now, now, Em. You're upsetting my favourite grandson.'

'Well, that is the funniest thing I've heard in weeks, Steve. Upsetting him, am I? Never mind that your son leaves us both in the lurch to head for the sodding Alps. Never mind that he's trying to move a gang of Latvian labourers into the house where we were planning to raise our family.' Freddie senses my fury and raises the volume level still further.

'Don't wet your knickers, love. You're gonna have to accept it. It's stay here with the boys, or come home.'

I want to shout at him some more, but suddenly I feel very weary. And I know he's right.

84

The mortgage on this place was always border-line unsustainable, and now that Duncan's forking out for fondue sets and cow-horns and all the other essentials of Swiss living, I suppose it was only ever a matter of time.

But filling the place with strangers who don't even speak the same language? I'm on my own, with a seven-month-old baby. They might be the loveliest people on the planet, but what if they're not? I can't help suspecting this is all part of Duncan's plan to force me out.

'I promise they're OK,' Steve says, more kindly now. 'Freddie's my first grandkid, Em. I might not be the ideal father-in-law, but I wouldn't agree to do anything that would put him at risk, I swear.'

Maybe I have to save my strength for the things I can change, the battles to come. I push myself up from the chair and manage one final withering glance at my father-in-law as I leave the room. 'This isn't the end of it, Steve. Just so you know.'

I try not to cry, try to recover some fragment of the optimism I was bursting with only ten minutes ago. At least . . . at least things can't get any worse.

As I go back out of the communal hall, into the dark, I realise even that isn't true.

Some bastard has nicked the bloody buggy.

CHAPTER 7

SANDIE

'**G**lasses, Sandie, glasses, chop, chop!'
I'll give him chop, chop. He'll be lucky if I don't chop his head off.

There is a stage in your life when you're happy to be a minion, to have people speak to you as though you're an idiot, to start at the bottom, to learn from your betters.

This isn't it.

'Come *on*. I don't pay you that extortionate minimum wage to daydream.'

Prentiss is Canadian and he has turned on its head everything I'd previously thought about the citizens of that fine nation. He is an *arsehole*.

It's no good. I can't swear, even in my head, without Gramma's voice ticking me off. *No need for that, Sandra. Swearing proves to the world that you don't have the intelligence and vocabulary to express yourself properly.*

So, as I lean over the industrial dishwasher and feel the hot steam blanket my face, I try to put my loathing for him into more elegant words. Ignorant . . . yup. Tyrannical. Untalented. Intellectually and physically stunted.

How's that, Gramma?

Never quite that simple, though. I must admit that I'm not the easiest of employees these days. For the first time ever, I'm working just for the money (that oh-so-generous minimum wage, plus tips) and it doesn't suit me. I can't switch off the desire to improve the customer service experience at the Vaults Bar and Brunch-erie: sack pretentious Prentiss for a start, simplify the wine list to focus on award winners rather than flash labels, drop the silly 'mission statement' from the menu, and upgrade the revolting loos.

'Guests!' hisses Prentiss as a media-type couple enter the bar. *The Vaults treats every visitor as a valued guest, a friend invited into our home to enjoy the finer things in life.*

Which don't extend to the revolting loos. I have to drench myself in Arpège every night before I come to work, because I can smell the toilets from here.

I serve the couple one of our more offensive reds before returning to the dirty glasses. I chose this bar, a bus ride from Dixie's Digs, because I hoped the tips would be more generous in upmarket Crouch End. Silly me. The rich stay rich by hanging onto their money.

Early evenings are the worst for dwelling on what might have been, because I'm not busy enough to be distracted from the grim state of my life. Haven't heard a word from that Grazia woman since my armpit-cam debacle. And anyway, I don't

87

see how I can build a *career* out of snooping around shops playing the awkward customer.

The glasses done, I begin to slice lemons, ready for the gin and tonic rush. What exactly am I going to do with my life? Maybe I should go home, tell Gramma, and take the lectures and the sighs and the disappointment on her face.

The thought of it makes me feel faint (and I have never fainted, not even after seventy-two-hour shifts preparing Garnett's for the legendary Greatest New Year Sale on Earth).

I miss Garnett's as intensely as people miss ex-lovers: I miss the smells, the warmth of the solid wooden door-handles, the music of commerce. Not being able to go there feels like the cruellest punishment. Especially when I have nothing to be punished for.

The doors open and a few more customers arrive. They come in waves, from the winter-sauna heat of the tubes and the buses, and from the chill of the sleety rain outside, hoping to wash away their commute with booze.

Ten to eight. On a normal evening at Garnett's, I'd be checking up on the night-time shelf-fillers, briefing the cleaners, joining Luis for a quick natter, and trying to summon up the energy to haul my body onto the train. On my journey home, I'd make notes about product ranges or displays. If I had a real brainwave, something too big to implement myself, I'd get Toby to put it to the board of directors.

But I'm trying not to think about him, for fear of letting loose my inner grizzly bear.

'Have you left your brain at home today, Sandie? Guests!'

I mumble an apology and form my mouth into a smile before looking up. 'Right, who's next?'

'I think you'll find I am.'

It feels like a drop of icy water is trickling down my spine.

Marsha. In all her pert, pouting glory. She looks more pneumatic than ever, pumped up with self-satisfaction.

'I didn't know you worked *here*, Sandie.' She leans forward so that her cleavage rests on the counter like chicken breasts on a butcher's block. Then she stage-whispers, 'You have told them, have you? About Garnett's?'

The desire to slap her so hard that her implants pop out fights against the desire to pay my rent. The latter wins, but it's a close-run thing. I can feel Prentiss's eyes boring into me. I can't give him an excuse to sack me, or her the pleasure of seeing me sacked for a second time.

Professionalism has always been my armour. 'What can I get you, madam?'

She giggles. 'Oh, a good bottle of wine. Something *sensuous*. What would you recommend?'

I can smell wine on her breath. Drinking on the job? Or maybe she's already ditched the management position she stole from me only five weeks ago. I don't know which would be worse.

'I think you'll find that the Dolphin Quay Shiraz meets your requirements.' At £40 a bottle, with an authentic aftertaste of rusty nails, I wouldn't wish it on anyone but my worst enemy. Which, of course, Marsha is. 'Though it is a little pricey.'

She smiles, revealing pearl-white teeth too big for her mouth. 'Not a problem. My date will be paying.' She looks theatrically over her shoulder. 'Now where is that naughty, naughty boy? Ah, impeccable timing as ever. Over here . . .'

I look up, expecting a chinless banker.

Oh no. Oh, no, no, no.

Toby Garnett's trademark 'life is sweet' grin disappears when he sees me. In its place, there's an expression of tortured embarrassment. He stares at the floor, as though he's hoping I won't recognise him under that floppy blond fringe.

Too late.

'Marsha . . .' His voice is low. 'Perhaps we should go elsewhere.'

I wait for my brain to unscramble my feelings. I grip the bar as an ocean of emotions threatens to knock me off my feet: fury, betrayal, bitterness, jealousy . . .

Jealousy?

Before I have time to think too deeply about *that* one, Marsha pipes up again. 'Rubbish, Tobes. I love the atmosphere in here. It's so entertaining. Unpredictable. And the barmaid has just recommended a luscious full-bodied number for us to share.' She licks her lips. Ugh. Surely Toby must see through her.

Toby looks at me and his eyes narrow with something I can't quite fathom. Sympathy? Even . . . an apology? I feel an unbearable surge of hope. Perhaps seeing me again like this after five long weeks has made him realise what Marsha is, and how he's misjudged me. He's about to tell me it's all been a terrible mistake and one he's going to put right this instant. He opens his mouth and I know he's going to make everything OK.

'Now, the nice barmaid is worried that your budget might not quite stretch to a forty-pound bottle of wine, Tobes. Put her right, won't you?'

The bitch has broken the spell: now he won't meet my eye. 'I really would feel more comfortable at the Old Dairy.'

He turns to go. I'm convinced that this is my last chance.

'Please, Toby. Wait. I need to talk to you.'

'There's nothing to talk about, Sandie.'

'But I never had the chance to explain.'

The other customers are watching intently. Toby glances over his shoulder, shakes his head, before reaching out for Marsha, grabbing her arm to pull her away. The look she gives me is one of total victory.

As I watch them disappear through the door I realise I'm hyperventilating. The chunky marble bar feels like a barrier between my old existence and the new one – on their side, life is bright with possibilities. On mine, life is one long washed-up mess of drink and dish mops.

'What does a man have to do to get a drink around here?' says the next banker in the queue.

I stare at him. *Think of the rent.* 'Sorry. What would you like?' Sandie Barrow, at your service, now and for ever.

Or not quite for ever, as it turns out. At the end of my shift – Prentiss wouldn't be stupid enough to leave himself short-handed – he calls me into the office and tells me he was having his doubts about my commitment anyway but an anonymous phone call has come through saying I was fired from my last job for dishonesty, and of course he wouldn't take an anonymous phone call seriously, but he will have to follow it up and wants to give me the chance to put my case before he does so.

I take my meagre back-pay without saying a word, and trudge home through relentless sleet. Safely back inside Dixie's Digs, I sit in front of my unlit fireplace, munching my way through a second packet of Gourmet Organic Camembert and Cranberry crisps (Prentiss allowed bar staff to take snacks home in lieu of drinks bought for us by clients). I don't feel hungry, but comfort eating is slightly less dissolute than comfort drinking.

The chewing doesn't stop the worrying, though. Why would Marsha want to destroy me so totally?

Am I really so hateful that someone would go to such trouble to rip me to pieces, bit by bit?

I must have done something dreadful in a previous life to have ended up here.

VALENTINE'S DAY

Time to go bisexual! At this critical time of year for giftware, cosmetics and lingerie, you're aiming to draw both men and women into your store. As in the act of love, male shoppers crave instant gratification: females prefer the slow burn, building to the ultimate climax. Offer both complete satisfaction – and your receipts will be better than sex.

MYSTERY SHOPPING BRIEFING
(02/9984 GL):

This national department store has invested millions advertising its Loved Up campaign featuring Valentine's gifts for all pockets. The assignment aims to test whether consumer experience matches expectations, through test visits by women in the target age range (25-45). The visits should include the following concessions:

- *For Your Eyes Only*
- *Garden of Eden*
- *Hearts 'n' Flowers*

Test visits should focus on display, customer-staff interface, and quality of advice/product knowledge.

CHAPTER 8

GRAZIA

London greets me like a neglected old friend, enveloping me in her smoggy embrace. *How could you have left me for so long?* The Chiswick flyover is an irresistible arc of silver, February sun on damp tarmac.

In the first month after Leon's death, before the money issues became apparent, I drove this way three, four times a week. I responded to every invitation, believing that surrounding myself with friends would keep him alive, somehow. But my value soon slumped: everyone had heard the story of his asthma attack. Old news. And once no one wanted to talk about him any more, there was no point in coming. What else did I have to say? I bored people; they bored me.

So here I am, back in the city, not to keep my husband's memory alive, but to try to keep our home. The letters from the bank are becoming less polite, and the letters from the solicitor gloomier. Leon never expected to die – who does? – but he couldn't have left things in worse shape. And 'muse' is not a job title often seen in the situations vacant columns.

When I begged Charlie for more work before Christmas, he laughed and advised me that the only way to make a good living from what he calls 'the spying game' was to run my own secret shopping team, yet so far they are costing *me* money. They cannot be trusted to get results, but Charlie has refused to send me more candidates until these two prove themselves. 'Start small, Gratz. Rome wasn't built in a day, you should know that, darling, being Italian and all.'

'In two hundred yards, turn left.'

The satnav's voice is male, authoritative but kind. It is crazy, I know, but halfway down the motorway I realised I was enjoying someone telling me what to do. I have missed it. The only independent decisions I ever made served my sole ambition in life: to escape Liguria and come to England. So I took the first job that came up at Malpensa International Airport – purely to increase the odds of meeting English husbands – and waited for my strategy to work. After that, Leon made every decision. It suited us both.

'You have reached your destination.'

Yes indeed. London. My destination since the age of fourteen. This part of town is less glamorous than my teenage fantasies back in Italy, but even so, there is nowhere else like this city. Despite the rubbish overflowing from wheelie bins, despite the pollution-stroked stonework staining the terraced houses, to me this road has so much more grandeur than a Parisian boulevard or a New York brownstone.

Charlie's assignments are about more than money: they are also my chance to sample urban pleasures again – hotels, restaurants, bars – the pleasures I could never afford on my own.

I spot fat Emily waiting with Freddie outside one of the smaller houses, surrounded by piles of baby paraphernalia. Maybe I am being unfair. I suppose she is not that fat, certainly nothing a good girdle could not correct. I prefer self-restraint, of course, but the right underwear might just pull the girl together. She could be pretty, if she tried, like a sweet shepherdess from the lid of a box of chocolates, all ringlets and rosy cheeks.

But no. I need her to stay the way she is. I chose her for how she looks: the undercover underdog.

I toot my horn, and she jumps. She approaches the Range Rover uncertainly, then smiles when she realises it's me. I press the button to lower the electric window.

'New car?' Emily says.

'You could say that.' I release the central locking before she has a chance to probe further. She fits the car seat in moments, loads the boot with the buggy and Lord knows what other items, and straps the baby into his seat, before hopping into the front.

'Oooh, it's like being in a tank up here. Look, Freddie!'

I peer in my mirror and see the boy waving his fists around in excitement. It feels strange to be

99

driving with him in the back: children make me nervous.

Emily babbles away about nothing as we head towards Kensington. She is clearly lonely living here; she admitted as much to me at that very first meeting. It all came pouring out about this husband who left her for a Swiss roll (I think this was a joke), and the family somewhere in the Wild West of England. I'm surprised she doesn't go home, but then perhaps she has her reasons.

I do not wish to know her reasons. I have never believed that a trouble shared is a trouble halved. Would it make me feel any better to tell Emily about the silent phone calls that have been plaguing me for the last few weeks? Not unless she is the one making them. And I think I know enough about her now to realise that staying silent is something she would find utterly impossible.

'. . . then there's this lovely little fruit and veg stall in the market, where they always give Freddie something free to crunch on, don't they?'

I was told the English were a quiet race. It was one of the things that appealed to me most. I was woefully misled.

I drive the tank into the car park, and by the time we unload the child, the buggy, the camera bags and all the rest, we are half an hour late for meeting Sandie. I spot her through the cafe window. She is flicking through a newspaper. There is no neediness about Sandie, no sense that she's desperate to make friends with you. Her aura is as solid and unyielding as chainmail. *Perfect* for antagonising shop assistants. Emily will be ignored and patronised by our targets: Sandie will try their patience.

She looks up as we enter the cafe. 'I was about to give up on you lot,' she says.

'My fault,' Emily says. 'And Freddie's. Sorry. I swear it'd be easier to transport a herd of elephants than an eight-month-old baby.'

Sandie's hard expression melts a little. 'It can't be easy.'

I clap my hands. 'No time to waste. I checked both cameras before I left, but you should still get into the routine of making sure they're working before assignments. Charlie will not pay for blank tape.'

'I thought all three of us were filming today. Where's your camera then?' Sandie asks.

I tap my black linen shirt. 'In here. Between the two top buttons.' They lean forward to look. 'You will not be able to see it. The lens is in the fabric, with the recorder housed in a belt strapped to my chest.'

'Gosh,' says Emily, 'that's real secret squirrel stuff, isn't it?'

'I did not want to have to carry one of those ugly bags so I had it made by the man who supplies undercover cameras to the BBC. You are clear on your tasks, yes? Emily, you start at the Garden of Eden and For Your Eyes Only concessions, and play dumb.'

She nods. It will not be hard for her, after all.

'Though also ask about exchange or return policy and gift-wrapping, yes? Sandie, your task is to make a nuisance of yourself. So, begin in Hearts 'n' Flowers, and ask about allergies and life span for cut flowers and anything technical. Try to needle the assistants into a reaction. Then, later, you'll swap places.'

Emily looks uncomfortable. 'I don't think I'll be any good at needling people.'

'No, no, you only swap locations. You stay dumb and Sandie, you stay awkward. Do not worry. It is only shopping. And I will be *right* behind you.'

Emily says she's feeling shy and doesn't want to be shadowed until she is into her stride, so I begin with Sandie, following her to the flower stall at the entrance to the store.

It is designed to look like a separate business, as though an enterprising florist has been to the flower market this very morning. Pah! People are so naive. I would never buy flowers from a giant retail group, any more than I'd buy my clothes from a discount store, or my wine from a corner shop. When we lived in London, my little black book of shops was encyclopaedic: under F, four florists, in the north, west, south and east. My favourite store, Art in Bloom, just off Marylebone High Street, was more alchemist than florist. Viktor could capture emotion in a bouquet. If I commissioned him for one of Leon's exhibition openings, he would always ask as much about the mood we wished to evoke as the colour scheme, and I do believe his arrangements influenced the guests, seduced them into buying.

But the English today are obsessed with convenience, preferring speed to quality, *just in time* over timelessness. Once, they prized old names, old values. Thirty-seven thousand shops in London and ninety-nine per cent, it seems to me, selling the same tat.

The Hearts 'n' Flowers stall could have been plucked from an amateur production of *My Fair Lady*. Underneath a striped awning protecting the merchandise from non-existent rain (we are inside), the bouquets are showy but tired-looking, like nightclub hostesses. The stall is staffed by two young women in navy butchers' aprons, with hands too soft to belong to true florists: they lack the raw, cracked skin of people who have spent years with fingers immersed in freezing water. There is a table stacked with a rainbow of tissue paper, overblown foil balloons and massproduced soft toys.

I smile as I imagine what Leon's reaction would have been had I bought him a bouquet of droopy roses and a teddy bear with orange plastic eyes. Most likely a long, moody rant about the commercialisation of feelings, the attempts to boil down the infinite scope of human experince to a few marketing opportunities.

But just occasionally, my mercurial husband

would surprise me. The dead-eyed ted might spark a passionate declaration of undying love for me and for popular culture, become the inspiration for a series of paintings. 'It's going to be the best thing I've ever done, Grazia, the best, I tell you!'

Ah, Leon. It was *always* going to be the best thing you'd ever done.

'I need help here. I want a budget bouquet that looks expensive.'

Sandie's voice is belligerent. Instantly, the two assistants exchange rueful glances. Good. Let us see how far she can push them. I hover at a distance, my camera recording her actions as back-up to her own dubious camerawork.

'These are nice,' the blonde girl says, gesturing towards some desiccated carnations.

Sandie shudders. 'They're revolting.'

'Oh,' says the blonde, 'well, I like them. For a boyfriend, is it?' she asks, her tone suggesting that she finds the idea of Sandie having a boyfriend implausible.

'Yes.'

'What's your budget?'

'Fifteen pounds.'

The brunette snorts. 'Well, you're not going to get a fat lot for that.'

I check Sandie's camera positioning. It is adequate: the bag faces the right way, with the side slightly angled upwards. Every sneer will be centre-frame.

'Can you at least try?'

The blonde sighs with weary resignation, the chorus of a thousand shop assistants whose hearts are not in the job, who believe customers simply get in the way of gossip. 'I guess. What's he like?'

Uncertainty crosses Sandie's face. Stupid girl. I told her to have a story worked out in advance, as it is clear she has no boyfriend in real life, despite her potential to be attractive. Her clothes are too old-fashioned, too buttoned up. And so, I suppose, is she.

'My boyfriend's very choosy,' Sandie says eventually.

The brunette raises her eyebrows. 'That doesn't help. Favourite colour?'

'Um . . . pink?'

'Pink?' Blondie does not disguise her contempt as she picks a single cherry-coloured gerbera from one bucket. 'You could have one of these . . . with a fluffy kitten.' She grins at her colleague.

'Look,' says Sandie, and her exasperation seems genuine, 'I just want something classy and reasonably priced. Is that so difficult? Surely a concession like this caters for all price points.'

I hold my breath: I must warn her that this is not the language customers use. But the blonde seems oblivious to everything except the irritation in Sandie's voice. 'Cream might work,' she says, leaning towards another bucket. 'These are cream roses. Not too girly. We could do those and maybe a box of toffees. Men always have a sweet tooth.'

105

Sandie frowns. 'How long can I expect the flowers to last?'

Brunette is bored now, desperate to get rid of her. 'Well, they're hardly going to be immortal for fifteen quid, are they?'

I smile to myself. Wait till Brunette's managers see *that*. Sandie hands over her money, trying to keep the bag angled towards the assistants. Unlike Emily, she is not a natural. But she is stubborn as a carthorse and independent, too, so maybe it will not be too long before I can let her work unsupervised.

She takes her flowers and turns away from the stall. As she passes, our eyes meet just for a second, and to my surprise, she winks.

To my even greater surprise, I find myself winking back.

CHAPTER 9

EMILY

O K. I *can* do this. I *have* to do this. Not only do I need the money, I'm also the patron saint of shoppers, a fearless one-woman campaigner for retail justice. Emily Prince, undercover in the underwear section.

So how do I stop myself shaking? The footage will look like it was shot during an earthquake. I have to focus.

Entering the store is like entering the court of Dame Barbara Cartland. Everywhere is pink and smells of flowers. Well, not *real* flowers, but a sickly fake scent somewhere between loo cleaner and the Parma violet sweets my granny used to crunch relentlessly between her false teeth. Duncan always said I imagined I was living between the pages of a romance novel, but this is too cloying, even for me.

Freddie grunts in disgust at the syrupy surroundings, and I try to navigate round this rose-tinted world. For Your Eyes Only is my first stop, and my camera purrs reassuringly as I follow the signs. First floor. I take the lift, which offers no hiding place from the soft-focus assault. Posters advertise Valentine beauty treatments (maybe if I'd opted for

Cupid's Bow Intimate Waxing, I wouldn't be a single parent) and *Love Shack* plays through the speakers.

For Your Eyes Only is a shop within a shop, hidden behind a rectangle of screens picturing Bond-style silhouettes of naked women holding guns. I step warily inside and feel momentary relief at the escape from Pink World. The relief is rapidly replaced by claustrophobia. There's a lot of black in here, and a lot of spot-lit mannequins with heads and limbs missing. Sure, they have pistols tucked into their scarlet mesh pants, but they're hardly going to be quick on the draw without arms.

I do a slow half-twirl to record the scene on my camera. Shame that secret shoppers are banned from giving an opinion about anything, because I'd have plenty to say about the sheer bloody idiocy of this department: the lighting is unflattering, the underwear looks slutty and uncomfortable, and I've never aspired to be a Bond girl anyway, as it seems to entail being bonked by a man who won't remember your name in the morning, and will abandon you to be bumped off by a villain with bad teeth.

'So, what can we do for you?'

The man who emerges from behind an Uzi-accessorised mannequin is quite a sight. He wears an all-black body suit, as modelled by the Milk Tray man. Very *slinky*. Very gay, too, I suspect.

'Um . . . I don't know that I want anything, really, just having a nose around.'

'You came to the right place to nose,' he says, 'but it's an even better place to buy. Hello, young man.' He drops to his knees to shake Freddie's hand. 'Cute. So, are we after something to excite his daddy, then?'

I bite back the urge to say that only lederhosen excite his daddy these days, but I'm a professional. My personal life does not intrude. 'Maybe . . . but I doubt that most of the stuff in here would offer me quite enough *support*, if you know what I mean.'

He nods sagely. 'Strictly between us, I know exactly what you mean. Our buyers are very keen on crocheted dental floss, yet I've never met a grown woman who shares their enthusiasm. But can I show you the nicer stuff?'

He doesn't wait for a reply, but leads me and my camera towards a black lacquer drawer unit by the back wall. 'Now, with your colouring, I'd say sky blue would work a treat. How do you feel about sky blue?'

'I don't know. All my underwear seems to be flesh-coloured these days.'

'Oh, I'm a big fan of flesh-coloured; nothing like it under clothes, but distinctly creepy when you're intending to get naked with the light on. Makes you look like Barbie, all smooth and genital-free.'

'It'd take more than pants to make me look like Barbie.' And anyway, the last person to show an interest in my genitals was the health visitor.

He laughs companionably and opens a drawer.

'Ah, if I had a pound for every woman who comes in here doing herself down. I wouldn't be working in a shop, put it that way. The secret of good underwear is *accentuating the positive*.' He holds up a pair of French knickers in pale blue satin, and without thinking, I reach out to touch them.

Then I jump back, remembering the silk pyjamas at Christmas. I'm not being caught like that again.

The assistant laughs. 'They don't bite!'

I remind myself of my responsibility to the shoppers of the world, and think myself back into the role Grazia has created for me: clueless consumer champion. 'I'm not really a fan of shiny fabrics. Do you have anything else?'

He shrugs amicably. 'What about cotton? Not as showy as silk, but it has that clean-cut aura about it that lots of men find very attractive.'

As he proceeds to pull out different drawers full of frivolous lingerie – a cute pink gingham set that should come with its own mop-cap, a white cotton bra and pants that conjure up wholesome 1980s tennis players, and a boyish navy vest and shorts – I feel a bit mean. There he is, working his socks off trying to sell me knickers, and I don't have any intention of buying – Charlie warned us in advance that our budget for this assignment was limited to fifteen pounds. And judging from the price tags, that would only buy me a single silk stocking, or possibly two thirds of a thong.

But I suppose I just have to remember that my work might get the salesman a promotion.

'Are you all right, darling?' He looks genuinely concerned. 'You look a bit out of it. Do you need to sit down or anything?'

'No, no, I'm fine. Sorry. I feel a bit faint, that's all. Shopping always makes me feel overwhelmed.' That much *is* true. 'I'm really sorry but I'm not in the mood for buying today.'

He shrugs again. 'Ah, well. There was me thinking I was irresistible. Take care, darling. Hope you get a real treat tomorrow.'

'Tomorrow?'

'Doh! Valentine's Day.'

To stop myself moping over my terrible Valentine's prospects, I charge straight over to the Garden of Eden concession. Grazia is hovering nearby, waiting for me.

The department store's version of Eden is bordered by purple plastic grapevines woven through trellis. Shiny plastic cherubs peek through the gaps in the fence, and a sign at the entrance shows a horny cartoon devil, with a speech bubble reading: OVER SIXTEENS ONLY.

I shudder at the thought of what's beyond the trellis, and glance down at Freddie, who, thankfully, is dozing away in his buggy. This one is grubby and second hand, an eBay replacement for the one stolen outside the flat. Secret shoppers can't be choosers. 'Keep your eyes shut, mate,' I whisper, and then push the buggy inside

Blimey.

I hope whoever gets to watch the secret camera footage is broadminded. I used to think I was, but there's something about walking into a space full of . . . um, well, *dildos* that brings a blush to my cheeks. I don't know which are worse: the true-to-life pink ones or the metallic space rocket ones. Either way, they make obstetric instruments look erotic.

Maybe this is some kind of secret shopping rite of passage. I pan the bag-cam round the room, trying to capture the full range of merchandise, which also includes oils, lotions and videos. It's the least sexy stuff I've ever seen, but I suppose it takes all sorts . . .

'He's not supposed to be in here.'

Now, I wouldn't be surprised to see the woman in front of me working in a library. But selling sex toys? She's probably only forty, but a very old forty, with tight grey curls and a po-faced expression. I bet she takes *People's Friend,* and prefers hot chocolate to choc-flavoured nipple gel.

'I did see the sign, but he's so little. I don't think he's in any danger of being corrupted.'

She folds her arms across her brown cardiganed chest. 'Not your job on the line, is it?'

Little does she know. If I leave without completing the assignment, I won't earn a penny and probably won't get any more work. 'Well, he's asleep.'

'He might wake up.'

'What about . . .' I cast around for a solution, or a 'safe' corner without any blush-worthy items.

Then I spot something, '. . . one of those blind-folds? He won't see a thing with one of those on.'

'They're not blindfolds, they're Luxury Lust Masks, designed for bondage, domination and sado-masochistic activities. Extra thick fabric to ensure maximum sensory deprivation,' she mono-tones, as though she's describing the features of a dishwasher.

'Yes, but he doesn't know that, does he?'

She shakes her head. 'I can't let him use it and then sell it to another customer. It's not hygienic.'

I'm seriously insulted on my son's behalf. 'You're saying that the people who'd use one of those might be in danger of *catching* something from an eight-month-old boy? I'd say that's the least of their worries.' But then I bite my tongue. I must stay detached. 'OK, OK, I'll buy one.' And actu-ally, the thought of using it later for maximum sensory deprivation – alone and in the privacy of my own home – is rather an appealing one.

£10 later, and my son is the proud owner of his first ever bondage mask. Quite a milestone, really, and something to tease him about when he brings his first girlfriend home. When I place it over his head, the soft fleecy lining pressing against his fluttering eyelids, he barely stirs and his baby features lend the jet-black blindfold an air of supreme innocence.

The woman says nothing. Surely salespeople are meant to try a *little* harder at the sales thing.

I offer her another chance to redeem herself on

camera. 'So what's your most popular present, then? I want something for my other half, nothing too shocking.'

She sighs. 'Handcuffs sell very well. Though you get what you pay for. We've had complaints about the furry ones, that they slip off too easily. Mind you, we've had complaints about the deluxe ones, too. Lose your keys and it takes the fire brigade to get you free. It's happened, believe me.'

'What, they come back and tell you? I'd be too humiliated.'

'Oh, no, very keen on their rights are perverts.'

'Perverts?'

'I don't know what else you'd call someone who buys this kind of stuff,' she says defiantly.

I give up. Some people deserve all they get. 'You know what, I think I might go the traditional route, now I think of it. Carnations. You can't go wrong with carnations.'

She sighs, and as I manoeuvre the buggy out of the 'garden', she's already taken out a large feather duster and begun to clean between the toys.

I turn round and aim my camera at her, a last lingering shot, just in case her good housekeeping is enough to save her job.

Missions accomplished. We're in the car heading back to Lime Village and Sandie is chattier than before, as she tells us how she out-grossed the Garden of Eden woman with technical questions about the vibrators. Even Grazia is smiling.

'What happens to the footage now, Grazia?' I'm sitting in the back with Freddie, who's still wearing his bondage mask. I tried to take it off him earlier but he wasn't having any of it.

'I check it over first, then I send it off to Charlie. I think he sends it straight off to the store head office. I do not know if he ever watches the material.'

'Then what happens?'

'Nothing, generally.'

'So you never know if your stuff got anyone sacked – or got someone a promotion?'

'Never.'

I feel a bit flat. 'It's like when a film or a book ends without tying up all the loose ends.'

Sandie, sitting in the front, turns back to me. 'I know someone who was sacked once, after a secret shopping visit.'

'Really? What did they do?'

'She was on cosmetics, working for a top-notch French brand. She made over this really awkward secret shopper . . . and she spat in the foundation, *and* the tissue she used to blot the customer's lipstick was one she'd just blown her nose on. All caught on camera.'

'Oh, gross.' I don't ask what I want to ask: why did Sandie leave Garnett's? The way she reacted when I recognised her, denying it at first, has convinced me there must have been some scandal, something at least as bad as the spitting salesgirl.

A weird silence fills the car and I contemplate my evening ahead. I've faced my fears, taken up the consumer challenge and seized the day. I can't bear the thought of celebrating with beans on toast and the whiff of Latvian stew wafting up through the floorboards from my housemates.

Grazia pulls up outside the flat. 'I will contact you when there is another assignment, depending on the response to this one.'

'Right,' I say, not moving. *Go on, Em.* What's the worst they can do? 'Um, I wondered . . . well, we haven't had the chance to view our footage and as we're still learning, maybe we could learn something from watching it together. Perhaps over a takeaway? Not if you've both got other plans, of course.'

There's an embarrassed pause. I've done it now. Exposed myself as Nobby No Mates. How humiliating.

Actually, no. It's not humiliating. If they want to be rude, then sod 'em. I *do* have other mates. They just happen to be a hundred and fifty miles away. OK, so I haven't invited them up from Somerset to stay yet, but I will. One day. When I get my shit together. When I have the London life I told them I was going to have. And if these two are too hoity-toity to want to know me, then that's their lookout—

'I'm free. And I'd quite like to look at the footage.' Sandie turns to Grazia and waits.

Grazia sighs. 'I suppose it might be helpful. I will only be sitting in a traffic jam at this time of the evening otherwise.'

All right, so a little bit more enthusiasm wouldn't go amiss. But these are my first house guests since Duncan left, and that feels like a baby-step forward.

'Cherry brandy or amaretto?'

Turns out I'm pretty under-equipped for house guests. I chucked anything I might be tempted to drink down the drain at Christmas, as a precautionary measure against maudlin behaviour, so all that's left are revolting liqueurs (I figured that if I was desperate enough to drink those, then I probably needed to).

My secret shopping colleagues have ignored the smell of damp and the horrible wallpaper, but a peep at my drink selection is too much for Grazia. She heads for the door.

'I will not be long.'

She leaves Sandie and I alone, tongue-tied, like kids left to amuse themselves. 'So, have you lived here long, then?'

'Just over a year,' I say. 'The little Londoner here was born a few months after we moved in.' Freddie's still lying in his buggy, snoring softly. Definitely like father like son.

'It's . . .' she hesitates, 'cosy.'

'Don't worry about being polite. It's cramped and damp and it's definitely not my dream home. This is not the way I expected to be living, put it that way. We own downstairs, too, had plans to redevelop the place, but . . .'

I run out of energy to explain and music drifts

up from downstairs. Soulful folk music played on mysterious Latvian stringed instruments.

'That's my neighbours. Only a temporary measure. They're builders from Latvia. They're normally pretty quiet, to be fair—'

I'm interrupted by a loud crash, followed by a shout of 'JANIS!' and then something unintelligible. The folk music stops and a few seconds later it's replaced by rhythmic Euro-pop.

Sandie gives me an odd look: I suppose it's pity. 'You should remind them about the baby. It's not fair on you.'

I smile at the word *fair*. Any fool knows life isn't fair and a bit of harmless music is the least of my bloody worries.

There's a knock at the door and Grazia comes inside with two bright blue carrier bags from the off-licence. 'The metal shutters on the outside were off-putting, but the owner had a remarkably good grasp of what makes quality wine,' she says.

'What, did you manage to fit in another assignment for Charlie?' I ask.

'Of course not. But this secret shopping . . . it is a hard habit to break.' She hands us each a bottle of Italian beer from the first bag, and produces a Swiss Army Knife with a bottle-opening attachment from her posh handbag. Then she retrieves the tapes from each of our bag-cams.

'What's in the other bag?' Sandie asks.

'Champagne,' says Grazia. 'But we only drink that if the footage is worth celebrating.'

CHAPTER 10

EMILY

I've never really had a talent before.

Not unless you count hopscotch, which isn't exactly crucial in adult life. No, Duncan's always been the gifted one, with a brain like a calculator. It made him the talk of the pubs in our town, with drinkers lining up to toss him long divisions like a seal catching fish.

A big fish in a small pond, and me swimming behind, his faithful minnow.

Who could have guessed that behind my dizzy blond exterior beats the heart of a fearless under-cover investigator? With a dozen assignments now under my belt, I do seem to have the knack.

It was obvious, even to me, when we watched the footage after the Valentine's shopping expedi-tion. Sandie's material was fine, despite a few blurry camera moves that left us feeling seasick. But mine was in a different league, each separate mission like a short film, the locations crystal clear, the assistants' faces centre-stage. The sales-woman's dumbstruck reaction to my purchase of the bondage mask made everyone laugh out loud. Perhaps my lifelong nosiness, my curiosity about people's secret stories, has finally found a useful outlet.

Grazia pronounced the material worthy of the champagne she'd bought and we toasted our future together as Charlie's Shopping Angels. It'd be foolish to think I'd gained two *proper* friends, but there's something about the secrecy and danger of discovery that creates a certain camaraderie.

It's been a busy few weeks since I passed Grazia's test. I've become quite the girl about town. I've ordered burgers with extra mayo and without pickle, in four different branches of the same fast food outlet, and recorded how many times I was offered a bigger portion. I've investigated whether staff in a national chain of shoe shops are following correct verruca-prevention procedures and giving customers the hard-sell on polish and insoles. I've also started doing assignments from the discomfort of my own home, inviting a specialist bathrooms salesman round to check out safe showering options for an imaginary elderly relative who might be coming to live with me.

OK, so it's not exactly the glamorous London lifestyle I dreamed of back in Somerset. But compared to my existence before Grazia talent-spotted me, it's a revelation. Fun, satisfying, and just the tiniest bit *risky*. Being undercover adds a frisson to the most tedious shopping trips. In fact, I play mystery shopper now whenever I go out, imagining a secret camera is recording every sneer from the bus driver and every shrug from the chemist. *I'll show you*, I tell myself, *you can't get away with treating Emily Prince this way!*

Except, of course, they can. And they do. Somehow I attract bad service. I used to think it was simply becasue I lived in a place where everybody knew my history. But I was wrong: after all, no one I meet these days knows me as the Little Mermaid who Wet Herself.

Well, no one except Duncan. The rain on my parade, the blot on my landscape, the . . .

'Emily!'

. . . the one part of my former life that I can never escape.

He strides across the cafe towards Freddie and me, and several yummy mummies nudge each other, Five-foot-five of boy-next-door charm. He looks well rested – no unbroken nights for Duncan any more – and immaculately dressed in preppy, perfectly pressed leisure wear. Either Heidi is a whiz with an iron as well as a spreadsheet, or he's splashing out on expensive laundry services.

He hesitates for a moment when he reaches the table, as though he can't decide whether to hug me.

I put him out of his misery with a curt, 'You're early.'

Duncan crouches down next to the buggy and begins to unclasp Freddie, who watches, wide-eyed. Does he still recognise his daddy, or is it simply pleasure at the prospect of being released from his reins?

'That sounded suspiciously like a moan, Em.' As he leans down, I smell the familiar musky aftershave, notice the trendy Alpine peaks in his field-mouse-coloured hair. He lifts Freddie out and kisses him on the forehead, before manoeuvring himself into a chair. 'I've been here approximately thirty seconds and you've started already.'

He smiles his charming smile.

'Are those new teeth, Duncan?'

The smile broadens. 'No. Got them whitened. What do you think?'

'Dazzling.'

'Why does that not sound like a compliment?'

I shrug. This is meant to get easier, isn't it? At some point, we'll move on from the sniping of separated spouses, towards deep indifference. But not just yet.

'I was going to get you a coffee, but seems you've already got one,' says Duncan. 'Though at least all that food explains why you want me to increase the maintenance payments.'

The remains of my lunch litters the table: a choc-latte with added marshmallows, a cheese and mushroom panini, a blueberry muffin. Oh and a pack of cappuccino-flavoured coffee beans. They're unopened – even I couldn't eat all that in one sitting – but I thought they might come in handy as a pick-me-up on secret shopping days.

And they also took my bill to £8.98, just under the £9 maximum spend that my assignment briefing specified. It's not Duncan's precious bloody money that's paying for me; it's Charlie's. Not that I intend to share this fact with my husband. Far more fun to wind him up. And anyway, I rather like the idea of keeping the mystery shopping a secret from him: that'll be a first for Blabbermouth Emily.

'So now I'm not allowed to eat anything but beans on toast? While you splash out on having your teeth whitened?'

'I need to maintain certain standards in my job,' he says pointedly.

'And I don't?'

He raises his eyebrows in reply.

'I'll have you know that my standards are very high, Duncan.'

'If you say so, Em.' He's staring at my chest and I know enough to realise he's not admiring my cleavage. I look down and see a blob of something congealed on my black sweatshirt.

'I might not be entirely free of stains, Duncan,' I say, 'or entirely crease-free, either, but in my job as Freddie's mum I have other priorities.'

'Like scoffing all the pies?'

'What's that supposed to mean?'

'Oh, nothing . . .' He's already lost interest and is scanning the room for pretty women. I used to tell him off for it, but he told me that it was instinctive, and that wandering eyes were better than wandering hands. And, to be fair, I don't believe he was ever unfaithful before Heidi. I'd have found out. Rowminster was that kind of village. 'Don't suppose you'd get me a coffee, would you? Only I've got my hands full with this little chap.'

He's not looking at me. In fact, he's checking himself out in the large mirror behind me, trying out different poses for his 'hunky yet caring single dad' look: *that* smile, then the slightly rueful frown, the wistful gaze. It works better when he's sitting down, of course. Much harder to look hunky when you're standing up and women can see that you're shorter than they are.

I swear I never used to be bitchy. Or bitter. I'd better leave before I begin to hate myself.

'Sorry, Duncan. I'm just going. I'm sure you'll manage.' I push my chair out, ready to go.

His eyes flick away from his reflection, up towards me. 'Oh. Don't go yet. We need to catch up on stuff.'

'Like what? You've got all you need to look after Freddie for a couple of hours.'

'Well, we should talk about his progress. And the flats. And the future.' He wrinkles his nose, as though he's trying to remember something important. 'Oh, and about you, of course. How you're getting on.'

I sit down again. 'If you're going to pretend that you care, Duncan, please don't bother.' Yet despite my defiance, the neediness in my voice gives me away, the unspoken plea for him to tell me I still matter to him. That he meant it when he told me I was the funniest, best girl on the planet. Even if he doesn't mean it any more.

124

He pulls the same rueful frown he was practising in the mirror a few moments ago. 'I'm not pretending.'

'What do you want to know?'

'Um . . . well, how you're keeping? How Freddie's sleeping? All the stuff I've been missing.'

I feel terribly weary. I mean, I'm not an idiot. I know he's not coming back. Yet every time we meet up, it hurts all over again. I don't really care that Duncan's missing out on having a son: but I care about Freddie missing out on having a full-time dad. 'He sleeps fine, most of the time.'

'Good, good,' says Duncan. Yet if I asked him, he wouldn't have a clue what 'sleeping fine' really means: two hours, four, sixteen? He'll never see the tiny changes I notice, the funny new expressions that Freddie's never made before, or the sounds that seem to creep nearer to a first word every day.

I know Freddie won't be the first boy to grow up this way, but I still feel that it's a tragedy.

'He's becoming more his own person all the time,' I say, suddenly wanting Duncan to understand how special our son is. 'I know it sounds daft, but he's already got this fantastic sense of humour.'

Duncan studies Freddie's face, as though he's expecting him to launch into a stand-up routine. 'Excellent.'

Go on, I think, ask me something else. What he loves to eat, what music makes him jiggle his plump arms above his head, which toy is his favourite.

But Duncan seems distracted, and there's a long pause. I'm about to fill it when he says, 'You know, Em, we're going to have to formalise things soon.'

'Things?'

'Arrangements. Make some calculations about the money. The way things are at the moment, it's not really sustainable. I'm running three households, more or less, when you count your flat and downstairs and Geneva, and things aren't great in insurance right now. Too many natural disasters. My bonus is going to be virtually non-existent.'

'Really?' I do hope he isn't expecting my sympathy. 'I thought the Latvians were meant to improve your cash flow.'

'Not quite that simple, Em. Not giving you any trouble, are they?'

'No. They're a bit noisy at times, you know, crashing around, but I never see them. Though I don't like them being there.'

'Good. Good. I mean, yes, I know it's not ideal but . . .' He reaches for the unopened packet of coffee beans and removes the cellophane with one hand, the way he always did with fag packets before he gave up smoking. 'I can keep going for a few months longer, but then we're going to need to think about longer-term arrangements. And you're going to have to tell your parents.'

'No! You know what'll happen. They'll be here before I've finished my sentence, dragging me back home.'

'Well, you're going to have to go back sooner or later, aren't you?' He says it casually, then scoffs a couple of coffee beans.

'Says who?'

He grants me a tolerant smile. 'Oh, come on. I know you had high hopes of London, thought the streets were going to be paved with gold and all that jazz, but it's time to face facts.'

'And I suppose you're going to help me do that, are you?'

'Now don't get all chippy with me, Em. Remember, I know what you're like. You need company. London's no place for you, now you're on your own.'

You'd think that after all this time, he'd be incapable of surprising me. But his complete lack of tact, and his failure to acknowledge that I am on my own *because of his infidelity*, renders me speechless. While I am trying to recover my voice, he chomps another handful of coffee beans with his traffic-stopping teeth, and then goes in for the kill.

'I'm not going to put a time limit on it today, Emily. But you can't behave like a little girl for ever. Freddie's your responsibility – well, our responsibility, of course – but you're his mum and you need to do what's best for him. I'm sorry if that sounds harsh, but it's basic biology. It's got

127

to be better for him to be near his grandparents than here, where you know nobody. I'm thinking of your welfare, as well as Freddie's.'

'Well, that's good of you, Duncan.'

'Don't blame me for pointing out the obvious.'

'But I like London.'

'Go on. What do you like about it?'

I've always hated it when he puts me on the spot. He's faster than me, and he knows it. The right answer always comes to me about thirty minutes after he asks me. 'Um . . . the shops?'

Duncan sighs impatiently. 'OK. There are some nice shops. But what's the point, if we don't have any money to spend because it's all disappearing into the money pit of those two flats? So apart from shops, what does London offer that Rowminster can't?'

'Freedom.' It comes out as a whisper, but still loud enough for him to hear me. As soon as I see his scathing face, I wish he hadn't.

'Oh, Emily. Freedom for what? You can daydream anywhere.'

I stare at the floor of the cafe. It's filthy, the lino stained with coffee and squashed sweets. Even in the midst of my misery, I make a mental note to mention it in my secret shopping report.

When I don't answer, he reaches out and touches my arm. I shoot backwards and his soothing smile falters for a fraction of a second.

'I've been patient, haven't I? Cut you lots and lots of slack, because I know I don't come out of this as the perfect husband. But you can't expect me to put my life on hold for ever.'

'And what if I don't agree? What if I want to stay here? In my *home*?'

His expression grows more patronising. 'Then there'd be questions to ask about your commitment to Freddie. If you keep putting your own needs first, I'll have to investigate my rights with regard to custody and so on. I might not be as hands-on as I'd like, but his welfare is my prime concern and if I need to get more involved . . . so be it.'

'You think I'd harm my own son?'

Duncan strokes the soft blond curls on Freddie's head, though I know my son hates anyone fiddling with his hair. 'Not on purpose. Oh, look, it won't come to that, Emily. It's just . . . well, life is an awful lot easier when we're singing from the same hymn sheet.' Freddie wriggles so hard he nearly falls off Duncan's lap. 'Come on, then, Fidgety Fred. Let's get you out in the fresh air. Daddy'll tire you out in the park, so Mummy can put her feet up later. She deserves a nice rest, eh?'

I take the 94 bus to the West End, unencumbered by Freddie and his wipe-clean plastic entourage. I'm going to spend the next three hours worrying myself to death anyway, so I might as well earn a few quid at the same time. I've arranged to do another quick assignment in a bank branch near Oxford Circus, then I'm going to keep Sandie company while she tests a wedding list service in a department store. I'm going to pose as her best friend: not that the assignment specifies a back-up, but she's still feeling a bit nervous about filming, so I offered to go, just in case.

Anything to take my mind off Duncan's afternoon with the Little Londoner and my own inability to stand up to his threats.

The bank job goes OK: the bland surroundings remind me of my own years pushing paper around. Assignments like this are more like memory tests than anything else: some clients don't want to fork out for filmed material, so instead I have to keep it all in my head. How many minutes do I have to wait in the queue? Are the counter staff well turned out (please note their name badges and any breach of uniform or excess facial hair)? Are the carpets hoovered and the leaflet racks fully stocked with offers of easy money and dread disease insurance? Apart from a non-working biro, the staff pass with flying colours, and I earn myself fifteen quid.

Get rich quick it's not, but I need to start saving if Duncan's planning to play hardball. Though he can't be serious about custody, can he? Ninety-nine per cent of me is sure he wouldn't see it through, but my husband has a seriously stubborn streak. I still remember the time when he ran a half-marathon just because his dad took the piss out of his weak knees. Duncan couldn't walk for a week afterwards but he said it was worth the pain to win the argument.

'Hey, daydreamer? You look miles away.'

Sandie is waiting for me alongside the Clarins counter.

'Yes. Sorry. All a bit overwhelming.'

'This is why we call the entrance to the store the Decompression Zone. It's where you get your bearings. And a good first impression, hopefully.' She smiles. She's made an effort today: she's wearing some fab, spicy perfume, and a touch of lipstick, which is all it takes to make her look gorgeous. No Spidered Out Cream required to even out her radiant complexion. I'd be dead jealous if it wasn't for the fact that she clearly has no idea how stunning she is.

'Well, you make a good first impression, that's for sure. The lipstick suits you.'

She pulls a face. 'I thought an engaged woman needed a certain glow, but I'm a bit worried I've overdone it.'

'No way. You definitely glow. Let me see the ring . . .'

She holds up her hand and I admire the antique gold ring. 'From my gramma. She gave it to me for my twenty-fifth birthday. She'd been saving it for when I got married, but then realised it wasn't going to happen any time soon,' she whispers.

'Think yourself lucky. Husbands are overrated, Sandie.'

'Was it that bad?'

'Duncan was horrible, just *horrible*. I'd forgotten how crap he makes me feel.'

'Oh. Poor you.' She looks uncomfortable and I fight back the urge to spill the beans.

'Shall we get stuck in, then?' I hold up my enormous handbag camera. 'This is definitely one of the best bits about getting married: having people buy you all the things you've ever wanted.'

The Wedding List Suite is on the first floor of the store. Suite's a bit of an exaggeration, but it's a very pretty room, with a dainty pink stool for our List Coordinator, Eileen, and a red sofa pushed against the wall for the happy couple. In the absence of any husband-to-be, I join Sandie on the sofa, and the squidgy cushions push us together in the middle.

'I didn't know you cared!' I say, and Sandie laughs nervously. She holds her handbag-cam on her lap, and I've placed mine on the coffee table. One way or another, we'll catch Eileen's performance. So far, it's Oscar-winning.

'I love my job,' she says, her plump face flushing happily as she pours two glasses of cava for us. 'Making people's dreams come true.' I'll be happy if I look as good as Eileen when I'm in my fifties: she has the cosy look of the fairy godmother from Disney's *Cinderella*, all soft edges. She smells like a powder puff.

'I haven't completely decided where I want my list . . . our list to be held, yet,' Sandie explains. 'I was thinking of John Lewis, or Garnett's. But I thought I'd find out what you had to offer.'

'Champagne truffle?' Eileen holds out a purple

heart-shaped box of chocolates, but her podgy hand fails to cover the many gaps in the velvet-lined interior. I suspect that there are more tangible – and tasty – benefits to her job than making couples' dreams come true. 'I don't blame you for shopping around, Miss Barrow. It's an important decision. But we think we've got something extra.'

She turns her swivel chair and reaches into a small chest of drawers behind her. Turning back, she hands us each a satin-covered oblong box. 'This is our secret weapon. Go on, open it up.'

Inside, nestling on a bed of horse-shoe patterned tissue paper, is a mobile-phone-sized device, with a touch-screen. As I lift it out, it comes to life in my hand.

WELCOME TO THE ULTIMATE WEDDING LIST PLANNER flashes on the screen, accompanied by a quick burst of 'Here Comes the Bride' from the tiny speaker.

'The Interactive Wedding List Planner is the biggest innovation in this area for decades,' says Eileen. 'It uses barcode technology to instantly relay your wishes to our central database. No forms, no catalogues. All you need is a large group of friends with bottomless wallets!'

I sneak a glance at Sandie, who is examining the handset. 'So how does it work?'

'Well,' says Eileen, 'I could give you the manual. But it is ever so much more fun to try it out yourself.'

★   ★   ★

Five minutes later, Sandie and I and the handsets are on the shop floor. Eileen has her own handset and shows us what to do.

'It's easy as anything. Whenever you see something you fancy, you just swipe the barcode and it beams each item through to your personalised list. It'll even point you towards matching accessories, or suggest where you could go next.'

Sandie scowls. 'That's all very well, but what happens when we get back upstairs and I realise I've spent the national debt of Colombia in less than half an hour?'

Eileen nods. 'We've thought of that. You can choose to have the running total displayed on the screen. But I think that does make it less magical, so I always prefer option two, where the computer automatically generates alternative lists with similar items, but for a lower budget.'

'Clever,' says Sandie.

'I can tell you're dying to have a play, so shall I leave you girls to it? See you back upstairs at two thirty – I'll put the kettle on, ready.' And off she bustles.

I switch my camera off: no point recording now she's gone. 'This is going to be such fun, Sandie. Where do we start?'

'I'd like to equip my luxury kitchen first of all,' she says, and I follow her towards Homewares. This is a less flashy store than Garnett's: no themed shops-within-shops, just brightly lit displays of carefully chosen products, and lots more Eileen-a-likes patrolling the aisles, kindly and firm, like old-fashioned hospital matrons. When they spot the Wedding List handsets, we get extra-warm smiles. I'd love to move in here: I bet they'd serve me toasted crumpets when I wasn't feeling well, before tucking me up under a fifteen-tog duvet with Egyptian cotton bed linen.

'So, are you thinking traditional or modern crockery?'

Sandie shakes her head. 'I can't say I've ever given it much thought. What did you go for?'

'Traditional. Cream Royal Doulton. Duncan wanted an all-black dinner service, but I refused. I'd waited ten years for that bloody wedding and I was having it exactly as I wanted.'

Sandie picks up a white plate made from such fine china that I worry it might shatter between her fingers. 'Ten years? I always imagined that you'd been married for ever.'

'We were together for twelve years, all together, but he only gave in and agreed to make an honest woman of me two years ago.'

'What brought that on?'

'I think he realised I was the only woman in Rowminster who'd put up with his constant flirting. Also, we both wanted kids, so that was my bargaining chip. I said I wouldn't come off the Pill till I had a ring on my finger. I got pregnant within three months of our wedding, just before he finally got a job in London. He'd been trying for years.'

'All change, eh?'

'Yes. Too much change, I guess. He'd decided to settle for the life we had back in Somerset, then, after all that time, there were so many new possibilities. First-class flights, expense-account dinners. Gorgeous young secretaries.'

'But he was married.'

'Well, yes, but he was always a flirt. I used to think that didn't matter, that I was the one he came home to. But I was getting fatter and fatter and obsessing about which buggy to buy for the new baby.'

'It's no excuse for leaving, is it?'

'No. But understanding why he went isn't the same as excusing him. We weren't enough for each other any more. We both had dreams. But mine was of family life in London, and his . . . well. Turns out his dreams didn't feature me any more.'

'Do you regret getting married?'

'No, because without that there wouldn't have been Freddie.' My throat tightens as an image of my baby crying, while Duncan chats up mums in the park, flashes through my mind. I focus on a chunky Rennie Mackintosh-style teapot in aquamarine. 'I like this – I always think that if you go for a plain dinner service, then you can afford to be flashier with the tea service.'

Sandie nods, taking the hint about changing the subject. 'Let's swipe it then.' The handset makes a satisfying ring, like two champagne glasses knocking together. 'Oh, I like that. Let's do it again.' She swipes the matching sugar bowl, and eight cups and saucers. 'This is really smart thinking, you know, Emily. Fabulous way of giving the customer a little reward with every new purchase, yet without any hard sell. Genius.'

The handset answers with another ring and a message appears on the screen: *If you like coffee as much as tea, our range of espresso makers suits all budgets and tastes.*

We walk on, past some wholesome earthenware soup dishes, towards the chrome glamour of kitchenware. 'Do you miss your old job?'

'It's that obvious, is it?'

'Well, your face did light up as soon as we got onto the shop floor. I adore shopping, but I also find it bloody stressful. I couldn't choose between all these lovely things, even if I did have the money to pay for them. I feel myself going quite dizzy. Whereas you seem to have gone all Zen-like.'

'Really? I don't think anyone's called me Zen-like before. But I am in my element. It's about making a potato masher,' she picks one up, 'seem like the answer to all your problems.'

I take it from her: it's shaped like a giant garlic crusher, in letterbox-red enamel. 'A *potato masher*?'

'Yup. Creamy mashed potato with a pool of melted butter on top. Eaten round a scrubbed pine farmhouse table, with an open fire in the grate and a gale howling outside. Wearing a cardigan and slippers. How does that sound?'

'Very nice. But I wasn't picturing any of that

until you described it to me, even though I have such a vivid imagination that living in the real world is a daily challenge. So does that mean the shop has failed?'

'No. It just means that a potato masher isn't the answer to *your* problems today. I only want to sell you a masher if you need one, or want one. I want to sell you things that you'll love using or wearing or looking at, so that you'll come back over and over again.'

I put down the masher and we walk underneath a huge wrought-iron rack, from which are hanging copper saucepans, huge steel woks, shiny colanders and vicious-looking cheese graters.

'I still don't quite get it. I thought the point of stores was to sell you as much as they can. More sales, more profits, surely?'

Sandie stops. 'In my view, it's not sustainable. Got to be a long-term relationship. Of course you want to seduce the customer. Create desire for what you've offered, close the deal and get them to take you – or your products – home, perhaps suggest accessories or complementary purchases. But it's no good if the customer wakes up in the morning feeling regret, guilt, betrayal, when they realise this isn't what they wanted and they don't want you or what you're offering after all.'

'Right. Well, I know all about that.'

Sandie sighs. 'Sorry. I didn't mean . . . that was insensitive of me.'

RIIING! The handset's screen shows a new

138

message: *Electrical items are amongst the most popular wedding gifts: take a look at our range of matching toasters, kettles and blenders.*

'Ah, don't worry about it. I know you're talking about shops, not marriages.'

'Yes, well, what I know about marriage could be written on the back of a postage stamp. But what it has in common is that customer relationships are also based on trust. Once you lose that trust you're finished . . . ooh.'

'What?'

'Over there,' she whispers. 'See the woman in the headscarf?'

I look towards the cutlery section where a middle-aged shopper in a dark green mac and Queen-at-Sandringham patterned brown scarf is examining teaspoons. 'Yep.'

'Well, I think the store might have been a bit too successful in creating desire in that particular customer.'

Sandie turns slightly, so it's less obvious that we're watching, and the woman opens her handbag for a hankie, blows her nose, and replaces the hankie. But the teaspoons – three of them – have disappeared from her hand.

'Did she just do what I think she did?'

Sandie nods. 'Yes. We have a magpie in our midst. And not a store detective in sight.'

I look round. 'But how would you know? Store detectives are normally in plain clothes, aren't they?'

'I could spot a store detective at a hundred paces.'

'What are we going to do?' I feel quite excited: I don't think I've ever seen a crime being committed before. I keep glancing across at the woman, who has now moved onto studying the knives. 'I think she's going for the full set.'

She shrugs. 'It's not our responsibility, Emily. And if we reported her, we'd compromise our own assignment. Shrinkage is a fact of life in shops. The smaller the item, the more likely it is to be nicked. Do you know what the most commonly stolen product is?'

'Booze?'

'Razor blades. Followed by teeny, tiny expensive pots of eye cream. Perfect for selling down the pub. Of course, the biggest thieves of all are shop staff.'

RIIIIING!

The handset springs into life agian: *If you've finished equipping your kitchen, why not pay a visit to decorative accessories and original art? Create a home, sweet home for you and your true love.*

For some reason, the message makes me smile. 'Hmm. I think it takes more than a few pictures to create the perfect marriage. But you can't blame them for trying . . .'

EASTER

Whether you're selling Easter eggs or egg-shell paint, capitalise on the first glimpse of spring to persuade your customers to treat themselves, their families and their homes. Bright colours and bright smiles equal bright sales figures.

MYSTERY SHOPPING BRIEFING
(04/1024GL)

Bells & Whistles is a homes and hardware specialist with a future! We're expanding our operations in the Home Counties, targeting ABC1s with disposable income and a love of good design. Our product range has evolved from nuts and bolts towards higher value items, refreshed seasonally to reflect latest trends and colourways.

At this key time of year for spring cleaning and DIY, we wish to check our performance in key territories in the Thames Valley. Our priorities are compliance with 'meet and greet' measures, product presentation and merchandising, point-of-sale behaviour, sales enhancement, and till protocol.

CHAPTER 11

EMILY

The shopping education of Emily Prince continues apace. In the last three weeks, I've been shopping for the morning-after pill (checking that the pharmacist didn't make me feel like a slut). I've been buying – and then returning – posh suitcases for an imaginary Easter holiday on a Greek island. I've eaten still more fast food (last Tuesday I travelled to seven branches of the same burger chain, all along the Central line. That night I dreamed of flocks of chicken nuggets).

There are fringe benefits. Literally. I've had my hair done for the first time in a whole year and, thanks to excellent positioning of my bag-cam, managed to get a perfect view of the stylist's appalled expression as she inspected my split ends (though to be fair, she trimmed Freddie's lovely blond baby hair for free, and put a curl in an envelope for me as a memento of his first cut). Grazia wasn't impressed by my new sleek bob – I think she *prefers* me to look messy – but seemed reassured when I turned up for the next assignment slovenly as ever. The only styling product on my hair was pureed apple, helpfully applied by my darling boy.

And today I'm back in the sticks. Grazia's picking us up from Beechford Station before we blitz the Berkshire branches of Bells & Whistles. As usual, the head office bods are obsessed with monitoring procedure and point-of-sale – the very things I'm realising most shoppers really don't care about. Every instance of fab service I've come across since starting to shop for a living has nothing to do with procedures: it's about individuals. Individuals like that sweet guy who tried so hard to sell me the right underwear, or the lady pharmacist whose sympathetic glances at a howling Freddie, as she sold me the morning-after pill and offered me a free condom sample, made me well up at the milk of human kindness. Those people don't need a handbook to tell them how to 'transact' – they instinctively understand what customers really want.

I suppose our job is to discover the ones who couldn't care less. Though I can't help feeling a bit guilty when I catch out a grumpy assistant – insisting people stay relentlessly cheerful at all times for the minimum wage does seem a bit unreasonable.

I haul the buggy over the railway footbridge and look round the station car park for Grazia's four-by-four. Nothing. Then I hear the toot of a horn.

Not *another* new car. Courtesy of some Sugar Daddy, I guess. Grazia's too foxy to be on her own (though I bet she scares a lot of men off with that Black Widow look). This car is midnight-blue, with low-key assassin's lines, the perfect secret-shopping mobile. I do the business with Freddie and his car seat and his buggy – the boot is fantastically generous: all the better for the easy stowage of dead bodies, presumably – then I climb into the back. Sandie's already inside.

'Ahhh.' I breathe in the scent of new car and leather, and settle into the seat, which is at least a hundred times more comfortable than my sofa at home. 'You're going to have to keep prodding me, so I don't fall asleep. Are you best friends with a car dealer or what, Grazia?'

'A woman has her secrets,' she says, mysterious as ever. I've spent a lot of time with her now and while she and Sandie know all there is to know about my fantasy world, my failed marriage, my cellulite *and* my Latvian lodgers, I'm still completely in the dark about them. I really ought to try to be more discreet. Perhaps if I keep going undercover, I'll learn to control my blabbering habit.

As if . . .

'I think this is my favourite car so far,' I say, 'though I'd be happy with *any* wheels. Duncan insisted that we wouldn't need one in London because "everything's on the doorstep". And don't get me started on bloody bendy buses.'

Grazia smiles tightly. 'Yes, that is probably best. Now, girls, we begin today at the biggest store and work our way down to the smallest. You've read your briefing papers, yes?'

Sandie and I nod obediently.

'Good. I shall say no more now, but I think you should know that today I have a suspicion that the stakes are higher than before.'

'What do you mean?' Sandie asks.

'I will tell you once our assignment is completed. To do so now could prejudice the outcome. But it is important that you carry out your duties to the letter.'

The Reading store passes with flying colours. Pristine displays, bright greetings and fast service: they steer me gently towards the most expensive saucepans in the shop, suggest a special zero-gravity cleaning cream for the NASA-approved non-stick coating and point out the three for two offer on spatulas in spring-fresh shades.

Sandie is in awe at the Bracknell branch: the salesman is so persuasive that she almost buys a drill and complete set of titanium bits, even though she doesn't own her flat. And the compact Workingham shop proves itself by recommending the latest organic planet-friendly paint range to Grazia, retailing at twice the price of ordinary emulsion.

'Not an unpleasant experience,' she announces over coffee at a cafe where we surreptitiously film the froth on our cappuccinos (Grazia always manages to find a secret shopping assignment around lunchtime: she seems to have mastered the art of never paying for *anything*). 'The process of being relieved of my money was very efficiently managed. However, I could not escape the feeling that I was being fleeced.'

Sandie nods. 'I must admit, I wasn't sure whether to admire them or feel like a well-milked cash cow.'

After lunch, we head for our final port of call. I thought Berkshire villages were all hanging baskets and bustling marketplaces, but Heartsease Common is too soulless to win a *Britain in Bloom* competition. Grazia says it's commuter-belt territory for people who don't want city life but whose budgets don't stretch to the full portion of rural bliss.

The common that gives Heartsease its name is a large field-cum-cricket pitch, with more bare earth than grass, and a colourful assortment of rubbish scattered across it: crisp packets, free newspapers, and a suspiciously large number of empty beer cans. On one side of the common, there's a sorry row of shops, featuring a windowless supermarket, a chemist, an estate agent, a bookie's, and two pubs.

Sandwiched between the bookie's and the chemist is Bells & Whistles. The store has the same navy and white logo and lettering as the branches we visited this morning, but that's where the resemblance ends. The storefront is mean and narrow, built in Victorian times when I suppose window dressing was less important. In contrast to the careful displays at the modern stores (the Bracknell store featured a *Singin' in the Rain*-style extravaganza with dancing mops, and buckets full of daffodils), there's barely room for a single broom. The window itself is mottled with age, and strips of peeling paint seem to be all that's holding the glass in place.

We park some distance away. The whole village feels so deserted that I feel conspicuous in Grazia's mafia-mobile, and I let Sandie go in first. Freddie's asleep so I climb into the front of the car. Grazia switches the radio on, and finds a classical station playing something terribly highbrow.

'Do you need the toilet?' Grazia asks.

'No, no, I . . .' I was trying to look intelligent. Shan't do that again. 'What wonderful music!'

Grazia leans over and switches the radio up a notch. Not in a mood for conversation, then.

I peer across the common, towards the store. It looks so shabby and dishevelled, and I feel sorry for it. *Get a grip, Emily.* You've got enough to worry about without getting emotionally involved with a tatty shop. And anyway, looks aren't everything. Perhaps this branch has brilliant service, a cosy interior?

I wonder what Grazia meant about the stakes being high. Maybe one of the store managers has his hands in the till, and we're looking for evidence. Or perhaps Charlie is checking up on us, spying on his shopping spies. After all, we don't

148

have a clue what he looks like. He could be following us.

Freddie's soft snores begin to rise in pitch, an early warning signal that he's about to leave the Land of Nod. I can't imagine what he dreams about, but he's usually pretty grumpy when he emerges, so I climb out of the car, open the back door and reach for his hand. I like to make sure my face is the first thing that he sees.

He shakes his head, stubbornly clinging on to sleep. There'll be hell to pay tonight, when he's wide awake and wants to play. Secret shopping isn't as child-friendly a job as it appears, and I feel guilty about dragging him in and out of random stores. In the better-off bits of Lime Village, offspring are tended to by au pairs or intellectually stimulated at baby yoga while their mothers are enduring Reiki or light lipo-suction. A year ago, I thought that would be me, lapping up luxury London. Instead, I now keep my eyes down whenever I pass a yummy mummy in the street, embarrassed by my total un-yumminess.

'Grazia, I know this is a bit of an imposition, but could I leave Freddie with you when I go in? He's so sleepy that I'd rather not move him.'

I see her face in the mirror: her lipsticked mouth purses.

Sandie reappears before Grazia can find an excuse to say no. 'Well, *that* couldn't have been more different from Bracknell.' Sandie stands next to me, leaning back against the car, shaking her head slightly.

'You look a bit shell-shocked.'

'That's one way of putting it. Really, that was seriously weird—'

Grazia gets out of the car. 'It is better not to prejudice Emily's view, I feel.'

Sandie raises her eyebrows still further. 'I wasn't planning to—'

'It's OK,' I say. 'But the suspense is killing me now. I'd better get over there. Won't be a moment, Freddie-boy. Be good for Sandie and Grazia.'

Without the buggy, I feel like dancing a jig as I cross the common (taking care to avoid the empties). I feel flirty and giddy and young again.

But the store looks like it's seen better days. Close up I realise why the window display is so unspectacular: the space is being treated as an extension to the shop floor, with piles of paint pots and damp-scalant stacked up against the glass. It's very dark and cramped beyond the glazed door, and I know it's going to test my camerawork to film anything interesting. I wriggle past a stack of zinc bins in the doorway, relieved I don't have to try to force the buggy in there too.

'Hello, dear.'

The voice comes from my left. A woman well past retirement age is knitting behind a high wooden counter. She stares at me, mouth slightly open, plastic needles darting back and forth so fast that I actually see a purple sleeve taking shape.

The sleeve looks terribly itchy, and I suppress the desire to scratch myself. Instead, I walk forwards, tracking her with the bag-cam. 'Hello there.'

She's *really* wrinkly, and doesn't appear to be wearing the distinctive blue Bells & Whistles uniform, unless it's under that chunky green cardigan. I'm mesmerised by her necklace, with beads the size of ping-pong balls. 'What can we do for you, then, dear?'

I hesitate before answering. The assignment sheet for this secret shopping expedition seems hilariously inappropriate. Would anyone really believe that I was 'just browsing' in this peculiar place? Heartsease Common is somewhere you speed through on your way to somewhere else. Time to *improvise*.

'I can't remember what I came in for.'

She nods, as if this is totally normal. 'Sometimes,' she says, 'I forget what I'm after between the living room and the kitchen. Or I'll pick up my handbag and then I'll forget what I wanted from it.'

'Ageing is a terrible thing.' I say, playing along. She gives me a sharp look. 'Sorry. I didn't mean . . .' I tail off. 'Perhaps if I look around, it'll come to me.'

She returns to her knitting with an aggressive sniff.

I hide behind a wooden shelving unit. I could have walked into a Dickensian curiosity shop, complete with authentic Victorian smells: mothballs and timber and polish. All oddly comforting, but a world away from the bright lights and bright citrus air fresheners at the other branches. This place could be a museum to shops-gone-by. Even Rowminster doesn't have places like this any more.

I pick up a bottle of weedkiller and pretend to read the ingredients while I reformulate my secret shopping mission. OK, so I bought non-stick saucepans in the other branches, but surely it won't *really* matter if I ask for something different here. After all, it's the service and the advice and, above all, the painless removal of the customers' money that the staff will be judged on. Though as the staff seems to consist of one grumpy granny, I'm not expecting this branch to score top marks for that either.

So what should I ask for that would require advice? I squeeze myself into the next aisle along. Traps for a sudden influx of mice . . . humane or spring-action? No, that's too easy. Perhaps I need tips on creosoting a fence: should I prioritise ease of application or durability? Maybe I should deliberately pick something that the knitting lady seems most likely to know about. Despite her manner, I feel the same protective instinct towards the shop that I had sitting in the car. I hate kicking anyone when they're down.

I turn the corner into the third aisle, still trying to formulate a shopping list. Of course, I could buy something useful for the Lime Village flat, but if I begin to think about all the remedial work it requires, I might lose the will to live. Instead an imaginary secret shopping house takes shape in my head. Perhaps it needs fertiliser for the adorable rose garden? A brass fireside companion set for making real fires on these chilly spring nights? Replacement Edwardian-style handles for my lovely panelled doors—

'Hello there. Have you remembered what you came for?'

It's a man.

A tall man.

A tall, good-looking man.

Bloody hell. Is this what happens to me when I come out without my baby? I turn into a giggly schoolgirl, flustered by the first man I encounter.

I think myself back into my role as super-observant secret shopper, and focus on the evidence. He's a good six inches taller than Duncan. Wiry, though not skinny, with Celtic colouring: dark curly hair that just dips down across pale eyes, though I can't tell in the gloom whether they're blue or green. An open face, instantly readable, with a scattering of freckles across his nose, or maybe it's a scattering of sawdust. The striplight in here is so dim that I just hope the camera is picking up what I'm seeing. Oh, and he's not in the classy grey Bells & Whistles uniform either. He's wearing a stripy shirt and a rough brown apron straight out of *Open All Hours*.

Having reviewed the evidence, I can confirm he *is* goodlooking, if rather geeky. He's the kind of bloke Duncan would have mocked at school for being a swot, while secretly wanting the swot's position at the top of the class for himself.

He's still looking at me, his smile now very slightly strained at the edges, as he waits for me to answer his original question. What was it again?

'Um . . . it's a bit overwhelming.'

'Don't tell me, you've seen jumble sales more organised? But appearances can be deceptive, madam.'

Madam? Oh God, now I feel about a hundred years old, but the voice is distractingly deep. 'Really?'

'A place for everything, and everything in its place. What if I asked you some questions, to try to jog your memory. Might that help?'

'I suppose it might.'

'Great.' He looks disproportionately excited by the idea of the guessing game, like a puppy desperate to chase a ball. I guess it must get quite boring in here, day in, day out. 'Indoors, or outdoors?'

I close my eyes, playing along. 'Um . . . indoors, I think.'

'Right! Do you think it belongs in the living room, the kitchen, the bathroom or the bedroom?'

He waggles his eyebrows theatrically as he mentions the bedroom and I find myself blushing again. The sooner this is over, the better. 'The kitchen. Yes, of course! It's a thingy I want, for the tap. I have a dripping tap and I need to fix it.'

'A washer!' he says, triumphant. 'Well, we've no shortage of those. Follow me.'

And I do so, trying not to notice that his bottom does look spectacularly pert in baggy blue denim.

What an inappropriate time to rediscover my hormones.

'I don't suppose you've got the old washer, have you?'

I shake my head.

'Not a problem. Shall we play spot the tap?'

I shake my head again, amused by his boyish-ness. 'Is everything a game for you?'

He gives me a strange, shy look, then laughs. 'Ah, life's a game, isn't it? Isn't that true, Jean?' He pokes his head through a gap between the shelves.

'It's a riot,' she mumbles.

'A riot! Exactly. Now . . . taps.'

As he pulls different blister packs of kitchen taps off metal hooks, I get another chance to study him. Despite his Tigger-like demeanour, there are little lines round his eyes, and a dozen or so white hairs just above his ears. I'd say he's slightly older than me and unlike Duncan, he's not the type to smother himself in Just for Men the instant he begins to go grey. He handles the taps carefully, as though they're much more valuable than they actually are, and as he does so, I can't help specu-lating about how he'd handle—

'Are any of these like your kitchen tap?'

'Um . . .' I try to focus on the job in hand. Rather than his hands. 'Well, that's a bit like it.'

'Bigger, smaller?' He pulls more taps off the hangers. I don't remember seeing a single tap in the other stores, unless they were hidden behind rows and rows of scented candles.

'More old-fashioned, I think . . . oh, wait, it's *that* one.'

He smiles in quiet satisfaction. 'Great. Knew the Inspector Clouseau approach would pay off in the end. Right, you just need the washer, which will be . . .' he runs his long fingers along a shelf full of tiny cardboard boxes containing bolts and nails and washers, 'this one.' And he presents me with a tiny orange rubber ring, with the kind of flourish normally reserved for diamond solitaires.

'How much?'

He whistles. 'Ooh, seeing as it's you . . . fifty-two pence. But if you want to splash out on a spare, for the other tap, then I can do you two for a quid.'

'All right. I'll be a devil.' There's something about his manner that makes me feel like a character in an Ealing Comedy, and it's a nice place to be, a place where everyone's honest as the day is long and neighbours always have time for tea and a natter and a fondant fancy. He takes the washers to the till and rings in the price. I hand over my money and he waits for the receipt to print.

'Jean?' he says. 'Jean, did you not replace the till roll?'

She looks up from her knitting. 'I've been rushed off my feet.'

He sighs. 'Can't get the staff. Listen, do you

156

really need a receipt? The till has a mind of its own; it could take half an hour to fit the roll. I promise if it's the wrong one, I'll swap it. I know I'll recognise you if you come back.'

'I . . .' I hesitate. *Yes, I do need the receipt, to claim it back*, but insisting on one will probably compromise my mission. 'Don't worry. Just hope I can fit it now.'

'Ah!' he says. 'Well, if you need any advice, don't hesitate to call.' He scribbles down the store number on a scrap of paper. 'Ask for Will. And if you really need it, I can pop round. I do it for all my favourite customers!'

I smile. 'Really, I'm sure I'll manage. Thanks, though. Can't remember the last time a man offered to fix my washer . . .'

He chuckles. 'All part of the service.'

As I leave the store, I hear Jean stage-whisper, 'You're worse than the local tomcat, Will Powell.'

'If only it were true, Jean,' he whispers back.

I walk back towards the girls with my two washers, still feeling flushed. A figure paces outside the car: Sandie, swapping her mobile from ear to ear, as though it's red hot.

'What's up?' I ask Sandie, and then I panic: what if it's Freddie? I push past her to fling open the car door. Freddie's in his seat, scarily still.

'Freddie, Freddie! Wake up—'

Grazia frowns. 'He is fine! He has not moved since you left, but he can snore to wake the dead.'

I lean into his body, warm as toast, and wait for the blood to stop rushing in my ears: sure enough, snorting snores – as musical to me now as a string quartet – fill the car.

'Sorry. When I saw Sandie outside, on the phone. I thought . . .'

Grazia's face softens a little. 'Nothing is wrong. Well, not with Freddie. I think for Sandie, however, a crisis is unfolding.'

We both look up to see Sandie holding her phone inches away from her ear now: I can't hear exactly what's being said, but a high-pitched voice is coming from the speaker.

'So, how did it go?' Grazia says.

'It was . . . peculiar. Nothing like the other shops. Cluttered, dark, a bit smelly. But I still liked it, like the shops I went in when I was a kid, the ones they closed down.'

She nods. 'Exactly.'

'Exactly what?'

'I fear that the same is in store for Bells & Whistles, Heartsease Common. Charlie mentioned that the company is engaged in what they call a brand evaluation and rationalisation programme.'

I feel slightly seasick. It didn't mention *that* on the briefing paper. 'Rationalisation. As in, closing shops down?'

'Yes. I did not mention it before, to avoid affecting the results. However, I would guess that the more traditional stores are the ones that are seen to be the weak links in the chain. There can be very little profit made in a store like this one.'

'That's awful. And what we've just filmed, that could be used as a reason?' I see the events of the last few minutes through the eyes of a ruthless head office penny-pincher: old Jean and her knitting, Will making silly jokes and spending an uneconomic amount of time looking for washers worth peanuts, not to mention the many breaches of procedure involved in the missing till roll . . .

'Emily, it is our job. We are offering a service to retailers.'

'No!' I say, my voice rising despite myself. 'We're here to catch bad service, rude shop assistants, that sort of thing. The people in that shop aren't rude, they're helpful, kind, caring.' *And one of them is also exceptionally handsome.*

Grazia shrugs. I suppose there is nothing she can say.

'Shit, shit, shit!' Sandie flings open the car door and jumps inside. 'Have we finished the filming now, Grazia? Because I need to get back to London ASAP.'

'Trouble?' I ask.

'Trouble,' she repeats. 'Yes. That was Gramma. Trouble with a capital G. It doesn't get any scarier than that.'

159

CHAPTER 12

SANDIE

Trouble comes in a size ten A-line plaid skirt and a navy pair of wide-fitting K shoes.

'You get sacked and you don't tell your own grandmother! What has happened to you, Sandra?'

Gramma stands just outside the Women Merchants' Hostel, her immaculate appearance making the rest of the street look trashy and dissolute. Bus, train, tube: she's negotiated them all without picking up a single stray hair or scuffing the patent leather of her courts. She is a marvel.

But I don't have the luxury of marvelling for long. Instead, I need to get her away from Dixie's Digs before the porter hears that I got the push from Garnett's and I end up homeless as well as jobless.

'Gramma, I am sorry, OK? But can you keep your voice down? Let's go to the cafe. We can talk properly there.'

'So now you won't have me in your flat. Either you are ashamed of me, or you are ashamed of how you live. Which is it, Sandra?'

'I'm not ashamed of anyone, but my room is tiny and the walls are paper thin and some of my neighbours work night shifts.'

'Work! At least they have work!' Outrage peppers every short syllable. And this is the woman who warned me against the undignified 'grizzly bear' of rage.

'Please, Gramma.' I reach out for her elbow, to usher her away. But where to? My favourite cafe, where the retro padded booths might have offered some privacy, is not such a great idea: in full flow, my grandmother can be deafening.

I look around for inspiration, which comes in the form of the little blue sign pointing towards the park. I start walking. Sure enough, she follows, keeping up the chorus of disapproval.

My gramma has reached the 'what was the point in going to university when you ended up working in a shop?' part when we arrive at the refreshment stall just inside the park gates. I keep my fingers crossed that my brainwave will work.

'. . . you, the first Barrow to make it to college, wasting three years of higher education to become a glorified checkout . . . a glorified . . .'

It's worked.

Gramma's voice tails off as she spots the stall: behind her thick bifocals, I see her eyes swivel towards the organic cakes. The sweet-tooth gene is deeply embedded in the DNA of the females in my family, and despite my grandmother's late-onset diabetes, she never can resist a doughnut.

'You must be hungry,' I say. 'Why don't I treat you? Things always look better after tea.'

I fork out £10 for two teas, two doughnuts and a sticky flapjack with toffee topping – a roof-of-the-mouth jamming combo that should buy me just enough silence to explain.

Oh God. How do I begin to explain?

We sit down on a bench. I hand over the flapjack and take a deep breath.

'OK. Gramma? Hear me out, please. I lost my job in December—'

'Gnooo!' Gramma interrupts, through a mouthful of oats. Whatever happened to 'chewing and chattering never mix, Sandra, except in a zoo'?

'I said don't interrupt. Please. I lost my job in December, and I was in shock for the first few weeks, and I knew you'd be devastated and angry and I had enough to deal with myself. And then the longer it went on, the more difficult it was to tell you.'

My grandmother squints into the sunshine, her back ramrod straight. It's hard to tell what she's thinking as she chomps her way through her flapjack, gagged by toffee.

'I was sacked from my job. I don't want to go into the details except to say that it was completely unjust, but there's nothing I can do about it. Not now, anyhow.'

As I speak, it hits home. It isn't just *not now*. It's *not ever*. Before the thought of being condemned to a lifetime of menial jobs silences

162

me, I plough on. 'But I am surviving. I've found work, I'm paying my rent and I'm doing fine.'

Gramma stares at me, her eyes narrowing. She's always had a sinister ability to read my mind, like the time I stole a tube of Love Hearts and she guessed, even though I'd eaten them all. Mind you, that could have been because they turned my tongue washing-powder white. She wipes the sugar from around her mouth with exaggerated care before checking her false teeth in a mirror compact. Gramma's nearly seventy, but she looks twenty years younger.

'What is the work you've found?'

Good question, Gramma, although I suspect she already knows, thanks to that X-ray brain of hers.

'I am waiting, Sandra.'

'It's a kind of . . . policing role.' My grandmother has the greatest respect for the police. She got to know all the local bobbies by their first names when my mother was a wild teenager, because they were always delivering her home. Then Mum did a flit to Jamaica, and returned pregnant and defiant, going back to the Caribbean without me within weeks of my birth.

It has always been my grandmother's greatest fear that I'll take after my mother.

Gramma shakes her head. 'Kind of? Stop being vague, Sandra. You're not a security guard, are you?'

'No, no. It's more low key than that.' How do you explain secret shopping? I know I have to put a good case, or I'll be bundled back on the train to Birmingham like a truant. 'It's about standards of service and so on. You know how standards are slipping, Gramma?'

She nods.

'Well, the latest thing is for shops to employ people to act as customers to monitor standards. That's what I'm doing. It's good fun.'

The last bit isn't a lie. It *is* surprisingly good fun, especially now my camerawork has improved. The only problem is—

'Never mind fun. What does it pay?' Gramma asks.

That's the problem. 'Um, well, it's not as much as I was on, but the harder I work the more I earn.' Though if I worked ninety hours a week, I'd struggle to do more than survive here in London.

'Sandra, do you mean you're *self-employed*?' In Gramma's world, a guaranteed paycheck and a full pension are the signs of a well-ordered life. I do understand why it matters so much to her. I never knew my granddad – he died when I was a baby, just two years into the retirement he'd worked so hard to earn – but I've heard the stories of the hand-to-mouth existence they led as unskilled immigrants from Jamaica. I've never been to the place where I was conceived. I was curious, of course, especially when I was a teenager, but Gramma insisted we went to cultural places instead. She saved up to take me to Paris and Florence on the coach from Birmingham. *Far more useful for your education, Sandra. I have high hopes. You won't let me down.*

'I'm freelance, yes.'

'Oh, Sandra, Sandra. This is no good! We'll go back to Garnett's, insist they change their minds. Maybe I didn't always approve of you working in a shop, but at least you had security. A final salary pension scheme.'

'That . . . might not be quite so easy.'

'Where there's a will, there's a way. You need to stand up for yourself, girl.'

'Gramma, what exactly did they say to you when you went to Garnett's?'

'Well,' she says, dusting sugar off her fingers, 'now, let me think, so I get this right. I couldn't see you in the store, and I wanted to take you out for lunch and all—'

'That's very nice of you. But it's a long way to come just for lunch.'

She looks shifty. 'Well, I've also had a few funerals lately, with more in the offing, and I need a new hat. So I booked a cheap rail fare, which I thought would pay for itself if I used that staff discount of yours.'

'Sorry.'

'Never mind. I can use it when we get you your job back. Anyhow, when I couldn't find you, I went to ask and they pointed me towards someone they said was your replacement. I nearly fainted dead away.'

My grandmother has never fainted in her life. Despite her tiny frame – I presume I inherited my height from my father, whoever he was – she has

165

Samson's unyielding strength. 'This replacement. What did she look like?'

'Cheap. I think her name was Marie. Or was it Marisa?'

'Marsha?' I suggest.

'That's it. Brassy, showing far too much cleavage. Not what you want to see when you're shopping. Anyway, this creature tells me you haven't worked there for months now, and that it really wouldn't pay to ask why, but between her and me and the gate-post, you aren't going to be getting a job handling money for a long while.' Gramma sighs, the shame of reliving the moment showing in her face. 'Oh, Sandra, what have you done?'

This is the moment I've dreaded ever since I was frog-marched to the HR office. 'None of it's true, Gramma.'

'None of what?' She's steely.

I take such a deep breath that I feel dizzy. 'They let me go because they believed I had stolen from them.'

'You?' says Gramma, shaking her head. 'I thought you had learned your lesson after you took those sweets!'

After the Love Hearts incident, Gramma made a badge reading I AM A THIEF, fixed it to my favourite blouse with Blu-Tack and made me wear it for a whole day. Even after it came off, I could never quite get the sticky blue paste from in between the threads.

'I didn't do it,' I say, knowing that a denial always

sounds unconvincing. 'Why would I slog my guts out for seven years, only to throw it away for a few quid?'

'What kind of language is that, Sandra? Using slang is the refuge of a lazy thinker.'

I stare at my grandmother, an uncomfortable feeling whirling inside me. It's that grizzly, angry bear, the one that keeps taking me by surprise. 'Don't I ever get the benefit of the doubt? Don't you ever think that the rest of the world might be in the wrong, and your granddaughter might be in the right? That the last few months might have been the worst of my life and that I've only been trying to protect you? That maybe using the odd slang word might be the very least you'd expect me to do under the circumstances?'

Gramma's face stays frozen. Her strength seems brittle, as though she might shatter without warning.

And then my Barrow angry bear disappears, leaving only guilt behind. I have never, ever lost my temper with her. I've never had reason to. However much she nagged, I always knew she had my interests at heart. It's not her fault the values she drummed into me – tidiness, courtesy, loyalty – were more suited to the fifties than the ruthless noughties.

Gramma holds up her gnarled hand, the only part of her that really shows her age. 'If you tell me it's a mistake, then I believe it's a mistake.'

'Thank you.'

She nods. 'No matter. So now that you've shown

me the skeleton in your cupboard, there's no reason for you to stay here in London. Come home, Sandra.'

It is tempting. My own bedroom, complete with Take That posters. Homemade jerk baked beans (the original fusion pick-me-up). Maybe the chance of a job with a friend of a friend, thanks to my grandmother's redoubtable nerworking skills . . .

'I wish it was that simple. I really do. But—'

But moving back in with Gramma means Marsha's won. I can't do it. And maybe there's another reason to resist. Maybe it's time I learned to live in the noughties, before it's too late.

Gramma picks up her handbag – an enormous snakeskin one, which could easily house three secret cameras – and pushes herself up from the bench, discarding half a doughnut. 'Enough. You stay here if you like, with your freelance job and your tarnished reputation. But you'll be home before the summer's out, you see if I am wrong. Goodbye, Sandra.'

It takes all my will not to follow her, but I'm not ready to admit defeat. And although I cannot for the life of me imagine how I'm going to do it, I still believe that one day I'll be walking back into Garnett's of Oxford Street with my head held high. She might not admit it right now, but this is what Gramma's taught me. *Without your good name, all is lost.*

SPRING BANK HOLIDAY

Spring has now officially sprung. It's time for shoppers to get digging – into their pockets. Capitalise on your customers' desire to save the planet and get in touch with their inner Felicity Kendal by promoting all things green: whether that's garden tools or eco-fabrics.

MYSTERY SHOPPING BRIEFING (05/1024GL):

Our client, a major player in the leisure field, is interested in the operating practices of Shire Oaks Horticultural Paraphernalia and Plant Depository. The client requires unbiased data regarding sales levels, thru-flow and staff performance. It is imperative that this assignment is carried out with the utmost discretion.

CHAPTER 13

GRAZIA

In my bedroom in Italy, I dreamed of English gardens. A million shades of rain-fed green. Pink peonies as big as rugby balls. A duck pond, and a hedge carved in the shape of a peacock. A man with floppy hair wearing a linen suit, playing croquet on the lush lawn, waving at me as I sipped tea and ate tiny sandwiches. Ah, Leon, you never did master the rules of croquet, but you looked so good in linen.

Now English gardeners are digging up their hollyhocks to go Mediterranean.

'Grazia, Grazia!' Emily calls me from behind a row of spindly olive trees. 'Have you seen the prices of these? Two hundred and fifty pounds for something that looks dead.'

Emily's pronouncements can be a little blunt, but today I agree with her. There is nothing appealing about these withered grey specimens, or the poorly made mosaic tables, or the fauxterracotta urns modelled on remains from Pompeii. I want scented roses and weathered enamel watering cans and Wellington boots. Give me the order of the Chelsea Physic Garden any day of the week.

'Gardens were once about serenity, Emily. Now they are all about fashion.'

You only need to look at the wealthy clientele of the Shire Oaks Horticultural Paraphernalia and Plant Depository to realise gardening is now cool and profitable. Plants that don't match this season's arbitrary colour palate will be torn from the earth, to be replaced by on-trend hot pink or velvet brown.

We are *very* secret shoppers today. Reading between the lines, our mystery client has an aggressive interest in taking over this store, so our job is to discover whether people are actually buying the overpriced shrubs, or just coming here to gossip over stewed coffee and stale cake.

Are they buying! We have filmed queues of women on daytrips to the country, spending hundreds or even thousands on plants. Their people-carriers are transformed into mini-jungles, though who knows how their new gardens will look. Advice here is dubious to say the least. We caught one of the assistants on camera mixing up her clematis with her chrysanthemums.

Inside the 'Al Fresco Collection' showroom, Sandie is quizzing another assistant about sustainable hardwoods, winding him up nicely with her special blend of slightly superior politeness. My girls are getting good, no doubt about it, and I feel what I imagine is something like maternal pride whenever I view their footage.

'Freddie, take your finger out of that compost!'

Emily moves the buggy away from the all-too-tempting pots of soil. 'Well, this might all be the height of fashion, but I couldn't afford a bloody weed in this place.'

She wears her middle-class poverty like a clown costume, parading it to make people laugh. I wonder what she would think if she knew that my home – the home Leon and I worked so hard to make perfect – is now under notice of repossession.

Facts must be faced. I could employ a hundred shopping operatives and it would make no difference. The debts that came to light after my husband died had to be cleared immediately. We had been living beyond our means for years, trying to maintain the same life as Leon's more famous contemporaries, without the earnings.

I was left with buttons. And, Leon, you would never have realised – because you never paid a bill in your life – that buttons do not cover the ridiculous mortgage payments. Or the heating bills, thanks to the huge windows and the high ceilings that you insisted upon. Yesterday's letter from the bank offered a helpline and the services of an 'arrears manager', but the plain facts are that my outgoings exceed my income, and nothing can be done.

Nothing except . . .

Oh, Leon, what choice would you make? It is an exquisite one: sell the home we made, or sell your paintings – let them be scattered around the world among heartless collectors who care more about ego than about art?

'Done!' Sandie reappears, tapping her bag-camera. 'Completely hopeless. People who shop here deserve all they get.'

I lead the way back to my latest car, a neat Audi. 'Shall we go back to Rose Cottage and check the footage?'

'Sounds good,' Sandie says, climbing into the car.

Strange. Though the money is a drop in the ocean, my secret shopping recruits are providing me with something I had not realised I lacked: company. I have actually begun to look forward to the missions. All we have in common is the reduced horizons that force us to earn our money this way: Leon would have labelled Sandie a worker ant, and Emily a hysterical dumpling, yet I feel strange kinship with them. Even little Freddie makes me smile, and I have never understood children.

I drive out of the village, towards Beechford. Sandie is telling us about the customer at the information desk who demanded to know whether the roses she was buying had been pre-screened for tetanus. The sun is shining after a fortnight of rain, and the Berkshire countryside is at its most verdant. Not an olive tree in sight, but plenty of rabbits disappearing into lush hedgerows as they hear the car approaching. The road bends as it enters Heartsease Common.

'This is where we came to do the filming at Bells & Whistles,' Sandie says.

'Oh, yes. The irresistible Will in his sexy dungarees,' Emily chips in.

We pass the row of run-down shops.

'Oh no,' Emily says, as we all stare at the store. 'Not already.'

The cramped window display has a new addition: a large sign reading CLOSING DOWN – EVERYTHING MUST GO!

'That's our fault, isn't it?' she says, her voice bordering on tearful. 'I know you said it might happen, but I didn't really believe you. We've closed it down.'

I put my foot down, cursing myself for coming this way. But I am surprised that the shop's head office has acted so quickly. It's only four weeks since we filed our report.

'It would probably have happened anyway,' Sandie says, with the resigned tone of a parent breaking the news about a dead goldfish. 'Overheads, staff costs, figures – that's what it's really about. We were just the final—'

'Nail in the coffin?' Emily sounds even closer to tears.

'You cannot think like this, Emily,' I say. 'We are only doing our job.'

She whispers something – I think it's *like the Nazis* – but I choose not to respond. We travel to Rose Cottage in silence, but she avoids my eye when I try to smile at her in the rear-view mirror.

By the time we reach home, I am so irritated by her sulking that I would like to turn her away at the door. But she's already unloading Freddie and he laughs, realising this is the place where he gets the fizzy water that makes him giggle.

Inside, the atmosphere is still tense. Emily cannot bring herself to speak more than two words when I bring out the coffee and my best amaretto biscuits. She takes a gulp of the coffee straight – though she normally drowns it with milk and adds three sugars to take away the bitterness – then slams the cup down so hard it is a miracle it does not smash.

'Is everything all right, Emily?'

She stares at me, her eyes cold. 'No. It's not. I feel like an executioner.'

'If that is so, then the store signed its own death warrant.'

'But what else were they supposed to do, Grazia? They were doing their best. That shop might not be much to look at, but it's obviously a lifeline for that village. And the service was better than I had at any of the other—'

'You cannot be a bleeding heart, Emily. Take the money and forget about it.'

Sandie leans forward. 'Grazia's right. It's not our fault that they couldn't be bothered to replace the till roll, and hadn't changed the window display since 1978. I liked the place, too, but it's not really on to knit when you're being paid to work.'

Emily pouts. 'I thought that was homely.'

'Stores are not there to be homely,' I say. 'They

176

exist to make money. Even in the art world, which I know best of all, commerce is the driver. It is basic economics. A gallery only provides champagne and canapés to sell art. Likewise, a hardware store can only justify personalised advice on tap washers if it contributes to the bottom line. Selling comes first. Always.'

I do not tell her that this fact escaped Leon for years. That a better understanding of the basic laws of economics might have saved me from my current financial meltdown.

Emily looks to Sandie for support, but Sandie shakes her head sadly. 'It's not our decision. The owners are God, the rest of us serfs. What they say goes. It's about the bottom line.'

Emily's lower lip wobbles.

I hesitate: what is the right way to treat an emotional woman? Sympathy or a firm hand? I spent so many years tending to Leon's needs that I have lost the habit of responding to others. 'If this is upsetting you so much, Emily, perhaps you should reconsider this line of work. It is no place for someone who wishes to occupy the moral high ground. You should think about it.'

She winces, as though she has been slapped, but the lip has stopped wobbling. Sometimes cruel to be kind is the only way.

'Oh, don't worry, I will,' she snaps. She stands up and begins to gather Freddie's necessities together. 'We'll be off. Don't worry about a lift to the station. I need some fresh air.'

She marches out, although the impact of the dramatic gesture is lessened by all the fussing she needs to do to get Freddie ready to leave. Finally the door slams. The thought that it could be the very last time I see Emily is uncomfortable. Unsettling.

'Will she give up, do you think, Sandie? It is not for everybody, after all, especially given the limited financial rewards.'

Sandie shrugs. 'No, but I suspect that for Emily there's more to being a shopping angel than money. Well, not just for Emily. Perhaps for all of us?'

I consider this. If I know that the income will never be enough to save the house, then why does Emily's exit matter so much? The possibility that I might have begun to care about these women astonishes me, but it is the only plausible explanation. Life is strange indeed.

CHAPTER 14

EMILY

All the way home I fantasise about a hot bath. Maybe I want to wash away the guilt. Grazia's words echo round my head as the train chugs its way back to London. *No place for someone who wishes to occupy the moral high ground.* Of course, I've had bloody years of being patronised by Duncan, but after a while, I switched off. Whereas Grazia's lecture really stung.

Either I jack in the job, or I accept that I can no longer afford to make a stand about anything: Emily Prince, hired gun, conscience not required.

What I don't quite understand is why I was trying to make a stand. I've never been a campaigner: I didn't even take part in the 'Save Our Chips' protest when the council abolished school meals. Yet the plight of Bells & Whistles, Heartsease Common, has outraged me far more than the plight of the whales or dinner ladies. I'm indignant on Will Powell's behalf, although I've only met him once. He seemed like one of life's triers, someone refusing to accept the inevitable, fighting the odds.

Maybe it seems all too familiar from my own life.

Yet I know I can't afford principles. Do I want to end up out of a job only a couple of months after starting, to waste all that hard-won filming experience? In the last few weeks, the money's begun to come in, paying for extra treats for Freddie, a pizza delivery for me. But it's not just the money. By keeping it a secret from Duncan, I've grabbed back a tiny bit of control over my disaster zone of a life, with its stolen buggies, broken tumble dryers, lost house keys, fashion mistakes and cellulite. Can I afford to lose that, all for the sake of a shop I'll never see again, and a couple of staff members who must have seen the writing on the wall?

But as my train stops at yet another picture-postcard commuter village, I can't help picturing that sorry row of shops at Heartsease, with an ugly boarded-up store where Bells & Whistles used to be.

Freddie grizzles throughout the Tube journey, attracting venomous looks from commuters, but he falls asleep as soon as we get home. I squeeze his buggy into the bathroom, leaving him safely reined in by the straps and hoping this doesn't make me a terrible mother.

Our bathroom isn't a place for lingering. The black suite and gold taps are straight out of a porn movie, but this evening I have more innocent pleasures in mind. I unearth some organic bubble bath from the back of the bathroom cabinet, and pour half the bottle into the running water. I can't remember the last time I managed a deep soak, so I definitely deserve several months' worth. It's also a luxury that will be impossible soon. My baby's growing up: he keeps pulling himself up on random pieces of furniture, determined to take his first steps. Once he's started, I know he won't stop. I just wish someone else was going to share that moment with me.

Stop it, Emily! Be grateful for having a healthy son, and a hot bath ahead of you. Every magazine I've ever read insists that a glass of wine and a designer candle are essential requirements for 'me time', but all I can find is the old bottle of cherry brandy and a few night-lights. I take out the silk pyjamas from Christmas, ready for slipping into later. As I undress, it feels bloody nippy for May, but the hot water will wash away my troubles.

Freddie's still snoozing. I reach my hand out to test the bathwater temperature.

'Shit! Shit! Shit!'

It's so cold that I'm surprised lily-fragranced icicles haven't formed in place of bubbles. My teeth begin to chatter with shock. I hold my hand under the hot tap and confirm that only cold water is pouring out. This is *not* good news. I wrap a towel around myself and head for the airing cupboard, though I know more about ruddy astrophysics than I do about central heating. Sure, I've watched Duncan do fiddly things to extinguished pilot lights in the past, but amazingly, since I've been an accidental single mother, the boiler has behaved impeccably. About the only thing in my life that has.

I open the cupboard door and a red light winks back at me.

That wasn't there before. My heart sinks and it's all I can do not to burst into frustrated tears. I *know* this is a ludicrous overreaction to a simple domestic malfunction, but that bath was the first thing I'd looked forward to in ages and the loss of my soak feels like a disaster of Titanic proportions.

Grow up, Emily. If Duncan could sort out the boiler, then so can you. There's a yellowing notice attached to the metal. LOW PRESSURE IS THE MAIN CAUSE OF BOILER MALFUNCTION. TO RESTORE PRESSURE, COMPLETE THE FOLLOWING ACTIONS. DO NOT DEVIATE FROM THE SEQUENCE OR COMPLETE FAILURE WILL RESULT.

Complete failure . . . yeah, that sounds familiar.

I squint at the instructions, typed in tiny print, and take a deep breath. TURN THE BOILER SWITCH TO OFF.

I do as I'm told. DEPRESS THE REPRES-SURISE BUTTON FOR BETWEEN 8–10 SECONDS.

I count the seconds.

WAIT FOR A FURTHER 10–15 SECONDS.

I wait.

Why has the bloody thing broken today? It's been the only thing in the flat I can rely on, since the incident with the tumble dryer, and the great buggy robbery.

Shit. I've lost count. I let go of the repressurise button, and peer at the instructions. HOLDING A RECEPTACLE UNDER THE BASE OF BOILER, OPEN THE BLUE TAP GENTLY.

Funnily enough, I don't have a receptacle handy, so I grab a towel, locate the blue tap . . . and hope for the best.

'Euuurgh!'

Lukewarm water spurts out, covering my arms and face, narrowly missing my eyes. When I lick my lips, I taste rust, and I struggle to close off the tap again.

Now the tears come, hot and heavy as the rusty water. I imagine Duncan sitting in a huge Jacuzzi tub with bloody Heidi, sipping champagne, nibbling each other's toes. Frustration pours out with the tears. Yet I'm determined to get this bloody boiler working, just to prove I can cope.

TURN THE BOILER ON. DEPRESS IGNITE SWITCH TO IGNITE PILOT. BOILER SHOULD FIRE.

I do as instructed.

The boiler doesn't fire. Of course not. I never really thought it would.

'Bastard bollocking boiler!'

The bastard bollocking boiler simply blinks back. What am I meant to do now? It's times like this when I feel completely alone in the world. I might as well be, with my dad a hundred and fifty miles away, and Duncan even further, deep in fondue land.

If only I lived in Heartsease Common. I'm sure that lovely Will would fix the boiler in a trice.

Now, what made me think of *him*?

'Oh, Freddie, I need a man. Where am I going to find myself a man?'

I walk through into the bedroom to find my dressing gown, wondering how much cherry brandy it'll take before I could consider a cold shower.

And then I hear it. The unmistakable thump-thump-thump of a Euro-pop track sneaks through the floorboards.

Men. Just below me. Three of them.

I put on my dressing gown and slippers and pad down the stairs. I've avoided them in the three months that they've been here – talking to them seems like fraternising with the enemy. Although I suppose it's hardly their fault that they ended up with dastardly Duncan as their landlord.

I knock on the door, softly at first, but I don't think they can hear me because of the Euro-pop. There's also a strange whine, like a saw cutting through wood: they must be bringing their work home with them. I rap harder and harder, and am just beginning to lose hope when the door opens so suddenly that I nearly punch the man behind it in the face.

'Is fire?' It's the oldest of the three, Kaspar, in spotless blue overalls. He averts his eyes when he sees I'm in my dressing gown, and I pull it around myself.

'No fire. That's the problem. It's my boiler. I wondered . . .'

I realise from his frown that my hand gestures aren't getting the message across. He calls into the flat, and it sounds like a long line of consonants without either vowels or a pause for breath. The volume of the music goes down and after a few seconds, Big Janis appears, his blond moustache bushier than the last time I saw him. His hands are covered in dried paint and he smells vaguely of white spirit.

'Mrs Prince, what is matter?'

He says it so kindly that I want to cry. But I try to be assertive, rather than pathetic. 'I am a bit stuck. My boiler seems to have stopped working and there's no hot water and I tried to fix it but I don't have any money to get a plumber . . .' Pathetic seems to be winning, '. . . and all I wanted was a hot bath . . . and it's been the most horrible day and . . .'

Big Janis is staring at me and I notice for the first time what sad eyes he has, spaniel-brown and moist.

'You upset. Come, come,' and he beckons inside the flat. I refuse to cross the threshold, but peep through the gap. Instead of the rubbish-strewn, testosterone-loaded boys' pad I was

185

expecting, it looks very homely: yes, there are tools and building supplies stacked in one corner, but there's a scarlet woven cloth on the round table and now I can smell coffee and roast meat. My mouth waters.

'I've left my son upstairs; I can't possibly come in.'

He nods, and although I've no way of knowing how many words he recognises, it *feels* like he understands on some deeper level.

'You go up. We come! We fix! Two minutes!'

I hesitate, unsure whether I want three strangers in my flat. But then I remember I have no prospect of that hot bath without them. Back upstairs, I rush around, putting on some clothes and un-buckling Freddie, who wakes up and begins mumbling away to himself about something that sounds very erudite but doesn't resemble English. Maybe it's Latvian.

My flat is a disgrace compared to theirs, so I begin to throw stuff into bin bags: clothes, free newspapers, toys, shoes, and the remains of various biscuits and snacks that never quite made it from the shopping bags into the kitchen cupboards.

There's a gentle knock on the door and after I've crammed the last lot of junk under the sink, I answer it. Big Janis comes in first, carrying a huge metal toolbox; behind him, Little Janis carries a cardboard box. Finally, Kaspar's hands are enclosed in two huge oven mitts, cradling a casserole dish.

'Can we come?' Big J asks, and I nod, slightly dazed.

He looks around him and heads purposefully for the boiler cupboard. Kaspar puts his crockpot on top of the hob and switches on the gas. Little J kneels down next to Freddie on the floor, the cardboard box between them.

The scene is so surreal – my home occupied by a Latvian taskforce, a cross between *DIY SOS* and the Three Wise Men – that I'm frozen to the spot. But Freddie takes it all in his stride, happily pulling the lid off the box and then pushing it back. Little J lets this hide-and-seek go on for a little while before taking my son's tiny hands in his huge ones: together they reach inside the box and pull out . . . a hand-carved Noah's Ark, chunky but beautifully smooth, the grain of a wood I don't recognise brought out by painstaking sanding. Slotted into grooves on the deck of the ark are Mr and Mrs Noah, along with a full set of coupled-up animals, all in different types of wood.

Freddie, of course, ignores the ark completely and picks up the box lid, holding it against his face like a mask and giggling delightedly.

I kneel down beside them both. 'It's beautiful,' I say to Little J. 'You made it?'

He frowns at me, and I take a zebra, with its grooves that resemble stripes, and I mime someone carving.

'Yes,' he says, smiling.

'And this is really for Freddie?' I say, pointing at him.

'Yes, yes.'

'Thank you. That's so lovely. Freddie, look. This is all yours.' I hold up the zebra and hope that he'll take it, rather than the cardboard lid. Finally he grasps at the animal and shakes it in the air, giggling louder. Little J beams back.

And then I notice the smell, a sweet, satisfying meatiness – beef? No, pork. Kaspar sticks a wooden spoon into the crockpot, then lifts it to his lips to taste. I thought Eastern European cuisine was nothing but gristle and cabbage, but my mouth seems to be watering. The men chat to each other, their voices low and respectful and calming, even though for all I know they're discussing their plans to murder me and sell Freddie on the baby black market.

'Is done.' Big J appears at my side, a spanner in his hand.

'My boiler? You've fixed it?'

'Easy.' He snaps his fingers and mutters something to the men. He waves towards the crockpot. 'You have dinner? Pig with caraway. Speciality of Latvia.'

'I can't take your food,' I say, though the smell makes me want to faint with desire. That's what comes of existing on Pringles and Pop Tarts.

Big J smiles, revealing cracked teeth. 'Yes. Yes. You not hungry?'

'Well, yes, I am a bit, but—'

'Then you eat. You share house, we share food.'

They gather at the front door, ready to leave. I wonder why they're helping me. For the first time, it occurs to me: maybe they're lonely too?

'You could stay if you like. Join me?' I say, realising that the sound of voices, even in a language I don't understand, is preferable to the suffocating silence I've been drowning out with the TV for months now.

Big J shakes his head. 'Not tonight. But soon, maybe. You invite us.'

He mumbles to the others again and they each nod a polite goodbye, then clatter down the stairs, leaving behind a working boiler, a wooden ark and the smell of cooking pork.

Strange, but after I've closed and bolted the door, the flat seems a little less lonely, knowing my new men are there, just beneath my feet.

BIKINI SEASON

The temperatures may still be in the teens, but shoppers are dreaming of the beach – and bikini bodies. Pair self-tan with swimsuits, cellulite-busters with sarongs. Create the scent of summer: fresh flowers are high maintenance; aromarketing is more effective and less messy. Bergamot, for example, has been proven to stimulate shopper desire and increase sales.

MYSTERY SHOPPING BRIEFING (05/2015GL):

Factory is a premium women's clothing brand, aimed at a mainstream yet discerning market. As well as producing high-quality ontrend merchandise, Factory has pioneered an approach to customer care that marries ethnographic information (based on extensive observation) and quantitative data.

Following in-depth staff training, the client is now undertaking research to ensure employees are implementing the Factory approach consistently and appropriately.

CHAPTER 15

SANDIE

Secret shopping without Grazia always feels illicit, somehow, like drinking underage.

Not that I ever did drink underage, of course. Gramma told me that if I wanted to end up like my mother, then alcohol would only speed up my descent into degradation and despair. A one-way ticket, she said.

But avoiding alcohol or behaving like a good girl hasn't saved me from . . . well, if not despair then certainly all-round disappointment.

Today's mission involves shopping at four different branches of Factory, an upmarket (i.e. slightly snotty) London-based chain of boutiques. The brief is full of jargon, and there are lists and lists of things for Emily and me to observe as we make separate trips to buy a summer outfit. Everything from the nature of the meet-and-greet smile ('this must be a *genuine* smile – in which the folds of the eye will be spontaneously lifted. A forced smile is not sufficient to welcome our valued customers') to the number of sheets of tissue paper to be used to wrap each type of garment. I've always thought that retail is a science, as well as an art, but this seems to be taking it to extremes.

'I've always been far too intimidated to shop at Factory before.' Emily nibbles at her thumbnail, although she's just polished off a full cooked breakfast. We're in the British Home Stores cafe, dosing up on tea before going into battle. Of course, we've saved our receipts and set the stopwatch to report back on hotplate service times. If Grazia's taught me anything, it's that there is such a thing as a free lunch (and breakfast, and dinner). Freddie's here, of course, singing to himself and enjoying the view from his highchair.

It was Emily's idea to meet up. She made some excuse about her bag-cam making odd noises, but I don't believe a word of it. I just think she wanted to calm things down after her funny turn at Grazia's last week. I've decided not to say anything unless she brings it up, though I am relieved she's back on board.

'Don't forget, without your money, they wouldn't exist.'

She laughs. 'If they were relying on *my* money, they'd be bankrupt.'

It's true: neither of us exactly fits the target customer profile. According to the documentation, a Factory girl is thirty-something, working in a middle-management job. She's called Sophie or Ellie, has a husband called Josh or Cameron, and possibly a cute toddler with a retro-chic name. She might treat herself to one signature piece per season from the Designers Lounge on the top floor at Garnett's, but for the rest she'll be buying her neutrals and her tailored everyday suits from Factory, and lying to her husband about how much it cost to buy the new season's black trousers, which are identical to last season's pairs, bar a slight change to the pocket stitching.

It doesn't say that last bit in the brief. Call that insider information.

'They should treat you the same, Emily, whether you arrive on the bus or in a Rolls-Royce.'

'Oh, wouldn't that be lovely? That's what I used to think life would be like living here. I thought that all I had to do to be Liz Hurley was get a London postcode. I'm still waiting.' Emily smiles her little-girl smile, but I'm not fooled.

'It must be isolating at times. Being here, with the Fredster, not knowing anyone.'

She looks surprised – and so am I. Usually I try my best to stick to safe topics of conversation, like camera shake and microphone rustle. It's the way I've always been: keep colleagues at a distance. Simpler that way.

'Yes. It's certainly not what I was expecting when we came here, but then again life's like that, isn't it? We're like skittles, never knowing when the next bowling ball will hurtle along and knock us for six.' Then she grins. 'Duncan was always telling me off for saying things like that.'

'Why?'

'He said it made me sound like a yokel.'

'Seems a bit harsh.'

'Maybe he was right. Maybe that's why he dumped me, when he realised I was too unpredictable to fit in with his new circle of city friends. Let's face it, Liz Hurley wouldn't be seen dead in the BHS cafe, would she? She'd be in Bluebird with Elton John.'

'There's nothing stopping you going to Bluebird.'

She smiles at me. 'Nothing except money. And I have a feeling that if Grazia had an assignment in Bluebird, she'd keep it to herself.'

I nod. 'You're probably right. So, weren't you tempted to go home when you realised you'd never be Liz Hurley?'

'At first I was. But I spent twenty-nine years in Somerset. All that time, I never knew whether I could cut the apron strings. If I go back now, that's me for life. I just know it.' She unwraps a chocchip cookie and proceeds to break it into two pieces, offering me half. I shake my head. 'You're not a Londoner either, are you? There must have been times when you've been tempted to go home.'

'Not really. My grandmother's desperate for me to head back to the Midlands, but I'm not ready either. Even if it does mean living on cereal and instant noodles. Mind you, if I had a kid, I think she'd drag me home at knifepoint.'

Emily winces. 'Oh, don't. The only reason that hasn't happened to me is because my parents don't know that Duncan's left me.'

I stare at her. '*What?*'

She shrugs. 'Duncan's working over in Switzerland anyway, so I just haven't got round to mentioning that Heidi, his boss, is also his lover.' She smiles tightly.

'Oh my God!' I can't quite believe what I'm hearing. It's one thing being a single mum, quite another keeping up that level of deception. 'You're a tough cookie under that fluffy exterior, aren't you?'

She points at the few crumbs that are all that remains of her biscuit. 'Yeah. A tough cookie who lives on cookies. Mind you, it'll be bread and water for tea unless we go and earn our money, eh? There's no putting it off any longer.'

'Right you are, comrade. See you back here afterwards for lunch?'

My assignment passes off without incident: true, Tsara the assistant could have been a little less po-faced, but her suggested outfit for an office party on a Thames riverboat was sensible, if sedate. Tsara made a token effort to get me to take out a store card, and only pouted a tiny bit when I 'suddenly' decided that I had one last shop to visit before I committed to buying.

The biggest problem I have when I'm secret shopping is *not* getting involved. It's so tempting. I jam my hands in my pockets, so that I don't start rearranging a display of handbags or refolding stacks of cashmere jumpers. And I do literally have to bite my tongue to stop myself approaching a manager to suggest a different soundtrack, or to compliment a staff member on going the extra mile.

Instead, I save my expertise for my assignment reports, sneaking in my suggestions between factual observations about response times and furniture cleanliness. 'It is not our job to give opinions.' Grazia always says, 'we are eyes and ears but we are not required to exercise our brains.' So I couch my ideas and observations carefully, hoping that I might still have an influence, even if no one ever knows my name.

I spot Emily on the street outside Factory when I leave, waiting to go in. Then I complete a quick visit to a mobile phone shop, where a young lad with dreadlocks gives me the most comprehensible explanation yet of 3G. If I phrase my report right, he might get a pay rise.

Emily takes longer than expected, but when she returns to the cafe, her eyes are wide, like a child trying not to cry after falling over.

'What's happened?'

She blinks rapidly, wheels Freddie and his buggy next to our table, and scoots to the drinks machine. She returns with a cappuccino loaded with cocoa powder, and eats all the foam off the top before speaking. 'I bloody needed that.'

'Was it really so bad?'

'Probably the worst experience since I joined the Shopping Angels. Oh, Sandie, they're such *bitches* in there.'

I must admit that I'm a bit sceptical. The shop certainly wouldn't win any prizes for touchy-feely warmth, but maybe Emily's extra-sensitive at the moment. She is still quite big after having her baby, and perhaps it was the sizing that upser her: after all, in one shop you could fool yourself into thinking you're a twelve but Factory's more accurate sizings would leave you in no doubt that you're actually pushing a sixteen. I had my own moment of truth with the skinny trousers that refused to fit over my hips. Luckily for me, I am probably the only woman on the planet who doesn't equate size of bum with self-worth. My gramma's outlook might be old-fashioned, but it's also heavy on common sense.

'Was it what they said, or what they did, or . . . ?'

She frowns. 'You think I'm exaggerating, don't you?'

'No, no. But we all have days when we're feeling on the vulnerable side.'

'Right!' She begins to unzip the top of the bag-cam. 'Let's see, shall we?'

'Emily, you can't play it here.'

'Can't I?' But she does move the bag out of sight, onto her lap. She manoeuvres the tiny LCD screen so we can just see it through the gap. 'No one's looking, and anyway, how do they know it's not my holiday video?'

She passes me the bag and her voice plays through the tinny speaker, identifying the footage as Grazia taught us to. 'May 16, 11.07 a.m., Job Number 10784, Operative GL1.'

I move closer, squinting at the screen. The camera tilts up to show the exterior of the store, the sign and the shop window: the shot is clear and steady and I feel mildly jealous of her camera-work. I've practised in my spare time, but I can't seem to eliminate the odd wobble. Yet on her footage, the dummies are in perfect focus as they engage in a game of tennis on an AstroTurf lawn in the window. I thought it was a striking display: summery, with a touch of English wit to match the quintessentially English clothes. Like houses, shops need kerb appeal and this branch is irresistible.

Emily's camera moves towards the door, the lens right up against the frosted glass. The door opens and the exposure changes automatically, taking a fraction of a second to adjust to the light inside the shop . . . just in time to catch the crucial first encounter with the store staff. I know from my years at Garnett's that this moment more than any other will influence the customer's perception of the place, which is why head office bods go to such trouble training their employees to get it right. The Factory manual is more specific than most:

Factory shopfloor staff should acknowledge all customers with a friendly smile and a short greeting. The 'welcome phase' should however recognise that each customer requires an 'orientation interval' during which time no direct offer of assistance should be made. However, the welcome should leave the customer in no doubt that assistance is available and willingly offered if required. The level of smile must be scored by mystery shopping operatives on a scale of one to ten, where one is no smile, and ten could not be wider.

It's Tsara again. But instead of the rather anaemic three-point smile that greeted me, Emily gets a long, shocked stare, as though an ill-bred zoo animal – an elephant, perhaps – has had the audacity to set foot in the branch.

The stare continues for five . . . ten seconds. Tsara looks furious at the incursion into her territory. Finally she regains control of her jaw, clamps it firmly shut, and turns away.

So much for leaving the customer in no doubt that assistance is available and willingly offered if required. If a real customer was greeted like that, I reckon they'd be back out on the street and heading for Evans before you could say plus-size. Which is presumably what Tsara wants.

Emily, however, is made of sterner stuff. The camera pans the entire store, showing that the other assistant is busy doing something fiddly at the till. I watch as the shot takes in a row of dresses hanging off a thin transparent rail, itself suspended from the ceiling by transparent cord. The clothes appear to float in mid-air.

Emily browses for two minutes, as per the assignment instructions. The Factory retail analysts have broken down their clients into three behavioural types according to browsing behaviour and purchasing power: Casual Shopper, Serious Shopper and Loyal Shopper. Each category of shopper has an appropriate 'customer care response' and if Tsara was following the rules then she'd be all over Emily after two minutes. Now I'm all for ignoring daft head office micromanagement if you have a better way of doing things, but this isn't an assistant taking the initiative. It's an assistant being an utter bitch.

When Emily turns towards Tsara, Tsara turns away.

'Excuse me . . .' Emily's voice is polite, but too loud to be missed. Tsara busies herself straightening pairs of black linen trousers that are already perfectly straight.

Now Emily and her camera approach Tsara, so close that she can no longer pretend she hasn't noticed. Probably Tsara had assumed that by this point the frumpy customer with the buggy would have slunk away in disgrace, but this shopper is on a mission.

'I'm sorry to bother you,' Emily says – because, after all, it's a bit unreasonable of her to expect a shop assistant actually to *assist*, 'but I've been looking for an outfit to wear to a summer wedding, and a friend suggested trying here.'

Tsara's face is a picture of amusement. 'Oh, yes? This friend – is she like you?'

'In what way?'

'The same size.' Tsara looks more delighted with

herself by the second, her voice plummy and disbelieving. 'Only, you see, we don't cater for the *larger* woman. So sorry. The kind of sophisticated tailoring we showcase at Factory doesn't work on the fuller figure.'

'I'm only a size fourteen.' Emily's voice is quieter now.

'If you say so.'

'I do say so. Do you really have nothing that would suit me?'

Tsara considers this. 'Let's not get ahead of ourselves. Right now I am more concerned with finding something that will *fit* you.'

And off she flounces, turning her back on Emily again. For the first time ever, the camera wobbles.

Emily pans to where Tsara is whispering to the other assistant at the till. Both disappear into what must be the stockroom and I can hear laughter. Finally, Tsara returns, various black and pink garments hung over her skinny forearm.

'Shall we get you into the fitting room? Sorry, it might be a bit of a tight squeeze, but they're really designed for our regular customers.'

And the camera heads into a cubicle that isn't small at all, where Emily places the bag-cam on a chair facing the curtain. We decided early on that we weren't giving Charlie or anyone else reviewing the footage the cheap thrill of ogling us in our underwear.

Only when she's fully dressed does Emily turn the camera back on herself.

'Oh, Emily.' I turn away from the camera, back to the *real* Emily, sipping her cappuccino and looking less pale than she did five minutes ago. 'She's seriously suggesting you wear *that* to a wedding party?'

That is an enormous black T-shirt, black leggings, and a boxy pale pink jacket with 1980s-style shoulder pads and ugly plastic buttons. Each item is several sizes too big for Emily and I find it hard to believe they could possibly come from Factory. Unless they keep a special set of clothing in the stockroom, specifically for the purpose of humiliating anyone over a size twelve.

Emily takes the camera back. 'Have you seen enough? I don't really want to relive it any longer than I have to.'

'Go ahead, switch her off. If one of my staff behaved like that, I'd have had them up on a disciplinary.'

Emily shrugs and turns off the power, places the camera on the floor, and moves Freddie into the vacant space on her knee. She begins to feed him with pink gloop from a jar, licking her finger when she spills some. 'Oh, yum. That's surprisingly good. Though maybe it proves her point. Duncan always called me his little piglet.'

'What a rotten thing to say.' I shake my head, although I don't really understand why she overeats. Gramma always drummed into me the importance of eating only when hungry, other-wise, you guessed it, *you'll end up like your mother.*

204

'Still, look on the bright side: Tsara is bound to get her comeuppance now.'

'Hmm. Do you think it makes up for us closing down the hardware shop? Seems so unfair for Factory to thrive while that place is for the chop.'

'You're not still worrying about that, are you?'

'Aren't you? I keep fretting about all the little old ladies whose gutters are going to overflow because lovely Will won't be there to clear them. Oh, *Freddie.*' Strawberry pudding now covers every part of his face, but seems to have missed his mouth entirely.

'It's not our fault that they can't balance the books.'

'I suppose that's true. But I still feel crap about it. Come on, Freddie, open wide.' She smiles at him, then looks up at me 'I've been thinking that I might go back. To Heartsease. To confess.'

'Oh, Emily. What good would that do? The decision's made.'

She sighs. 'I know it won't make a difference to the end result, but it might make me feel less underhand.'

'There is that, I suppose.'

'Would you . . . would you come with me, Sandie? I'm not all that brave. You wouldn't have to come in. Just wait outside. In case it gets tricky.'

'I'll think about it. If it really means that much to you.'

'It's the least I can do. That guy, Will, worked so hard to find me my washer. I know shops are about making money, but why can't they have a role in their community too?'

'There's no profit in good service any more.'

'I'm not so sure. Wouldn't millionaires like their washers individually wrapped and tied with a little bow?'

I laugh. 'Posh people have staff to buy their washers for them. Posh people probably don't realise washers exist.'

'Well, maybe washers were a bad example. But look at Garnett's. It's not the cheapest, yet the service is good, so people shop there even though they can get things for less elsewhere.'

It makes me queasy, thinking about Garnett's. 'Depends on your definition of service. Customer care always took second place to sales.'

'You don't really mean that, Sandie. I *know* you cared! I saw it with my own eyes.'

I allow myself a short burst of nostalgia. 'Well, yes. There was that time when I arranged for an entire house-load of furniture to be flown to Abu Dhabi while these newlyweds were on honeymoon . . . Oh, and then I sourced a spare part for this woman's food mixer from the manufacturer in Germany, though she bought it forty-four years ago. But despite that I still ended up getting the sack, which probably proves how little service matters.'

Emily's spoon stops midway towards Freddie's mouth. 'So you *were* sacked. I knew it. I never could believe you'd leave a job you obviously loved.'

I sigh, furious at myself for letting my guard down. But sometimes it's almost beyond human endurance, keeping secrets. 'Yes. I *was* sacked. I was falsely accused but . . . well, I might as well have done it. I'm completely unemployable either way now.'

She smiles sympathetically. 'What was it? You don't have to tell me, but bottling it up isn't good for you. Not that I'd know. I'm incapable of keeping anything to myself. Well, except for Duncan's dastardly desertion.'

It hits me, now. I bottle things up because I have no mates to confide in. *Keep yourself to yourself, Sandra; nobody needs to know your business.* And, true to Gramma's instructions, I've kept myself separate, as though I'm better than other people because I am so self-contained. The only time I've dared to make a connection with anybody was with Toby and what a disaster that turned out to be.

'You know, Sandie, you don't have to pretend everything's OK. I'm your mate.'

I feel touched, if a little embarrassed. 'Thank you. If I ever do feel the need to bare my soul, you'll be the one I bare it to.'

She nods. 'I'm serious. About the mates thing. Since I started doing the secret shopping, I've begun to feel I belong in London, because there are people here who would miss me if I wasn't here. Maybe I don't belong at Factory, or at the Bluebird cafe, but I have my own identity again.

I'm not just Freddie's mum, or Duncan's chubby, silly wife.'

I think it over. 'Perhaps that's my trouble. I still see myself as an employee of Garnett's, or my gramma's loyal, God-fearing granddaughter, the girl who always does as she's told. But I don't have a clue who Sandra Barrow is.'

Emily reaches over and touches my hand again. 'I know who she is, Sandie. She's a hard worker, bright as a bloody button. And I'd bet my entire collection of Mills and Boons that she's a seriously loyal friend, too, if only she'd let her guard down.'

Her kindness embarrasses me. But it also makes me feel a little less alone.

CHAPTER 16

GRAZIA

Three o'clock. No one awake but me and the owls. Are you there, Leon?

I remember when you couldn't sleep, we'd discuss the big questions: God, the meaning of art, the pursuit of happiness.

OK. Let me rephrase. You would talk, and I would listen. An insomniac husband is a curse. I never admitted it to you, but I craved an uninterrupted night, without those 'accidental' nudges from you, which I always knew were designed to wake me up. Once I was awake, of course, I could not let you suffer alone: you seemed so vulnerable. In the twilight, I saw you as you used to be. Plain Leon Trevor Smith, the East End boy whose artistic talent brought him nothing but schoolyard fights and family taunts, until he found like minds at Goldsmiths. And now you're gone, each shared minute in the grey of the early hours seems a blessing.

The one thing we never discussed in the midnight hour was what would happen when one of us died. Ridiculous, really, but then again with a relationship like ours, it was inconceivable that we'd be separated.

Here is a twist that would make you smile: I have developed insomnia myself. I don't lie awake seeking answers to existential questions. I have more practical concerns. About money and loyalty and your legacy. Is it disloyal to investigate how much money I could raise from the contents of your studio, and from that final painting – and is there any point, when I cannot imagine selling them?

And which would ultimately distress you more, Leon? Your pictures hanging on a billionaire's wall, or strangers living in our house? For hours I navigate this maze of options, only to find each leads to a dead end. And despite my pleas, you never answer.

Who am I kidding? Leon is not here. No one is here but me, the owls . . . actually, that is not quite true. There is someone else. Someone who cares enough to want to snatch away from me any possibility of sleep. Once, twice, three times a night, the telephone rings, mundane yet threatening, echoing through the empty house like a sound effect in a horor movie.

No one is ever there when I pick it up, so now I let it ring out. It is strange, but each time it sounds, at least I know someone is thinking of me. Sometimes, in my more fanciful moments when I have taken red wine or sedatives to help me rediscover this lost place called sleep, I imagine Leon is trying to call me, using all his psychic energy to connect with me, yet failing at the last moment to get through.

Except, of course, Leon never did believe in the afterlife. I certainly don't have much life after his death.

'Ooh, this is such a treat, Grazia. I've never had my nails done before. Well, except by my best friend at school, and then we got detention for wearing red varnish.' Emily wiggles her fingers and toes in delight.

My lack of sleep makes me short-tempered. 'Quite so. Red varnish is common, only to be worn by prostitutes and actresses.'

Sandie nudges me, then nods towards the manicurist . . . whose nails are painted pillar-box red. My cuticles tingle in anticipation of the punishment she'll inflict in revenge.

'What colour *should* we wear, then?' Emily asks.

'Rouge noir, with a hint of black, is more sophisticated. Or a French manicure. Glitter can only be excused in the under-twelves.'

Emily's face falls and she puts down a tiny bottle containing ludicrously bright pink varnish with iridescent sparkles. Freddie sits wide-eyed, singing mysterious tunes to himself, charming everyone around him even though he can't yet speak.

'Only on the toes can you afford to be flamboyant,' I tell Emily. 'What colour have you chosen, Sandie?'

She frowns. Her hands are tightly clasped in her lap, and her feet are unexposed. 'I don't like people fiddling with my extremities. Especially my feet. I've never had anyone touch my toes before.'

'Then get those socks off. A good pedicure is one of life's pleasures,' I say, then whisper, 'especially when it is free.'

She does as she is told, reluctantly.

'A quick whiz with my diamond foot file and we'll have you sorted,' says Red Nails, gleefully. I suppose one must find job satisfaction where one can.

Today was supposed to be about improving job satisfaction for my two recruits – one of Charlie's special treat assignments – but I fear it is not working for Sandie. We're on an undercover visit to a tiny nail bar just off Covent Garden, a temple to spit and polish. Or hopefully just polish. There are vintage movie posters on the walls, a baby-pink fridge containing miniature bottles of champagne, and white china dishes filled with silver sugared almonds. Even better, the manicurists seem to know what they're doing. The American parent company will be happy with the footage and we can all relax.

Except that I cannot quite relax. Maybe it is simply my insomnia making me irritable, but I am convinced there is more to the strange atmosphere than Sandie's reluctance to reveal her feet.

The manicurist fills three coral bowls with warm water, and instructs us to soak our hands. It is oddly freeing to be unable to do anything but talk and sip champagne through a straw. When Red

Nails produces matching basins to soak our feet, the immobilisation is complete.

'Ah, blissful! Makes a change from spying in snobby clothes shops,' Emily says. Her eyes are closed, so I can't fire a warning look. I hope she does not forget herself: she is not what you could ever call discreet.

I try desperately to think how to change the subject. The girl removes my fingers from the bowl and begins to massage them with a rich cream that smells of almonds. What could we talk about? Contemporary art? Japanese film? Hardly. What do we have in common, after all, beyond these cloak and dagger missions?

Red Nails is surprisingly tender, and the unfamiliarity of someone else's hands on mine feels peculiar at first, but soon becomes soothing. I allow my own eyes to drift downwards, giving in to the firm touch of her fingers and the sound of cool jazz.

When she stops and places my fingers back in the bowl, I open my eyes just in time to see Sandie and Emily exchange furtive glances. Instantly, I know my hunch was right: they are keeping secrets from me. The intensity of feelings that this knowledge produces in me is a shock: irritation, isolation, even *jealousy*. *I* am the boss here. I created this team. I must not be kept in the dark.

The telephone rings and Red Nails crosses the room to answer it.

'There is something going on. Tell me, tell me,'

I hiss to the girls, hoping my voice is too low to be picked up by the tape, but knowing I can record over it easily enough: after all, it is what Emily did on her first time out, at the shop in my village. I pretended I did not know, of course, but I respected her for trying to cover up whatever that horrible woman must have been saying about me. Yet how does Emily repay my faith? By colluding with Sandie. You can trust no one.

Emily's guilty expression lasts only a few milliseconds but it is enough.

'What are you talking about, Grazia?' Sandie does a better job of sounding innocent.

'Between the two of you. Thick as thieves. I can tell. Are you plotting to take over from me?' I sound more paranoid than I intended, but what was it Leon always said? Just because you are paranoid, does not mean they are not out to get you. Though it has to be admitted, Leon smoked a great deal of weed over the years.

Sandie shakes her head, a sulky pout dominating her face. 'I don't know what you're on about—'

'Sandie, we should explain,' Emily interrupts her. 'It's not fair to keep this from her.'

The manicurist is too absorbed in a complex domestic argument with a man called Waaaayne to notice us. Sandie shrugs, and switches off her bag-cam: when Emily does the same, I know it must be serious.

'We're going back. To Bells & Whistles,' Emily says, looking straight at me. 'Now I know you think I'm silly and emotional, and I admit it, I am, but I've been feeling so bloody guilty about it. It's the only way I can get it out of my mind.'

Despite the warmth of the soaking water, my hands and feet go cold. 'You're going to tell them? About the filming?'

'Well, yes. I think he deserves to know—'

'No!' Instinctively I raise my hand to cover my face, splashing soapy water in my eyes. 'Ouch.'

Red Nails looks up, alarmed, and puts the phone down. 'You OK?'

'Fine. Something in my eye.'

'Oh dear. Let me,' and she wipes my eyes with a cotton wool pad. I must remember to correct my make-up before we leave: I will not be seen in public with smudged mascara. Even at Leon's funeral, I was immaculate. When one has lost the bloom of youth, then good grooming goes some way to compensate.

'It's not as bad as it sounds, Grazia,' Sandie whispers.

'Easy for you to say! What about your confidentiality agreement? What if the manager . . . tells his superiors that he's received a visit from . . .' I try to speak in code, so Red Nails will not realise that we are secret shoppers, '. . . from *Charlie*, and then the superiors report it back to Charlie himself. Do you want to lose your job?'

Emily shakes her head. 'No, but I can't bear this secrecy, all the lies.'

'I forbid you to go.'

She screws up her eyes in concentration. When she opens them again, I see something I have never seen in her before: defiance. 'You can't do that, Grazia. I know I'm a total pushover, and I don't want to seem ungrateful, but I have to do this . . . thing.'

Red Nails gawps at her. Speaking in code makes us sound more like secret agents than secret shoppers. I place my hands in the bowl again, and try to focus on damage limitation. She is right, of course – I cannot stop her. Maybe I am panicking over nothing. By all accounts, the shop was already on a hit list, so hopefully the manager will put it down to experience. Worse tragedies befall people. I should know.

And yet I need to be certain.

'Emily, Emily,' I say, 'your concern for the client is very touching. I understand that this one has moved you for some reason. So under the circumstances, I think you should go. On one condition.'

'Which is?'

'I want to come with you.'

CHAPTER 17

EMILY

I feel naked without my secret camera. It's my security blanket, almost as important to me now as Freddie's soggy rabbit is to him. But then I'm not really going shopping.

I am shopping *myself*.

The closer we get, the more worried I am. This might make me feel better but, like a guilty spouse breaking the news of an indiscretion, there's a chance I'll only make it worse for the person we've betrayed.

Betrayed? I remind myself for the thousandth time: I was just doing my job. But the very least Will deserves is to know why.

'Ready?' Sandie's in the front seat of Grazia's latest set of wheels – a plasticky purple people-carrier that could transport a rugby team.

'Ready.'

Grazia catches my eye in the mirror, then looks away. I think she was flabbergasted when I defied her order not to return to Bells & Whistles. But not as flabbergasted as I was.

We arrive at Heartsease Common in the middle of an early summer downpour, the shop blurred by rain. We park on the far side of the common, just as we did the first time we came here. I'm going in first, because it is my idea. The others are going to wait here with Freddie, I think it'll be better if I go in babyless: I can focus on what I want to say, and maybe he'll take me more seriously. However, in the best tradition of the real Charlie's Angels, the others will be available as back-up, in case things get at all heated. Not that I'm expecting argy-bargy, but it's hard to know how anyone would react to some girl turning up and revealing that she spied on you, filmed you covertly and got you the sack.

My stomach lurches.

After a few steamy minutes while I shelter in the car, the storm eases off.

Right. I walk the long way round, avoiding the sodden common, past the tired collection of shops, until I reach Bells & Whistles. After last week's sterile perfection at Factory, the poor old shop looks more like a jumble sale than a tempting retail experience. But then again, this *is* a hardware store, not a boutique. Since when did a customer have to be seduced into buying tile grout or wing nuts?

A large handwritten sign is stuck to the window with tape: STOCK CLEARANCE, TWO MONTHS LEFT, EVERYTHING MUST GO.

I take a deep breath and step into the gloom: the smell of mothballs and sawn wood tickles my nose. There's no Jean behind the counter. Surely they can't have laid her off already? My guilt reaches new levels as my eyes adjust. It's even messier than before. Piles of random objects are perched precariously on the shelves, and the lino floor is crowded with baskets overflowing with odd items: a dozen nozzles for garden hoses, some tester pots of bright red paint, a puncture repair kit. Someone – I guess it must be Will – has attempted to make the sale more appealing by adding more signs. THREE FOR THE PRICE OF TWO ON EVERYTHING IN THIS BASKET! one screams, while another notice alongside a row of weedkiller sprays admits that ALL REASONABLE OFFERS WILL BE CONSIDERED.

I wonder how he took the news. Perhaps he tried to make a joke of it, or maybe he begged the cruel owners to reconsider, explained how much there was to lose, how Jean would never find a job again at her age, could end up on the streets, penniless, forced to sell her body or her hair or her entire collection of hand-knitted jumpers . . .

'. . . It might seem pointless to you, Jean, but I refuse to let standards slip!'

Voices from somewhere out the back of the shop.

'Oh, get over yourself, William. It's only a bit of dust.'

'The customers will notice. We can't let them think head office was right to close us down, can we?'

'I don't see what difference it's going to make now.'

I hear a deep sigh.

'Fine. Thanks for the support, Jean. I'll do it myself. *As usual.*'

He emerges from the back of the store, through the multi-coloured fly-strip curtain. He's holding a broom that seems under-sized against his tall frame and . . . oh, yes, my memory hasn't been playing tricks; he's every bit as attractive as I remember. Dark hair, light eyes in that impossible-to-pin-down colour. But there's a vulnerability about him this time: a slight slope of the shoulders, maybe, or a touch of wariness.

He spots me and confusion crosses his face, followed by a glimmer of recognition, and then a broad, boyish smile. He *is* very easy to read. I've rather lost faith in my judgement after making the mistake of marrying Duncan. But then again my husband was the master at using that sly grin to hide his indiscretions. And, I suppose, his un-happiness. Happy men don't leave their wives and babies.

'Washer, wasn't it? For your tap?'

'Well remembered!' I say.

'Did it go in OK?'

'The washer?'

'Yes,' he says, 'because they can be absolute devils to fit. And we weren't totally sure if it was the right one, were we? Is that why you're back? I'm sure we can locate a replacement somewhere in this chaos—'

'No. No. That's not why I'm back.'

'Oh, right. Bargain hunting then, maybe?' He waves towards the ceiling, where a dozen or more garden umbrellas are suspended as if in mid-storm. 'Parasols are a steal.'

'No. Listen, Will – I can call you Will, can I?'

'Call me anything you like. Though you never told me *your* name.'

'Emily,' Perhaps it's good for the healing process for him to know who to curse. 'Will, the thing is . . . there's no easy way to say this but . . . this is partly my fault.'

He looks puzzled, perhaps a little amused. 'What is? You've lost me, *Emily*.' He tries out the name, nods in satisfaction at how it sounds. It does sound good, I must admit: his low voice could belong to a high-flying doctor from one of my romance novels. Sexy, with just a hint of geek . . .

I blush. It is so hot in here.

'It's partly my fault that the shop is closing down.'

He frowns, less amused now. 'I don't follow. How could you possibly have anything to do with it? This place was on the hit list before I took the job. I thought I could stop the rot, but sometimes you have to admit defeat. It's not me I'm worried about, it's—'

'I'm a secret shopper, Will. I filmed you.'

'*Filmed* me?'

'Yes. You, and Jean. I filmed the advice you gave me on the washer, and the business with the till roll running out, and Jean knitting away behind the counter.'

It takes a few seconds for him to understand. Again, I can see his thought processes reflected in his face. Confusion, recollection, understanding, *anger*.

'You *spied* on us?'

'That's one way of putting it. It . . . it's my job. It's not personal. Just a job. But I swear I didn't know what was going to happen.'

His frown is so deep now that I can't see his eyes. 'So, let me get this straight. You came here to catch me out?'

'No, no. We visit stores for a whole load of reasons. To check on good service, to make sure people are following procedures.'

'That's what I said. To catch me out.'

'We're only doing what ordinary shoppers do.'

'Except you're filming it all.'

'We're consumer champions,' I say, in a very small voice, knowing how pathetic it sounds.

He shakes his head slowly. 'I hope they pay you well.'

I decide now isn't the time to tell him that it's not much more than the minimum wage. 'We all need to earn a living.'

Will turns away from me, straightens a row of PVA glue tubs. 'Do you know how long this shop has been here, Emily?'

'No.'

'Ninety-two years. Arthur Bell founded his first ironmonger's on this site. That was in the days before the marketing types spent a fortune testing the brand and decided to add "Whistles". Imagine all the people who came through those doors, Victorian tradesmen. Domestic servants. And more recently, first-time buyers and widowed pensioners who can't afford to get a workman in . . .' He refuses to meet my eye.

'Yes. I know.'

'But that history, that service, that's not important to the bean-counters. We're not conforming to chain standards, they told me. Failing to meet targets in terms of customer churn, range sales and overall profitability. Never mind that we managed to save a partially sighted lady two hundred pounds last week because we cleared her drains with a twenty-quid drain rod. Or that I give regular talks to the local primary school about gardening and pet care and—' And then he stops. 'Ah, what's the point? This place was always a poisoned chalice. I should have left the company rather than come here, for all the good I've done.'

'I'm sorry.'

He stares at me in surprise, as though he's forgotten I'm here. 'What is it I'm meant to say at this point, Emily? "No use crying over spilled milk? Plenty more fish in the sea?"'

'Um, I think that's when you've broken up with someone,' I suggest, and then curse myself for saying something so crass.

But he manages a wry smile. 'Why did you come here?'

'I suppose I thought owning up might help.'

'Help who, precisely?'

'Well . . .'

He waits for me to speak, but I can't. It was *stupid* to think that coming here would make any difference to anything. I don't have the common sense I was born with, sometimes.

'Ah well, I'm sure you thought it was a good idea at the time,' he says, and his voice is softer. 'OK. You wanted to help. Tell me one thing. If you've got all this expertise, this classified, secret shopping knowledge. What *should* I have done here? Could I have saved the place?'

I peer around the shop, with the gloomy lighting and the squillions of items for sale and the dust and the worn-away flooring. The scale of the task would rattle Hercules. 'I don't honestly know. Probably not.'

Will nods, as if he knew it all along. 'That makes me feel a little better. Now, I don't suppose I can interest you in a whole bag full of washers, can I? Everything must go . . .' Then he slaps himself on the forehead. 'Not that you ever needed a washer, did you?'

I smile, despite myself. 'No. I didn't. Sorry.'

There's a pause and I'm about to find an excuse to leave when I look through the window and spot a mini-delegation crossing the muddy grass. Grazia's spike heels are sinking into the damp grass, and Sandie is carrying Freddie, because his buggy won't fit through the narrow shop doorway. She's not used to his weight, and is puffing as he tries to wriggle loose. They don't look anything like a crack team of retail professionals; more like a bedraggled convoy of refugees.

'Right,' he says. 'Well, thanks for stopping by. I'd say "Do call again," but you know how it is. We probably won't be here.'

'Umm, Will . . .' I gesture towards the window. 'I don't think we've quite finished with you yet.'

CHAPTER 18

SANDIE

The trouble with Emily is that she's all emotion, and no logic. And I've been too busy thinking about *her* to realise that we're not the cause of that little shop's problems.

But we might just be the solution.

I push the door open with my elbow, clutching Freddie. The guy looks shell-shocked after Emily's confession. I wonder how he's going to take what I've got to say. If someone had turned up in my department at Garnett's and started to tell me how to run the place, I wouldn't have been remotely grateful. I might have been rather put out.

No. That's a fib. They'd have been lucky to escape with their lives.

Funny, it's been so long since I've had any power that I can't really remember how it felt to be in charge. I miss it.

Emily steps out of the way as we troop into the shop. Her cheeks colour. 'Will, I'd like to introduce you to my colleagues. You might recognise Sandie.'

He stares at me, and then the penny drops. 'Oh.

226

Not you too? I always thought there was something weird about *two* strangers coming in the shop on the same afternoon.'

The elderly woman from last time appears from the back of the shop, clutching her knitting. She nods warily at each of us in turn.

'Hi,' I say, embarrassed. 'I wasn't sure you'd remember the day we—'

'The day you came to spy on us?' Will says ruefully. 'Ah well. We've got a lot of stock to shift, so all customers are more than welcome these days.' Then he spots Freddie. 'Especially customers in dungarees. Hello, old chap. Who are you? And where have you hidden *your* secret camera?'

'He's come unarmed today.' Emily blushes more deeply and reaches across to take the wriggling baby. She holds up her son's chunky pink fist to wave back. 'Hello. This is Freddie. He's my son.' Her voice is oddly defiant.

Will does a double take, but recovers fast. 'Pleased to meet you, Freddie. Good to have another man in here, for sure. It can get a bit hormonal at times.'

The woman glares at him from behind the counter, her knitting needles a blur of pent-up aggression.

'Jean, Jean. You know I love you, really. I don't think we've met?' he says, shaking Grazia's hand.

She nods in acknowledgement. 'I am Grazia.'

'Pleased to meet you too, Grazia, even under these peculiar circumstances. I take it you're connected to these three? Unless word's got round that we're the *only* place in the south of England to be offering three for two on bumper kilogram packs of Fishy Friend guppy food?'

Grazia raises her eyebrows. 'We are not here for fish food. Or for jokes. I am the team leader. Since Emily here was so keen to visit, I felt I should be here too. In case of problems.'

'Problems? What, other than the fact that we're about to be unemployed? And, in my case, homeless. Jean? I'm not dreaming, am I?'

She shakes her head. 'No one ever tells me what's going on around here.'

I step forward. Now or never. 'Look, we didn't know our film would close you down. But now we really want to help.'

Everyone stares at me. Except Freddie, who is fascinated by the rapid movement of Jean's knitting.

'Oh yes? Are you sure you haven't already *helped* rather too much?'

'Look, I'm a straight talker. I used to work in retail myself, and I can always tell the difference between someone who really cares and someone who's doing it for the money. And this place has individuality. That's rare in retail.'

'Rare?' He laughs, and it catches in his throat. 'I'd say it's pretty much extinct.'

'The point is, Mr—?'

'Will.' He smiles shyly. Quite the hunk in an overall. I wonder what on earth he's doing in this backwater hardware shop.

'The point is that you could still change your directors' minds.'

'It's kind of you to offer, but we shut in eight weeks. Not even a royal visit could save us now—'

'That's it! I bet we could get Prince Charles here,' Emily says. 'He's really into rural communities, isn't he? And maybe we could get the guy who runs the corner shop from *Coronation Street*, and—'

I cut her off in her prime: she's not exactly enhancing our credibility. 'Yes, all right, Emily, that's got potential. But it's more fundamental than that. First we do need to make sure we have something here worth saving, don't we?'

Will's face falls. 'And you don't think we do at the moment?'

I take a deep breath. 'If I'm honest, not entirely.'

'I thought you said individuality was a rare thing in retail?'

'Yes, but it's no use if customers are still rarer. I know it's not nice to hear when you've devoted your time to the place, but I can see why this branch is on the head office hit list.' I wince in anticipation of his reaction. 'Can't you?'

'I hate to admit it,' he says, quietly, 'but actually I can. I did my best when I was sent here, but everyone knew it was the worst posting you could get, the Bells & Whistles equivalent of downtown Baghdad.'

'Bloody charming!' Jean points at him with her knitting needle. 'After all we did to help you when you arrived. I mean, it's not as though you were exactly in great shape, what with—'

'Oh, Jean Genie, I don't mean *you*. But you've got to admit, they've been running the place down for years.'

She nods, sullenly. I suspect managing Jean's moods is a full-time job in itself. 'Will, I can't pretend that we can definitely save the shop. But even if we can't, wouldn't it be at least a bit satisfying to show everyone what could have been?'

Emily is shifting from one foot to another, as though she needs the toilet. 'There's so much we could do,' she chirrups, 'What if we were to remake Van Gogh's *Sunflowers* out of nuts and bolts in the window?'

The more I get to know Emily, the more I realise she has a child's view of life, her mood changing minute by minute. Everything's either *dreadful* or *blissful* or *terrible* or *wonderful*. I can't imagine there's ever a boring moment in Emily-world.

Even Will can't help smiling. 'Hold on a minute. Let me think. It's all so much to take in.'

But Emily's unstoppable. 'Or we could do a calendar, like in *Calendar Girls*, and get people to pose surrounded by your products, like in *American Beauty*.'

Will shakes his head. 'Enough. Look, I appreciate your enthusiasm, but the truth is that I've given so much energy to this place, I don't think I've got any left.'

'Are you a man or a mouse?' Grazia hasn't said

anything for ages, and I was sure she was waiting to get outside and sack me for daring to interfere. But instead she pushes past me, towards Will, fiercer than I've ever seen her. 'We are offering you valuable assistance and you talk about lack of energy. Are you so easily defeated?'

'Hang on a minute,' he says, riled. 'In case you're forgetting, it was you lot who condemned this store.'

'Ah! So you do have a little fire in your belly after all. So why not use it?'

'I don't need fire in the belly,' he says, quietly. 'I need better premises. Head office support. A complete restock. But since none of those are coming, I mainly need a new job. Oh, and a new flat because I'm hardly going to be able to live above a shop I no longer manage, am I?'

Emily bites her lip. I decide to try one last time. 'You're going to be here till the end anyway, aren't you, Will? So why not spend the time productively? Better than rolling over and playing dead, surely?'

There's silence: Jean has even stopped knitting.

I know what he's going to say before he says it. His eyes seem to come back to life. 'There's never any point in arguing with a woman, is there? Never mind three of them.' He reaches out to stroke Freddie's cheek. 'Best you realise that now, young man. Save you a lot of time later on. OK. Suppose I do decide to fight back. What's the grand plan?'

I smile reassuringly. 'I find a cup of tea is always a good start.'

I suspect now is not the time to admit I don't actually have a clue where to begin.

CHAPTER 19

EMILY

Image is everything. That's what Grazia says. I've never really had an image, but perhaps it's time to adopt one. Duncan's due at the flat this morning, and after his patronising attitude and veiled threats last time. I feel the need to get strategic.

'What do you think, Fredster?' I parade in front of my son in my sweatpants and slippers. He giggles, then throws his soggy rabbit at me: his aim is improving all the time. 'Is your mummy yummy or scummy? Which is going to work best?'

This must be a good sign, wanting to play my husband at his own game. I am *strong*. I have no interest in winning him back, and I am not playing the wronged wifey any more.

Deep down, I think I always knew he wouldn't be in my life for ever. How could I claim ownership over dashing Duncan, the Casanova of South Somerset? OK, so perhaps I did believe for a while that our lopsided marriage might be cemented by the move to London, but that illusion was shattered on the labour ward, in my haze of pain and loneliness. As I sat up in bed when it was over, trying to work out the fiddly mechanics of feeding Freddie, gazing into his eyes with shock and awe and triumph and exhaustion, I *knew* this was how it was going to be: me and my little Londoner against the world.

Except tonight I'm spending my first night away from Freddie: Duncan's taking him overnight. I suppose it has to happen some time, though I'd rather we waited till my baby turns eighteen. That's years, not months. Duncan's found one of those kid-friendly hotels with round-the-clock nannies and organic baby food on the room service menu. Which means I have twenty-four hours *alone* stretching ahead of me. OK, I'll spend twenty-three hours of that worrying, but there's the teeniest part of me that sees possibilities. I could drink Mojitos in Soho, soak up some higher culture than CBeebies. What I will probably do is sleep.

I look around the flat. Duncan needs to know that I'm coping – so that he doesn't start on about me going home again – but I can't have him thinking we're living in the lap of luxury on his cheapskate maintenance. So I punch the life out of the sofa cushions and pile most of Freddie's toys into a corner, and he toddles over with his baby-walker. I think it'll only be a week or two before he takes his first steps alone: my baby won't be a baby much longer.

'Now, then, Freddie, has Mummy forgotten anything?'

All the kit's ready for the father-and-son sleep-over: nappics and lotions and changes of clothes and buggy and car seat and the rest, along with four handwritten pages of what to do and when, because he won't listen when I try to give him instructions.

Back to my own image. Got it. I'm going for *couldn't-care-less*. I select a *who-gives-a-shit* navy cotton skirt long enough to cover my pale legs; a *no-bloody-time-to-iron* navy-and-white striped Breton top and some *high-heeled-because-now-I-don't-have-to-pander-to-your-insecurities-about-your-height* sandals. OK, so I have shaved my legs (the blade had gone rusty from under use), and applied make-up. But I ended up wiping most of it off because I'm out of practice and Freddie kept giggling at my face.

And now we wait. I pace the room, plumping the cushions back up again. This edgy feeling is one I'd forgotten. After nine months of living without my husband, nine months with nothing to prove and no one to keep happy except Freddie, I don't like this.

'Where's Daddy, then, Fredster?' I check the clock: six minutes late. I suppose that's excusable, as he's travelling from Geneva, via Heathrow. To pass the time, I take out my Save Our Shop note-book, where I've been jotting down my ideas for the Heartsease Common campaign. I've been coming up with some brilliant thoughts, even if I do say so myself: a rainbow painted across the common, in the store's wide range of fabulous emulsion colours; a Battle of the Handymen and Handywomen contest; a human-chain protest outside the Bells & Whistles HQ in Reading, with a line-up of celebrity supporters. Maybe we could blockade their lorries.

But Sandie's such a spoilsport. She keeps going on about 'getting the basics right first'. We've been back to the shop twice in the past nine days, and each time she commandeers Will, huddling over the figures with him, talking profit margins and unit costs and other bollocking jargon. Maybe she fancies him. He is the ultimate in geek-chic, after all: Hugh Grant would play him if they made an Erin Brockovich-style movie of the campaign. I do quite fancy him myself, though it's only because he couldn't be more different from Duncan.

I know a crush isn't dignified at thirty, but it's the nearest I'll be getting to a man for the foreseeable future. Who would look at me? So much for nine months on, nine months off. Freddie will be one next month, yet I'm still in rock-bottom physical condition.

'But at least I'll always be *your* ideal woman, eh, Freddie?'

Thud. The shared front door slams shut and it must be Duncan because the Latvians always make sure they close it softly, in case Freddie's asleep.

My stomach tightens as I wait for the knock on

the door. I check my hair in the mirror, smooth the bumpy line of my lipgloss with my finger. *Emily, Emily, why are you still wasting your time?* You're meant to be over him.

The key turns in the lock, and I feel irritated. This isn't his home any more. It's mine and Freddie's and he's taking liberties letting himself in and I'm going to tell him so. He's had things his own way for far too long.

The door squeals open.

'Duncan! Before you go any further, I'd like to point out that you don't live here any more, so I'd appreciate it if you'd knock before barging in—'

And then I realise he has company. *Female* company.

Oh shit.

Duncan turns away from me, but not fast enough. I see the raised eyebrows, the 'didn't I tell you this was what she was like' grimace that he shares with his companion.

But my eyes are drawn to her, as Duncan cups her elbow and leads her from the dark hallway into *my* home. She blinks in the light, like a fawn.

Except . . . she's not fawn-like at all. Or, in fact, Heidi-like: no flaxen plaits, no mountain-dew fresh complexion or embroidered pinafore dress. The woman's older than me – late thirties, maybe forty – dressed in un-Alpine black, with Toblerone-coloured hair in a short, unforgiving crop. She's extremely thin, and taller than Duncan in her dominatrix heels. Perhaps he doesn't dare to insist she wears flats, like he always did with me.

She does at least have the grace to look uncomfortable about this situation.

'Before you say anything, Em, Heidi wanted to wait outside in the hire car, but I said she had no reason to be ashamed. You two were going to have to meet sooner or later, eh?'

I'm beyond speech. So is Heidi. The boys have no such misgivings. Duncan races towards Freddie and my baby's face registers confusion, then delight. I feel a sharp stab of betrayal as his father lifts him into his arms and uncontrollable giggles fill the room.

'What a great big champ! Aren't you growing big and strong?'

I want to say *no thanks to his daddy*. But I don't. I'm above all this . . .

'He's looking well, Em,' Duncan says. Duncan's looking well, too, with his on-trend leisurewear and his still-sparkling teeth. He sinks onto the sofa without a second glimpse at my precisely positioned cushions, and play-wrestles with Freddie. He's rougher than I am, but maybe that's what dads are for. Wrestling, footy and farting competitions.

'Yes,' I say, desperate now for them all to be gone. 'He's a good boy. I've put together everything he needs. He'll want feeding at four, nappy change usually follows soon after. I bath him at six, but you can afford to go about half an hour either side. But please don't disrupt his routine too much; it's taken months to get him sleeping through.'

Duncan doesn't seem to be listening. 'Oh, don't worry about that, Em. I know I'm a bit of a bloody liability, but Heidi's worked as an au pair. We'll be fine.'

She nods. 'I was an au pair in London. To learn English.' Her accent is crisp and authoritative. 'It was some years ago, but babies are all the same, huh?'

I'm torn between wanting to scream at her that my baby *isn't* the same, and feeling relieved that Freddie will be under the care of at least one responsible adult.

'So, you're meeting your mum and dad at that hotel at Windsor, then? The one that's geared up to . . . families.' I feel a catch in my throat as I speak.

Heidi looks at me sharply – or maybe it's just the way her face is arranged. Duncan shakes his head. 'Well, um, there's been a bit of a change of plan. Mum couldn't face the drive – you know how her legs swell up in the car – so we decided we might as well head down . . .'

'You're not going home! You can't! Not the three of you!'

Duncan sighs and adopts that oh-so-patient face I used to see on a daily basis. 'Em. We've tried doing things *your* way, at your pace, but it's getting ridiculous, all this subterfuge. And the thing is . . . well,

I'm not coming back, Em. You know that, don't you?'

His voice is gentler than usual, and it isn't a shock. Of course it isn't. But at the same time I do feel quite weak and tearful. This *really* is it. 'Yes. I know.'

'Well, then. I know you don't want to tell your parents, but you can't keep it from them for ever. Apart from anything else, Freddie deserves to see both sets of grandparents.'

His piety infuriates me. 'Oh, you're so grown up, aren't you, Duncan? So mature about it all: what's best for our son, what's best for our parents. But what about what's best for me?'

He looks around the room. 'Well, I can't imagine what's keeping you here.'

I take a deep breath. 'You can't make me do what you want any more, Duncan. You tried forcing me out by moving the Latvians in and now that hasn't worked, you're trying to send me home, so you can do what we were planning to this place, turn it into a perfect home, and then probably move your—' I was about to say floozy, but I can't think of a less appropriate word for the stringy woman in the doorway, '. . . girlfriend into the *love nest*. Well, sorry, but no. You can't have everything your own bloody way.'

Again, Duncan gives Heidi the raised eyebrows 'see-what-I-married' expression. She has the decency to look away. 'Em, no one is going to force you to move home, although I'm sure being here on your own isn't great for your mental health—'

'And whose fault is that?'

He ignores me. 'But we have to put Freddie first. I can't go skulking around the country, avoiding my own hometown, hiding Heidi, keeping up a charade because you can't stand up to your own parents.'

I want to say, *why not? Why does everything have to be on your terms?* But actually, he's right. Bastard.

'Now,' he says, his voice smooth, as though he's trying to placate a dangerous dog, 'I know it's not the kind of news you can break on the phone, so . . . why don't you get it over with? Hitch a lift with us to Somerset. It'll help Freddie stay calm on the journey, and then you can visit your mum and dad, tell them face to face. Apart from anything else, won't it show how amicable it all is, if we arrive together?'

'What, you *seriously* want to take Heidi for tea with my parents?'

He tuts. 'Now you're being silly. No, we can drop her off at the pub or something. Then when you've broken the news, I can either leave you to stay with your folks and give you a lift back tomorrow, or drop you at Bridgwater for the London train. How's that for a plan?'

Oh, it's supreme, Duncan. Congratulations. You have painted me into a corner, stitched me up like a kipper, given me the choice of frying pan or the fire. I wonder how long it took you to think that one up.

'I don't want to do this, Duncan.'

'No,' he says, 'but that doesn't mean it doesn't need to be done, eh, Em? Sooner we get there, sooner it's over with.'

And I know he's right and I feel my weekend of irresponsible non-motherhood morphing into a messy family drama.

CHAPTER 20

EMILY

Travelling in the back of the car has sent me travelling back in time. At a guess, I am now thirteen years old, a primordial soup of hormones and resentment. The only difference is that instead of being wedged in between my sister and the dog in the back of a Vauxhall Cavalier that overheats every twenty miles, I am wedged in between my son and several suitcases, and I'm overheating every twenty seconds.

How dare he? My anger with Duncan increases the closer we get to Somerset. I suppose I shouldn't be that surprised by what he's done. He's been using similar techniques since we met in the first year at Rowminster Comprehensive nineteen years ago. Even as a weedy eleven-year-old, he managed to kiss all the girls in my class except me. When we were reunited working at the bank seven years later, he insisted he only kissed them to get my attention. For a while, he actually made me believe it.

Heston, Reading, Chievely, Membury, Leigh Delamere: I tick the service stations off in my head as they whiz by. I'm trying to work out what to say to my parents, but my mind goes blank whenever I reach the point where they ask, '*And when did all this happen?*'

'*Nine months ago. I've just been waiting for the right time to mention it.*'

Oh yes. That's where it gets tricky.

'Need me to stop, Em? I know how small your bladder is!'

I squirm in the back seat. I suppose Heidi's bladder has the capacity of a small reservoir, and her pelvic floor muscles could match the Thames flood barrier when it comes to holding back the tide. Her smile muscles seem underdeveloped in comparison, but I suppose you can't have everything.

'I'm fine, thank you.' I'm lying. I really could do with the loo right now, but I'm not going to give him the satisfaction.

Duncan switches on the radio and U2's 'With or Without You' fills the car. He tried chatting about the weather earlier in the journey, but Heidi and I both refused to play ball. I suspect that Heidi's quite pissed off. It's bad enough having to spend a weekend with her boyfriend's baby, but having the boyfriend's wife tag along is a twist she clearly wasn't expecting. I know she's a scarlet woman and I should hate her guts, but I don't. All my hate cells are focused on my husband.

Eventually, with my bladder approaching bursting point, we leave the motorway and drive into Bridgwater. Heidi gawps. I'm guessing that her image of the West Country is all thatched pubs and rosy-cheeked scrumpy-drinking farmers, rather than corrugated iron industrial units and whey-faced scrumpy-drinking wasters. Duncan speeds up until we turn off the main road and Somerset stereotypes are restored. Sheep stare after us as though they've never seen a car before. A chocolate-box pub lists so badly it looks like it's had one too many. Cardboard signs advertise farm shops selling 'organic Cheddar, tomatoes and potatoes'.

And then we're on the edge of Rowminster, and I feel myself regressing still further. It's only now that I realise how exhausting it was living in my hometown. Every time I left the house or went to work, I had to live up to the legend of dippy, smiley Emily, the younger of the Cheney girls, 'you know, the one who played the Little Mermaid and wet herself in the 1985 carnival, before chipping her tooth a year later when she toppled off the Alice in Wonderland teapot', as though nothing had changed since I was cute enough to be a float mascot.

That's why I am not ready to come home.

Duncan pulls up alongside the little recreation ground with its swings and slides, overrun by hyperactive kids and bored teenagers. This is where we used to hang out every summer before we were old enough to get served in the Anchor. There was never much to do.

'I reckon it's best to leave you here, Heids, just for a bit. I don't think the pub's such a good idea. Tongues will start wagging before they've finished pouring you half a lager and lime.'

Heidi shrugs. 'OK. I understand.' She takes a black laptop bag with her when she leaves the car.

'And you don't think the sight of a woman dressed in black, examining spreadsheets in the park is going to get tongues wagging too, Duncan?'

He catches my eye in the mirror. 'Well, they'll all know soon enough, won't they?'

'Emily! Big D! Little baby F!'

My father is bounding up the driveway towards us before we can open the car door. He's been painting the fence: his clothes and hands are stained with brown creosote, only a shade or two darker than his face. He's just shy of fifty-five, but looks younger, thanks to his Hawaii-five-o tan and his thick strawberry-blond hair.

'What a lovely surprise, munchkin. I was beginning to think you'd disowned us in favour of your swanky London friends.'

'If only, Dad.' I climb out of the back seat to kiss him, then begin to unload Freddie.

My father slaps Duncan on the back. 'She's travelling in the back now, is she, while you taxi her around? Got you where she wants you!'

Duncan laughs nervously and Dad looks puzzled. Duncan doesn't usually *do* nerves. This is a man so cocky he'd play the joker with his own

246

firing squad, confident of being able to win them round before a bullet was fired.

'Dad, we're dying for a cup of tea.'

He nods. 'Understood. I'll get the quartermaster on to it!' And he disappears into the house.

I lift Freddie out of his seat and catch a particularly intense wave of filled nappy whiff. 'Here,' I say, calling over to Duncan, 'I think you should take him. Create a good impression when you drop the bombshell about Heidi.'

He pulls a face. 'Why does it have to be me who has to tell them?' Then he realises what he's said, and grimaces. 'OK, give him here. At least your dad won't punch me if I'm holding his grandson.'

As the baby of the family, I've never felt grown-up. Not on my wedding day, not even when I presented my son to his grandparents for the first time.

But there is something unquestionably *adult* about sitting in Mum and Dad's living room with your estranged husband squeezed next to you on the sofa, preparing to tell them that you're now a single mother.

'The thing is,' Duncan begins, once we've got the cooing over Freddie out of the way, 'things have changed a bit since we moved to London.'

'Things?' My mother's nose wrinkles, as though she's smelled something bad. Freddie's nappy, probably.

'I take full responsibility. It's nothing to do with Emily.'

Well, that's very gracious of you, Duncan.

'Come on then, spit it out, whatever it is,' my mother says.

'Thing is,' Duncan repeats, 'the trouble is, I think, that me and Emily were just kids when we got together. Literally. I mean, we met at eleven. First date at eighteen, which counts as a kid in my book, living together within two years—'

Dad laughs. 'I could have tanned your hide, run you out of town. But I guess it all turned out all right in the end.'

'In the end is about right,' says Mum. 'Took your bloody time to get round to getting married, didn't you? Ten years must be a Somerset record.'

If it wasn't for the fact I am dreading my parents' reaction, I'd almost be enjoying Duncan's discomfort.

'Yes, well, we both wanted to be sure . . .' Duncan insists. 'But you never know, do you? Relationships are subject to so many more pressures these days. And personally, I don't think a relationship has to last an entire lifetime to be a success. Bringing a healthy baby into the world, for example, is an achievement all by itself.'

My father looks bemused, but I think my mother's cottoning on. 'Marriage is meant to last a lifetime,' she says. 'That's the point. Do stop talking in riddles, Duncan.'

Duncan turns to face me, panic in those come-to-bed eyes. I look away.

'I . . . um, I've moved to Switzerland.'

'Yes, we know that,' Dad says, 'but it won't be for ever, will it? Absence makes the heart grow fonder, eh, Emily?'

'Well, it *might* be for ever, you see, Don. I have, well, sort of . . .' he pauses, and I'm pretty sure he's just realised what the bad smell is. His eyes begin to water. 'I've left Emily.'

My parents' faces mirror each other perfectly: maybe that's what happens when you've been married for decades. First they frown, then they both lean forward, close enough to tear Duncan limb from limb.

'You've left her for someone else? Or you've left her because you want to be on your own?' Mum always gets straight to the point: she worked on quality control at Clarks for two decades and in all that time I don't think she let so much as a faulty buckle leave the factory floor.

'Someone else.' Duncan whispers.

'What? Speak up, lad!'

'For someone else!' He shouts this time and now I don't feel quite so detached from the situation.

Dad's lips have disappeared, as they do on the rare occasions he gets angry, but when he speaks, he's adopted a *man of the world* tone. 'You know, lad, you can't go abandoning your wife and child for the first girl to flash her teeth and tits at you.'

'Dad!'

He waves me away. 'Every marriage has its ups and downs but it's the glue, isn't it? The glue that holds families together. And you have to bear in mind that—'

'Dad, I'm serious. It's too late for all that. He isn't going to change his mind, however thick you lay on the old-fashioned wisdom.'

My father looks put out. It's my mother who has scented blood.

'Too late? What's that supposed to mean? When exactly did this happen?'

Trust her to hit the bullseye. 'Um, a few months ago.'

'How few?' She's as ruthless with me as she was with poorly stitched sandals or rumpled insoles.

I sigh. 'I didn't want to worry you.'

'WHEN was it?'

'All right, all right. It was October, Mum, when he went to live in Geneva. I mean, I didn't know for sure that Duncan had found someone else, but I think I *knew* inside –' I touch my chest – 'that he wasn't coming back. And he confirmed it a month later.'

'But . . .' Her mouth pops open and then closes, like a goldfish. 'I . . . but . . . that's . . .' she counts on her fingers, 'nine months ago. Your son was less than two months old. How *could* you? Wild animals stick around for longer!'

Duncan encircles Freddie with his arms: whether it's intended as evidence of his continuing affection towards his son, or a self-defence manoeuvre, I'm not sure. 'I know I've been a shit, Diane. But I do still want to be a father to Freddie, even though I don't want to be a husband to Emily.'

I feel winded by his bluntness.

'So, you've been completely on your own – a single parent – for nine months?' My father seems to be struggling with the whole concept of me surviving alone.

'It was my choice not to tell you, to be fair to Duncan.'

'Why the hell should we be fair to Duncan? Has he been fair to you?' My mother is in full lioness mode now.

'Well, no, but—'

'You've obviously had some kind of breakdown, otherwise you would have come home to us,' she says. 'Still, you're here now. Don, ring round the committee. If we can get hold of the trailer and a couple of lads tomorrow, we'll have everything shifted by teatime. You can have Jane's room, and Freddie can go in your old room, and I bet I can talk Gordon at the bank into giving you your old job back, only part-time, but what you need is a routine—'

'Mum, please listen to me. I'm not going to come back, not yet. I actually quite like London—'

'I think she should come back, too,' Duncan says. 'I've been saying that. It's no place for a woman on her own with a baby.'

'Oh, belt up, Duncan; you lost your right to an

opinion when you left me for Miss Cuckoo Clock. The fact is, I am coping just fine. I've got myself a little job. Made some new friends.'

'That's the first I've heard about it. Who's looking after Freddie? You can't go farming him out to some chain-smoking childminder without consulting me.'

'Don't you speak to my daughter like that, you . . . *deserter*,' my mother hisses.

I stand up. 'Look. This is exactly why I didn't want to tell you. I'm coping, OK? The first time in my life I've had to manage alone and I'm doing fine. I know that'll be a big surprise to you all – it was to me, too – but I don't feel ready to give up my freedom yet, thanks very much.'

The silence that follows is curiously satisfying. Then my father stands up, too, and walks across the deep pile. Without a word, he puts his arms around me and I can smell creosote as he crushes me against his overalls. 'My little girl's all grown up,' he says eventually. 'You make me feel like a *very* old man.'

The train from Bridgwater back to London is almost empty, and I lean back in my seat, letting the sound of the wheels send me into a trance.

Everything feels unreal, not least the lack of a buggy and a baby. It's like losing a limb, but without the physical pain. I'm numbing the un-reality with a beer from the buffet car and I put my feet up on the seat opposite. I might be a grown-up, but I feel like a naughty fifth former.

It was a battle of wills to get away – Mum was all for calling the GP to administer a knock-out horse sedative – but I was, surprisingly, eventually backed up by Duncan, who was desperate to return to Heidi to play happy families. As we left the house to drive towards Bridgwater, he even had the cheek to say, 'That didn't go too badly, did it?'

And then looked perplexed when I didn't speak to him for the rest of the journey.

So, twenty hours left with nothing to do but worry about my son.

I think I need *major* distraction . . .

CHAPTER 21

EMILY

I didn't set out to get drunk. Let me make that absolutely clear. But I *am* out of practice at the business of drinking and so it is high time I got back in the saddle.

'If I get another bottle,' Sandie asks, 'will we drink it?'

'Sandie,' I begin, not knowing quite how I'll finish my sentence, 'it is one of the laws of nature that an opened bottle of wine placed before three drunken women will be emptied!'

'I am not drunken,' says Grazia, although she definitely is. We've been in the Maypole Bar and Grill for two hours and her accent has thickened so much that she now sounds like a mafia moll. 'Being drunk is not elegant.'

'No, but it's a giggle,' I say. 'Definitely another bottle.'

My first night out in nearly a year, and I'm making the most of it. After two beers from the train buffet, I plucked up the courage to call Grazia and Sandie: I think they were so shocked to hear from me out of hours that they sort of said yes by accident. I'd already guessed that they wouldn't be doing anything else on a Saturday night.

Within minutes, Grazia had called me back with a list of potential venues for a spot of secret shopping *and* secret drinking – 'I make it a matter of principle that I never pay for anything if I can get Charlie to foot the bill.'

The Maypole is brightly lit, full of young trendy people with loud clothes and louder voices. I walk past every time I go to the Tube and it's always made me feel terribly old. Now we're inside, it doesn't seem nearly so intimidating, mainly because no one is interested in us at all. We've got the checks out of the way: inspected the loos (spotless, with working hand dryers), asked some tricky questions about the wine list, assessed staff uniforms, and ordered and rated some fusion tapas to line our stomachs. The hard work over, we can enjoy our night out.

But my hopes that free-flowing wine might also free my comrades' tongues are ill-founded. Drink just magnifies our personalities. So, of course, I am chattering nineteen to the dozen about Heidi and Duncan, but Grazia merely sticks her perfect aquiline nose higher in the air, and Sandie stays infuriatingly selfcontained. She looks in the direction of the Portuguese waiter, and he's at her side in an instant, with the new bottle of Pinot Grigio appearing seconds later. Grazia makes a brief note of the time it took in her notebook, along with a description of his appearance. Then she turns to me.

'So. This husband. How much is he worth?'

'I beg your pardon, Grazia?'

She sighs impatiently, as though this is a perfectly reasonable question, not a mammoth dose of nosiness.

'Money. It is the first question your divorce lawyer will ask.'

'Um. Well, I was rather hoping to avoid lawyers. Can't you do all the paperwork on the internet these days?'

She raises her eyebrows. 'If you wish to be *fleeced* then go ahead. But with a child to raise, that would be insanity. I have friends who attempted to keep their divorces straightforward, but it does not work. Never, ever.'

Sandie tops up all our glasses. 'She's right, Emily. He is in the wrong, and after the way he's behaved, you can't predict what he might do to stitch you up.'

'Hang on. He's not *that* bad. He hasn't robbed a bank, or sold the house under my nose, he's just done what men have done since time immemorial.'

'Emily, do you know what you are saying?' Grazia's exasperation shocks me: she's always seemed far too cool to care about anything. 'You are defending him. Why? He deserves nothing but your contempt.'

I pull a face. 'I don't see the point in getting angry. It's not how I do things.'

Grazia takes a sip of wine. 'You are sure it is

not because you are afraid what will happen if you allow yourself to be angry?'

'Oh, that's ridiculous!'

But *is it?* I think back to the dozens . . . no, hundreds or even thousands of times I nearly lost my temper with Duncan during our marriage. Each time, I stopped myself by remembering an incident when we'd just started dating, and I shouted at him for flirting with another girl in the pub and humiliating me in front of our friends.

He laughed in my face. There was no attempt to soothe or placate me, no apology. He simply couldn't take my anger seriously. As a way of proving that I had no power at all, it was pretty unbeatable.

'The divorce needn't be nasty,' Sandie says. 'You just need to decide what you want from him, and make sure you get it.'

My two partners-in-shopping nod at each other in agreement. 'It is all about taking responsibility,' Grazia says. 'The trouble with marriage is that it leaves you so ill-equipped for divorce. A certain kind of husband will chip away at your ability to behave like an adult, until you are entirely dependent. And then when he leaves, he leaves you bereft.'

'Maybe. Though I'm not convinced I ever had the ability to behave like an adult.'

'Time to acquire it, then,' she says firmly.

I should be grateful for their advice, but I feel

rather irritated. 'Fine. But aren't you trying to take over from Duncan, telling me what to do?'

'No, I do not think—'

'And anyway, what makes you such bloody experts? Sandie, you don't even have a boyfriend, and Grazia, we've only got your word that you had the perfect relationship with your husband before he died—'

And then I stop, shocked at my own cruelty. 'I'm sorry. I don't know what came over me. It must be the wine, or what happened today, or . . .'

'Or maybe you are not quite as nice as you seem, Emily?' Grazia says, her black eyes boring into me. Then she smiles. 'Bravo! I am pleased to see there is some spark there. I must point out, however, that perfect is not a word I have ever used to describe my relationship with Leon. Tempestuous, yes. Inspirational, yes. Unique, undoubtedly. But perfect . . .' Grazia's lean, sculpted face sags, making her seem very vulnerable.

'You must miss him terribly,' I say, trying not to think about what the woman in the village shop said about his young female visitors.

When she eventually speaks, her lips barely move, as though she's trying to hold in the pain. 'Yes, I miss him. I also miss myself. My role. People dismiss the muses of artists as passive creatures, but it is so much more than striking poses or saying witty things at parties. Nurturing the soul of an artist is both exhausting and addictive. And now . . . what do I have left to do?'

I try to think of something to say that might reassure her, give her hope for the future. But I do see her point: compared to inspiring great artistic works that will be admired for centuries, secret shopping must be a comedown. 'I suppose that marriage doesn't necessarily leave one well equipped for widowhood, either.'

Grazia nods sadly. 'This is true.' She turns to Sandie. 'It seems to me that one of us has avoided any such problems. I am curious. Tell me, are you a lesbian?'

Sandie's jaw drops. 'Um . . . well, no. Why? Does it matter?'

'Not at all. But it seems you have escaped these ties. Emily and I are both still beholden to our men in one way or another, yet you are a free spirit.'

Sandie laughs now. 'Hardly. I'm the least free-spirited person I know. Can you see me prancing round a boggy field, high on Ecstasy and free love?'

'No, but you could if you wanted to,' I tell her, 'or you could climb Everest or volunteer in an elephant orphanage or go to Hollywood to seek fame and fortune. You're an independent woman.'

'Or a sad specimen with no life. Anyway, I'm not single because I hate men. I'd quite like a boyfriend, but when I was at Garnett's, work was my grand passion. There wasn't room for anything else.'

She stares glumly into her wine. I don't like the maudlin direction my precious night out is going in. There must be some way to turn it into a happy ending?

'Ah, but the working all hours was to help you forget a tragic past, was it? It's like one of my love stories. Heartbroken Sandie poured all her energy into her career. But then . . .' I falter.

'Go on, what happens next?' Sandie says. 'I'd love to know.'

'Well, usually some dashing but improbable doctor with a mysterious history turns up at work and before the heroine knows it she's falling for him and then there are lots of misunderstandings, but then they get it together on the final page. Brilliant fun.'

Sandie shakes her head. 'But why would a doctor come to work in a department store?'

'Oh, now you're being silly. They were only doctors because the heroines were nurses. In your case, it'd be . . . I don't know, a dashing designer launching his latest collection in the store, surrounded by his pick of glamorous models, but he only has eyes for . . . no, that won't work; aren't designers mostly gay? So maybe he's the new manager, come to revitalise the dowdy old shop, facing lots of resistance, and you're his right-hand woman and . . . well, it's obvious what happens. Snogging in the stockroom. Waltzing up the aisles!'

I realise I am *truly* drunk.

But Sandie's laughing properly. 'Well, it's funny you should mention it . . .'

'What? I'm right?'

'Half right,' she says. 'If you forget the happy ending. I *did* have a bit of a thing about my boss. No, not really my boss. You know that Garnett's is an old family firm? Well, Toby was the great grandson of the original Mr Garnett. Why am I talking about him in the past tense? He still is. And he's still working at the store, unlike me.'

'What happened?' I tuck my legs underneath me on the suede banquette, ready for a good story. 'Was that why you were fired? Love across the class divide, his father sacking you because he didn't want a commoner to get a place on the board . . .'

'Um, Emily, this is the twenty-first century, remember? Last time I looked I wasn't wearing clogs and facing destitution in the workhouse. No, it's far duller than that. Toby and I spent a lot of time together, but we never actually got it together. He was always far too busy being snapped falling out of taxis with 'it' girls at five o'clock in the morning.'

'He sounds *adorable*,' Grazia says, deadpan. And then she laughs, a throaty sound that is surprisingly contagious.

'He *was* adorable. *Is* adorable, I mean, but completely not the sort of guy who'd ever go for me. Except I did think for a little while . . .' she

261

sighs. 'I thought at least he respected me. I was the only person who could get away with teasing him, while everyone else fawned all over him.'

'That's *always* a sign, in a love story,' I explain. 'People who share a sense of humour end up sharing a bed, ninety-nine per cent of the time.'

'Well, in our case, we shared strategy discussions, and the odd supper . . .' Sandie stops, pretends to slap her forehead. 'I was a fool. First sign of trouble, he dropped me like a stone.'

'What *did* happen?' I ask, wine making me brave.

'I was set up.' She sounds matter of fact. 'I think it was my deputy. She hated me. Someone made it look as if I'd been stealing from the store. Took the key to my locker, placed a fat envelope of cash inside, and then left an anonymous note accusing me of stealing. Do not pass Go, do not stop to collect references. That was bad enough. But the worst thing was that Toby didn't question it. He just assumed I was guilty.'

I refill her glass, right to the top. 'Poor you! There's nothing worse than betrayal.'

'Betrayal. Yes. That's what it was. Oh, and in a brilliant twist, my deputy now has my job *and* I think she's dating Toby. Hopeless.'

'You know, nothing is ever hopeless,' Grazia pronounces. 'A woman can do anything she applies herself to.'

'Well, that's definitely true of Marsha,' Sandie says.

'No, what I mean is, you must apply yourself to

resolving this situation. Or it will dissolve you from the inside, like acid.'

I stare at Grazia. Obviously her taste in fiction is rather more Gothic than mine. 'She's got a point, Sandie. What if you made contact with this Toby guy again? You don't have to name names, do you? Just explain what you think happened, remind him of the good old days.'

'Already tried and failed when he came into the bar where I was working. He's made up his mind. I'm the ungrateful wretch with her fingers in the till.'

'But, Sandie, a bar's a bloody hopeless place for a serious chat. Do you know where he lives?'

'Bachelor pad in Chelsea when he's working, and the Garnett's ancestral pile in Gloucestershire when he's not. In between extended trips to Henley and Ascot. All in the line of duty, of course,' she adds, with a wry smile.

'Oh, it gets better and better. Destitute girl turns up at the gates of the master of the house, soaked to the skin, starving, penniless. She's turned away by the forbidding butler until the master spots her from a window as she's about to collapse on the gravel drive, races down, drags her into the house in front of the open fire, feeds her . . . I don't know, scones and cucumber sarnies, and then admits undying love! Sorted!'

'Err . . . thanks, Emily. How can I resist my destiny?'

'So you will look for him?'

She shakes her head in disbelief. 'Of course not. That part of my life is over, isn't it? I have to move on.'

I nod: despite my romantic fantasy, I'd have given up by now, too. But Grazia, clearly made of stronger stuff, wags a determined finger. 'No, no, no. You are clearly not moving on, so you must take the bull by the horns. Life is for grabbing by the balls, my Leon always said.'

'Is that what *you're* doing in your life, Grazia?' I ask, as gently as possible.

She looks startled. 'No. No, I am not. Leon would be very angry with me. But I have nothing to grab. And bravery is easier when one has company.'

I need to rescue this evening before we end up weeping into our wine. 'But we do have company, don't we? I'm hardly a great example of bravery, but knowing you two has made me a bit less of a coward. Without the secret shopping, I'd have headed home months ago.'

'Actually, I think you are pretty brave, Emily,' Sandie says.

I giggle. 'Yeah, right.'

'I couldn't have coped with being left in the lurch with a baby, in a strange city where I knew no one. OK, it's a different kind of bravery from the mountaineer sort, but it does take a special kind of strength.'

I'm sure it's the booze, but I feel choked. I,

Emily Prince, am a woman of courage, the Saint Joan of single parenthood! A survivor. As I lean across the table to pour myself a celebratory glass of wine, my mobile vibrates in my pocket. Who would text me at this time of the evening?

Duncan's name pops up alongside the little envelope on the phone screen and my thumb is clumsy on the keys as I try to read the message.

It has to be Freddie! Oh God . . .

SORRY EM, KNOW IT'S LATE, BUT THOUGHT YOU'D LIKE TO KNOW – FREDDIE HAS JUST TAKEN HIS VERY FIRST STEPS! ATTA-BOY!

Before I can stop them, tears flood my eyes.

'Emily? What's the matter? Is something wrong?'

I look up at Sandie, feeling excited, and insanely proud of Freddie, and scorchingly jealous of Duncan, all at once. 'My baby's just walked for the first time. Isn't that the most exciting thing you *ever* heard?'

And I reach out to throw my arms around them. Sandie resists at first, but I am going to share this moment with my friends, even if I can't share it with my boy, so I don't let go and before long, we're group hugging like victorious Italian footballers.

'This calls for champagne,' Grazia announces, when we come up for air.

I nod happily. 'Hang on, though. Are you sure you can claim that back from Charlie?'

'Almost certainly not,' she says.

'But what about your rule about never paying for anything?'

'Rules, Emily, are made to be broken, in exceptional circumstances. And I think that the first steps of the youngest member of our mystery shopping crew count as exceptional. Would you agree?'

ANYONE FOR TENNIS?

Even the shopper who hasn't lifted a racquet since school will respond to a Wimbledon theme in June: strawberries, cream and Pimm's No. 1 Cup. Draw them in with retro-tennis dresses, plain white plimsolls and the promise of mixed doubles with the sexiest players off Centre Court. More balls, please!

CHAPTER 22

SANDIE

Bravery or madness? I can't decide whether the decision I've just taken is inspired or dangerous.

It was a spur-of-the-moment thing. I'd intended to send the 'fruit and chocolate gift bouquet' to Gramma – it was the sole reason I schlepped all the way to Chelsea, because this assignment was only worth ten pounds. I've been feeling guilty about not living up to my grandmother's expect-ations, and about the fact that I can't bring myself to phone her, and endure yet another lecture on my scandalous freelance lifestyle and impending ruin.

Actually, my impending ruin seems to have been postponed. Feedback on my secret shopping reports is so positive that creepy Charlie emailed me personally: the suggestions I've been sneaking in between the lines have been welcomed by the retailers, and I'm being allocated some more interesting assignments, along with all the bread-and-butter jobs that pay the rent. *Play your cards right, Sandie, Charlie said in his message, and the world could be your oyster. I'm thinking swanky hotels, fancy restaurants, perhaps the odd international flight. Stick around, kid. Best not mention it to your colleagues yet; can't have the green-eyed monster wrecking your working relationship, eh?*

So far, then, secret shopping has kept me busy, given me two new friends, and now it might even develop into something like a career. But the sick feeling returns every time I have to pass Garnett's on my way to a job. there's a whole store full of people there who think I'm a liar and a thief.

It was playing on my mind yet again this morning as I entered Chelsea Greens, the chichi green-grocer offering fruit and chocolate bouquets. At first I thought this was just a typical over-the-top SW3 description for a gift basket containing a pineapple, a few prickly lychees and a box of naff Belgian chocolate shells.

But no. As I entered the store, I nearly walked right into a bouquet the size of a hanging basket. A bouquet sculpted from fruit: pineapples, straw-berries, oranges, grapes and kiwi . . . oh, and lots of dark chocolate. There was something comical about it, but also something quite mouth-watering.

The assistant – for whom, judging by her cheekbones, a single grape constituted a square meal – took my order and all was fine until I gave her the delivery address.

She laughed. 'Birmingham? Oh. We don't deliver to *Birmingham*.'

It was as if I'd suggested despatching a fruit bouquet to Mars. 'Why not?'

'We only deliver within a three-mile radius,' she explained, 'mainly because this is such a *Chelsea* thing, but also because cut fruit goes off so awfully quickly. So, do you want to cancel the order?'

I shook my head: I've made it a rule that I *always* complete an assignment. And as I racked my brains for someone I knew in the area, a terrible, scary, irresistible plan began to form in my mind.

'No. I take it you *do* deliver to Chelsea Harbour?'

The closer the van gets to the river, the more convinced I am that this definitely counts as madness.

'You OK?' asks Benny the delivery driver, as he takes another speed hump at Grand Prix speed. 'Only you look queasy and it's impossible to get the smell of vomit out of car upholstery.'

'Don't worry, I've never thrown up in my life. And we're nearly there, aren't we?'

Benny was reluctant at first when I asked if I could hitch a lift and help hand-deliver the bouquet 'as a surprise'. But then I begged, telling him some sob story about a long-lost colleague, and he relented. It is partly true, of course. My long-lost colleague will be very surprised when I turn up.

We pull up at the gatehouse. I've never been here before, but I was always sending couriers with documents for him to sign, so the address is etched in my memory. The porter takes the van's registration number. 'Don't tell me. You're delivering

271

for the party at the penthouse, am I right? Go into the underground car park, take the service lift; the code is 9871.'

At least I know now that he's in. We're waiting for the lift when I suggest to Benny that I take the bouquet up myself. 'I'll sign for it.'

Benny huffs and puffs a bit. 'You are the customer, I guess,' he says eventually and heads back for the van.

In the service lift, I try to check my reflection in the brushed metal surface, but I can't see past the tropical fruit. The scent of pineapple is over-whelming, and now mango juice is dripping onto my black shirt.

What the hell am I hoping to achieve? Toby has been playing on my mind ever since the night in the pub with Sandie and Grazia. Back then it seemed simple. Maybe, just maybe, I could change everything – convince him that he's made a mistake. The prospect of returning to Garnett's, my name cleared, shop-floor staff breaking into a round of spontaneous applause as I take my rightful place again, keeps tantalising me. I've clearly spent too much time with Emily.

'Please enter your code.' The lift's electronic voice is insistent. I feel dizzy and deliberately enter the wrong code, while I calm myself down. I have to try this, don't I? There's a reason I can't forget Toby, a reason why I've been googling his name, and why his address popped into my head in Chelsea Greens. Maybe there's some higher force at work, the god of secret shopping sending me to Chelsea to complete the most important mission of my career.

Oh dear. I'm *definitely* channelling Emily now.

'Incorrect code. Please enter your code.'

Right. I enter the correct sequence of numbers this time and feel a lurch in my stomach as the lift rises. No turning back now.

But is this what I really want? To go back to the old days? Sandie the Sensible, Sandie the Workaholic, Sandie with no friends and no life outside the four walls of a department store? Maybe I should stop the lift, abandon the fruit bouquet and head home.

I'm just hot, dehydrated, not thinking straight. Retailing is in my blood. I love it. This is worth fighting for, even if I do keep hearing Gramma's folk wisdom in my head: '*It's like the moth and the flame, Sandra, and you know what happened to the moth.*'

The lift stops, and I hold my breath while I wait. Somewhere on the other side of those doors is the man who can make or break me.

They part smoothly and I step into a small lobby, where a brisk woman with a clipboard looks me up and down before inspecting her list. 'Chelsea Greens, right? I'd recognise those bouquets anywhere.'

I nod. While she flicks through the pages of her list, I try to see past the pineapple slices into the flat. The glossy black kitchen is straight ahead, and a white-haired chef is piping mint-green mousse into flower-shaped pastry cups.

'Can't see you down here.'

'That's because Mr Garnett only called us an hour ago. Wanted a rush job,' I say. 'If you ask him, he'll confirm it.'

She frowns at me. 'Wait.' As she disappears into the kitchen, I hear her call out, 'Toby, Tooo-by! Where are you?'

What is he celebrating? It can't be his birthday; that's in March. Record-breaking profits at the store?

His engagement to Marsha?

No, stop being so ridiculous. Toby would no more marry her than he'd marry Sandie Brains. According to Google, he's now number nineteen in *Cosmo*'s Top Fifty Most Eligible British Bachelors. He's also Toff of the Month on the Top Toff Totty Blog, a bizarre website for stalkers and gold-diggers who'd like a title or a share in a stately home along with a solitaire engagement ring. The only thing Toby lacks for these aristocratic wannabes is a title. The Garnetts are nouveau riche, with less than a century's worth of money behind them, acquired through grubby trade at that. Bambourne Manor, the so-called ancestral home in Gloucestershire, only came into the family in the twenties, after the first Mr Garnett struck lucky with his department store (and even then, the upper crust were always of the opinion that he stole all his ideas from that jumped-up Yankee, Gordon Selfridge).

I lean against the wall, and a photograph catches my eye: it's Toby on the deck of a yacht, surrounded by pretty girls. His blond hair is blowing in the breeze, sunglasses on his head, and he looks at the camera with the supreme confidence of a man who has never had to fight for anything.

Oh God. I should have written to him instead. A letter is *so* much better: less confrontational, more measured, and also my inner grizzly bear is far less likely to make an appearance. I need to get out of here. I hit the lift call button.

'Now, what would I ruddy well want with a bouquet made from fruit?'

'Well, that's what I thought . . . excuse me, EXCUSE me, miss.'

Too late. I turn, the bouquet shielding most of my face.

'Dear God, what a vulgar monstrosity,' Toby says, close now. 'I definitely don't want that . . . Sandie?'

I let the bouquet drop a little.

'Bloody hell.' Toby shakes his head, uncomprehending, as though he's spotted a penguin in the Kalahari Desert. Aside from the confusion, he looks good: tanned, fit, with that floppy fringe bleached lighter than usual, presumably as a result of the month in Antibes that the girls on Top Toff Totty have been getting so excited about on their website.

'You know her?' Miss Clipboard raises her eyebrows.

'I know her,' replies Toby, his eyes not leaving my face.

'I didn't want to ambush you, Toby, but I needed to talk. This was the only way.'

He keeps staring. Mango juice continues to drip down my arm, and a chocolate-coated pineapple petal drops to the floor.

'That porter has some explaining to do. Don't worry, Toby, I'll call security, get rid of her—'

'No, no. You take that bloody bouquet,' he tells Miss Clipboard. 'Stash it somewhere. Anywhere. Stuff it down the waste disposal, I don't care. And *you*,' he turns back to me, 'follow me.'

The woman takes the bouquet, tutting loudly, and I do as I'm told, trying not to feel stung that he's trying to hide me away, because he's ashamed of me, just as he always was at Garnett's. He marches through the gathering of cooks in the stainless steel kitchen. The place reminds me of an operating theatre. The living room is full of pretty waitresses, and there's a large tin bathtub sitting on the oak floor, jammed with ice and magnums of champagne. There's a giant cinema screen, bigger than the one in my local Ritz cinema, but the real showstopper is the vast terrace, and beyond that the view . . . the Thames sparkles below, barges and pleasure boats reduced to the size of clockwork toys.

But he doesn't stop: he pushes through a door into a large bedroom. *His* bedroom, I suppose, the dream destination of subscribers to Top Toff

Totty. The bed could sleep seven, with a chocolate-brown suede headboard that must have used the hide from a herd of cows. He slams the door behind us.

I hear a yowl from behind the bed.

'Oh, bloody hell, Monty, get a grip.' Toby leans down and squeezes under the bed, resurfacing with a terrier puppy in his arms. 'It's a girl, not a serial killer. Well, I don't think she's a serial killer. You're not here to bump me off, are you, Sandie?'

I hold out my hands in a gesture of peace. 'No.'

'What in God's name *are* you doing here? First you steal from us, now you sneak in like some bloody stalker, gatecrashing my Wimbledon party before it's even started. Are you trying to get yourself locked up?'

I say nothing, which seems to make him un-comfortable. He motions towards a chair and I sit down. He paces the floor, still cradling the dog, which has stopped whimpering but continues to quiver.

'Come on. Say something. I can't wait to hear your explanation.'

'I never had a chance to defend myself, Toby.'

'From what I recall, you had plenty of oppor-tunity. You just chose not to use it.'

'I was in shock.'

'Shock at being caught out, no doubt!'

Something about the pompous way he says it gets under my skin, and I feel my grizzly bear stirring. 'Toby. I understand why you're angry. But if you think about what happened before Christmas, it makes no sense. I'm Sandie Brains, for goodness sake. Sensible's my middle name. I don't *do* crazy stuff.'

He squints, thinking hard. I recognise the expression from the hours I spent when we first worked together, teaching him how Excel worked. By the time I'd finished, he was better with figures than any of the old codgers who ran Garnett's.

After what feels like hours, he sighs. 'All right, Sandie. Against my better judgement, but in recognition of our work together, you've got *ten* minutes. After that, I want you out of my flat and if I ever see you in future, I'll call the police. OK?'

The grizzly bear grumbles in protest, but I nod my agreement.

'I need a bloody drink,' he says, lifting the puppy gently onto the silk bedspread. He crosses the room and flicks open a sepiashaded globe to reveal dozens of bottles and decanters. He pours a large tumbler of something for himself and, as an afterthought, holds up another crystal glass. 'Want one?'

I'm about to say no, but I am still shaky and it occurs to me that on this occasion drinking before noon might not be the slippery slope towards certain alcoholism (as Gramma always insisted) but a sensible way of calming my nerves before my big speech. 'OK then.'

He hands me a glass of amber liquid. I sniff. *Sherry.* Ah well, in for a penny . . . the raw warmth hits my tongue and the back of my throat and it's all I can do not to gag. But then, seconds later, it begins to taste rather nice. I take a second sip.

'Toby, the thing is—'

He holds up his hand to stop me and walks over to the French doors, which lead to another fabulous terrace. 'Don't tell me. You were framed.'

'Well, yes. But if you knew that, then why—'

'Have you ever been prison visiting?' He has his back to me, which seems rude, but I guess a lecture on manners won't help my case right now.

'Um. No. Why, have you?'

'Yes. I used to visit my Uncle Roland.'

'Oh. Am I allowed to ask what he was in for?'

'Fraud.' He gives me one of his meaningful looks. 'Of course, he didn't do it.'

'Of course.' I take another gulp of sherry.

'None of them had done anything. The prisoners. That's what I remember most clearly. I was only thirteen, and it was rather daunting at first, even though it was one of those open prisons, you know, for white-collar criminals and the odd career burglar judged too old to shimmy up drainpipes. Actually, in some ways it reminded me a lot of boarding school. Except the food was better in the prison, from what I saw.'

He refills his glass. 'When I went to see my uncle, the lags would whisper their sob stories to me when they served me tea and home-baked scones. It seemed the whole place was filled with victims of injustice.'

'Well, I suppose people do slip through the net occasionally.'

Toby sighs. 'Yes. My father found out, eventually, about the visits. I wasn't supposed to be going at all. But, you know, Roland was my favourite uncle. I didn't believe any of the things they'd said about him.'

'Which were?' I have a bad, bad feeling about this.

'Which were that my favourite uncle had been using his position on the board at Garnett's to steal from the store for fifteen years. So, all the time he was being *oh so generous* with his christening gifts for me and the day trips to the races and the polo and what have you, it was with stolen money.'

'Ah.' It rings a vague bell: some scandal in the early nineties that the store had spent most of the decade recovering from financially. Very hush-hush.

'Ah indeed. I protested my uncle's innocence vehemently. Until my father sat me down and showed me the accounts. Not that accounts have ever been my strength, as you know.'

'Yes.'

'But he made sure I understood what that particular set of accounts meant.' Toby walks towards me now, uncomfortably close, as though he's about to kiss me, or punch me. 'My father had a stroke the year after his brother was sentenced. He was in the midst of trying to sort out the financial carnage. Hasn't worked since, doctor's orders. But it doesn't take a doctor to work out what might have caused the stroke, does it?'

'I'm sorry.'

He doesn't seem to hear me. 'He's never been quite the same. Even now, fifteen years on. He's so . . . stooped.'

The sherry goes down the wrong way, and I cough. He blinks, remembering I'm here. I decide it's now or never. 'Toby. That sounds horrible, but I'm not your uncle. Someone at Garnett's bore me a grudge and planted that money in my locker. If you think about it, the only evidence against me was the cash and the envelope, and I always bring my bills to work with me, so it wouldn't have been difficult for Mar—' I stop myself. 'For someone to have gone through the staffroom bin. I worked so hard for Garnett's; you saw it yourself. Why would I devote myself to the place for seven years, for the sake of a few pounds?'

The look he gives me makes me realise that I've lost him. 'Why would my uncle steal from his own brother for fifteen years? I've never found the reason, but I've heard every single excuse, courtesy of my friends living at Her Majesty's Pleasure.'

'Right.' The booze has made my head spin, but the situation is crystal clear. 'I suppose I'd better go.'

'I suppose you better had,' he says, refusing to meet my eye.

I walk slowly and deliberately to the door, and

then stop, searching my brain for some last words. 'I don't blame you for not trusting me, Toby, but I didn't steal from you or from Garnett's or from anyone. Maybe one day you'll realise that.'

He walks towards the bed, picks up the little dog and grimaces. There's a wet patch on the silk where the puppy was lying. 'Bloody hell, Monty, you dirty boy.'

I leave the room, past the caterers with their vats of strawberries and cream, past a man unwrapping a three-layered cake in the shape of three life-size tennis rackets, past Miss Clipboard, who is flapping over the state of the bathrooms.

And as I slip unnoticed into the service lift, I can't stop thinking about the moth and the flame . . .

CHAPTER 23

GRAZIA

The English male loves a naughty girl, with a kiss-me-quick hat and wet T-shirt and overflowing bra. Me, I have never been naughty. I used to worry that Leon – an Englishman through and through – would look for mischief elsewhere. But Leon always told me that I was made not for naughtiness but for *sin*.

So I am surprised how much I am enjoying this ridiculously naughty deception of Charlie and the Bells & Whistles management. It could be a plot from one of those coarse *Carry On* movies. *Carry On Up the Plunger*, or *Carry On Screwing*, perhaps. I do not believe for a second that our campaign will change anyone's mind. Nor am I convinced that Sandie or Will believe it. At times it seems that we are all involved in a charade to protect Emily from the truth, as though she is a small child.

But we are having such fun. Imagine that. Fun!

Leon, I can almost hear you scoffing. *Almost.* Because I know I do not really hear you, of course, but I remember your voice so well I can conjure it from thin air. We did not lack for good times together ourselves, of course. Gallery openings, concerts, first nights . . . there was no hot ticket you could not acquire, no cultural event that could not be enhanced by your presence.

My presence, if I am truthful, was profoundly unimportant, decorative at best. A muse may inspire in private, but she serves little purpose in public. She is serene, blank. She is never so vulgar as to giggle.

In fact, when I giggled last week, I hardly recognised the sound coming from my mouth. We were experimenting with window displays for the Save Our Shop Last Chance relaunch; the three of us began to waltz with our mops and Emily started singing that Whitney Houston song, 'I Wanna Dance With Somebody', and it seemed like the funniest thing in the world.

Still, it is nearly over. After four weeks of work, this afternoon is the Save Our Shop Last Chance gala party, with invited guests and a picnic on the village green to celebrate the improvements to the store. Fate has provided us with a perfect summer's day, and the stage is set for yet more fun.

And then, it is time to face the music. I have been pretending for too long that there is no tomorrow, yet tomorrow is catching up with me. The decision must be made: sell the house, or sell the paintings? I must choose between the devil and the deep blue sea. But first, a meeting that may help me make up my mind.

The journalist called a week ago. A 'source' had provided her with my ex-directory number. She was preparing a feature for a broadsheet newspaper on how Leon's death had proved to the Young British Artists that they were far from immortal, and had 'altered the trajectory of the work that will be produced over the next three decades'.

Maybe I should have said no, but when was the last time anyone wanted to talk about Leon? And preparing for her visit has distracted me from the bills and the anonymous phone calls.

The house is now immaculate. We used to have a cleaning woman but she was one of the first casualties of my reduced circumstances. Since then, I have let things slip, for what did it matter when my only visitors were Sandie and Emily? But a journalist is different. A journalist will scrutinise and form judgements about Leon, based on circumstantial evidence. No dust or smears will sully his memory.

So now the house is back to what it was always intended to be: a perfectly lit theatre for my husband's creativity. The rest is simply distraction. As I dusted around the many valuable things I bought to make our house a home – the Corbusier chairs, the custom-enamelled Aga in Leon's favourite shade of Prussian blue, the Lalique crystal vases – I had an urge to throw them in a skip, donate them to charity. On my knees, scrubbing and polishing our three bathrooms, I laughed at the days . . . no, the weeks I wasted sourcing the right Italian marble for the floors. The marble, the bricks and mortar – none of it matters. The art is what counts.

Of course, I will not unlock his studio for her. It still feels too soon.

I see the journalist on the security camera first. A new blue hatchback draws up on the lane outside the gate and the kind of hanger-on I saw a thousand times at exhibitions emerges from the driver's side. She turns three hundred and sixty degrees, orienting herself, then runs her fingers through her sharp butter-blond bob, smoothes her black shift dress with her fingers. There is nothing unique about her, but she has groomed and gym-trained herself into something resembling grace. Art voyeurs – that is what Leon always called them: the people who could not do, but liked to watch.

Before she has a chance to use the intercom, I activate the electronic gates and she jumps. Good. She's a little too slick, too confident. I must try to unsettle her, to regain control.

Three further cameras track her progress: she barely looks at the house, which is unusual. Perhaps she has done her research, seen the piece in *Wallpaper*. I allow her to ring the bell and take a very deep breath before coming to the door.

'You must be Della. Welcome to Rose Cottage.'

'Thank you for allowing me to visit you, Mrs Leon,' she says, her voice languid and slightly accented with a trendy London drawl. 'So these are the famous roses?' She reaches out to touch the wall painting with immaculately manicured fingers. Rouge Noir. Naturally.

'Please do not touch. These were hand-painted by my husband and as such, the wall is a work of art.'

She withdraws her hand. 'A shame to keep it hidden from the rest of the world, isn't it?' Then she laughs.

I stare at her until she falls silent. 'I expect you are thirsty. Come.'

Della follows me into the house, through the hall, into the salon. But a strange thing happens. Instead of the Pavlovian response I have seen one hundred times from visitors – they always look out through the sheet of glass to the garden, look up at the triple-height ceiling, then, finally, notice the painting – her eyes hone in on *Muse 7* without hesitation.

Though, after all, it is what she came looking for.

'It's . . .' she's lost for words.

'Overwhelming? Yes, it is rather, isn't it?' I say, feeling a little more sympathetic. 'Let me get you a drink, then we will talk.'

It takes me several minutes to make the espresso, but when I return, she is in the same position, staring at the painting. Finally, she turns to me. 'More people should see it, you know. Isn't that what he would have wanted?'

I consider this. 'I find it difficult to know what

he would have wanted. I do not believe my husband ever considered the possibility that he might die. He had an incredible capacity to ignore the inevitable.'

'And yet wasn't he right? Doesn't an artist achieve immortality through his work?'

I sense she is not expecting an answer. 'Do take a seat.' She does as she is told. 'I must say, your call came out of the blue. People seem to have lost interest in Leon. They have short memories.'

'That's not true of everyone,' she says, taking an espresso cup from the tray. 'I'd say it's time for a revival. It's the two-year anniversary of his death in August, isn't it? Because . . .'

Her voice fades as that last image I have of him, flat on his back in his studio with a gaping mouth, overwhelms me. The room spins.

'. . . and of course the ideal way to stimulate new interest in Leon is to run a piece about his final work, don't you think? Especially as so few people have had the privilege of seeing it.'

She stands up again and walks back towards the painting, her voice buzzing in my head like a wasp's, but the words are blurred, hypnotic. It is very hot in here this morning, the sun on the glass turning the room into a stifling greenhouse. She points at details on the canvas: the soft sharpness of my vertebrae, the thorns on the rose tattoo. *See, I want to tell her, I was beautiful. Inspiring. It's not all about youth and breasts and blond hair . . .* I realise she's stopped talking.

288

'Well. What do you say, Mrs Leon?'

'I'm sorry, I . . .' I hold my hands up in apology.

'I was asking whether you will allow me to approach a handful of publications, to pitch the article. Of course, I'd give you full copy approval. But he must not be forgotten. As his wife, surely, it is your duty to ensure that—'

The trance is broken. This cocky young woman is in *my* house telling me about *my* duty to *my* late husband, when all she wants is the fee and the kudos for the exclusive.

'I will think about it. Now, I have an appointment, so perhaps you'd like to go now?'

'But I've only just arrived. I've come a long way.'

'Well, there is no more to say at present. No point in doing any interview until I have made my mind up that it is the right thing to do. I am sure you understand.'

She seems to be weighing up whether to attempt to change my mind. 'All right, but please do consider it. I honestly believe he would not have wanted to sink into obscurity.'

I manage to stop myself asking how the hell she thinks she would know what he wanted. She thrusts a business card into my hand as she leaves.

When she reaches the other side of the gates, she slumps back against the car, unaware she is being watched. And I feel the same, floppy as a rag-doll, at this most minuscule invasion of privacy.

I suppose it is something I must get used to.

Whether I sell the paintings or the house, I can hide no longer.

I am in no mood for a party, but nonetheless, I climb into my latest car – an electric Japanese prototype with planet-saving features but zero style – and drive towards Heartsease Common. I cannot let my friends down.

Friends. I used to think a married woman – particularly one with an artist for a husband – did not need friends. Too many conflicts of interest, the inevitable tug of war between obligations to *him* and obligations to *them*. Women always expect more than one can give from friendship.

But if a wife does not need friends, a widow does. I remember in that bar Emily turned around my own words: marriage does not equip one for widowhood.

Leon, she was right. Protecting your memory is not enough. Life with only obligations to a memory is no life at all. I must formulate alternative plans that involve more than existing.

The road bends round to reveal the common. That miserable patch of grass looks less miserable now that it is packed with people. It is only midday, so these must all be volunteers. *Please* let there be more visitors than volunteers.

I park up and look for Sandie and Emily. But it is little Freddie I spot first, toddling along at breakneck speed. Sheer momentum keeps him going, though I think he knows he *will* fall as soon as he loses his nerve, so he runs and he runs. It takes courage to make your way in the world, when so much of it is a mystery.

'Freddie!'

I crouch down and open up my arms. When I first knew him, I would never have done this. I would have been scared he would not come to me. He beams, and races in my direction, forgetting how to brake and colliding with me so we nearly topple over. He squirms delightedly when I envelop him in a hug.

'Hello, Grazia!' Emily joins us. 'You look fab.'

'You are looking good yourself.' I am not lying: something is changing in Emily. It is nothing I can put my finger on – no sudden weight loss or miracle cream – but she glows, just a little.

'Do I?' She smiles as broadly as her son. 'That's a first. Shame we can't be in any of the photos.'

'You have made it clear to the photographers?'

She nods. We must not be photographed, in case the pictures are seen by Charlie. None of us can afford to lose income.

Except, of course, it will soon be irrelevant for me. Whatever I decide to sell, secret shopping is unlikely to play a part in my life in future.

'. . . and the guy from *Corrie* is definitely making it later, but Joanna Lumley's sent her apologies and—' Emily puts her hand on my arm. 'Are you OK, Grazia? You're really pale.'

'What? Oh. A little hungry, perhaps. I have not eaten today.'

'Bloody hell. I can't imagine going a day without eating. Still, we have the answer. There is nothing a slice of Women's Institute finest ginger cake won't put right. Follow me to the catering tent!'

In Emily's world, cake appears to be the answer to all problems.

SUMMER IN THE COUNTRY

The city's beginning to swelter; we're all craving the country life. Dust off the bunting, pop up the picnic tables and let's have fun al fresco . . . fetes, fairy cakes and the Floral Dance will send Cath Kidston wannabes into a frenzy of spending.

CHAPTER 24

EMILY

I'd got used to life being a non-stop grind, and then suddenly it's an absolute whirl.

Dozens of letters written, hundreds of emails sent, thousands of phone calls made and answered, and what feels like a million crazy ideas conceived and mostly dismissed. All for the sake of a cramped shop in the middle of nowhere.

But we've put the Heartsease Common branch of Bells & Whistles on the map. And not just the shop: the fight seems to be bringing this funny little village together. Petitions have been circulated; neighbours who've never spoken to one another have come together to offer help, to keep campaign costs down. With half an hour to go before the Last Chance gala party kicks off, there are twice as many people as I expected. A bouncy castle is inflating, the pointy purple turrets rising into the air like the tentacles of a sea anemone. More traditional sideshows are scattered around: Speak Your Weight scales, a coconut shy, a brightly coloured helter-skelter for the kids. Trestle tables frame all four sides of the common, and 4x4s are pulling up to unload antique bed linen and posh candles. Even better, food stalls are setting up: there's a whole pig roasting on a spit, a Mexican taco tent, *and* an organic ice cream stall (I can vouch for the Berry Bliss). The smell is fabulous. We have Sussex wine and – at my insistence – Somerset cider to drink. Each stallholder has drive and ambition, just like Will: the event is a celebration of beautiful things and passionate service.

Freddie and I wear matching fluorescent yellow bibs to mark us out as official organisers – it makes a change from being undercover. The men from the rugby club in the next-door village are building a stage from orange crates, and an old hippie in Dylan-the-rabbit dungarees is testing the PA system.

'ONE-two. One-TWO. Heartsease, can you hear me?'

A few of the rugby boys shout back something unintelligible and probably highly offensive. The PA man laughs back, glad his speakers are working. I feel at home: if I closed my eyes I'd be right back at one of the raucous carnival-club fundraisers Mum and Dad used to organise when I was little. Except the ice cream back then was all E-numbers, and the stalls sold second-hand baby clothes and *Beano* annuals with broken spines.

'Looking good, isn't it?' Sandie's next to me, the brains of the operation. Dunno what that makes me. The bleeding heart, maybe?

'It's bloody brilliant. I didn't sleep a wink last

296

night; I was so convinced something would go wrong. Floods, or plagues of locusts, or little green men turning up to ruin it.'

'No way. We've thought of everything – even little green men couldn't undo our work!'

She's right. We have a contingency plan for rain, hail and electrical storms. We have back-ups for power failures, and every cable is taped to the ground to avoid tripping. A St John's Ambulance van is on hand for cuts and bruises, there's a Missing Child Masterplan downloaded from the Internet, and a dog refreshment bar so that our four-legged friends don't overheat. We have dotted the i's, crossed the t's, predicted every eventuality—

'Hey, how are my two favourite angels getting on?'

Well, every eventuality but one. I appear to have fallen in love with Will.

I realised I was in love with Will two hours and – I check my watch – twelve minutes ago. It was *that* sort of bolt from the blue. Just before eleven o'clock this morning, we were on our hands and knees, scrubbing the paintwork outside the made-over shop. He was singing 'The Grand Old Duke of York' to keep up our momentum. He has a strong voice, mellow and sexy even when singing some daft nursery rhyme, and something made me look up from my wire brush and soapy water.

It was like seeing him for the first time. Concentration crumpled his brow as his lips mouthed the words and his maybe-green-maybe-blue eyes focused on the grimy window ledge. I drank in everything: freckles like a scattering of sand from a day at the beach; curls of dark hair at the nape of his long neck; pale grey shadows under his eyes, from too much worry and too little sleep.

And I knew that what I'd been dismissing as a silly crush was something much, much worse.

'You're very quiet.' He's changed into a ring-master's costume hired from a fancy dress shop in Windsor. The jacket is navy, lined with purple silk, with tails that reach the floor. It's definitely seen better days – it's both shiny *and* moth-eaten – yet he carries it off. There's definitely an air of the showman about Will and I wonder for the umpteenth time why he's landed here in dowdy Heartsease Common, where the only people to appreciate his charm are miserable old Jean and a few little old ladies.

And me, of course.

'Just last-minute nerves, I'm sure.'

'That's not like you, Farrah Fawcett.' Will has given us all Charlie's Angels nicknames: it seemed very silly at first, but now I'm quite fond of being Farrah. Sandie is the brainy one, as played by Kate Jackson, and Grazia is streetwise Jaclyn Smith. 'Anyway, with my three angels on the case, there's no need to be nervous. And let's not forget Master Frederick, too.'

Freddie's toddling towards us, followed by

Grazia. Will reaches out to take my son's hand and the sight of those tiny, chubby fingers in that large palm is almost too much to bear. All I wanted was a family: Duncan and me and baby makes three. I believed that love could conquer all. The class hunk and the little mermaid would live happily ever after, because that's how it works in the stories. But now I think it wasn't true love at all: more a combination of puppy love and pride at landing the class charmer. Will isn't charming, well, not in the way Duncan was. Yet what I feel for this man with his corny jokes and his ring-master's costume feels like the adult sort of love. Twisty-turny. Complicated. No, make that *impossible*.

I've fast-forwarded my way through the relationship in the last two hours and . . . fourteen minutes now. And I've concluded that it can't possibly work. I run through it again in my head.

Could he fancy me? I've wracked my brains for signs and, astonishingly, it's just possible that he might. He's always sweet, always making silly little jokes. But if I concentrate hard, I can find evidence that he's singled me out for special attention, that the smiles are that bit broader when they're directed at me. OK, to counter that, he has a forcefield of self-deprecation surrounding him, but according to the collected wisdom of my Mills and Boons, this must be down to some terrible tragic secret. Of course, the right woman will breach his defences.

So, he might fancy me. I certainly fancy him. But getting from there to doing something about it involves baring my soul and quite possibly my body too. I try to put Duncan's teasing out of my mind but it's impossible. *Oh, Chubster, you're going to have to do something about that flab, aren't you? Anyone would think you're still expecting.* Yes, it would take a lot of alcohol to make me confident enough to bare anything to a stranger, but isn't that the way it's always been? Most of my friends were drunk as skunks the first time they got off with their men . . . and I'm going to have to get off with someone again one day, surely?

But there's the biggest obstacle of all. *Am* I really going to do that again? It seems to me that there's only room in my life for one member of the opposite sex and he's two feet tall, with a love for me that's only matched by his love of penguins and carrot sticks. He's had enough disruption to last him a lifetime, without some ever-changing line-up of Mummy's Special Friends darting in and out of the master bedroom like characters in a sitcom.

Maybe I am using Freddie as a shield against all the messy uncertainties of love. But there's more to it than that. I am not fighting to stay in London just to fall into the arms of another man who can tell me what to do, how to behave, who to be. And I need to use all my energy to fight the pressure to return to Somerset. One thing's for certain: if Duncan's threatening to get nasty over my plan to stay in the flat as a single mum, he won't pull any punches if there's a new man in my bed, and in Freddie's life.

I know what he's like.

'Emily?' Sandie's touching me on the arm. 'You're not flaking out on us, are you?'

'No, no, I'm absolutely fine. Raring to go, in fact.'

Will holds out his cloaked elbow, like a suitor offering a debutante the first dance. 'Come on then, Farrah Fawcett. Shall we get this show on the road?'

I allow him to take my arm and try to ignore the tingle where his skin meets mine. *Enjoy it just for this afternoon, Emily.* Where's the harm? After today, there's no need to see Will ever again, no need to tempt myself with what could have been, what might still be. I can return to the secret shopping, to making my own way. Me and the Fredster against the world. Two's company; three is definitely a crowd.

The afternoon passes in a crazy, joyful blur, a day of sun-soaked images to preserve for ever in my mind's photo album . . .

There's Freddie draped in an entire stall's worth of multi-coloured costume jewellery by two Trustafarian girls (Duncan would have hit the roof: 'I will not have a son of mine seen in public wearing dangly earrings. He might turn *gay*!').

There's Will being filmed for regional TV news

with the actor who plays *Coronation Street's* current villain, and a bevy of glamorous grannies – Jean has tracked down all the pensioners Will has helped over the last eighteen months and they've all turned up, pledging their willingness to lie down in the road in front of Bells & Whistles HQ, naked if necessary. We had to be quite firm with one Woodstock veteran who wanted to strip off there and then.

There's Sandie, wandering from stall to stall, chatting to the traders about their products and sneakily rearranging displays whenever their backs are turned.

There's Will on that same orange-crate stage, with a queue of villagers waiting for Heartsease's own superhero, the incredible 'Will-Power' who can work magic on their battered kitchen appliances or blunt garden shears.

There's Grazia facing an entire press-gang of middle-aged women trying to talk her into joining the mid-Berkshire branch of the WI . . .

There's the crowd with necks craned as they peer up at the blue sky, as acrobatic pilots from the air show a few miles down the road take a detour to lend their aerial support . . .

Oh, and there's me and Will on the Test your Love Rating stall (*definitely* not my idea under the bloody circumstances), watching as this totally unscientific tin-and-plastic contraption shows our compatibility is: RED HOT – OFF THE SEX-ON-LEGS SCALE!

Hmm. It'll be hard to forget the sheer ruddy embarrassment of that moment, not to mention the definite frisson. I searched Will's face, trying to interpret his expression, usually so transparent. He laughed, and blushed, and then put one (friendly? More than friendly?) arm around my waist. Then he kissed me on the cheek, before pulling away again, as though his joke had gone too far.

It's the closest we've ever been.

And now I keep remembering the smell of him: minty breath, squeaky-clean soapy skin, and the shape of those lips like an invisible tattoo on my skin. The only cure for this madness is to go cold turkey.

'It has gone well, has it not?'

Grazia appears at my side, offering me a left-over strawberry smoothie.

'Yep. I'd say it went bloody well. People are going to be talking about it for ages, and that's what we wanted, isn't it?'

She nods. Her red lipstick is a bit smudged, and her suit creased. It makes her look a lot more human.

'It is what we wanted, Emily . . .' She hesitates. 'But promise me you will not be too disappointed if this fails. Because, you know, I am not so sure they will change their mind. The management.'

Her gentleness surprises me, but also irritates. Sandie's the youngest, yet I know they both see me as the *baby* of the group, to be mollycoddled and protected. Not so different from the way I'm treated back home.

'It's OK, Grazia. I know. But it's been fun, hasn't it?'

'Yes. It has been fun. Although nothing lasts for ever.'

'No.' There's such finality about the way she says it. She can't know about my feelings for Will, can she? Perhaps I've been making a fool of myself, mooning over him, without realising. 'What do you mean, Grazia?'

'My circumstances may be changing soon. The secret shopping may not be my main concern. It may be time for me to bow out.'

'Oh!' I try to think of something to say to conceal my shock. 'Right. Why?'

'Many reasons,' she says, with the deliberate vagueness she does so well.

But today she's not getting away with it. Her news makes me feel rudderless. Without Charlie's Shopping Angels, London seems a cold place. 'I think you owe me more of an explanation than that.'

She looks surprised. 'Perhaps. Some things are difficult to explain. But it is hard being on your own, is it not?'

'Bloody hard. I mean, there are good bits too. I wouldn't want to be back with Duncan, but being completely without support – that's been tough.'

'A child, I think, makes things both easier and more difficult.'

'Yes. It's definitely harder to feel lonely when

he's around. Though, well . . . I still do feel isolated, sometimes. When the bills come in and the boiler packs up, it'd be nice to have someone to help. Not that my husband was ever any good at fixing boilers.'

She smiles. 'Neither was mine.'

I begin to giggle, and she joins in, and for a moment, the differences between us seem so much less important than the similarities. The last few WI women look up from what remains of the cake stall.

We only stop laughing when we're gasping for breath. 'It does seem a waste, though, Grazia. All that time training us up, getting good with the camera. Learning how to wind up shop assistants.'

'Oh, you do not need to worry on that account. You will still be working. Charlie will replace me – *plenty more where you came from*; I am sure that is what he would say. Which is how he can get away with paying low wages.'

'Well, you're not in it for the money, anyway, are you?'

Grazia frowns. 'What makes you say that?'

'Um, well . . . the designer house. The clothes. All those swanky cars.'

'The cars are assignments. Secret shopping missions. Charlie knows I cannot afford to run a car, so he sends all the test drives my way.'

'Oh. Right. But your husband was a big name, wasn't he? I mean, I am clueless about art but Sandie said—'

'My husband's death was not anticipated. There was no point in mentioning it before, but my financial situation is not sustainable. Secret shopping is no longer sufficient. More drastic measures are called for.' She is matter of fact, but I sense how much this admission must be costing her in dignity.

'Grazia, I had no idea.'

'Exactly as I intended. I have no desire for the world and his wife to know my business. But it is not so bad. I have options. I can sell the house. Or Leon's work. As yet, I have not decided which.'

'Oh, you poor thing. What a terrible choice. I don't know what I'd do in that situation. Except cry a lot, probably.'

'I will manage.' Grazia moves away, only by a few millimetres, but enough that I realise the brief intimacy between us is over. 'And so will you,' she says firmly.

But will I? Today's revelations – realising my feelings for Will, and now hearing Grazia's plans – are making me question whether I have been fooling myself, thinking I can cope alone. 'It seems such a shame. I like working together. Me, you, Sandie. The secret shoppers taking on the big, bad universe.'

Grazia smiles at me. 'Yes. We are a good team. But, you know, Emily, you do not need other people to be strong. Real strength comes from inside.' And she touches her breastbone through her black shirt.

I nod. 'Yes, Yes, I know.' Yet a little voice in my head is pleading. *Don't leave, Grazia.*

'It will not be immediate, Emily. I have arrangements to make. And decisions.'

I look at her haughty face and for once I see doubt there. 'You have to do what you have to do, Grazia.' There's a long pause and I feel awkward, like I'm intruding. 'Actually, Freddie and I should get going.'

'I thought you were staying until the bitter end.'

'Completely forgot that I had something to do back at the flat. You know what a scatterbrain I am!' And I walk away before she can tell that I'm fibbing. I have had enough drama for one day.

I find Freddie being fussed over by one of the WI women, and when I go to lift him up he puts up only token resistance, mumbling sleepily in that funny secret language of his. I plonk him in his pushchair and look around for Will.

Time to say goodbye . . .

He's by the Speak Your Weight machine, standing close to Sandie. I try not to analyse their body language, the intensity of the conversation, the expressions in their eyes, but I can't help myself. I'm jealous of their easy friendship. Jealous of Sandie for a few laid back moments with Will.

Definitely time to make myself scarce.

'We're off now,' I say, bounding towards them with the buggy. 'It's been a great day but Freddie's fit to drop!'

'Oh, that's a shame,' Will says and I try to read

the level of his regret. 'I have some wine upstairs in the flat, to say thank you to my shopping angels.'

The urge to stay on is powerful, but I must resist. God only knows what kind of a tit I'd make of myself after a glass of wine. 'Ah well. All the more for the two of you to enjoy together!' I find myself winking. What the *hell* am I doing?

Sandie frowns. 'Hardly just the two of us. I bet Grazia will want some. And I suspect Jean won't say no either.'

'Exactly!' I say, wishing the common would crack open right now and swallow me. 'A bottle won't go far. I'll raise a cup of tea to you when I get home.'

Will takes my hand. It's all warm and firm and . . .

'Thank you, Emily. For *everything*. I know we can't predict the outcome, but none of this would have happened without you.' His eyes pull me in and I have to work hard to drag myself out again.

Worse, I realise he's about to put his arms around me for a hug goodbye. If that happens, I don't know if I'd ever be able to let go. So I reach down and pull my son out of the buggy, using his sleepy body as a shield. 'It's the least we could do, isn't it, Fredster? Let's hope it's paid off, eh?'

'Yes,' Will says. 'Let's hope so.'

I want to ask what he really thinks the chances are, what he plans to do if it all goes wrong, whether he might come to London, I want to tell him that Lime Village is very affordable and yet within easy reach of the West End.

I bite my lip, and begin to walk away. But I can't quite bear to let him out of my sight until I'm off the common and he's no more than one little stick man among the final stragglers.

And I know that's going to be the hardest image of all to erase from my mind.

CHAPTER 25

SANDIE

The penguins don't need to dress up for the occasion, but I have. I'm wearing my usual sensible shoes and jeans, but I've splashed out on a black T-shirt with a rabbit embroidered on the front, which the guest of honour seems to appreciate. Oh, and I've squirted on Eau Dynamisante for energy. Think I'm going to need it . . .

I'm not invited to many parties – as Marsha never tired of pointing out – but she can keep her swanky cocktail receptions in the fleshpots of Mayfair. Because this afternoon I am attending an event so exclusive that there are only three names on the guest list. Me, Emily and Master Frederick Prince, one year old today.

We've timed our arrival at London Zoo to co-incide with feeding time at the Penguin Pool: judging from the crowd, we're not the only ones.

'Excuse me, excuse me,' Emily whispers, trying to force Freddie's buggy through the sea of legs. 'It's my little boy's birthday and he's got this passion for *Pingu* videos.'

People move reluctantly, mumbling to themselves.

I guess that a kid with a birthday is no novelty at the zoo. We reach the front at last, just as a keeper begins to throw glinting fish towards a mass of stumpy Rockhoppers. Their fabulous yellow feathers quiver like grand hats in the breeze at Ascot.

'There, now, Freddie. Lots and lots of Pingus!'

Freddie stares uncertainly at the beady-eyed penguins, then back at his mother. And then he begins to howl at the top of his voice, a sound of sheer terror that ensures our journey *out* of the crowd is faster and easier than on the way in.

'That went well, then,' Emily says, once we've got settled again in the Oasis cafe over a pick-me-up pear-and-cranberry shake for Freddie and two strong coffees for us grown-ups. She tucks the receipt into her purse, and scribbles the name of the cashier on the back, to send to Charlie: I think Grazia pulled strings to get us the zoo assignment, because she knew Emily would struggle to afford much of a celebration otherwise.

I hide the carrier bag holding Freddie's birthday present under the table. 'I guess now's not the time to bring out the giant cuddly penguin then?'

'Perhaps not. Sorry, Sandie. He's so fractious today. That's the thing about kids. You've just got the hang of one tricky stage, thinking you're getting the motherhood thing sussed, when, bingo! They're onto the next one.'

'I guess that only works to your advantage if you have more than one.'

She raises her eyebrows. 'Well, that's hardly likely, now, is it? Unless I corner the market in immaculate conceptions.'

'Sorry.'

'Ah, bollocks, I'm kidding. I'm really chuffed you agreed to come today. He won't remember it, but I will, and it would have been no fun on my own. Besides . . .' she hesitates. 'Well, there's something you need to know.'

'Oh yes?' I wonder what the latest confession will be. Ever since I gave her the sketchiest details of my horrible experience at Toby's apartment, Emily seems to have developed a greater determination to tell me all her secrets. I'm sure she sees our tête-à-têtes as the conversational equivalent of a tennis match, lobbing nuggets of gossip across the net. The trouble is, I don't have many juicy revelations to send back in return.

Maybe I just don't have the emotional depths of other people. OK, I was upset by Toby's behaviour. Well, fuming, really. But I need to move on, give the secret shopping my all. Now I've got the hang of the filming, I'm good at it. Sometimes I wonder whether we could do a better job without Charlie. Maybe we could even do what we did for Bells & Whistles, too: save shops rather than condemn them.

Cloud-cuckoo land, of course. With my tarnished reputation, no store would employ me.

'I hope you won't be too shocked.'

'Don't worry. I'm a big girl now, Emily.'

'Grazia's giving up the secret shopping.' She pauses. 'And I'm wondering whether I should do the same.'

Whatever I was expecting – a squirm-inducing description of some post-natal condition, maybe, or a blushing confession to the monster crush on Will that she thinks she's kept under wraps – it wasn't this. 'Oh. When did she tell you?'

She wipes Freddie's face with a tissue. 'At the weekend. She said something about being short of money. I mean, you'd think that living in that ruddy great house, she'd be loaded. But apparently she's as broke as we are.'

'I'd never have guessed that.'

'Me neither. Anyway, she's got to do something more drastic than the shopping to keep going. She says there'll be someone else taking over, but I'm not sure I could face working for someone else, having to prove myself all over again. I know Grazia can be blunt, but underneath the black widow clothes and red lipstick, she's a big softie, don't you think?'

'Yep. She is. But what would you do, Em, if you gave up?'

Just as she finishes cleaning him up, Freddie blows a raspberry, splattering both of them with more cranberry-pink liquid. 'I suppose you're allowed to be messy on your birthday, aren't you, mate?' She giggles. 'I don't have a bloody clue what I'd do, Sandie, but the thought of finding another job makes me want to crawl into bed and never get up again. The last year has been such a rollercoaster – I'm amazed I'm still here, sometimes – and I don't know what I'm trying to prove any more.'

'That you can be independent? Stand on your own two feet.'

'But what's more important – independence or sanity?'

'I didn't realise it was a case of either/or.'

'In an ideal world it wouldn't be. But I don't live in an ideal world and I'm beginning to wonder whether Duncan's right and I just don't have what it takes to survive in the city.'

She goes off to find more tissues, leaving me trying to work out why the prospect of secret shopping without Emily and Grazia makes me feel so queasy. It's not as though Charlie would sack me, after all the positive comments he's been passing on, tucked in with my pay slip. He might give me Grazia's job.

But we're the *angels*. We go together, complement each other: my passion for everything about retail, Grazia's take-no-prisoners attitude, Emily's wide-eyed enthusiasm and fancy camerawork. Even Freddie's disarming smile, and his constant wrestling to free himself of the constraints of his buggy.

I've gone and let myself get involved, allowed myself to see them as friends. Gramma used to insist we kept ourselves to ourselves, and now I understand why. Alliances make you weak.

Emily reappears with a wad of serviettes.

'So you want to go back to Somerset, then?'

She sighs. 'I. Don't. Know.'

'Look, tell me to mind my own business, but you've always said that if you go back now, you'll never get away again.'

'Hmm,' she says. 'I did say that, didn't I? Meant it, too. But it's like a boxing match. I'm in one corner of the ring, and in the other there's Duncan, and my parents, and the building society, all wanting me home, and it's a bit of an unequal fight. I'm on the ropes, Sandie.'

'Do you really think you should be taking a blind bit of notice of Duncan?'

'Easier said than done *not* to. And although he's been a . . .' she leans over to me to whisper, 'total bastard, I do sort of see his point. He can't pay rent on the swanky apartment in Geneva *and* on a house he's never going to live in again. So if I move back to Somerset, then there'll be more money for Freddie. Because you're getting more expensive by the day, aren't you, big boy?'

'It seems a shame to give up on your dream.'

She ruffles his hair and he raises his fist to unruffle it. 'The thing is, there's no way my life in London is ever going to resemble the one I dreamed about. Not unless you know any sugar daddies looking for dippy, overweight mothers-of-one.'

'And what happens to the London flats if you go home?'

'Duncan sells them, I suppose.'

'You have seen a solicitor about the divorce, like we said?'

She wrinkles her nose. 'Um, well, not yet. There's no rush. Duncan's got no more desire to go to court than I have and so if we live apart for however long it is, we'll be able to do the easy-peasy sort of divorce – you know, what's it called, the separation one, rather than the nasty kind. Better for Freddie, after all.'

'But not necessarily better for you. Duncan could take advantage. What's to stop him selling the house and spiriting away some of the profit so that he doesn't have to pay you your share when you do divorce?'

'Ah! Well, I had thought of that, but he doesn't think there will be much of a profit and I agree. The area was meant to be going up in the world, but I don't think it's improved since he bought it.'

'Since *he* bought it?'

'Well, we both bought it, didn't we? It's just that, as I wasn't earning, there was no point putting my name on the mortgage. Anyway, it doesn't matter, because the house is in a worse state than when we moved in, what with Freddie treating it as a demolition derby theme park, and a base-ment full of lodgers. We might not sell it at all.'

I shake my head in despair. Still, it's her life: what gives me the right to tell her what she should do? 'Just don't sign anything without legal advice, eh? Will you promise me that much?'

She nods, distracted now by the zoo guidebook.

'Yes, yes. Don't worry about us, Sandie, we'll be fine. Now, who's for Meet the Monkeys? Maybe that'll go down better with the birthday boy.'

On the Tube back to Lime Village, I become increasingly convinced that Emily's not telling me the full story. I see the way she is with Freddie, hear the excitement in her voice as she keeps up a running commentary about all the stops: Oxford Circus – 'not a *real* circus, but ten times more exciting'. This girl hasn't fallen out of love with London. There's definitely more to this than she's admitting: something else has happened, I'm sure of it, but for once, she's not telling.

We arrive back at her house and in the bright afternoon sunshine it does look dowdy and run-down. But I watch my property programmes – it's not as if I have a social life to keep me busy in the evenings – and I know that the presence of this many skips and scaffold poles signals an area on the up. From what I know of Duncan, I'll bet he knows it too, even if he isn't choosing to share that information with his estranged wife.

Newspaper lines the windows on the lower maisonette, fixed on with yellowing tape.

'What are your Latvian lodgers so keen to keep hidden, then?'

'I wondered that,' she says, pushing her buggy up the steps. 'Thought they might be dismembering bodies. But they're such lovely lads, I bet it's just because they can't afford curtains.'

'Really?'

We enter the hallway and I'm sure I can smell paint. 'I can't believe you've had time for decorating as well as everything else.'

'I haven't,' says Emily, sniffing. 'I suppose there is a whiff of gloss, now you mention it.'

The smell grows stronger. The two of us lift the buggy up the staircase to the top flat and Emily opens the door. 'Oooh, a card! For you, Freddie!' Then she looks at me. 'That's a bit odd. The postman can't get in here. Don't say Duncan's been snooping around again. He let himself in last time he came, bloody cheek.'

Emily tears open the envelope. 'It's from the Latvians! Bless them.' She holds up the card, which is on cheap paper, featuring an old-fashioned watercolour of a steam train. 'We should go down and thank them, before I collapse in a big heap. I'm completely zonked.'

She lifts Freddie into her arms, then we trapse back down the stairs. She knocks on the door, which takes ages to open, and when it does, the paint fumes are so powerful they make me sneeze four times in succession. Freddie giggles.

A hunky man with a moustache beams at each of us in turn. 'Hello! Happy birthday,' he says, in heavily accented English. He leans forward to kiss Freddie on the cheeks, an action which, to my surprise, doesn't provoke a screaming fit, but a grin. 'Come. We have present!'

He ushers us inside.

'Fuck a duck!' Emily says, with feeling.

Far from being the laddish squat I'd imagined, the flat is immaculate. There's hardly any furniture, except three camping chairs and an old table, so I instantly notice the features of the room: high ceilings accessorised by an ornate plaster rose, whitewashed floorboards, a grand moulded fireplace with a chrome firebasket beneath. Beyond an arch, there's an all-white kitchen with glossy units and a brand new fridge freezer, still in its wrapping. Sunlight shining through the impromptu newspaper 'blinds' gives the space a soft-focus glow, and with all the white surfaces, I almost expect technicians with gleaming hair and lab coats to appear. Instead, two more Latvians come into the room and fuss around Freddie, as though he's the baby Jesus rather than a fractious, though undoubtedly cute, one-year-old.

But Emily's not smiling. 'Janis, what have you done?'

The hunky Latvian nods. 'You like?'

'Well, yes, it's great, but *why*? And *when*?'

Janis looks nervous and his moustache begins to twitch. 'Your father-in-law, he explain? We pay no rent, we make flat nice. But we try to work when you not here, or work very, very quiet, for you and baby sleep, like father-in-law tell me.'

'They did all this without you realising, Emily?'

She pulls a face. 'Well, they made a bit of a racket sometimes, but I just switched the volume up on the telly. Thought maybe they were bringing their work home with them.'

Emily turns to Janis. 'I knew nothing about this, Janis. Nothing.'

He backs away and begins a rapid-fire conversation with his flatmates involving lots of nodding and gesticulating.

Right at the back of the room are sleeping bags I hadn't noticed before, neatly rolled away. The kitchen work surface has an old kettle and a stack of square packets that are all too familiar from my own kitchen: instant noodles, the cheapest way to fill your stomach. These guys are being exploited, no doubt about it. But why?

'Duncan really didn't mention this at all? Or his dad?'

'No.' Emily paces, her feet tap-tapping across a perfectly fitted oak floor. 'What is he playing at? You don't suppose he wants to move back in, be closer to Freddie?'

From what little I know about Duncan, parental responsibility isn't high on his list of priorities. 'Maybe. Although why would that need to be a secret?'

'As a nice surprise when it's finished?' But she doesn't sound convinced.

'What if . . . what if he wanted to sell the place under your nose, Emily? Put pressure on you to go home to Somerset, then once you'd moved out, get them to refurbish upstairs as well, and then sell it for a huge profit without telling you.'

'He wouldn't!' She shakes her head, but then her face changes: her cheeks colour, and her lips disappear. I think the penny might finally have dropped. 'What am I saying? Of course he would. Oh God, Sandie. He's an even bigger bastard than I thought. Right. I'm going to ring him right this minute and give him a piece of my . . . oh, is that for Freddie?'

The oldest of the three men approaches us, holding a parcel wrapped in white tissue paper. Emily opens it dumbly, her hands busy but her eyes barely registering what's inside.

The last piece of tissue paper falls to the floor and the gift is revealed: a pair of wooden penguins, every detail precisely carved. 'Oh,' she says, finally looking properly. 'Oh, they're lovely, Kaspar.' She turns to me. 'They carved Freddie an ark, so these will go with it. Thank you!'

The hunky one brings over a tray, with five glasses the size of thimbles. The third guy pours yellow liquid out of a bottle, and hands one thimble to Emily and one to me. The men clink glasses with us, careful not to spill any, and down the drink in one. We follow suit, and the aniseed flavour burns my throat, but it's not unpleasant.

I look at Emily: her eyes are wide and rather wild, though she's maintaining a forced smile for the Latvians. Freddie's oblivious to the whole thing, his chin dropping onto his chest, and rhythmic snores beginning to escape from his nose.

'Thank you. I'm afraid we have to go back upstairs now; it's all a bit much for Freddie,' she says brightly, before adding, under her breath, 'not to mention for his poor bloody mother.'

The men bestow further kisses on the sleeping child, on Emily and then on me. Their door closes, and though the hallway is gloomy, Emily's eyes blaze like a tiger's.

'That *bastard*,' she says, her voice low but the vitriol sky-high. 'That bastard husband of mine thought he could get one over on me, didn't he?'

'We don't know for sure that he wasn't going to tell you . . .'

'Of course he wasn't going to tell me. Well, two can play at that bloody game. Time to keep some secrets of my own, don't you think?'

'Like what?'

'Like the fact that little old Emily has definitely ruled out sloping back to Somerset with her tail between her legs. Like the fact that it's about bollocking time she stopped relying on other people to make her decisions, and started fighting her own battles. And that's just for starters.'

'Right,' I say, feeling a rather selfish pleasure as I realise I might not be losing Emily as a colleague quite yet. 'But how exactly are you going to fight?'

'I'm going to fight dirty!' she says, running back up the stairs to her flat. 'And I'm going to fight to win.'

FOURTH OF JULY

The Americans like to celebrate their independence from us – so let's join in, with stars, stripes and BBQ sauce. The iconography of the USA is timeless, adding a fresh, primary-coloured verve to your merchandise. Bigger? Better? Better make it Independence Day.

CHAPTER 26

EMILY

Grazia says possession is nine tenths of the law. Now, Duncan might be the maths prodigy, but even I can work out that if I play this right, my bloody husband doesn't stand a chance.

I can't explain how liberating it is to shrug off the cloak of niceness I've worn for so long, like some goody-two-shoes from *Harry Potter*. The pleasure of scheming against my rat-bag of a spouse is greater than I'd have guessed, more energising than a thousand vitamin pills. All my uncertainty about London and what exactly I'm doing here has evaporated: the point of being here now is to win.

'I am pleased you have followed my advice on the mushroom, Emily,' Grazia says, lifting the lid off one of the pots of trade paint lined up on the dust sheets. 'It will give a feeling of space, without being as bland as the dreadful magnolia you English are so keen on.'

I have a plan, and like all the best plans, mine is devastatingly simple. Step One begins today. With the help of Kaspar, Big Janis, Little Janis,

Sandie *and* Grazia I'm doing up my flat: not quite to the standards of the basement one (Duncan made sure no expense was spared there. Tosspot!), but enough of a makeover to make living here a lot more pleasant.

Step Two: I work out which of the flats Freddie and I like the best, because we're going to choose one as our home, post-divorce.

Step Three: wait till idiot conman husband next suggests that I return to Somerset. And then go in with ALL GUNS BLAZING.

It'll be the last time Duncan Prince takes me for a fool.

I peer into the paint can that Grazia's opened. 'Well, I wouldn't have picked it without you. It really is the colour of Campbell's mushroom soup. Then again I've always been rubbish at colour.' It's true: I had such terrible taste in clashing clothes when I was little that my sister convinced Mum I might be colour-blind. The school nurse was called, but my eyesight was fine. I just had zero taste. Oh, and nits, as it turned out.

Luckily, Grazia is the most tasteful person ever, so she's taken charge of the overall colour scheme, while Sandie's been supplier in chief, using all her professional knowledge (she did eight months in the Homes to Die For department at Garnett's) to source the best deals. Given that my budget would barely kit out a dolls' house, this is vital.

Sandie thought I should involve Will in my scheming, too, but I said I thought he'd have too much on his mind waiting for news on the shop. Well, I could hardly tell her the truth.

And the truth is that I can't get him out of my head. I haven't seen him in the fortnight since the gala party, but I can't look at a paint chart without trying to match up the shade of his maybe-blue, maybe-green eyes.

'Where shall I put this chandelier, Emily?' Sandie comes through the door, barely visible behind an enormous cardboard box. The chandelier, all cut glass and chrome, is bigger than I remember it from the shop. We spotted it at an assignment in a designer furniture warehouse in Hayes. It is the chandelier of my London dreams, chic and sleek and overblown, and I very nearly didn't have it at all. It seemed too extravagant, given my Lilliputian makeover budget. But Grazia overruled me: 'It is a design classic; it will put the room on the map.' And it *was* discounted by seventy per cent, due to some wonky crystals that you won't see once it's hanging from the ceiling.

'Put it in the bedroom, so it doesn't get splodged.'

She nods, and does as she's told.

I'm getting better at bossing people about, though alas it doesn't work with Freddie. He seems to have hit the Terrible Twos a whole year early – his father would be proud of him for learning to put himself first – and does exactly as he pleases at all times. What he pleases mainly consists of running on those newly discovered legs towards whatever is most interesting, most dangerous, or both.

So today, we'll be putting almost as much effort into keeping Freddie out of trouble as we will into facelifting the flat.

The boys downstairs, or my Latvian Superheroes as I now prefer to call them, are processing up and down the stairs with an array of tools and materials. Big Janis has ordered everything we need to do up *my* flat, on the builders' merchant account Duncan had organised for doing up downstairs. It's genius. Every free paintbrush, every bonus tube of filler represents another tiny victory over my evil ex.

The day of Freddie's birthday was the turning point: Big Janis was gutted when he realised the role he'd inadvertently played in my husband's deceit. OK, I'm not totally sure he understood the ins and outs, but they were all so eager to put things right. We bonded that afternoon. The photos came out: Kaspar's teenage grandchildren sulking on old-fashioned bicycles, and the two Janises with their families, huge group portraits showing at least four generations.

'Is it time to take the young man downstairs yet?' Grazia asks.

There's another minor miracle. When I first met Grazia, she went out of her way to avoid my son, as though he might bite (actually, it's not that unlikely – he's nipped me a couple of times this week, eager to try out his baby teeth). Now she seems to relish time spent with him, singing him Italian songs, and daring to tickle his feet.

Maybe this is all the Fredster's doing. His amazing powers have transformed my life. Sometimes I get so focused on the twenty-four/seven grunt-work involved in keeping him clean and fed, that I forget how incredible he is.

I pick him up and hold him tight, despite his determined wriggling, and feel his warmth and his energy.

'Who's Mummy's top boy? Who?'

And a little bit of me feels bad about stitching up his father, because Duncan gave me Freddie, didn't he?

I dismiss the thought. Duncan doesn't know the meaning of loyalty, so why should I? 'Right, let's get you out of the danger zone, mister, before you end up tiled and grouted.'

I don't know why people moan so much about having building work done. So far, this is the *best* fun. In the basement flat, Grazia and Freddie are covered in paint – face paint, which she bought because she guessed that he'd be frustrated at not getting his hands dirty. I think he's about three years too young to appreciate her efforts fully, but so far he's enjoying the attention. Grazia has turned them both into big cats: my baby is now a smudgy leopard, and she's a tiger, with an unlikely mane of dark, wiry hair. Yet somehow she still looks completely elegant, even though her face is a maze of orange and black stripes.

They're playing nursery rhymes at top volume to drown out the banging and crashing above thier heads. But I like the noise. Every smash and crunch is evidence of progress. As they dismantle the rooms where I've been depressed and dumpy and down-hearted, I feel my own mood lightening.

'How's it going up there?' Grazia asks me, watching Freddie as he builds towers from plastic cups and knocks them over again with sheer destructive delight.

'Hard to tell. The poor flat has all its nether regions exposed, all the wallpaper ripped off, the carpet ripped up and the kitchen cabinet doors in a sad little pile by the door. But it's brilliant.'

'Ah! Progress. I remember watching Rose Cottage being made, how it felt to create something wonderful. You feel it too. Breathing new life into space.'

'You think I'm doing the right thing, then?'

'I *know* you are doing the right thing, Emily. London is the place to be. It never disappoints. A child born in London has the greatest gift in the world.'

I think about the hoodies I see every day, riding on the pavements, shrieking obscenities: they don't seem to view life here as a gift. But I still understand what she means. 'What about you, Grazia? Any nearer to reaching your big decision?'

She sighs deeply: it sounds wrong coming from

a tiger. 'No closer. But closer to *having* to make it, you understand? Time running out, letters from the people I owe money to arrive every day. House or paintings, paintings or house? It keeps me awake at night.'

'It would.'

Freddie howls with fury at the refusal of the plastic cups to do what he wants them to do. I walk over to the Latvians' swanky new fridge and pull out the carrot batons I prepared earlier. He claps his hands in excitement. There. Most of the time I'm convinced I'd fail every motherhood test going, but I must be doing something right to have raised a child who gets excited about raw vegetables.

As he munches, I head back upstairs. Sandie is meant to be supervising the workers, but the bearded trio work so efficiently together that she's relegated to making the tea.

'Are we on schedule?'

'So far, so good,' she says. 'I just wish I could do something a bit more constructive. It's a tall order to get it all done in three weeks.'

'Hmm. They did say it'd be OK, though. I don't think they'd let me down.' It needs to be done while Duncan's on holiday with Heidi in the Maldives. According to Janis, Duncan's planning to return at the end of the month, and get estate agents here to value both flats in secret, knowing I'm bound to go home to Somerset for my mum's birthday.

'They're good lads, Emily. If anyone can do it, they can.' Her voice is sing-song and reassuring, but I don't need reassurance. I am invincible.

I can't resist a look at the bathroom. Oooh! It wasn't exactly a luxurious spot for lingering before – the black bathroom suite looked satanic *and* showed the dirt – but now it's a cave with bare brick walls and thick pipes projecting upwards from the uneven floor. They really have got their work cut out. But I know they'll sort it. They are superheroes, after all . . . and absolutely everything is going to turn out fine!

Duncan won't know what's hit him when I present my fait accompli – give me one of the flats, or sell them both and split the profits (giving me enough to buy a new place). I haven't decided which of the two I'd like – perhaps the downstairs one, with the garden for Freddie to play in as he gets older – but whatever happens, I am staying in London.

And once I have a place of my own, I'm going to furnish it exactly as I choose. Sod neutral colours and tasteful tiles: I want orange chairs and purple cushions, bright red bed linen, paintings in primary colours. No one can stop me. And so what if it reduces the value of the flat: I plan to stay in London for ever, as a bona fide girl-about-town.

Back in the living room, the boys are working around each other wordlessly, never colliding or swearing. It's ballet in boiler-suits.

Suddenly the boys stop what they're doing and look towards the door. A man in brown overalls stands in the doorway, and it takes me a second to realise . . .

'Will?'

He takes a step forward.

'Will?' I repeat. The temperature in the room seems to rise by ten degrees. 'What are you doing here?'

'I know I'm gate-crashing,' he says, his voice muted.

'No, no, not at all,' I say, feeling like a prize bitch. 'Come in. I'm just getting a bit of work done on the flat.'

'Yes. Sandie mentioned it. But when you didn't invite me, I thought you didn't want me here . . .'

'It's not that. I just thought you had enough on your plate, without me asking you to help rebuild my flat.'

'After all you chaps did? It's the least I could do.'

There's something subdued about his manner, though I can't quite see his face. 'Well, it's great to have you here. Quiet day at the shop, then?'

He stares at me for so long I think he hasn't heard me. But when I open my mouth to repeat the question, he nods. 'You could say that. That's why I came. We've lost, Emily. We've lost the campaign. Bells & Whistles, Heartsease Common closes as planned in three weeks' time.'

★   ★   ★

Big Janis pours us medicinal shots of Riga Black Balsam. 'Is very good for shock. Is made with herbs!'

Sandie takes a sip and grimaces. 'Is made with vodka, too, isn't it, Janis?'

He smiles back conspiratorially. 'That also is true.'

Will won't sit down. He's pacing the room, his face distorted by anger. The MD came down in person this morning to tell him – the first time anyone senior had bothered to visit the Heartsease branch in ten years – and gave him an enormous bollocking for involving the media.

'He stood there, playing with the keys to his bloody Porsche, and expected me and Jean to feel sorry for him,' Will says. 'He had this whiny voice and told me off like I was a schoolboy. "You wouldn't believe the trouble your antics have caused. I was on Grand Cayman when you organised your pathetic little protest, and I had to spend hours crisis managing. Do you know the cost of mobile calls to the UK on a sat phone? Bloody astronomical." I half expected him to present me with the bill.'

'So what did you say?' I ask, trying to focus on the horrible situation, rather than the way anger lights up his face.

'I said I thought he could probably afford it. Whereas the people of Heartsease couldn't afford to lose their lifeline, at which point he told me that he wasn't running a sodding charity, and I told him that it wasn't about being charitable, and asked if he'd looked at my new figures and the projections Sandie had done. The ones that proved we could make money if we had more autonomy, were allowed to order in products to suit local demands.'

'And had he?' Sandie asks.

'He said he didn't have time to read half-baked figures produced by idiots from the sticks who think they can do his job better than he could.'

Sandie gasps.

'Sorry.'

I shake my head. 'What a moron. Then what did you do?'

'I . . . well, I punched him.'

It's my turn to gasp. 'You? But you're such a—'

'Wimp?'

'No, that's not what I meant. You're gentle.'

'More fool me. No one got anywhere in life by being gentle. I've always taken it before. It's in the job description, isn't it? Keep a stiff upper lip when top brass try to push you around. But the way he spoke to Jean and me . . . I didn't see red exactly – more like black – and next thing my fist was jabbing out. There was quite a crack when it made contact with his cheekbone. It didn't feel that hard at the time, although now . . .' He rubs his knuckles, which are beginning to bruise. 'I've never punched anyone before.'

'Pah! Be proud you stood up for yourself. I am a supporter of violence under appropriate

335

circumstances,' Grazia pronounces. 'Sometimes a punch in the face really is the only way to get a message across.'

'He got the message all right. He was shouting and wailing that he was going to sue me, and then he began to sway—'Will stops mid-sentence. 'For a minute I thought he was about to drop dead.'

'I'm sure any of us would have done the same.' I say. After all. I am the newly reinvented Feisty Emily, who takes no shit from anyone.

'Hmm,' says Sandie dubiously. 'Maybe. Though I'm not sure violence ever solved anything, myself. I'm amazed they didn't sack you on the spot.'

'Yes, me too,' Will admits. 'Actually, he did sack me. But then his assistant pointed out that they'd have a devil of a job finding someone else willing to clear the shop ready for handing the keys back to the estate agent. And anyway, I have legal rights as a tenant in the flat upstairs.'

His eyes are sad. It's all I can do not to give him a big hug. Instead I say, 'What are you going to do, Will?'

'Who knows? I don't think the MD's going to give me a reference. Then there's the little matter of being homeless as well as jobless.'

I *just* manage to stop myself offering him my spare room. 'Perhaps you could join Charlie's Shopping Angels?'

Grazia shakes her head. 'Charlie will not employ

male shoppers. He says they stick out like spare pricks at an orgy.'

Will tries to smile. 'Ah well. I'm sure I'll find something.' But his voice lacks any conviction. I don't think there's anything sadder than a man who has lost his sense of purpose.

'Come on, guys. It's so obvious.' Sandie waits until she's got our attention. 'There's a flat here that needs making over. Will is the King of DIY, the possessor of true Will Power. OK, he doesn't speak Latvian, but there's an international language of building. What do you say, Will?'

She turns to me, smiling. Was that a *wink*?

'Well,' he says. 'I'd be delighted, but only if Emily wants me here.'

And what am I supposed to say to that except, 'Of course! I would be so grateful. The more the merrier.'

I gulp down the last of my Black Balsam, wondering whether I can get through the next week or two without confessing undying love.

CHAPTER 27

GRAZIA

Leon, *Leon*. I know you disapprove. I swear that this morning I felt your censure, unforgiving as a hanging judge.

Art, as you were so fond of saying, should never be a commodity. But it is impossible to live life without *some* commodities. Will the electricity company accept my past glories as a muse in lieu of payment for this quarter? Can I eat artistic integrity?

These are my dilemmas, Leon, and your condemnation from beyond the grave is no help whatsoever.

'Grazia! My darling!'

'Selina.' I reach for her chilly hand – bloodless and smooth as the floor-to-ceiling white marble in her gallery – and she shakes it limply before letting it fall.

'It has been *too long*,' she says, emphatically. No matter that it was Selina who ignored the one desperate phone call my dignity allowed me to make in the first days following Leon's death. Or that it is only now, after I called to express a vague interest in obtaining a valuation of *Muse 7* and a

338

few other works, that she deigns to return my call.

'Yes. It has been a while.'

'Come through, come through.' She moves through the gallery swiftly, a calculated streak of blood-red silk against the bare white walls. Leon used to joke that Selina saw herself as the ultimate work of art, *darling*, a vintage piece created in the 1950s, barely showing its age, a rare one-off in a world of unoriginal copycats.

The irony being, of course, that Selina resembles every other woman of a certain age in the art world. Spare, sour, Botoxed to the point of immobility.

We enter her office, a large room of extreme blandness. Just occasionally, could these people not allow themselves the slightest deviation from sparse minimalism? A mug with a name on it, perhaps, or a Mickey Mouse mouse mat? Selina produces two crystal tumblers of sparkling San Pellegrino apparently from thin air (there is certainly no sign of a fridge) and hands one to me. 'So. *Muse 7*. I shan't ask why . . .' she says, though the pause she leaves at the end of the sentence is an invitation to disclose all the dirt.

'Leon is not the first artist to pay little attention to matters of Mammon.'

She leans forward, the red dress gaping to reveal xylophone ribs beneath her St Tropezed skin. 'Really?'

'As you know, Selina, his death was sudden.

We didn't have time for inheritance planning or life assurance policies. It has caused . . . difficulties. Difficulties that I am now attempting to resolve.'

'Yes, but the paintings, Grazia. Surely there must be other things to consider besides the paintings?'

'Anyone would think that you don't want the commission.'

Her jaw drops. I'm astonished it still can, her skin is so taut. 'Ah, the commission is neither here nor there to me. If you do decide to sell, of course, I hope that you will choose a friend over a stranger. I simply wished to check you know what you're doing.'

'I do, thank you. At this stage, I am merely investigating my options.'

I do not add that my investigation has a certain urgency, that an appointment with the bank follows this one. One has to work so hard to see a bank manager these days; they much prefer to ruin your life by letter, without having to see the pain in your eyes.

Selina offers me another pregnant pause, but I choose not to fill it. She nods to herself, accepting that there will be no gory details to share at her members' club.

'Following your call, I made a few discreet inquiries, contacts who have expressed an interest in the past in this kind of work. I must warn you, Grazia, conditions are not as good as they might have been this time last year. Budgets are tight amongst corporate collectors, and in the private arena there is a trend towards the abstract. These things are cyclical, so it would probably be my advice to wait, if that is an option.'

'It is not an option.'

Now her body shifts away from me slightly, like a doctor confirming a diagnosis of something contagious.

'I have complete confidence I can sell anything you wish to dispose of, Grazia. We may not be able to be very choosy, that's all. There is a sheikh who is very keen to acquire anything by the older Young British Artists, for example.'

A sodding sheikh? I hear you, Leon. I hear the contempt that someone who did not understand you might mistake for racism, not realising the pleasure you take from righteous indignation. *A scumbag prince who wants to buy status, like he can buy wives and slaves and entire countries if he wants them.*

Fine! It is easy for you now. But what else am I supposed to do?

I blink. Selina is staring at me.

'I don't think it's my business to tell you what you're supposed to do, Grazia. I simply act on your instructions.'

I realise I spoke my reply to Leon out loud. 'I am so sorry, Selina. I appreciate all you are doing, and the delicacy you are showing. So this sheikh is the only lead so far?'

'There will be others, I am sure of it. And now

341

that I appreciate the urgency, I shall redouble my efforts. Other than *Muse 7*, what else is there? Believe it or not, there's quite a market right now in paraphernalia, too. Someone sold a used palate last month in New York.'

I hear Leon laughing savagely. Shut up. *Shut up.* I have not made up my mind; I cannot think with you crowding my head. 'There must be some items in his studio. I have not been in there since . . .'

Selina smoothes her skirt. 'Perhaps I could visit? It might be easier for you.'

'Thank you.'

'How would you feel about viewings at home? Naturally we'd be delighted to exhibit here, in the private space, but you might prefer for the work to remain in situ for as long as possible.'

The thought of workmen loading those precious paintings into some anonymous lorry sickens me. Can I really do this? I hear myself answering automatically. 'I would like to limit viewings, if possible. I have already had one visitor, a journalist, wanting to do a piece.'

Selina's bagless eyes widen. 'A journalist? Now, that could be useful, in terms of drumming up interest . . . let me ponder. I will call you.'

'Soon?' With this one word, my humiliation is complete.

'By the end of the week,' she confirms, leaving me to show myself out.

The bank has a very different take on *minimalist*.

My 'personal banker' is based at a grimy branch near Euston station, a far cry from the bank's plush Mayfair HQ where one of Leon's paintings dominates the reception area.

For a man so resistant to art as a commodity, Leon was realistic about what it took to fund our dream house. The 'donation' of a large piece he'd never liked changed the status of our mortgage application from outlandish to approved. He even snarled his way through the official unveiling, shaking hands with plump bankers over tepid Laurent Perrier and miniature Yorkshire puddings. If he was still alive, he could pay the arrears with an afternoon's worth of doodling, but it is not an option for a mere muse.

Debbie, my personal banker, is the same age as Selina, but she is graceless, overweight and stuffed into an off-white trouser suit. Her office is small, the laminated bookshelves crowded with family photographs and knick-knacks from holidays: a carved wooden camel on spindly legs, a miniature sombrero.

'Hello there. Mrs Smith, isn't it?'

I hesitate. 'My husband used only the name Leon.'

'Well well,' she says. 'Though the account's in the name Smith, isn't it? Anyway, I did try to explain on the phone. These days, we don't have much leeway.' She nods towards the computer. 'That's where the power is now.' Her voice is high pitched.

'I appreciate that,' I say, 'but I wanted to discuss options with you.'

She raises her eyebrows – a strangely affecting gesture after Selina's frozen forehead. 'Fire away. I used to work for the listening bank, you know. Do you remember the jingle? *Come and talk, talk to the listening . . .*'

'As you know, my husband died intestate. I had not previously appreciated that funds were so low.'

'My mother was in the same boat. Gambling. She didn't have a clue until she went through my step-dad's stuff. In the olden days, the pay packet went straight to the wife, and she doled out spending money. No credit, neither. I blame the banks.'

'You are the bank.'

Her nose wrinkles. 'Nah, I'm just a wage slave. So, anyway, have you tried getting a job? Mum got herself a nice number doing shelf-filling in the evenings. She got herself a brand new social life, too.'

'I *am* working.'

'Oh, right,' she says, running a finger down a bank statement. 'Not much coming in, though, is there?'

'No,' I admit.

'What did you do before you were married, then?'

I think back: it seems like someone else's life. 'I worked at Malpensa Airport in Milan. Ground staff. But I am too old now—'

'And you never worked during your marriage?'

'My husband was an artist. I was his muse, and I looked after him.'

'Ah, not many ads in the Job Shop for a muse, eh? That's the trouble with men today. Still expecting all the molly-coddling their dads got, but not keeping their side of the bargain and providing for us in return.'

I am about to tell her that I am not part of *her* generation, that Leon and I were above anything so bourgeois as providing for one another, that we were kindred spirits, not parties to some shop-soiled business deal, but then I stop. Was it really not part of our duty to look out for each other, to be sure that we would be protected if the worst happened? Not very bohemian, certainly, but the actions of adults.

Not that we ever did behave like adults.

And Leon . . . no one could ever accuse him of expecting too much from me, could they? My life with him was perfection. Wasn't it? All artists have moods, and as my role was solely to look pretty and accommodate his needs, then it was hardly a sacrifice to do what he wanted, to move to the place he found most inspiring, to live in surroundings decorated and accessorised as he dictated . . .

Dictated?

But it was a benign dictatorship, surely? And if friends fell by the wayside . . . no, if I chose to abandon friends to serve the needs of art, then it was *my* choice.

'Mrs Leon?'

Debbie's voice intrudes into my consciousness, but I swat it away mentally. I am thinking,

thinking, *thinking*. Maybe the only choice I had in my relationship with Leon was whether to stay, or go. Maybe once I decided to marry him, the rest was irrelevant. Anything to avoid one of those monstrous sulks that he could maintain for weeks and weeks, turning Rose Cottage into a prison of recriminations.

'Mrs Leon, I don't think there's much we can do. There's no magic trick I can perform to change the figures. I'm afraid that unless you have new information to share—'

After so much agonising, I feel certain, suddenly, that I am doing the right thing. 'I have paintings to sell. The proceeds will clear the arrears. Perhaps clear the entire mortgage.'

She leans forward, nearly knocking over a tiny Greek urn. 'We'd need a written valuation, to stop the repossession proceedings.'

I nod. 'Can you give me a few days?'

'End of the week is the best I can do. The computer, you know. Mind of its own.'

As I leave her office, the air feels fresher and flower-scented, despite the trucks and buses rumbling by. London, my true love.

For the first time in almost two years, I do not hear Leon's voice in my head, telling me how to behave. No. That is wrong. It had been telling me what to do for longer than two years. More like twenty-two.

Strangely, I do not mourn its absence.

CHAPTER 28

SANDIE

The porter at Dixie's Digs tracks all our comings and goings, though his eyes never appear to leave his *Daily Star*. It's quite a skill. He should have worked for MI5. Maybe he does.

But today he's not playing secret agent. He stands up as I walk into the lobby.

'Miss Barrow? Miss Barrow, can I have a word?'

I can't ever remember hearing him speak before. His voice is monotonous, like the buzz of a cruising mosquito.

'Of course,' I say, desperately trying to remember his name. Dennis? Danny?

'I have received . . . correspondence. About your current employment status.'

I feel like I'm inside an elevator that's crashed down one hundred floors, leaving my stomach behind on floor ninety. I look down at my jeans, T-shirt, scuffed trainers – the uniform for this morning's mission consuming a borderline inedible all-day breakfast at a burger chain – and realise how far I've let my guard down. Too far.

'Oh yes?'

He looks at me, his age-browned eyelids lifting to reveal sprightly blue eyes. 'Miss Barrow, I didn't make the rules. I am prepared, in most situations, to overlook breaches that don't make themselves apparent. However—'

Derek! That's it. 'Derek, I can assure you that I am very grateful for my home here and would do nothing knowingly to put it at risk.'

The eyelids close slowly, like a lizard's. 'Miss Barrow, I believe you. I do. But this correspondence has placed me in a difficult position. It informs me that you may not currently be employed in the mercantile trades. This is information that I am duty bound to pass onto the trustees, if I suspect it to be true. Now—' he holds up a liver-spotted hand, 'I don't want you to say anything hasty. I want you to go and have a little think about your answer. No hurry. Tomorrow will do.'

He sits down again and lifts his newspaper back in front of his face. So I'm dismissed. I try to compose myself as I walk towards the ancient lift. That inner grizzly bear of mine seems to have developed a terrible need to roar.

I've just about collected my thoughts when the *Daily Star* moves down a few inches. 'Oh, and Miss Barrow. You might like to bear in mind that whoever it is who has decided to correspond with us appears to have a strong motivation for making these accusations. I find anonymous tale-telling

348

pretty disgusting, but this individual won't give up; instinct tells me that much.'

Then he lifts the newspaper again and I scuttle towards the lift, abandoning all pretence of calm. Oh, Marsha, *Marsha*, what did I do to you?

My little room has always been a refuge, but this morning it feels like a cell. I stand in front of the narrow built-in cupboard and pull out my old Garnett's uniform. I lay the clothes out on my bed: white blouse, crimson waistcoat, crimson skirt, polished black court shoes. It's as though the clothes have been discarded by a ghost.

Am I that ghost? Could it really have been me who pressed that blouse to perfection every night before bed, as though the world would end if a single crease remained? Did I shine my shoes to a mirror shine each morning, even though they'd always be scuffed again by midday?

At this moment, I simply can't imagine why I cared so much.

Appearances, Sandra, are never deceptive. You must never let things slide. People will judge you on how well turned out you are.

Well, Gramma certainly judged me on that. And, in turn, I learned to judge myself – and everyone else – by her unforgiving values. Maybe that's why Marsha hated me so much. No one could live up to my impossible standards.

'And look where it's got me, Gramma. A complete bloody failure, by anyone's standards!'

I pick up one shoe and throw it across the room. It hits the wall with a satisfying slap, and leaves a black polish mark against the wallpaper. I lift my arm to throw the other one, but the energy drains away.

Blaming someone else – someone who loved me, who tried her best to bring me up right – isn't going to get me out of this mess. For all the faults in Gramma's world view, she taught me not to give in. Barrow women are pragmatists. Survivors. I pick up my shoes and put them back in the cupboard, thinking, thinking, thinking. *I can get out of this. I just don't know how.*

The first task is to get out of the building without facing Derek. I check the corridor and then take the wrought-iron fire stairs that curl down the side of the building. I feel self-conscious, like a particularly rubbish spy. My feet ring loud as church bells with every step, but the only passer-by, an elderly woman with a Chihuahua, looks away as I hop over the fence onto the High Street.

I try calling Emily, but her mobile goes to answer phone, so I try Grazia and she's in town, having lunch at some swanky restaurant.

I *knew* she saved all the best secret shopping assignments for herself.

By the time I reach the West End, I have tried to find a solution and failed. I can't afford to stay in London. Time to get shopping out of my system for good. Time to accept that Marsha has won, that Toby will never have to eat his words. My dreams of setting up my own secret shopping service, doing consultancy, becoming Sandie the Shopping Saviour, are sillier than anything Emily could come up with. I need to give my notice, pack my bags, go home to Gramma. At least it will make her happy.

I get the Tube to Bond Street, then walk round the corner to the Italian restaurant. It's very low-key and almost empty, the ladies who lunch having long since left. I spot Grazia alone in the far corner, staring into space, a large glass of red wine and a coffee on the table in front of her

A craggy waiter approaches me, about to explain that they're closed, but I wave at Grazia and he nods morosely. I walk to the table and spot an untouched plate of petit fours, chocolate truffles and tiny pastries. My stomach rumbles. It feels like a long time since that all-day breakfast.

'So this is how the other half lives, eh?' I say. She jumps a little.

'It's a special occasion,' she says, but her face is sad.

'Birthday?'

'Rebirth day, perhaps.' She clicks her fingers, says something in Italian to the waiter and he scuttles off.

I remember Emily telling me about Grazia's financial situation. 'What's happened?'

'I have made a decision that I should have made

a long time ago.' The waiter returns with coffee for me and an empty wineglass. She waits until he's gone before speaking again. 'I am going to sell Leon's paintings.'

'Grazia! Are you sure? It's not something you can undo if you realise you've made a mistake.'

She seems to notice her wine for the first time and takes a determined swig, then pours half of what's left into my glass. 'It is not a mistake. It is time to move on.'

'What happened? I can't believe you just woke up one morning and decided to sell up. The paintings must hold so many memories.'

'Maybe I did just wake up,' she says, calmly. 'And my memories are in my mind, not on canvas. Besides, perhaps I no longer wish to be reminded of my husband all the time.'

'Well, if you're certain.'

'I am. Now the decision has been taken, I feel nothing but relief.'

'Yes,' I say. 'I think I know how that feels.' I take a swig of wine myself.

'Drink, drink. So what is your news, Sandie? You did not sound yourself on the telephone.'

I sit down next to her. 'You could say that.' And I tell her about the anonymous letter and the terms of my lease and my certainty that it's Marsha who did this. And then I tell her that perhaps it's for the best, that I'm stuck in this in-between world, unable to plan any further than Charlie's next bank credit. That it's no way to live.

Grazia nods, but her face is hard. 'So you are running away?'

'No, not running away. I am accepting the inevitable rather than fighting it.'

Now she tuts at machine-gun speed. 'No, no, no. This is unsatisfactory.'

'Well, I'm awfully sorry, Grazia, but there really aren't many options open to an about-to-be-homeless unemployed store manager without any references.'

'Pfft! You *must* fight. This Marsha, she must not be allowed to win.'

'She already has.' My inner grizzly bear growls at Grazia's bluntness.

'This is craziness. How will you live the rest of your life, bearing this injustice upon your shoulders? It will poison you from the inside out!'

The growling increases. Though it might just be my empty stomach. 'OK, what am I supposed to do about it? Rely on the conscience of the one person in the world who seems to burn with total hatred for me, and ask her to confess?' I ask, before stuffing a pastry and a chocolate truffle down in one gulp.

Grazia alternates between thoughtful sips of coffee, wine, then coffee again. Finally she slaps her hand down on the table. 'Conscience, pah! No one has a conscience any more. But the camera . . . the camera *never* lies.'

And Grazia smiles a smile so steely, so confident of victory that I feel my grizzly bear purr with anticipation. And I wonder whether Marsha, flouncing around the shop floor at Garnett's doing *my* old job, has any premonition about the force that's just been unleashed.

INTROCUCTION TO ASSIGNMENT 07/10729GL:

Advisory: this leading supermarket is a new client for Charlie's Shopping Angels. Any incomplete reports will be returned without payment. Please follow instructions to the letter.

This hypermarket is the flagship store, with 17,000 square metres of retail space. It promises customers 'Service Plus' – all the speed and convenience of a supermarket, combined with the product knowledge and support that would be expected from a specialist. It is designed to be a destination store, offering everything a customer needs in every aspect of their life: work, leisure, family.

Each assignment will involve adopting a different role, with very specific queries. Please memorise the details thoroughly. Under no circumstances should Mystery Shopper status be revealed. The customer profiles are:

Shopper A: new mother seeking advice on post-natal weight loss

Shopper B: professional requiring mobile

computing and telecommunica-tions solutions

Shopper C: shopper investigating investment vehicles for significant windfall

Please note that each shopper will also be required to monitor one food outlet, ordering food and beverages to a maximum value of £12 per person.

CHAPTER 29

EMILY

'Dear God in heaven.' Grazia brakes hard. 'Even in my worst nightmares I could not have imagined the brutalist horror of this.'

From a distance it could be a military base, a gigantic hangar that would easily house the airborne fleet of a medium-sized country. As Grazia drives closer, along a winding ring road, it's like entering a CBeebies world of bright colours and brighter smiles. Rows and rows of shiny parked cars seem to stretch into infinity, and yellow-dressed men with matching carts patrol the area looking for dirty vehicles to return to shininess.

'You big snob, Grazia. I can't wait to get inside.' It's true. OK, so this is not Garnett's of Oxford Street, but maybe supermarkets are my spiritual home. At least I can afford to shop here.

'At this moment I am unsure whether we will ever get inside. Can anyone see a space?'

'You're forgetting that procreation is the passport to parking. Just follow the pram signs.'

Grazia huffs and puffs a little, but within seconds

we find a parent-and-baby bay, wide enough for the largest of MPVs. As I unload Freddie, I notice Sandie and Grazia whispering. They're thick as thieves these days. Every time they come to my flat they end up in the corner together, muttering away until I come within range. Whatever the secret is, I'm not part of it, and I hate being out of the loop.

Grazia spots me watching them. 'Now, girls. Cameras all working? Mission instructions fully digested and then destroyed?'

'Oh, come on, Grazia,' Sandie says, 'we're old hands. If we haven't got the hang of it by now, we never will.'

I wheel Freddie round to them. 'You know, I counted up the other day. This is my one hundred and eightieth assignment?'

'Bull's eye!' says Sandie. 'Shame you don't get a carriage clock. Hey, Grazia, could you suggest that Charlie introduces a reward card for his more prolific operatives? We used to run something similar at Garnett's and—'

'I doubt that Charlie would take kindly to advice from you any more,' Grazia says, then frowns. 'Or any of us, of course. He likes his angels kept firmly in their place.'

She strides towards the store entrance without looking back.

'Is it my imagination or is Grazia behaving a bit oddly?'

Sandie shrugs. 'Can't say I've noticed. Shall I

meet you in the cafeteria in half an hour for an assignment debrief?'

'Yes, but . . .' Before I can finish my sentence, she's gone, too. It definitely *isn't* my imagination. Something's up.

But I can't stand around speculating. In secret-shopper land, time is money. I wedge my bag-cam into position under my arm, and navigate the buggy through the throng of people at the entrance. There must be half a dozen, all employed by the store: a couple of meet-and-greeters with floor-plans and kids' TV presenter faces; a sterner security guard; a woman handing out vouchers for haircuts in the in-store salon; a man dressed as an Edam cheese offering free samples, and a giant green bunny rabbit who scoots over to us as soon as he spots the soggy old rabbit sitting in Freddie's lap.

'Rabbit,' says the rabbit. He has a very deep voice for a rabbit.

'Buuur,' says Freddie delightedly. The rabbit hops around a bit for good measure.

Surely it can't be much longer before my baby says a real word – I don't think *buuur* quite counts. The hothouse infants of Lime Village are probably all conversing in Latin and Mandarin before their first birthdays and though I do truly want to be a laid-back mum, it's hard without someone there to share my anxieties. Not that Duncan was ever much of a listener.

The rabbit hands me a leaflet about the internet-phone service he's promoting and I enter the store.

It's like a roofed city. I can't actually see where it ends. Even on a weekday it's hard to move in the entrance, the bit Sandie always calls the Decompression Zone. Other shoppers stand slack-jawed and motionless, not sure where to look, never mind where to walk.

'Right, Fredster, onwards and upwards.' I push forwards, not sure where exactly I'm headed, but aiming for the gaps in the crowd. As I begin to acclimatise, everything begins to make sense. The whole store is designed to resemble a high street, complete with wooden benches and metal sign-posts that direct us to The Market Garden and The Cheese Ripening Room and The Granary Bakehouse and The Wine Merchant. And then there's a sign pointing into the air, to The Village Green.

I look up. It's so unlikely, so *playful*, that I giggle. A second level is suspended somehow above the rest of the store. There's a huge circle of bright green fake grass, with swings and a working Magic Roundabout, all pastel colours and nostalgic charm. Picnic-style tables are arranged around the edge, and food stalls are scattered on the grass. At the other end of this fantasy park there's a circular sushi bar with a conveyor belt – a magic roundabout for grown-ups.

'Later, Freddie. First we have work to do.'

I enjoy the sensation of losing myself in the crowd. For the last week, I've been struggling to cope with my house-full of people. The constant

360

banging and crashing of the Latvian superheroes isn't quite as invigorating as it was on day one of the building work, but the real problem is Will. Wherever I go in the house, he's there too. Now it's true that the two flats aren't exactly on the scale of Buckingham Palace, but even so, I feel I need to be on my best behaviour at all times. I've lost any sense of what's appropriate when dealing with a friend who is helping with the DIY, but I know it doesn't involve the things I want to do: tell him how cute he looks with mushroom paint splodges in his dark curls, or give him meaningful looks when Magic FM plays 'Love is in the Air', or check out his pert backside in those jeans. I repeat my reasons like a mantra under my breath: the acute risk of humiliation if my feelings are revealed; my appalling judgement where men are concerned; the need to put Freddie first; the way Duncan would react if I took a lover . . .

Still, the work will all be finished tomorrow. Life will return to normal for a few days, before the weekend when I put the final stage of my plan into action and face the wrath of Duncan.

There. The thought of that is enough to cool my ardour for Will.

I reach the Wellbeing Zone and check my watch: 12.33. *A colleague should approach you within two minutes. Please note the time and manner of first contact, and the name of the colleague. If no approach is made within that period, then you must approach a colleague yourself.*

361

The zone is designed like an old-fashioned pharmacy, with dark wooden cabinets and enormous glass jars full of knobbly ginger and gnarled twigs. At eye level, the products are more accessible: vitamins promising vitality or virility, plus packets of powder to help you gain muscle or lose fat.

One of the 'colleagues' notices me and crosses the store towards me. She has dark hair in a chignon and feline eyes, and her slim figure is enviable, despite the unsexy white lab coat. She's exactly the kind of shop assistant who just a few months ago would have had me scuttling out of the store like a bag lady. But now I am made of sterner stuff.

12.34. Assistant approaches me with a smile.

Could I describe that as a genuine smile? No, it's slightly superior, and the skin above the eyes doesn't lift. Still, they'll be able to judge that for themselves: the camera is focused on her face as she comes closer.

'Hello, are you looking for some advice on the products?' She looks down at Freddie, who is transfixed by her legs in their caramel-brown fishnets and high heels. He reaches out to touch them. 'And hello to you too. Isn't he cute?'

'He is, yes. I do need some help, actually. Since he was born, I've been finding it hard to shift this excess weight.'

She looks me up and down and I read her name badge: Jay. 'Yes. It's a common enough problem.' Her voice puts me on edge: I can tell she's dying to add, *a common enough problem for you lazy, lardy women with no self-control.* 'How much extra do you think you've put on?'

'Well, I used to be a size ten to twelve, and now I'm a fourteen on a good day.'

'And that must bother you?' Jay says.

Clever girl. By suggesting that it should bother me, she's softening me up to flog me more stuff. Deliberately undermining your customers won't be in the staff handbook, but in a way I admire her initiative.

I look down at my body, ready to dredge up a few nuggets of self-loathing. God knows I've felt crap often enough about my muffin top and my cellulite and my stretch marks. And Duncan's constant sniping about me being a chubster hasn't helped.

But it's strange, because as I check out my legs, I think they look rather shapely in these Primark jeans. All right, so it'd be nice to have Jay's perfect pins, but they'd look silly on my curvy body.

I move up to inspect my tummy . . . literally my soft underbelly, the bit I feel most self-conscious about. True, there's a sticky-out bit just above my belt that I didn't have before. But then I didn't have a baby before, either, and would I rather have a flat tummy and no Freddie? It's a no-brainer. And anyway, this season's floaty pink top covers it completely.

Boobs, then. Surely I can find something to hate there? When I stopped feeding Freddie they were floppy as dog-ears – yuk – but remarkably they seem to have popped back into shape. A bit bigger than they were, but is that necessarily a bad thing? The boat neck dips nicely to reveal a touch of cleavage that's nothing if not feminine.

'Are you all right?'

'What? Yes, well, obviously I'd like to be a bit slimmer,' I say. It's not a lie. I'm just not sure that it would make me significantly happier.

'Naturally,' she says. 'The first step would be a diet plan. Our in-store nutritionist can design one for you in ten minutes. In your case, it might be a good idea to go for the Accelerated Plan.'

'And why's that then?'

'Well, on account of the amount you need to lose.'

For a moment, I wonder if I'm kidding myself: if my positive self-image is in fact the ultimate in self-delusion, triggered by paint fumes and euphoria at nearing the end of the flat makeover. Oh, and my unwarranted suspicion that Will might *just* fancy me.

But I'm not kidding myself. I shake my head. 'Look. I'm a bit plump, OK? Not dangerously obese, not a drain on the bloody health service, not so fat I need three seats on the bus.'

Jay's skinny face is a picture. 'No, I never said—'

'It's that kind of body fascism that makes women hate themselves. Haven't you seen *How to Look Good Naked?* We should be proud of our shape!'

Jay sighs. 'Of course, madam,' she says, 'but it

was you who told me that you were looking for a weight-loss solution.'

Now I remember the camera. Bugger. My one hundred and eightieth assignment, and the first time I've ever forgotten that I'm playing a role. I try to recover, to remember my part. 'Oh. Yes. You're right. It's the hormones, you know. I used to be so placid, before Freddie came along. You were saying . . . about the in-store nutritionist?'

I think I got away with it. In fact, snotty Jay treated me with new respect after my little outburst. In the bad old days, I'd have walked away feeling lower than a worm, hating myself for not having the guts to stand up for myself.

'It's easy-peasy-lemon-squeezie to be assertive, isn't it, Freddie?'

'Eeee,' he agrees.

But instead of feeling bad, I've rewarded myself with a muffin, to celebrate the joyous abundance of my very own muffin-top. I'm sitting on the edge of the Village Green, Freddie snuggled next to me on the park bench, watching the life below. Shopping *is* life, after all. The quest for your heart's desire, the covering and the budgeting and the wishing and then the moment when it's finally in your grasp. And then the pleasure of finding something else to aim for.

Aisles tower over shoppers. From up here, the colours glow like fairy lights: a wall of turquoise Heinz beans tins, the dazzling orange juices in illuminated chiller cabinets the size of a minibus. Oh, and look at the fruit and vegetables: thousands of glowing red tomatoes stacked on top of each other, a mountain of deep green broccoli, and plump purple aubergines reflecting the faces of customers in their shiny skins.

I could spend days here and not get bored. Below me, to the right, I spot Sandie in the Wired Technology Store. She loves the job too, of course, though in a different way. I watch as she views each display as though it's a work of art in a museum, stepping back to appreciate the overall effect before getting closer, touching the products, unable to resist moving an item a fraction of a millimetre so that it catches the light in precisely the right place. She is *so* good at this.

'Mission accomplished?' Grazia sits down next to me, a hot chocolate and two biscotti on her tray. This is how it all began, isn't it? With an offer I couldn't refuse at the Spanish cafe in Hammersmith.

'Yup. The assistant was a bit pushy, but the service ticked all the boxes. What about you?'

'Better than I had anticipated. The financial advisor knew his onions, though he did not seem to believe me when I said my windfall was coming from the sale of paintings.'

'You told him the truth?'

She shrugs. 'The fewer lies, the easier it is. In any case, I could not imagine that someone working here would have heard of Leon.'

'You're such a snob, Grazia!'

'I am not!'

'Yes you are. I mean, you're a generous, adorable snob, but you still believe that anyone who shops in a supermarket is lacking style, don't you?'

'I prefer to support the boutique retailer, it is true, but that is based on personal experience. Britain is, after all, a nation of shopkeepers. Whereas supermarkets are so American.'

'Oh right, and when was the last time you came into a supermarket? Before today?'

She scowls. 'One does not have to experience salt mining to know that it is unpleasant.'

I giggle. 'Grazia, I can't believe you just compared shopping in a supermarket to a spell in the Siberian gulag. We might be a nation of shopkeepers, but we're also a nation of customers. I've been to loads of little cutesy shops where the owners treat you like dirt, and to supermarkets where I've been treated like a princess.'

'But the products, they're so . . .'

'Mass market? Affordable?' I reach down into my bag and draw out this morning's purchases. I pull out an admittedly unpromising flesh-coloured garment. 'Look. That'd cost you thirty pounds in a posh boutique. Here, a fiver.'

'Yes,' says Grazia, 'but what on earth is it supposed to be?'

I unravel it and hold it against my body: it looks like it'd barely cover my thigh. 'It's a Wonder-Slim Body-Suit. I took one look at the diet plans the nutritionist showed me and decided life's too short to live on celery and cottage cheese. This thing claims to shrink you a dress size, and lose you seven pounds. Though God knows where it bloody goes.' I put it back in the bag. 'But it's not just control underwear; take a look at this.' And I show her a gorgeous bra and pants set in pale blue silk. 'The pants are like boy shorts, to cover my tummy. And the bra fits perfectly. Seven quid. What do you say to that, eh?'

Grazia is smiling. 'I say that you have changed, Emily. For the better. They might be chainstore knickers, but I cannot imagine you having the confidence to pull them off when I first met you.'

I giggle. 'Who said anything about pulling them off?'

'Hey, girls,' Sandie says, plonking herself down next to me on the bench. 'Wanna see my new wireless-web and video-enabled super-duper mobile before I take it back to get a refund?'

'No. Actually,' says Grazia, her face now serious, 'I think we have something to discuss with Emily.'

'Oh. Right. Yeah . . .'

Uh oh. Now it's coming. Some bombshell that will make all of my achievements – my new-found self-assurance, my embryonic property empire, my plot to defeat Duncan – seem insignificant. Maybe Charlie's decided I'm surplus to requirements, or perhaps the girls are setting up their own secret shopping company but don't want me involved. 'What? I knew there was something up. Tell me!'

'You know that my change of circumstances means I won't be running the team any more?' Grazia says.

I nod and then cotton on. 'Oh . . . is Sandie taking over? What a relief. I thought it was something awful. Were you worried I'd be annoyed? No way. Sandie, you'll be brilliant, I mean, you know so much—'

Sandie shakes her head. 'No. It's not that. The thing is, Em, I'm going to have to give up the shopping too. I have to leave my lodgings and I can't afford to live anywhere else in London – there's no way I can pay market rent on what we earn; you know that.'

'You . . .' I blink. 'But we're the gang. We're the shopping angels.'

'Well, I know, but I've tried to work out a way round it and the sums don't add up.'

'But you could come to live with me! In the other flat. Even if Duncan does insist on selling one of them, I bet it'll take ages and—'

'No, Em. That's just a stopgap. I've been in denial for too long about the whole Garnett's business. I need to move on. The only way I can do that is by going home, looking for a new job in a new industry, where I can start from the bottom. Put shopping behind me for good.'

'You can't do that! It's in your blood. You've worked so hard; we all have.'

Sandie looks too miserable to speak.

'That is why we want you to carry on, Emily,'

Grazia says. 'I am going to suggest to Charlie that *you* take over from me.'

'Me? No way. I couldn't I'm too—'

'Too conscientious? Too clever? Too much of a natural with that bag-camera? Emily, I said earlier that you had changed because I believed it. Truly, Charlie would be extremely fortunate to find anyone else with half your ability.'

'Grazia's right, Em. You have to do it, to take on the secret shopping sword of truth. I'd hate to think that all our hard work ends here.'

I gulp. In books, the underdog always saves the day, but it never works out that way in real life. Does it? 'I don't know. I suppose if you two really believe in me, then I'll think about it. No promises, mind you.'

Grazia's eyes narrow. 'I shall take that as a yes.'

'No you don't! I said I'll think about it.'

She raises her eyebrows. 'There are times when I think that perhaps I preferred the Emily who always did as she was told.'

Sandie smiles. 'You know it makes sense, Em. You're a survivor. And you know what they always say. When the going gets tough . . .'

I nod. 'Yep. When the going gets tough, the tough go SHOPPING!'

We giggle, all four of us, and it's only when we've finished that Freddie frowns in concentration and, checking we're watching, opens his mouth.

'Shuppy!'

'Did he just say what I think he said?'

We stare at him. He frowns again. 'Shuppy,' he says, more confident this time. 'Shuppy, shuppy, shuppy, SHUPPPPPEEEE!'

And as I lift him onto my lap to give him a fabulously slobbery kiss, I wonder what his dad will think when he learns that Freddie's first word was 'shopping'.

SKOOL'S OUT FOR EVER

Well, at least until September, but with nothing to do and no homework, boredom looms. So be a busy mum's best friend. Climbing frames, paddling pools, cricket and croquet sets – plenty to keep your young customers amused and the tills ringing.

CHAPTER 30

EMILY

'I've been saving this outfit for when the Queen invites me for tea at Buckingham Palace on my hundredth birthday. But I think today is nearly as special.'

Jean steps out from behind the counter, modelling her best mauve twin-set, accessorised with bright purple shimmery lipgloss. Beside her, Will is dressed in smart jeans and a purple shirt (to match Jean's lip-gloss) which makes his chameleon eyes look like something from a pop art picture.

And Bells & Whistles, Heartsease Common awaits her fate with quiet acquiescence, like the fading nonagenarian she is.

'You look fantastic,' I say to Jean, a lump already forming in my throat. There'll be tears before elevenses at this rate. Mine. I leave the shop before they notice. Today is a day of two halves. This morning, Will and Jean are shutting up shop for good, and this afternoon we're having a drunken wake to remember the good times. OK, I feel a bit of a fraud, as I don't remember the good times and could justifiably be blamed for the bad ones.

But Will wanted all the angels to come, and as this also happens to be the end of the line for our little secret shopping team, it seemed as good a time as any to celebrate. I dropped Freddie off with my mum in Somerset – a birthday treat for Granny and for me – so I won't have to balance my desire to get roaring drunk with my maternal responsibilities.

When the angels first got together, none of us would have guessed that Emily the Country Bumpkin would be the last surviving secret shopper. But Sandie returns home next weekend, and on Friday Grazia will finally become the rich, merry widow the world always presumed her to be. Well, maybe not merry, but definitely rich: that's the day Leon's paintings go up for auction.

And me . . . well, I'm about to become a secret shopping supremo. How could I refuse? I'll be taking over Grazia's complete portfolio of regular jobs – including the ones she's kept to herself, like the glamorous car test drive assignments, the meals at Freddie-unfriendly Michelin-starred restaurants, and free nights at incredible-sounding hotels. Shame I'm single, eh? I'll also be scouting West London to find my own mystery shopper recruits.

Three months ago, I'd definitely have said no to any kind of responsibility, made some excuse to cover up my fear of failure. And a year ago, I'd have laughed if anyone had suggested I might work for myself, run a team. But now life is . . . well, if not exactly one hundred per cent sweet, then certainly a world away from last Christmas, when I broke down in the changing rooms at Garnett's, nursing a puking baby and wearing vomit-covered silk pyjamas.

And apart from the shopping, I have another new sideline as a Sarah Beeny-style property developer. The upstairs flat looks terrific. My days of blissful torture are over now the work has finished, though Will still pops up in my thoughts from the moment I wake till I fall asleep on the sofa. He probably features in my dreams too and I only wish I could remember them. I bet mine would be pretty steamy right now.

Sadly, I have no problem remembering my nightmares. They all feature Duncan. Right now, he's in Somerset playing at being Daddy, but tomorrow it's D-Day. Yes, tomorrow, I finally show my hand – and discover whether my apparently Dunc-proof plot has undiscovered flaws.

'Penny for them?' Sandie's crept up behind me.

'Just thinking about tomorrow's fun and games.'

She nods. 'How do you think he'll take it?'

'That's the million-dollar question.'

I'm prepared for guilt trips, for pleas of near-bankruptcy and accusations of conniving. Sticks and stones may break my bones but his words no longer have the power to hurt me. So why am I worried?

'And you're sure you don't want us there?'

I shake my head. 'Nope. I don't think an audience

would help. I'm pretty sure that wounded male pride is going to be an issue. Duncan's always had a bit of a thing about control.'

'What, worse than me?' Sandie says.

'Don't be silly. You're nothing like Duncan.'

'Honestly?' She sounds very vulnerable. Her eyes are blood-shot, as though she's been crying. Not that I can ever imagine her crying, but since she admitted she's leaving, she's gone all grimfaced, refusing to discuss her plans. I suspect it's because she doesn't actually *have* any plans. It's like her life stops dead after our very last group expedition on Thursday.

'You're a laid-back hippy compared to Duncan. OK, so you're a bit anal, but at least you don't get a kick out of undermining people.'

'I wouldn't be so sure about that.'

'Go on.'

She leans against the wall, kicking at a stone on the pavement. 'I've had time to think. About what's happened to me.'

'Always dangerous.'

'Yes, well. I had to try to work out why Marsha hates me so much. If I was the decent person I've always assumed myself to be, there'd be no reason to do what she did.'

I consider this. 'Ah, but you're assuming that she's a reasonable person, driven by logic. I know I only met her the once, but she seemed like Barbie's seriously poisonous younger sister.'

She frowns. 'I used to own Barbie's younger

sister. Her name was Skipper and she seemed a good sort. For a plastic doll.'

'You *know* what I mean. All I'm saying is, just because Marsha's got some weird obsession with you, doesn't mean you're to blame, does it?'

'Maybe not,' Sandie says, dubiously. 'Thing is, though, I have a hunch that we're all about to find out for sure.'

'You mean Thursday?'

'So it's not just me that thinks something's up?' She blinks. 'Has Grazia said anything?'

'No, but . . . she does get this evil glint in her eye whenever she mentions our final assignment.'

'I knew it.' Sandie groans. 'She's planning something.'

'Would it be a bad thing, though? To achieve "closure"?' I draw inverted commas in the air to show I'm half-joking.

'Oh, it'll definitely be closure if it ends with all three of us being dragged out of Garnett's by security. Last time I saw Toby he said that if I ever darkened his door again, he'd call the police.'

'I'm sure Grazia wouldn't risk that happening,' I say, but actually I'm not sure at all. Ever since she decided to sell off the paintings, I've seen a playful side to her. Although she's playful in the way a feral cat is playful, claws always at the ready.

A loud horn sounds behind me and I turn to see Grazia screeching towards us in a green open-topped sports car, hair blow-dried almost vertical by the wind.

'Good, I am not too late!' she says as she pulls up alongside us.

'Too late for what, precisely?' I ask.

'For the final moments, the tears, the heightened emotions,' she says, rather too gleefully. 'It is like a grand opera.'

Sandie and I exchange glances. There really is something terrifying about the new Grazia.

Despite Grazia's predictions, the last moments of Bells & Whistles, Heartsease Common are more reflective than explosive. Everything is charged with meaning. The last time Jean puts the kettle on, the last time Will dunks a plain chocolate digestive in his *Little Britain* mug, the last time Jean cashes up that ancient till, the last time Will locks the stockroom door. Ancient Bob Frobisher from Frobisher's estate agency, the last one left in Heartsease, wears a black tie when he turns up to pick up the keys. He lets Will turn off the lights, then attaches the key to a large Paddington Bear-style brown label.

'End of an era, son,' he says, touching Will lightly on the arm, like an undertaker comforting a mourner. 'And you'll drop off the keys to your flat at the weekend?'

'Yes.' Will shifts from foot to foot, clearly desperate to get away. Or get to the pub.

Bob walks up to Jean. There's a moment when I think he's going to touch her on the arm too, but then right at the last moment he reaches over and hugs her.

This goes on for quite some time and we all pretend to avert our eyes (though we can't help looking) until Jean pushes him softly away, her mauve-varnished nails sinking into his white shirt just above his rounded waist.

Bob sighs. 'I've waited thirty-seven years to do that.'

'Daft bugger,' she says, but she's blushing and her eyes are round and bright.

'Join us in the pub, Bob?' Will suggests, winking at me.

'Um . . . yes, yes, why not? Just as soon as I've locked the shop key in the safe.'

Bob hesitates and Jean steps towards him. 'Let me give you a hand,' she says. 'Can't have that going missing, can we?'

We watch them walk across the common towards the estate agency. Right now E.T. and Queen Victoria could land on the grass in a jumbo jet and I wouldn't be surprised. It's turning into one of those days.

Will, Sandie, Grazia and I walk in stunned silence to the Rose and Crown. The place is quiet for a Saturday, but this isn't really a destination pub. Jean has pre-ordered a farewell plated lunch of curly white bread sandwiches wrapped in clingfilm. I begin to make mental notes for my assignment report, before I stop myself. *You're off duty, Em; let your hair down.*

Will buys the first round. Since the purpose of this afternoon is to get gloriously drunk, the buyer of each round gets to choose the drink. He returns to the table with four pints of honey-coloured beer in thick-handled glasses. 'Local brew,' he explains.

Grazia tuts. 'I have never drunk bitter.'

'I thought you said you loved all things English?' I say.

'Yep, doesn't come any more English than bitter,' Will agrees. He holds up his glass for a toast. 'To Bells & Whistles and memories.'

'Not just memories, surely,' I say. 'We should be drinking to the future, too.'

Sandie takes a sip of her beer. 'No, let's not. We're not all about to take over secret shopping empires. Or make a cool million from paintings. Are we, Will?'

'Nope. The world is our oyster, apparently, though I'd rather my world was my duvet for the next week. Except I've still got to find new digs.'

He smiles a slightly strained smile.

'Do you think you'll stay in retail?' I ask, trying to steer the conversation away from beds. I'm already blushing.

Will wrinkles his nose. 'If anyone will have me. It's hardly a ringing endorsement of my management skills, is it, to have had my store closed down?'

'Everyone knows you took on a poisoned chalice,' Sandie says.

'All the more reason to doubt my abilities,' he says gloomily. 'Should have said no.'

'If it was so obvious, why didn't you?' I ask.

He laughs. 'Ah, that's a very long story.'

'We've got all afternoon.'

He considers this. 'I need to be a bit drunker to share that particular tale.'

Maybe I'm imagining it, but that look seems surprisingly intimate. 'In that case,' I say, suddenly daring, 'can I get you another drink?'

The afternoon passes in a haze of mixed drinks and sweet regrets. When it's her round, Grazia buys Campari sodas (with a sprinkling of dust from the bottle the landlord found in his cellar). Sandie splashes out on white wine spritzers. Jean, who arrives with Bob and spends the next hour cuddling him in a corner behind the fruit machine, chooses port, despite the scorching weather. Feeling reckless, I choose Long Island Iced Tea, but the landlord doesn't know how to make it and neither do I, despite it being my cocktail of choice on girls' nights out in Rowminster. So I tell him to pour half a pint of coke each and add a shot of vodka, rum, gin and whisky to the glasses. Not sure about the whisky, actually, but the taste has never really been the point. It's all about the effect.

We move outdoors when we realise there's an impromptu game of cricket on the common. I don't have a clue who's winning, but the sounds of willow against leather, and the cheers and applause from the spectators are soothing, although the more I drink, the more distant they seem. All that's stopping me stretching out on the grass and falling asleep is paranoia that I might snore.

Will returns from the bar with some crisps, and sits down next to me. 'I say, Farrah Fawcett, I'm feeling really rather dizzy. What could be the matter with me?'

'Is it possible you might be pissed, Mr Powell?' I say, opening up a bag of ready salted. 'That is, pissed enough to tell me your life story?'

'Very direct, aren't you, Emily?'

'Only in the afternoons,' I giggle. 'In the mornings I am shy as a kitten. In the evenings I am asleep before *Coronation Street* is over.'

'Well, I'm glad it's still the afternoon. If you fall asleep, I might take it personally.'

'You haven't answered my question.'

'Let me see. Around the rugged rocks, the rugged rascal ran.' He smiles. 'Peter Piper picked a peck of pickled peppers. Red lorry, yellow lorry, red lolly, yerrow lolly . . . ah. Failed the tongue-twister breathalyser test, then.'

'I can't do them when I'm sober.'

He pushes himself back up, his long body towering over me, and then reaches for my hand. I take it and feel his strength as he pulls me up. The world spins benevolently.

'This is the completely reliable method of detecting drunkenness, as practised by me and my brother Nick from the age of thirteen. First of all, you attempt to walk backwards in a straight line.'

I watch him try. 'Isn't it cheating to go that slowly?'

'OK, smarty-pants, you do it.'

Keeping my eyes fixed on a point on the horizon – well, it works for seasickness, doesn't it? – I try to go faster than him. It's tricky, the nearest I've got in ages to understanding how the Fredster must have felt when he was taking his first steps. The concentration involved is immense. I decide to give my boy extra hugs as soon as I see him, for coping with the trials of being a toddler.

'You OK, Emily?'

'I'm fine. Just thinking of Freddie. Haven't seen him for . . .' I check my watch and it takes a little while to come into focus, 'eighteen hours now. I know that sounds a bit pathetic, but that's mother-hood for you.'

'It doesn't sound pathetic at all. I love kids. My brother's got two, and they put everything into perspective.'

'That's the kind of thing a woman would say.'

'Clearly I'm very in touch with my feminine side. Which must be why I am such a hit with the ladies.'

'Oh, is that why it is?'

'Absolutely irresistible . . . to ladies over sixty who need their guttering cleaning out.'

Not just to ladies over sixty. I manage to stop myself saying it out loud, but I can't quite think what to say instead: my brain is Long-Island-Ice-Tea-ed.

'Sorry. I seem to have brought the conversation to an abrupt halt. Better move on to stage two of the drunkenness test. Tell me if I wobble.'

He begins to walk towards me and then, without warning, closes his eyes. His large hands move out to the side of his body, like a tightrope walker trying to keep balance, and he maintains a perfect straight line. He turns, eyes still shut. 'So?'

'I'd say you're not quite drunk enough.'

He opens them. 'Ah, but maybe if *you're* drunk enough, I can tell you anyway, as you won't remember.'

I take my cue. Begin to walk, then close my eyes. I feel oddly vulnerable, as the sounds of the cricket game grow loud again. But I have a stubborn streak and I am not about to let myself down by failing at such a basic bloody task. Just one foot in front of another. Left foot, right foot, left foot . . .

My body feels dislocated from my brain, and I try what Will did, holding my hands out to the sides, as though the air will help keep me upright. No, that's *worse*.

Perhaps I'm walking too slowly? I speed up now, going into marching mode, trying to forget the scariness of not knowing where I'm going.

Uh-oh. I'm really beginning to feel quite sick now. 'Will? Have I done enough? Will?'

And then I feel as though I am melting, like ice disappearing in a glas of hot water, and it's a surprisingly nice feeling . . .

'Emily?'

Strong arms grip me just as my knees go soft and I recognise the sweet, hoppy smell of Will's breath. The temptation to stay like this, cradled and safe, is powerful, but I manage to resist, and I open my eyes.

Maybe it's the frown on that strong brow. Or the tension in those full lips. Or the cloudiness in the indefinable eyes. Or perhaps it's the whole package. After all, the very first time I saw Will I realised he had a face that couldn't help but tell the truth.

And the truth, I now know for sure, is that he fancies me as much as I fancy him.

Which is why, as his face gets closer and closer to mine, I am not quite as shocked as I might have been . . .

Which is probably just as well, because the kiss has enough Will Power on its own to knock me off my feet.

Show-stopping kisses come a few times in a lifetime, at most. If you've any sense, you try to hang on to the person who's delivered the show-stopper, so they can deliver them daily, like milkmen did before supermarkets stayed open round-the-clock.

But of course, however many times you try, you'll never recreate the power of that first kiss. The dizziness, the holding on for dear life, the way the rest of the world fades away until there's nothing but lips and lust and little fireworks exploding at the periphery of your vision. Feeling lost *and* found, all at once. Oh, and lost in time.

After a kiss that might have lasted ten seconds or ten minutes for all I know, Will and I come up for air. He's slightly pink, and I suspect I'm even pinker. The bit of my brain that deals with speech has deserted me and instead I gaze at him, overwhelmed.

That truly was an unrepeatable show-stopper of a kiss. All subsequent kisses are bound to be a disappointment.

But, you know, there's no harm in checking, is there? Just to make sure . . .

A very, very long time later, we separate again. Maybe we've given our friends enough to gawp at, and our lips enough of a workout, and perhaps if we don't cool off a little we'll steam ourselves into meltdown.

Will takes my hand. His own hand is, of course, bloody brilliant with washers and guttering, but I happen to think hand-holding is its true vocation. His fingers fit around my fingers, no awkwardness. Our hands have a very profound understanding.

We walk towards a bench further along the common, out of view. I'm feeling increasingly drunk, though I'm fighting it. I want to remember every millisecond of this, but booze and perfect recall do not go together.

Once we're seated, we search each other's faces for the right thing to say.

'Well,' he says, at last.

'Well,' I agree.

I check myself for signs of guilt – I am a married woman and a mum, after all – but I'm not experiencing the slightest prickle of remorse. Anyway, this is a single afternoon of drunken fun. A boost to the ego, but nothing more. I need to make sure of that.

'Where were we again?' His voice is throaty.

'I think you were about to tell me your life story.'

'Ah, only if I was drunk enough.'

I giggle. 'Doesn't . . . *that* prove you are?'

Will considers this. 'Maybe. OK, what do you know about my life story already? I'd hate to repeat myself or risk boring you.'

I decide against feeding his ego by telling him that he could read out the ingredients on the back of the crisp packet and I'd be enthralled. 'Right . . . well, your dad was in the army, wasn't he? That's how you got good at DIY, to help your mum out. Your brother Nick is a barrister, which means he's posh. And as an officer's son, I bet you grew up in a huge house in the country with dogs and ponies.'

'You *have* been paying attention. Though you're wrong about the house. I mainly lived in a succession of nasty barracks. Which is where I really developed my DIY skills.'

'Yes, but didn't you mention an ancestral home in Shropshire?'

'A four-bedroom Edwardian semi within

rumbling distance of the railway. Hardly a mansion.'

'I grew up in a two-bedroom house! With pebbledash!'

'OK, you win the deprived childhood prize, Emily. I'm sure your life is far more interesting than my boyhood at a *very* minor public school.'

'Ah. Public school. See? And then you went to study law, like your brother, but I bet you spent your holidays on expeditions, didn't you, to prove yourself to your distant and demanding father?'

'With my public school chums, presumably?'

'Of course! Joined some mercenaries in East Africa. Organised a few coups between rugger matches, plundered a few gold mines. Then went into hiding as a mild-mannered shopkeeper, to escape the international hitmen.'

Will sighs. 'I wish it was so glamorous.'

'Well, why else does a man give up a glorious future in the law for the dubious thrills of the hardware business?' But as I say it, I realise. A woman. It has to be about a woman. My romance novels are never wrong.

'I didn't see not becoming a barrister as a great sacrifice. Nick had to study all hours and spent what little time was left sucking up to people who could make or break his career. And I was never as clever as Nick, but I will admit that hardware was never really part of the grand plan.'

'Was it a girl?'

He blushes. 'How did you guess? Yes, there *was*

a girl. Helena. A goddess. I'd had this monstrous crush on her throughout university and she was always out of reach.'

'I thought you could charm the birds from the trees.'

'Hardly. My education prepared me for afternoon tea with dowagers and matrons, but chatting up girls my own age was beyond me. I got better at uni, that's true, but Helena was still firmly out of reach.'

'What was so special about her?' I hear the edge in my own voice and hope Will hasn't heard it too. It's crazy to get possessive after a few snogs – even snogs as life-affirming as those.

'You know, I can't actually remember,' he says, leaning over to stroke my cheek. 'I wouldn't tell you anyway. Bad form to harp on about ex-girlfriends. But Helena was indifferent to me and there's nothing like indifference to drive a man crazy with desire.'

'Ah. That's where I've been going wrong all my life.'

'Don't be silly.'

'No, seriously, I couldn't do indifference if I tried.'

Will leans back slightly, studying my face for so long that I feel faint. Though, of course, that might be the Long Island Iced Tea. 'And that's exactly what I like about you, Farrah Fawcett. Cool is overrated.'

I smile. 'Whatever. Weren't we meant to be

talking about you, and the connection between Helena and hardware?'

'OK. You know the Milk Round – when companies snap up the best final-year students? Well, one lunchtime I heard Helena talking to her friends about going to some interviews for retail management. I'd decided already that I didn't fancy law school, but I didn't know what to do instead. So, why not try retail management? At the very least, I could finally have a go at chatting her up in the waiting room. We'd have something in common.'

'You chose your career because of a girl?'

'There are worse reasons.'

'I hope it worked.'

He frowns. 'Not exactly. We did have interviews on the same day, but she blanked me. She got a job at Selfridges. I got a job at Bells & Whistles.'

'You've been there ever since university?'

'Yep. How crap am I? So much for being a mercenary. My parents lie to the neighbours about my career progression because it's non-existent. Actually, it wasn't always non-existent. The first few years, I was the golden boy.'

'And then?'

'Um. Well, if I said it was a woman again, would you think I was a total sleaze?'

I sense immediately that this woman is more important than Helena the Goddess. 'Depends.'

'Her name was Abby. *Is* Abby. She's still alive and kicking. She's very good at kicking. We met at a bonding weekend for new employees at the Banbury Sleepeasy Lodge: she was big in head office; I was the bright young graduate trainee . . . the bar was free . . . you can probably guess the rest.'

I nod. I can guess the rest, of course, and I don't like it. I suppose this nasty feeling is jealousy. I haven't felt it for years. I'd become immune when I was with Duncan: I couldn't afford to let myself be hurt over and over again.

'It should have stayed there, really. In the Banbury Sleepeasy Lodge. But it didn't. We dated, then after a couple of years, we moved in together. You can imagine the tongues wagging. Every time I got a promotion to a new store, the whispers were that I was being promoted not because of who I was, but who she was.'

'It wasn't true, was it?'

He looks hurt. 'No. I would have resigned if I thought it was. My career was going really well; I had all these cool ideas, I was marked for big things. Things on the domestic front were less good. Abby was . . . tricky. Moody. I was working too hard. She wanted to get married. I wasn't sure. She issued an ultimatum, believing I'd never dare to disobey, I was her protégé, after all. But I did disobey. I went to work one day and didn't come home.'

'Oh.'

'I'm not a bastard, Emily. I felt really awful. But I couldn't give in to emotional blackmail either.

393

Still, she got her revenge.' He nods across the common, towards the shop, with its FOR SALE sign already erected above the door.

The penny drops. 'That's why you were sent to work here?'

He nods. 'Punishment posting. She made it clear that if I went back to her, I'd be moved again. I didn't. So she stitched me up, poisoning people against me at head office until there was no chance of ever getting promoted out of Heartsease. In a funny way it helped me, knowing she was getting even. Made me feel less guilty about being a shit. And the casualty of our power games is the poor bloody shop.'

'You did your best.'

'Not good enough, though, was it?'

'You were doomed from the start. But it doesn't have to be the same if you go elsewhere, does it? So long as you avoid getting too friendly with management.' I realise that my advice has more than an element of clingy self-interest.

He smiles. 'And remember not to punch the MD? Yes, I think I've learned both those lessons. Trouble is, *all* big companies are as political as the Roman Empire. You can't avoid getting involved one way or another. You're lucky, being freelance.'

I think it over. 'Yes. I certainly prefer it to working in the bank. Though it won't be the same once Grazia and Sandie have stopped. It'll be lonely without them to moan to.'

'Well, you'll just have to recruit some *staff*, won't you? Hey, what about me? I've got the professional knowledge; I bet I'd be a whiz with a secret camera.'

'Remember what Grazia said: Charlie doesn't take men. Though in view of my recent promotion, I could try to put a word in.'

'No, on second thoughts, I've learned my lesson about mixing business with pleasure . . .' He leans over and kisses me tenderly on the lips, pulling away to finish his sentence. 'And I'm hoping that any time I spend with you, Emily, will be *one hundred per cent* pleasure.'

CHAPTER 31

EMILY

leasure. Gorgeous word, isn't it?

Bliss. That's another favourite of mine.

Oh, and then there's ecstasy. Mustn't forget ecstasy.

None of those words have featured prominently in my ten months as a single mother. Not that there isn't plenty of fun involved in living with the Fredster, alongside all the hard work. But pleasure, bliss and ecstasy are unmistakably adult experiences, and I think I was well overdue for my share.

Will lies next to me, his face soft in sleep, lit by the dawn sun filtering through the gauzy curtains in Grazia's guest suite. I'll admit this has happened with indecent haste – with the emphasis on indecent – though, mortifyingly, I can't remember all the indecent details. Alcohol is Cupid's little helper when it comes to turning unrequited lovers into the requited kind, but I wish I'd been less drunk. I feel as dehydrated as a shrunken head from South America, and it hurts to move, or even to try to put the fragments of last night back into meaningful order.

I do remember Grazia driving Sandie and Will

and me back to Rose Cottage in the open-topped sports car, the breeze deliciously tingly on my face, Will's hand lingering equally deliciously on my knee. We'd always planned a secret-shopper sleep-over for tonight: just us girls, toasting *Muse 7* and the rest before the paintings make their owner a very, very wealthy woman. Having Will along for the ride added a certain *je ne sais quoi* to the evening.

Then I remember the Sancerre coming out from Grazia's wine chiller and although I knew I was more than drunk enough already, it tasted very good. I also sensed where the evening was headed and I knew I needed to maintain levels of Dutch courage to help me get there. It's one thing accepting that being a size fourteen is not a criminal act – quite another getting your flesh out for the first time. OK, so I did happen to be wearing my lovely new sky-blue bra and pants set, but I even felt self-conscious about that. What if he thought that I'd *known* this was going to happen?

I remember Sandie and Grazia in the background, the two of them pretending there was nothing unusual about seeing Will with his arm round me, then scurrying to the kitchen to compare notes. I don't remember which of them went to bed first, though I do recall a convoluted explanation from Grazia about how the sofa bed in the living room worked. I'm sure she realised by then that one bed was going to be enough for both of us.

Alone with Will again, I remember feeling shy at first. Then less shy. Then, as if by magic, nearly naked. I don't think he noticed my matching lingerie. We stumbled towards the guest suite, me holding my clothes up against my body like an actress in a bedroom farce.

I don't remember a conversation about whether we were going to *do it* or not. By the time we were nearly naked, I suppose it was academic. *Doing it.* What am I, a teenager? But to call it *making love* entails a whole list of presumptions. So *doing it* will have to do for now. My boozy memories are of the feelings, rather than the act itself. I can't claim that I have accurate memories of the body beside me, although I have a vague recollection of impressive hardware, and a thorough knowledge of how to use it . . .

My most immediate problem is morning-after etiquette. I shimmy one centimetre at a time, hoping he won't stir. I discovered on waking that I am, in fact, stark naked under the duvet, so when I reach the edge of the bed, I make a run for it, into the guest bathroom. It's stocked with everything you need after a night of sin: dental floss, heavy-duty moisturiser, basil-scented body lotion (OK, so it makes me smell a bit like a pizza but Duncan always spouted that old joke about the perfect woman turning into a Margarita after midnight). I finish my ablutions, then slip into a silky white dressing gown.

The bathroom mirror is ridiculously flattering.

I *know* I don't look anything like this in real life. My reflection is slimmer than it should be, my eyes brighter, my cheeks rosier, my lips plumper, my hair blonder. Much as I'd like to think this look is the result of my admittedly satisfying night of passion, I know it's more to do with the built-in backlight. I must find out where she bought it. I could do with believing I am this gorgeous every morning: maybe I could install one in the Lime Village flat.

I creep back into bed. It's not quite six o'clock, so I have another couple of hours to admire my sleeping partner, and to ponder the complications of dating Will. Though admittedly it's a little late for dates.

Under the duvet again, I feel the heat of his limbs just millimetres away from me and though I'm not sure I do want him to wake up – what if he's horrified to find me here with him? – the desire to feel his body next to mine is too great. It's not lust. Well, not entirely. It's a hunger for skin.

Not that I plan to take a bite out of him for breakfast or anything.

Tentatively, I shift my leg towards his. Oooh. Yes, that's it. *That*'s what I've been missing. Freddie has, of course, the most scrumptious legs in the world, but these are different. Muscly. Hairy. Attached to a man . . .

No sign of waking from my lover (now why does that word make me want to laugh?) so I wiggle myself closer. Arms, now. My arm sits alongside his and the warmth does things to my nerve endings that Duncan never managed to do with his entire erotic repertoire.

Now, that's lovely. Enough. Really, it's fine for at least two minutes. But now I feel impatient again. Never mind the embarrassment factor. I want this man awake. I want this man.

'Will.' I mouth his name, wondering whether my breath on his face will be enough. Nothing.

'Will.' Audible this time, but still a whisper. God, he sleeps soundly. Duncan was a fussy sleeper, demanding complete silence and blackout curtains.

'Wi-ill.' Now I sound like a sulky child trying to tempt a lazy chum out to play. 'Wakey wakey!'

I am beginning to wonder whether he's slipped into a coma, when in one big movement he rolls over on top of me.

'Now, why on *earth* would you want to wake a sleeping giant so early in the morning?'

'I can't think,' I say, though it's a struggle to say anything with his weight squashing me into the mattress.

'You're sure you don't have anything *particular* in mind?' His voice is teasing, his lips touching my ear.

'No.'

He keeps very, very still and it's more than I can bear. I'm just about to spell out in no uncertain terms why I was so keen to wake him up – it's too late to be coy – when his face breaks into the wonderful schoolboy grin.

'I've just thought of something!'

And then he disappears below the bedclothes and I feel a blush spreading, tingle by tingle, from my forehead downwards . . .

Eight thirty, and dragging myself from that bed is a monumental act of will. But sunshine floodlights the room, telling me it's time for me to revert to mummy mode. Nearly fourteen hours of non-maternal bliss with this man has been more therapeutic than a fortnight in the Caribbean, but all good things must come to an end.

'Why?' he asks, when I explain.

'You *know* why.' I try to sound more certain than I am.

'Shall I come over later? After the big showdown?'

I ignore the instinct to scream 'YES, YES, YES!' Instead I say, 'We ought to take things steadily, don't you think?'

He sits up in bed, dishevelled from sleep and, um, other activities, and I have to use all my resolve not to climb back in. 'If we'd just picked each other up from some seedy club, rutted like deer all night and now had nothing to say to each other, I'd agree. But we're friends, Emily. We know each other too well to pretend to play it cool.'

'I thought you said that was the secret. Indifference. Playing it cool.'

'Did I? Well, that was *before*. Now it's *after*. Makes all the difference. Come on. Come back to bed.'

'I need to be back before Duncan. You know that.'

Will groans. 'Ah, life's a bitch when your girl-friend's married.' He pushes himself up in bed and reaches across to me, parting my dressing gown and kissing my navel. It's never quite popped back into place after my pregnancy, though Will doesn't seem to mind. 'But my considered view from here is that the benefits definitely outweigh the disadvantages.'

I tap him on the head. 'I hope you're not trying to lead me astray.'

'Now that I have no job, I see leading you astray as my raison d'être.'

Finally I manage to drag myself away to the bathroom to dress, and from there into the kitchen, where Grazia is prompting the espresso machine into life. She's dressed in hotpants and a turquoise Pucci-print top, and I realise it's the first time I've seen her wear colours other than black, white and red.

'So?' She's tactful enough not to look me in the eyes.

'So far . . .' I say, as though my silly grin hadn't already given me away. 'So good.'

A lazy smile spreads across her face. 'Splendid! I am delighted. I have always thought our William Powell would make a better husband than store manager.'

402

'Husband?' I blush, because of course, I have entertained that fantasy at least seven times already overnight. 'Don't be daft. And anyway, he was a very good store manager. He was just unlucky with the store.'

'Already sticking up for him?' She does something clever with coffee grounds and the steam nozzle and passes me a cup of strong coffee, plus a croissant. 'Here. You need to be sharp as a tack for tackling that current husband of yours. And as, by the sight of you, you have lacked for sleep, you must make up for it with caffeine.' She gives me a lascivious wink.

'Do I really look that bad?' I take a bite of the croissant, and then another, and another. I seem to be quite peckish this morning.

'Not bad,' comes a voice from behind me. 'Anything but bad.'

I turn to see Will, adorable in rumpled clothes. 'I hope I look tidier than you do.'

'Tidier, yes,' says Grazia, 'but unmistakably a woman who has enjoyed a night on the tiles.'

Will and I are both blushing now. 'Let's just hope Duncan lacks a woman's intuition,' I say, 'otherwise I am in big trouble.'

'I find baby-pink lipstick is perfect for suggesting innocence,' Grazia says, pulling out a cutlery drawer filled not with knives and forks, but make-up. She tosses me a couple of lipsticks. 'Not surprisingly, it never suited me.'

'Thanks.'

'Now, can I give you a lift to the station?'

Will winks at me, then looks away.

'No, that's all right, Grazia. I'd prefer to walk; it's such a lovely morning. Maybe the fresh air will erase the signs of my wanton behaviour.'

Grazia raises an eyebrow. 'Maybe. But when you see that husband of yours, do not forget that there is no reason on earth why you should not have a lover. He was the one who deserted you. Keep that thought in your head.'

'Ye-es.' Except I know Duncan will never, ever be able to accept that his Chubster has a lover. Any more than he'll be able to live with the fact that I've stitched him up over the flats. I shiver, though the room is warm as toast.

Outside, the day is so bright I feel more exposed than I did in bed, but Will seems to sense my unease and holds my hand tightly, matching my walking pace step by step. We spot only one car on the entire walk to the station. Beechford is still sleeping. It feels like the day belongs to the two of us.

The next train isn't due for twenty minutes, so we climb the footbridge and look down the tracks towards London. Well, in between a few more show-stopping kisses.

'I saw *Brief Encounter* on TV a few weeks ago,' I say, when we take a brief snog-break. 'This station is exactly like the one in the film.'

'Oh dear. Doesn't bode very well for us, does it? He strikes an anguished pose, hand to forehead. '*This misery can't last . . .*'

'I thought it was lovely.'

'Emily! I didn't realise you were a doom-and-gloom romantic.'

'I liked the intensity.'

He pulls me towards him. 'Ah, well, intensity is something I think I can provide.'

I surrender to yet another kiss, hearing nothing but birds twittering in our honour overhead and . . .

'Will,' I pull away. 'Can you hear crying?'

'No!' He laughs. 'Oh, you really have bought into that whole doomed love idea.'

'I can definitely hear it. It even sounds like . . .' I shake my head at my own stupidity. 'It must be guilt, because it sounds exactly like Freddie.'

Will smiles indulgently, but just as he bends his head for yet another kiss, his face changes. 'Actually, I can hear crying too.'

We look around, then down, as the cries are joined by footsteps.

'Oh, fuck.'

Coming up the stairs, only just managing to hold onto our wriggling, howling son, is my husband.

'You cow,' he pants, sweat staining the T-shirt around his belly button. 'You conniving, cheating, evil . . .'

'Duncan! Please. Not in front of Freddie.'

At this point, my son turns his head and sees me. His face registers confusion, then delight. 'Mummeeee!'

'Freddie!' Despite the horrible situation, I'm thrilled to hear his second word.

He reaches out those chubby arms. 'Mummeee!' Then his head shifts slightly and he spots Will. 'Willeeeeee!'

Oh God. And his third.

Duncan's face freezes, mouth wide open. I keep expecting Will to back away, but he doesn't. Part of me feels relieved, though part of me wishes he would scoot.

'Not in front of Freddie?' Duncan laughs nastily. 'Seems to me someone has been doing plenty *in front of Freddie*. How long exactly before my son starts calling this bloke Daddy?'

'I promise you, that is not going to happen,' Will says calmly.

'Oh, well, that's OK then.' Duncan spits out his words. 'Because I'm really going to believe the promises of some posh wanker who is screwing my wife.'

I hope to God that Will doesn't make the mistake of saying that it's only happened once, because I don't think that's going to help.

Duncan takes the silence as all the evidence he needs. 'You tart,' he hisses. 'You manipulative cow. All those guilt trips, all that "poor little me" whinging and all the time you were getting busy with your own bit on the side.'

Freddie looks anxious, but Duncan seems to have a firm grip on him. And at least while he holds the baby, he doesn't have a free hand to punch Will. Duncan's not a violent man – well, unless you count a few scraps at school – but I don't think he's ever been pushed this far before.

'I know you're angry, Duncan, but I'm not sure this is the place to discuss it.'

'No? Where would you suggest? Your newly refurbished flat, maybe?'

My jaw drops. 'How . . . ?'

Duncan sneers. 'If you're going to try to stitch someone up. Emily dear, do it properly. I'd have changed the locks, at least, if it had been me.'

'I wasn't trying to stitch you up. I was just trying to get what I deserve.'

'My heart bleeds for you, it really does. What's she told you, eh, mate? That her hubby's a hooligan? Or a wife-beater, maybe?'

Will still doesn't move. 'No.'

'Oh. Come on. There must have been some sob story, knowing *my* Emily. She tells a bloody good tale.'

'The only concerns she's shared with me are about her financial security after the divorce. And about ensuring that you still have a role in Freddie's life.'

I wish I could warn Will that being reasonable doesn't work with Duncan.

'So that's it. I'm the absent father, some heartless bastard who couldn't care less about his son. That'll be why I got up first thing this morning to come to London and surprise Mummy, eh, Freddie? I was making the effort. Thought that just because we'd split up didn't mean we couldn't do things as a family. Promised Freddie a trip to the zoo.'

Freddie stops wriggling when he hears the word 'zoo'.

'I took him to the zoo already. On his birthday.'

'What, playing happy families with your Old Etonian?'

'Oh, is that the best insult you can come up with?' Will says. Duncan's eyes narrow to ruthless slits. He lets Freddie elbow his way out of his arms, and my little boy runs towards me and hugs my legs.

'Zoo-ee?' That'll be a fourth word. Go on, Fredster. Say Daddy. Say *Daddy*.

'Some of us are more into actions than fucking words,' Duncan mutters, his voice low so Freddie won't hear. He takes a step closer to Will, and has to stand on tiptoes to look into his eyes. But the height difference doesn't seem to scare Duncan off: if anything, it seems to fuel his anger.

'Duncan, please don't—'

When he turns to me, that familiar charming smirk is twisted by hatred. He looks like his father, bitter and cruel. 'You had it all planned, didn't you? Do up your little love nest, rob me blind in the divorce settlement, forget I ever existed and make sure my son does too? Shame I found your lover's address at the flat. Otherwise I'd be none the bloody wiser.'

I consider whether explaining that Duncan doesn't live in Beechford would help, but decide against it. 'It's not like that, Duncan.'

Duncan ignores me. 'Nice place you got back

408

there, posh boy. Though you could at least have given your girlfriend a ride home in that sports car, instead of ditching her at the station. Hey, Em. Maybe he's not the One. Sorry, but it's better to know. eh?'

He takes another step closer to Will, who is refusing to give ground. The height disparity becomes more obvious with every step.

'Look, Duncan, this isn't what it seems. Will and I are friends. He's been having a bad time – his business closed down yesterday – and I came to support him. Not alone. Lots of us.'

'A fucking orgy? That's meant to make me feel better?'

'No, not an orgy. A party. We had too much to drink.' I plead with my eyes. 'Way too much to drink. So, yes, things happened that shouldn't have happened. I've been lonely, Duncan.'

'You've got Freddie.'

Duncan's stopped foaming at the mouth, so I carry on. 'Yes. I know. He's the most important person in all of this.'

'Glad you realise that,' he says smugly. 'Because you know *this* changes everything. I mean, nothing comes for free in this life, does it? Getting drunk and sleeping around – it's not what I expect from my son's mother. I warned you before, I knew London was the wrong place for you. And I meant it, about getting the lawyers in. About fighting you if you insist on putting yourself first.'

'You *hypocrite*. How dare you talk to her like that.' Will jabs his finger towards Duncan, and rage fires up again in my husband's eyes.

'Will, this isn't your battle to fight. Please, can you go? It'll make things easier.'

His face registers pure hurt. 'I don't want to leave you with your little thug of a husband.'

It's the 'little' that does it. 'Don't you fucking well call me names, you bastard.'

'Duncan, stop it. *Please.*' I step forward, between them. 'There's nothing for you to get angry about. One mistake. We're all allowed one mistake, aren't we?'

'Mistake? You're saying that this . . . you two getting it together,' Duncan waves at Will, 'is a one-off? Nothing more?'

I close my eyes, try to think straight, and quickly. I don't seriously think he'll do Will any damage. That's not the problem. The problem is that Duncan bears grudges. If he believes that Will means something to me, he'll do everything he can to ruin my life – including trying to get custody of Freddie, just to spite me.

'Emily? I'm waiting.'

I keep my eyes shut, blocking out the world. Time for choices, Emily. Last night wasn't reality. It was very nice . . . OK, it was blissful. But I decided weeks ago that there's only room for one man in my life and that's Freddie. He's my priority, isn't he?

'It was a one-off, Duncan,' I whisper, not looking

at Will. 'I'd never do anything that might upset Freddie. He knows who his daddy is.'

Out of the corner of my eye, I see Will's shoulders slump. I'll ring him. I'll explain. *I'm sorry.* He'll understand, won't he? He's the most understanding man I've ever met. And he must have known that my life is too complicated already.

'So you're not going to see this wanker again? You promise?'

Will is backing away.

'I promise not to do anything to put your relationship with your son at risk, Duncan.'

'Not what I asked, Em. Try again.'

'I won't see Will again.'

Duncan sniggers. 'Hear that, wanker? Off you trot. Think of it as a lucky escape, eh? You don't wanna get involved with a single mum, anyway. Especially one like Em. Far more trouble than she's worth, take it from me!'

Will turns around, his eyes pleading with me. 'Emily, you can't let him dictate your life like this . . .'

'This is how it's got to be.' My voice is robotic. 'I'm sorry. Really, I am.'

He hesitates for a second more, then nods and walks very slowly along the bridge, just as the train to London pulls into the station.

'My train,' I say weakly to Duncan.

'Ah, bollocks to that,' he replies. 'We're playing happy families, aren't we? For Freddie's sake. So you're coming back in the car with me.'

I watch the train doors open. No one gets in or out, the doors close again and the train moves away, disappearing into the distance.

'Byeee,' says Freddie. Whether to the train or Will, I don't know.

This misery can't last.

But I'm not Celia Johnson. I'm Emily Prince. I'll get home, I'll apologise to Will, I'll focus on my son and my business and my London life. Everything will be all right.

Won't it?

AUGUST – THOSE LAZY, HAZY DAYS OF SUMMER

While your customers laze on a beach, it's time to get busy instore. Take stock of staffing and strategy before the Back to School promotions begin in the second week of August.

CHAPTER 32

09.57: GRAZIA

You can lead a horse to water but you cannot make it drink.

So Emily has love presented to her on a plate – William is quite perfect for her – yet she turns her back on him to satisfy the demands of a man who, on the evidence I have heard, never actually loved her. She is giving up everything: William, London, secret shopping. There is nothing so frustrating as watching someone waste opportunities.

Still. Am I really one to talk? For so long I turned my back on life, in tribute to a dead person who made no effort to understand me when he was alive. I was an accessory, a mirror for his brilliance. Yet I know I would not have listened to anyone, any more than Emily will listen to me. By the time she realises what she has lost, Will is bound to be long gone. Though she is young. There will be others.

But if I cannot rescue one of my shopping angels, I must work harder to save the other. I am no fairy godmother, but I am grateful. Something about our hours together triggered this most necessary change in me.

415

Planning the downfall of that witch of a shop assistant has been a pleasant diversion, a break from the painful preparations for tomorrow's auction. I cancelled Selina's visit to Rose Cottage three times before I finally allowed her to unlock the studio. I stood behind her, like a little girl scared of the dark.

The smell hit me first: paint, turpentine, the patchouli Leon burned to cover the heavy stench of weed he smoked in defiance of the fire risk. The dust made Selina cough as we stepped inside, but otherwise it was exactly as it had always been. Messy, chaotic, as though my husband could appear at any moment from behind the canvas with a cry of triumph or despair, depending on how his latest project was progressing.

As I stood there, Selina raced around like a contestant in *Supermarket Sweep*, greeting every new discovery – a discarded palette, a notebook of sketches so incomplete Leon would not even have called them doodles – with greedy pleasure. In the end, I left her in the studio to choose whatever she felt would interest collectors.

Others will appreciate you more now, Leon. I have my memories and they are enough, Although I have kept one picture, a traditional landscape, painted at night from Hungerford Bridge, astonishingly vivid for a watercolour. Oh, in those days, it all felt brand new. Do you remember how that was?

I hope you might be there, that somewhere, you do remember.

So I left Selina and her workmen to load a van with the contents of the studio, and I travelled to London to observe the witch of Garnett's. I dressed down, hid behind displays as she smarmed around the richest customers and barked at her assistants. I did not like her, but I understood her. I recognised the paranoid insecurity of a girl who knows she has limited talent and must make the best use of those rather cheap good looks before they turn sour. Sometimes, as Emily says, it *takes one to know one.*

I would almost pity her, if it was not for her behaviour towards Sandie. Destroying someone out of jealousy is wicked. She deserves to find out how wicked. But girls like that have raw cunning and no conscience (I should know, though I was never motivated by malice, only fear). So revealing the truth is never going to be as simple as appealing to her non-existent better nature. Stalking her in case she does something out-rageous on camera is equally unlikely to produce results. I have taken my time to formulate a plan, but I believe it has as good a chance of succeeding as any.

However, an element of luck will be required, as is the case with everything in life.

'Sandie, you are at leisure until I call you. It will be at least four hours, but I need you nearby. Go

417

shopping, perhaps? If all goes to plan, you should be welcome in the store again by this afternoon, but it would be as well to put on the beret when I call you back, so the security guards do not recognise you.'

Sandie nods passively. I have gone to some lengths to help her, yet she shows no gratitude. I believe she is rather numbed by the prospect of returning home.

'And you, Emily, are coming with me. Your clothing is not too uncomfortable, I hope?'

'It's fine,' she mumbles. I have dressed her in ill-fitting designer black, hand-picked from my own collection, so she looks like a dominatrix whose clothes have shrunk in the wash. She also wears a dark wig that only emphasises why baby-blond hair suits her girlish face. Overall, she looks awkward and diffident. Perfect. This is for the greater good.

'Ready?'

'Ready to respond to your every whim, boss.'

10.07: Emily

Déjà vu. Back at Garnett's and back down in the bloody dumps. I'm only here because I don't want to let Sandie down: it's the first time this week I've bothered to get up before midday, despite Freddie's determined prodding and jumping on my head.

This is my secret shopping swansong. Another

418

failed experiment in the life of country bumpkin and renowned village idiot Emily Prince. The Little Mermaid is going home. Well, what choice did I have? The letter from Duncan's solicitor arrived on Tuesday, and its contents made my options crystal clear. Stay on in London and try to fight Duncan and a load of clever lawyers for custody of a child he barely knows? Or return to Somerset, like everyone wants me to, with baby-sitters on tap, a ready-made circle of old friends, and an adequate allowance from my ex-husband? I don't even need to arrange removals: the Old Devils Carnival Club are coming to my rescue on Saturday afternoon. Duncan organised it all the instant I said yes: he didn't want to give me a chance to change my mind.

It's so easy, isn't it? All I need to do is forget about Will, forget about the show-stopping kisses and the accompanying glimpse of a different life. Did I say glimpse? Better to think of it as a mirage. That life could never have been mine. Could I really have paid the bills with just the secret shopping income? Duncan would have no qualms about pulling the plug on the maintenance. OK, he'd have to pay up in the end, but by the time the CSA could drag him back from Switzerland and into court, I'd be broke. And anyway, how long would it take for Will to find someone sexier, someone unencumbered by a small child and the overactive imagination that's got me into such trouble over the years?

Oh, if only I could switch that imagination off, because it keeps conjuring up pictures of life with Will. But that life is for another Emily, a braver version of me.

'Excuse me!'

A woman shopper pushes past, and I realise I am standing right in front of the escalator. I have to concentrate. There's a job to be done and I will do it, without getting sidetracked by the trivial tragedies of my life.

The store looks very different from how it did at Christmas: less fairytale kitsch, more clean lines and well-honed retail space. Though I guess I also see it differently, with the newfound skills that will be pretty redundant in the local shops back home. As the escalator carries me up, I survey the shop floor and feel a fleeting admiration for the cool efficiency of Garnett's. The doors opened only minutes ago, yet already people are being relieved of their cash.

I reach the Style Floor and head for Personal Shopping. There's a very young assistant at the reception, her auburn hair tucked into a French plait in an unsuccessful attempt to make her look older. I explain that my boss has an appointment booked with Marsha in half an hour but I need to see Marsha beforehand. She winces.

'Are you sure? Only generally she's not keen to be disturbed before ten thirty.'

'Oh God, she sounds like *my* boss,' I say. 'But I daren't let her arrive here unless everything's just so. Could be my job on the line. And she knows the management here so it could be *yours* too.'

The assistant weighs it up and sighs. 'And your name is?'

'Don't worry about mine. It's my boss's name you need to worry about. Grazia?'

'Grazia who?'

I feign surprise. 'I'm amazed you haven't heard of her. She's so well known that she never uses her surname. *Don't* ask for it, whatever you do.'

The assistant scurries off and I feel a bit sorry for her. But then I remember that if this goes according to plan, she won't have to suffer bullying at the hands of Mad Marsha for much longer.

Grazia's too-large stilettos have blistered my heels. There's a mirror behind the reception desk and I try to straighten my wig. Sandie was certain that Marsha wouldn't remember me from Christmas – 'she only ever notices eligible bachelors' – but I feel nervous all the same. The purr of the bag-cam settles me a little: I am on duty. All I need to do is follow the script, as I have so many times before.

After a minute or two Marsha appears, all pouty lips and push-up bra. Her face sends a shiver of recognition down my spine but she doesn't realise we've met before. Her blond hair is not quite coiffed and her mascara has black splodges in the corner of her eyes. Clearly it takes her a while in the morning to prepare for her *public*.

'Hullo,' I say, as meek as I can manage. 'I'm Grazia's PA. She's booked in for half past but I always come ahead to check everything will be to her liking.'

'There really is no need,' she whines. 'We do know what we're doing.'

'But I'd like to inspect the changing room even so. You got the list? San Pellegrino, kiwi fruit *only* in the fruit bowl, and only ripe ones that give when pressed gently with the thumb? Definitely no bananas. A selection of magazines including American *Vogue* and Italian *Vanity Fair?*'

Marsha's eyebrows rise two centimetres and I study her forehead. Unlike last time, I can see worry lines. Must be the stress of her promotion. 'Bloody hell, who does your boss think she is?'

'The MD of Italy's premier model agency. With a new office just opened in Covent Garden, *that's* who,' I say, hoping I haven't overdone it.

'Oh.' She looks momentarily flummoxed, then turns to her assistant. 'Why didn't you tell me?'

'But I tried to—'

'Evidently not hard enough. Right. Find that list and get to the food hall. Go on, move.'

'Do you mean no one's got any of it ready?' I whisper. 'Only Grazia really can be awfully . . . short-tempered.'

She shoots me a withering look. 'Stop having kittens; it'll be fine.'

10.43 Grazia

I time my arrival exactly. Late, but not too late. Grazia the model agency boss would have no compunction about keeping people waiting, but would be too busy to allow her schedule to slip. People to see; calls to make.

I stride towards Personal Shopping in my highest black boots, and spot Marsha immediately. She is shouting at one of the store assistants. So we have her nicely rattled already – precisely how I wanted her.

'Where is the hopeless girl?' I demand, thickening my Milan accent as I step up to the reception desk. 'Never around when I want her.'

Before Marsha can reply, Emily appears from the changing room, a large vase of lilies in her arms. The bright orange pollen has covered my black suit. Never mind. After tomorrow's auction, I will be able to afford a new one from petty cash.

'So sorry, Grazia, I was just moving the flowers, I know you hate the smell.'

'Look at you! Your suit is orange. You will have to change.'

Emily does a convincing job of looking devastated. 'But, Grazia, I don't have a spare jacket.'

'Buy one! That jacket makes you look obese, in any case.' I turn to Marsha. 'I had heard this expression before in English: *cannot get the staff.* It is only since I have worked in your country that I fully understand what it means.'

Marsha pauses for a moment, considering this. Her prettiness doesn't bear close scrutiny: the lips are too uneven, the eyes a touch too beady. She looks me up and down and I see an icy glint of recognition in her face. 'Quite. I do sympathise. But I am confident that you won't experience any such frustrations this morning. I *am* the best in my business. If that doesn't sound arrogant?'

We exchange smiles of mutual admiration. 'I like to think I can tell the difference between arrogance and confidence.'

She nods, accepting the compliment. 'Follow me.'

11.14: Emily

I wait outside the fitting room, like Grazia's bouncer. The French-plaited assistant and I share sympathetic looks whenever our respective 'bosses' bark another instruction from inside, sending one or other of us scuttling off to meet their demands. But Marsha's compliments to Grazia flow like honey, becoming sweeter by the minute.

I hope she's going to get what she deserves.

The assistant brings outfit after outfit, each bearing a more audacious price tag. It seems an awful lot of money to spend on black trousers, black skirts and black jackets. How strange that this is the life I dreamed I'd have when I came to London: sales people pandering to my every whim. Yet even if I could afford it,

I don't think I could ever get used to the syco-phancy. And tipping makes me squirm with embarrassment.

'EMILY!'

I head into the changing room, where Grazia stands in her La Perla undies, looking in far better shape than I do. What did Will think, I wonder, when he saw me naked? I suppose I will never know. I've tried to call him, to explain, but he doesn't pick up.

'Stop daydreaming, girl. Have you chased up the arrangements for Naomi's shoot in Brazil? I do not want a repeat of the Fiji fiasco.'

'Um . . .' I stare at my feet, as we rehearsed earlier. Marsha ostentatiously rearranges the clothes on the rail, but can't help sneaking a look at me as Grazia tears me to pieces.

'Idiot girl! You have forgotten?'

'I—'

'Out with it. You have forgotten, yes or no?'

'Yes. I'm sorry, Grazia. Truly sorry. Won't happen again. It's just I have had so much to do lately, with the basement flood and the San Francisco trip and—'

'Enough, enough! Your excuses are nothing to me. Nothing. And so are you. Personal assistant, ha! You would be lucky to find job as cleaning toilets. Finito! You are fired, Emily. I should have done this months ago.'

Marsha is staring openly now, so I can't get away with a half-hearted performance. 'But Grazia,

I *need* this job. You know about my debts. And what about San Francisco? You can't go on your own. You'll never manage.'

'Ha! I will manage better on my own. I will have accounts send you your salary till the end of the week.'

'But it's Thursday already.'

'Yes,' says Grazia, apparently relishing her role. 'See how generous I am! Now go before I have my friend Marsha here call security to get you out of my sight.'

I shoot her what I hope is a convincing puppy-dog look of wounded innocence, and run from the room. But not before checking out Marsha's reaction. Her mouth is open but her eyes are wide with admiration for Grazia's management techniques.

'Uh, these girls,' I hear Grazia say when I am halfway out the door. 'Where will I ever find one I can rely on?'

12.11: Grazia

I am a fast worker. In a little under ninety minutes, I have purchased £2,200 worth of clothes (though I will return every stitch before the day is out – black, I will tell customer services, is so ageing). I have sacked my personal assistant. And I have found myself the perfect candidate for her replacement.

'I will come right to the point,' I say, moments after ordering our lunch. I have taken Marsha to

426

a discreet starched-napkin-and-Waterford-Crystal place off New Bond Street. I like that I am potentially killing two birds with one stone: entrapping Marsha whilst secret shopping. The place also has the advantage of no background music, and very little chatter: perfect for recording a conversation on my hidden camera. 'I have concluded from recent experience – three personal assistants in as many months – that I am recruiting the wrong calibre of employee.'

'The right people are very difficult to find,' she agrees. 'One has to be ruthless when one is dealing with staff.'

'Ruthless. Yes. Interesting choice of word.' I pause meaningfully.

'You think?' she parries.

I play with the bread on my plate. 'Let me tell you something. I believe I have been looking in the wrong places for assistants. Of course, the bottom line has to be profit, but perhaps I have been trying to achieve results on the cheap. In Milan, one can find talented young women willing to learn for a pittance. Not here, it seems. In London, as in wine, cheap can be a false economy.'

The maître d' brings two glasses of Barolo.

'Yes,' says Marsha.

'I am going to replace the personal assistant position with a manager role. I am impetuous, but I also have good instincts, so think carefully about what I am about to say. I wonder if you might be the woman for the job, Marsha.'

She does not look surprised. I should hope not. I have been dropping hints for the last hour. 'Go on.'

'What I require is someone with fashion sense, ambition, supreme organisational skills and . . . well, you said it yourself. Someone with a certain *ruthlessness*.'

'And what makes you think I might meet your requirements?' she says, circling her finger round the top of her wine glass in a parody of seduction. 'Or that I would be interested in demotion?'

'Oh, I do not think this would count as demotion. Does your current role involve international travel each month? Control of a six-figure entertainment budget? Five-star hotels? Not to mention invitations to more parties than one person could ever attend?'

She maintains a poker face. 'I have worked hard to reach my position. Very hard.'

'Exactly as I would expect. I do plan, of course, to try other routes, but frankly the recruitment agencies I have used have left me very disappointed. When one sees what one wants, it is the act of a fool not to seize the day. If I have offended you, so be it.'

'I didn't say you'd offended me,' she says, as a waiter arrives with two rocket and parmesan salads.

'Good. So, Marsha, how hungry are you?'

'I'm sure this will be plenty . . .'

'No. I mean, how hungry are you for success?'

'Oh!' She blushes coquettishly. I have to work hard to contain the desire to slap her. 'Extremely.'

'So if I asked you . . . I don't know, to dose a rival model's coffee with laxatives at a casting, you would?'

She laughs. 'I thought they were all on laxatives anyway.'

I don't smile. 'Yes, but they do not generally take them immediately before they meet art directors.'

'Oh! I see. Right. Well, I suppose if it makes a difference to our girl getting the gig, then, yes. All's fair in love and modelling.'

I stare at her for some time before nodding. 'Good. What about spying? How do you feel about spying?'

'On rivals?'

'Yes, rivals. Or our own girls, to check they're keeping to their diets or not moonlighting or threatening to defect to other agencies.'

Marsha shrugs. 'I don't have a problem with that. If it's in the interests of the business.'

Our salads are untouched. I lean forward. 'I once tampered with the heel of a rival model's shoe. My client needed a break. So the rival got one.'

Her eyes widen with delighted horror. 'She broke her leg?'

'Sprained her ankle. But the effect was the same. Being part of the Grazia *family* means complete loyalty. Although . . .'

'Yes?'

'Imagine a situation where you have to choose. Between Grazia and yourself. Which do you choose? Who comes first?'

The waiter returns, moves our salads to the side and puts down two plates of buttery saffron capellini – angel hair pasta, my favourite. But I do not touch it.

'What a strange question. Are you playing games with me?'

It feels as though my blood has frozen in my veins. She cannot have guessed, surely.

'No games. I value honesty.' I force my voice to be light.

'Honesty.' She takes a sip of water, followed by one of wine.

'Yes.' My hands are so tight I am surprised I do not shatter the stem of my glass when I lift it.

'If I came to work for you, I would do my best, that goes without saying, but to ask me to put myself second . . . well, I don't think that's realistic. It isn't how I operate. Sorry.'

I clap my hands together, three cool claps of acknowledgement. 'Bravo, Marsha! I always ask this, as a test. Only idiots promise total loyalty. The last three girls were idiots.' I nod towards the pasta, giving her permission to begin. She cuts the pasta into small strips – what a graceless creature – and when she takes a mouthful, I go for the kill. 'Now prove it.'

She looks up, unable to answer while chewing, as I knew she would be. I continue.

'Marsha, I have revealed my modus operandi, my unique approach to morality. I have done this quite deliberately, to prove my intent. But it does leave me exposed. As an act of faith, I would appreciate it if you could do the same. Prove you are the right person.'

I focus on my food, but although this is the very best pasta in London, I have little appetite. All my buttering up has been leading to this moment. My real-life experience of the ruthless business world is restricted to watching American dramas and reading airport novels. The art world does its deals behind closed doors: muses are not part of the process. Do ruthless people have lunches like this? Is Marsha about to push her pasta away with a nasty laugh, scoff at my melodramatic acting, tell me she was not fooled for one moment, but thank me for buying her lunch?

I am gambling on the assumption that she has no more experience of the corporate world than I do.

'Prove myself, how?'

'What have *you* done, Marsha? Our worlds are different, but I cannot believe you have risen to your position – and are set, I am sure, to rise further – without behaving in a way that some may see as . . . distasteful, but that you saw as simply necessary.'

She sets down her fork, eyeballs me. 'I can't imagine what you mean.'

I must not waver. I saw something in her eyes

there. This is a game of dare. 'Fine. We are wasting one another's time. Feel free to finish your lunch. I have business to attend to elsewhere.'

But as I click my fingers for the waiter, she relents.

'OK. Your way, then. What about something that is in both the interests of the company *and* my career?'

'A good combination,' I say. 'Continue.'

'There was this manager,' she begins, and I keep my fingers crossed under the table, 'my boss, I suppose, though she had no right to be. Smug bitch. Did everything by the book. Grazia, you're a free spirit. You can imagine how frustrating that was.'

'Indeed.'

'She was jealous and chippy. Envied me my looks, the attention I got from men. So she bullied me, endlessly. Didn't recognise my selling skills, seemed to think we were running a charity, not a business.'

'How old-fashioned.'

'Exactly!' Her smile is chilling. 'She was also allergic to fun, and resented anyone who had it. Oh, and poisoned the big boss against me. It was more than anyone could take.'

'Power without ability often breeds insecurity. So what did you do?'

'Let's just say I found a way to *help* management see that she was a liability rather than an asset.' Marsha seems to think this is enough.

'If she was so poor at her job, how do you know it was your actions that ensured her exit?'

'Oh, I know. I made it clear how much she was costing us.'

I sigh impatiently. 'I do not have time for riddles, Marsha. What did you do?'

She pouts. 'I was coming to that. A sum of money found its way into her locker. Shops will tolerate just about anything except hands in the till. It was rather neat. I must admit. I got the idea watching a news item about identity theft. Well, if Sandie was stupid enough to leave her old post in the staffroom rubbish bin, then it was her lookout, wasn't it?'

'Identity theft? Tell me more.'

'I picked up envelopes, addressed to her. Then I worked out how much I thought she was costing us in lost sales each day – natural justice, you see – and popped it into the envelope. Wearing gloves, just in case, but as it turned out, that wasn't necessary. Then all I had to do was *borrow* her locker key and hide the money inside. Goodbye Little Miss Perfect.'

'Ingenious,' I say. 'So how did they discover the envelope?'

She giggles. 'Oh, I'd forgotten that bit. I used the suggestions box that Sandie herself had set up. Hoist by her own petard!'

'You really are very, very devious, aren't you, Marsha?'

She casts her eyes down flirtatiously. 'Why, thank you.'

'It's a rush, is it not? Stitching people up.'

'Uh-huh,' she says. Then she frowns. 'Actually, between you and me, I rather miss Sandie. In a strange way. Life is so much more interesting with someone to *hate*.'

I look at Marsha, sweet-faced, hard-nosed, and I pity her. But it only lasts a second. 'Oh, I am sure that if you stick with me, there will be plenty of people to hate before long. The job is yours.'

'Oooh!' she says. 'And I thought today would be just another boring Thursday.'

'Apparently not. I will have a formal offer hand-delivered to you by this afternoon. Provide me with your latest payslip: whatever you are getting now, I shall pay you five hundred pounds more per month during your trial period. We will review this after three months. Obviously I would like an immediate start. I take it your passport is up to date?'

She nods, speechless with excitement.

'Excellent. Make no mistake, Marsha. With me, you are going places. Going places you would *never* expect. Now, shall we head back to Garnett's together? I have some final business in customer services. And you need to hand in your notice.'

CHAPTER 33

SANDIE

How do shoplifters do it?

I am completely innocent of any crime, yet as I pull open the heavy doors that lead into the perfume department at Garnett's, it feels as though a big red cartoon arrow is suspended above my head. *Look! It's her! Hands-in-the-till girl!*

I walk briskly, eyes down, in case I see someone I know. Instead of faces, I spot familiar bodies. The matronly bulk of Marie on the Lancome counter. The skeletal frames of Louise and Toni from Bliss. Camp Callum's delicate hands as he rearranges the spot-lit display of Crème de la Mer.

The lifts feel too risky, with no escape route if I'm recognised. Instead I take the stairs, and let the buzz of being back hit home. Maybe it's the smell of beeswax on the wooden banisters, or the familiar sound of my sensible heels against the stone steps. I'm in civvies, but I might as well be in uniform: mid-calf skirt, white blouse, court shoes. Below the beret disguise, my hair is neater than it has been in months. I sprayed light, floral Anaïs Anaïs – the scent of innocents and au pairs – on my

435

wrists at the perfume counter in Selfridges during my long wait for Grazia's call. And around my neck . . . the garnet necklace Toby gave me last year. Why on earth did I put it on? It hardly brought me good luck before, did it?

I pull at the fine gold chain, feeling ridiculous, but it refuses to snap, so I have to unclasp it and stuff it into my skirt pocket. *Some people will never learn*, eh, Gramma?

Puffed from five flights of stairs, I reach the landing leading to the management floor, with its polite varnished signpost informing customers that the next level is Staff Only. I ignore it, but once I get to the top, I see the keypad locking the door. What was the code again?

It won't come back to me, but then I hold my hand up in front of it and my fingers instinctively push four keys. The door buzzes open and I step inside.

The management floor smells like a gentleman's club, of tobacco and leather cream. Hours pass like weeks up here, to Toby's frustration. 'They're dinosaurs, Brains,' he used to whisper to me over lunch in the canteen. 'They think the Internet is a flash in the pan, for fuck's sake, and they laughed till they wet their tweed trousers when they learned John Lewis had *wasted their money on a silly website.*'

Toby. His threat to call the police on me definitely wasn't hollow. I hope Grazia knows what she's doing.

I turn into the corridor that leads to the board-room. Hilary, long-suffering PA to the directors, looks up from her *Woman and Home*. The first person to recognise me. I hold my breath.

'Ah, Sandra,' she says, as though she'd last bumped into me only yesterday. 'Mr Garnett and his guests are expecting you.'

I hardly dare to breathe. Guests? I imagine a line-up of Toby and Marsha and a few beefy members of the Metropolitan Police, and my courage fails me. My hand trembles as I reach for the door knob.

She gets up from behind her desk and walks to the door. A whiff of Patou's Joy wafts towards me and her hand rests on my shoulder for a second. 'Nothing to be afraid of, dear.'

Hilary turns the door knob and ushers me through. Right at the other end of the boardroom, behind the enormous oak table, are Toby and Grazia and the HR Harpy. But no Marsha. And no police.

The door closes behind me. I'm still holding my breath as I walk the length of the room. *You're in the right*, I tell myself, *and if they don't see that, it doesn't matter any more.*

'Miss Barrow,' says the Harpy, po-faced as ever. 'Do sit down.'

'No. I think I'll stay standing, thank you,' I say, without knowing quite why.

Now I notice the items on the table. A silver tray with china teapot, sugar bowl with miniature tongs, a plate of Nice biscuits, and four cups. One for Toby, one for HR Harpy, one for Grazia and . . . one for me?

'Please,' says Toby. He won't look at me, but I hear it in his voice. It's all over. I feel quite faint and have to steady myself on a chair, before sinking into the worn leather seat. For a while, I can't really hear what HR Harpy is saying; there's a high-pitched hum in my ears.

'. . . to thank Mrs Leon for bringing this to our attention, although the slightly unorthodox methodology does concern me a little.'

'She was hardly going to confess any other way, was she?' Grazia stands up and plonks the loathed mock-croc-bag camera on the table. She sets it going and Marsha's voice fills the room, its whininess amplified by the wooden panelling. It makes me feel nauseous.

'. . . *all I had to do was borrow her locker key and hide the money inside. Goodbye Little Miss Perfect.*'

Toby is staring at me. 'I'm so sorry,' he mouths. I look away.

'. . . *you really are very, very devious, aren't you, Marsha?*'

'*Why, thank you . . .*'

Grazia leans over and switches the bag off. 'We would not want to wear out the tape, hah?'

'Under the circumstances,' Harpy says, her lips twisting as she speaks, we were planning to sack Miss Delaney. However, it would appear she has already resigned. Which, given the possible accusations of entrapment that this recording could prompt, may be the best outcome.'

'Right.' I mumble, struggling to keep up.

'It goes without saying,' Harpy continues, 'that you are reinstated with immediate effect. Subject to board approval, which I am sure will be a formality, we will meet your full salary for the months when you were on your . . . sabbatical. Some form of mutually agreed bonus will also be forthcoming, in recognition of the stress you have experienced. Although, as I am sure you will agree, no one but Miss Delaney is in any way culpable. We were acting on strong evidence, Miss Barrow. You would have done the same in our position.'

Harpy smiles twitchily, awaiting my acquiescence. Grazia raises her eyebrows. I feel nothing.

'I need to think.'

Harpy twitches again, her pinched face a picture of discomfort. 'It is important to us to get this settled, so if it helps your decision then we could also build in a further leave of absence. A month off, on full pay . . . two months, even.' Then she reaches into her briefcase and pulls out an identity card. *My* identity card, with the photograph of me from the day I joined the company, the card she confiscated before Christmas. She pushes it across the table. I wait for satisfaction to kick in, for the new-found power to make me feel euphoric. But there's nothing except emptiness. It's as though I've belatedly discovered that I won one of the postal chess games Gramma made me play as a kid, long after it ceased to have any relevance to my life.

Toby stands up. 'Would you mind if I asked the others to leave, Miss Barrow? I'd like to speak to you alone. Only if you're happy with that, of course?'

I nod dully. Grazia winks at me as she passes, while the HR Harpy bustles off, murmuring to herself about protocol.

The heavy door closes. Toby pulls out the chair next to me. His floppy fringe has gone, replaced by a blond crop. *'I need to look serious,'* I imagine him telling his barber, *'older, more responsible.'* Actually, it makes him look more like a boy-band singer than ever.

'Sandie, before I say anything else, I want to tell you how sorry I am.' He's not looking at me.

'For what, exactly?'

He squirms in his seat and focuses on the table. 'Well, for not believing you. For being disloyal. For letting my own hang-ups influence how I responded to you. For judging you . . .' he glances up. 'Shall I keep going? I don't blame you for wanting me to sweat.'

'Funnily enough, Toby, this isn't all about you.'

He sighs. 'No. No, of course not. Typical of me to bring it back to myself. But it's all been so sudden, you see. Lot to get my head around.'

'I've had eight months to get used to it myself.'

'Yes. I know. I still can't believe someone could be so conniving. I only wish the stupid bitch hadn't resigned. I'd have liked to sack her myself.'

I stand up. 'Is that how you talk about all your girlfriends?'

'Girlfriends? Oh, no. I realised pretty quickly that she was a gold-digger. But I blame myself for not realising she was a scheming liar into the bargain. To tell you the truth, I thought she was rather dim.'

I suppress a grin. 'I think it's possible to be cunning *and* stupid at the same time.'

'Indeed. But it's also clear that my judgement sucks, isn't it?'

I decide not to answer that one.

'Sandie, listen. I do know that we should have tried harder. Investigated the situation a bit more. The only person who did that was poor old Luis. Every time he saw me he would plead your case. In the end he resigned. Said he couldn't continue working for a company that had got it so wrong.'

'No!'

''Fraid so. He might want his job back, now. That's if you come back too, of course.'

I walk over to the window, look down at the service yard where vans in crimson Garnett's livery are being loaded with the best goods in the world, from the best store in the world. I feel wistful for the days when this meant everything to me, and fond of the Sandie who arrived here full of dreams. 'I thought coming back here, clearing my name, would be the best feeling in the world.'

'And isn't it?'

'Not exactly.'

441

'The best way to undo the damage is to come back for good. We need you. I need you. It just isn't the same place without your retail theories and your big ideas and your amazing range of perfumes.'

I'm glad I'm not looking at him, because my face flushes. 'The edifice doesn't seem to have crumbled in my absence.'

'Only weeks away, I assure you,' says Toby.

'And what about poor Luis and his Dulche de Leche sandwiches?'

Toby frowns. 'I'd be lying if I said I was missing *him*. Apart from anything else he's not my type.'

I laugh awkwardly, and silence descends. I turn round and Garnett ancestors look down from the walls, the familial fair hair too frivolous for those sombre paintings. Were they in the society pages too, the search for a wife documented by gossip columnists? Or is that just Toby?

It would be so easy to tell him how it felt, to show him how hurt I was, how lonely I felt, how devastating it was to be all washed up. But I won't. I have always had my pride. Gramma would approve.

Toby gets up and comes towards me. 'Please, *please* tell me if there's anything I can do. I mean, we go back a long way, don't we?'

'That's what I always thought. Until last year,' I say.

'Ouch. I guess I deserved that.'

'Some things haven't changed, though, have

they? You still only acknowledge me when we're alone.'

He looks baffled. 'Eh? I don't follow.'

I sigh. 'Don't you? Think about it, Toby. Lunches as far away from Garnett's as you could get. Briefings before the board meetings. There was nothing to stop you bringing me in, just once, to give me the chance to explain my own ideas.'

'But . . . but I always thought that was what you wanted. You hated the limelight, Sandie.'

'Is that why you virtually ignored me on the shop floor too?'

'I didn't! Did I? Really?' He shakes his head. 'Fuck, Sandie. I never realised. Well, we can put that right this minute. Come on. I'll take you downstairs. Call a staff meeting. Tell them how important you've been. Let's face it, Garnett's could afford to lose a dozen of me. But the store needs you.' He strides over to the door.

'Toby, wait.' And I realise that being borne aloft over the heads of my colleagues in a victory parade is not what this is about. This is about quietly being in the right. No more, no less. 'It won't make a difference. I'm not coming back, Toby.'

He doesn't say anything for a long time. I wonder whether he's heard me, but then he sighs again. 'I suppose I'm not surprised. Desperately disappointed, but not surprised. I'd like to argue with you, but I have no doubt our loss will be someone else's gain. You'd be fabulous at Harrods. Or Selfridges. Or you could go to New York or Tokyo.

We were lucky to hang on to you for as long as we did.'

'You know, buttering me up isn't going to change my mind.'

'I know, but I still mean every word. Obviously you'll get a reference and a half from us. But sometimes you need to go elsewhere for people to see your true worth.' He looks away, then at me again. 'Nice to have you back, even ever so briefly.'

Over Toby's shoulder, his ancestors keep an eye on him. Suddenly I feel rather sorry for him. I can walk away from Garnett's and its stuffy self-righteousness, but he can't. In his situation, perhaps I'd take to hanging round Bouji's too.

'Thank you, Toby.'

'In the meantime . . . how would you feel about some consultancy? Paid at the highest rates, of course, and with full credit for your ideas. No more hiding your light under a bushel. We'd have lunch, like the old days, except you'd invoice me afterwards. We could go to Paris or Shanghai. Research. See how they do things there.'

'I'm going home. To Birmingham.' But even as I hear my own words, I know I'm not going back. Toby might not have been right about Marsha, but maybe he's right about me. With an A-plus reference, I could go places. The world is my shop floor.

'Birmingham? Fuck. I didn't know things had got that bad.'

'Oi! I like it there.' But it's almost a relief to

hear him being offensive again. Apologetic doesn't suit him.

'I don't believe for one second that Birmingham will be enough for you. Garnett's is in my blood, but I get a funny feeling it's in yours, too.'

I pause. 'Maybe. But actually, there's something you need to do. Find Luis. Offer him his job back.'

'He won't come unless he knows we've resolved things with you.'

'Ring me if you find him, and I'll talk to him,' I say, knowing it's leaving the door ajar for Toby to call. And for the first time in months, I feel just the tiniest bit excited.

'I will find him, Sandie. Promise.'

I pick up the identity card on the desk. Me, twenty-one years old, eyes wide with hope. I put the card in my pocket, and my fingers close around the garnet necklace Toby gave me. It feels warm in my hand. 'I'd better go, Toby. But I know we'll speak again.'

Just as soon as I've got my head round having my future back . . .

CHAPTER 34

GRAZIA

My hotel room is not pretty. Charlie's overnight assignments are usually at more salubrious places than this travelling salesman's haunt, but then again there is no incentive for him to look after me any more.

My report will not be favourable. There is a musty smell, with a curious top note of lager. The carpet has a violent pattern in blues and purples to disguise stains, and the kettle is so heavily scaled that it takes ten minutes to boil enough water for a tiny, strong, instant coffee. I slept in my dressing gown and socks, even though it is thirty degrees outside, to avoid making direct contact with the bed sheets. I say slept. I barely slept at all.

But the view. Oh, the view! It is Mary Poppins' London, seen from the sky (or, in fact, from the twelfth floor of the hotel's tower block). I see rooftops and chimneys, here and there a tiny balcony with a box tree or geraniums. At four in the morning there were still lights on, jewels of life keeping me company. The country is darker than the grave.

I dress in a Missoni knitted tunic, white skirt.

No widow's weeds for me, I do not care what people think. This compulsion to wear colour is new. It makes me feel alive.

I assess the presentation of anaemic bacon and eggs, read the *Telegraph* (which has an excited preview of the auction) and then, at last, it is time. I check out of the hotel – and out of secret shopping for good. Of course, I could have booked myself into a suite at the Hempel last night, given Selina's estimate of profits, but somehow it felt right to mark this transition with my last ever assignment.

My cab travels one hundred yards before the traffic stops dead.

'Bloody roadworks,' the driver says. 'Bloody Ken Livingstone.'

Nothing moves. It has taken me two years to find the courage to sell, only to be kept from the sale by roadworks. My absence will not halt the march of commerce. But I do feel I am letting Leon down.

I tap on the screen. 'Thank you, but I will walk.'

He shrugs. 'It's a good mile.'

'And how long might it take in the cab?'

'Yeah, well, not my fault, is it?'

I pay him and climb out. Traffic on the pavement moves much more swiftly, though the heat is oppressive. Sweat forms on my brow and I imagine my foundation is beginning to run. I shall hardly present a dignified picture, but nothing is more important than being there.

Faster. Faster. I stumble on a paving stone, but right myself in time. Finally, I catch sight of the Georgian house where the auction is being held. Outside are my motley crew, waiting for me just as they did seven months ago on the platform at Beechford station. Are they older? Wiser? Emily's face is as mournful as a spaniel's, and Sandie does not look like a woman whose reputation has been restored. Only the irrepressible Freddie is in a mood to match our moral victory over Marsha, jabbering away in words ending 'eee'. More often than not, this word is *Will-ee* and each time he says it, his mother flinches slightly.

'I was so worried you weren't going to make it,' Emily says. 'I think they're about to start.'

We walk into the building, and I take ten deep breaths before I enter the saleroom. I begin to panic: what if Selina has misjudged the situation, and there is no one beyond that panelled door but a few disgruntled journalists?

'You can't stay here for ever,' whispers Sandie. 'Through there is your future.'

'I thought it was my past.'

'If I worked anything out at Garnett's yesterday, it's that the two are pretty much inseparable for most of us.'

With this, she pushes the door open and I see rows and rows of people, dozens seated, still more gathered at the back. The auctioneer and three heavies face me, along with twenty of Leon's pieces. But I do not see the paintings themselves.

I remember the times when he was working on each one. The winter we first met, when every moment seemed snow bright. Two springs later, when he insisted we move to Paris for his 'Left Bank' phase, even though I had only just arrived in London and was desperate to experience the city of my dreams.

The auctioneer nods an acknowledgement and people stare at me, nudging each other. Selina gestures to join her in the front row, where she's reserved me a seat. But there is no space there for Sandie or Emily or Freddie in his buggy, so I stay where I am.

'Lot two is an early abstract in gouache, entitled *News*. Vivid greens and blues are combined to produce a mesmerising effect.'

Leon painted it over three hot August weeks in St Ives, when I thought I might be pregnant. He did at least wait until we knew I was not – or was no longer – to tell me that he did not want children with anyone: his work needed to be number one.

The bidding begins in the high four figures and quickly passes the reserve of fifteen thousand. I was all for not setting reserves: having decided to sell, it seemed of no consequence how much I would get for them, the catharsis was more important. But Selina was adamant.

The bidders are no longer interested in me, so I can survey them more closely. Despite the August heat, almost everyone is swathed in black,

449

which may fuel sales, as Leon's colours come alive in contrast to the monochrome. The gallery has managed to exclude the hangers-on and the curious, so the mood is focused. Feverish.

As the bids float towards fifty thousand – even allowing for commission, that's half my mortgage arrears paid off from a single picture – I recognise a few people. There is the collector who used to come to every exhibition, wanting to buy the largest piece regardless of quality. Leon turned him down every time. 'Where do you think your obsession with size might come from?' he used to joke, looking down on the poor man, five feet eight in his Cuban heels. And over there is the stupidest dealer in London, a forty-something red-head who once dated Prince Edward and has been trading on that spurious royal connection ever since.

My eye is drawn towards a woman in the second row from the front. Her perfect butter-blond bob moves now and then, like a wave in a rockpool. I cannot recall how I know her: all I can summon up is a strong feeling of discomfort. Then the head turns, and the pinched features of the woman behind the hair come into view. She gazes back, and it is as though we are engaged in a staring competition. Finally she shrugs defiantly and turns back.

Della. Yes, the cocky journalist who, in a roundabout way, began all of this. Perhaps she has come to reprimand me: Selina chose to organise all the press coverage without her.

I feel a tugging on my leg and look down to see Freddie playing with the strap on my sandal. What would life have been like if I had stayed pregnant in St Ives? I am pretty certain I *was*, just that once. Would my life be better with a teenager to share my grief? After that one near miss, Leon made it clear that he expected me to 'find a way' to make sure such mundane concerns would no longer intrude.

The bidding finishes, and *News* is sold to someone at the end of a telephone in Berlin. Sixty-five thousand pounds. I have no ideas for spending this money, beyond halting the letters from the bank. My plan is to retreat to Rose Cottage, to lick my wounds. So why does that not fill me with excitement?

Two more pieces are sold – another abstract, painted the morning after a drunken episode at the Groucho, described by the auctioneer as *visceral* (I would describe it as dyspeptic). And one completely unlike anything else he ever did, a line drawing of a tree uprooted after the storms of 1987, as perfect as any botanical drawing. It only just clears its reserve, selling for three thousand, and for a moment I want to buy it back and with it, buy back that October day when we searched for *beauty in destruction, Grazia.*

But I do nothing. I do not trust myself to move; the heat makes me faint. People are shuffling in their seats. I watch as Della stands up to remove her black jacket, turning to look right at me before sitting down again. The neck of her dress falls low, revealing bony vertebrae that draw the eye down her scrawny back.

Towards a tattoo.

A tattoo of roses.

The auctioneer's voice is unbearably loud. My lungs stop working, but my legs carry me out of the room, down the corridor and out onto the street where I lean over the railings and retch, like a drunken lout. I fight for breath and finally it returns to me and I take great gulps, which make me feel sicker still.

Sandie has followed me outside. 'What's happened?'

But I do not have a chance to explain because behind her I see Della, skipping down the steps from the auction house in kitten heels. She walks towards me, face unreadable.

'We should talk,' she says and passes me, confident I will follow.

In an empty basement bar, we both order glasses of red wine, and sit on opposite sides of a low table in a dark corner. It is too dim in here to compare tattoos, even if we wanted to.

'It's not really about the money, you know,' she says, in that mannered drawl I loathed even before I knew what she had done. Though is it possible that I *did* know, deep down, that there was more to Leon's roses than a flash of inspiration?

'Are you actually a journalist, Della? Or was that a ruse, too?'

She sighs. 'Freelance. Though when I met Leon I was a staffer on *The Times*.'

'And when was that?'

'First time? 1998, I suppose. But nothing much happened for a few years.'

'Nothing much?'

Della wipes the lipstick off her glass with her little finger. 'Idle flirtation. You know what he was like.'

She is speaking as though we are friends comparing notes on an old conquest. 'No. I do not know. Tell me.'

'Come on, Grazia. It's OK if call you that? Madame Leon seems so formal, now, under the circumstances. Or should that be Mrs Smith?'

'Call me what you wish.'

'Look. Everyone knew what he was like. I saw him flirt with women, actually with men too, just for the sake of it, right under your nose. It didn't mean anything.'

'I suspect that if that were true, we wouldn't be sitting here now.'

She shrugs. 'Fair point. Let me rephrase. Ninety-nine per cent of the time it meant nothing. It was his game, wasn't it, that thing middle-aged men do to reassure themselves they haven't lost it.'

'I am not sure this is getting us very far, Della. When did you become *intimate* with my husband?'

'I forget. Remind me when you built your house?'

Rose Cottage. The roses around the door were

not Leon's creation after all. They were only ever a copy of some cheap tattooist's work on some cheap slut's back. Someone else's roses. And I will be reminded of that every time I enter my home, even now *Muse 7* is gone. Or whenever I undress. It hurts to breathe. 'Christmas 2001.'

'Right, well, it would have been that autumn then. It's not like I've ever been shy about showing my tattoo, but I doubt it would have inspired a wall painting *and* an enormous canvas on the basis of a quick flash at an opening.'

I want to hit her. No, I want to smash this wine-glass against the table and drag it across her smug face and ask her how that rates as a piece of conceptual art. Instead I say, 'So you had a fling. Did it last?'

'Did any of us?' Then she laughs.

'I did,' I say, quietly.

'Oh, I don't mean *you*,' she says. 'You were the wife, weren't you? It might seem funny to you, but I respect that. I meant the other girls. The multiple muses of Leon.' Then she laughs again.

For a moment, everything goes black. But only for a moment: I will not let her see my weakness. 'How many?'

'Are you serious? How should I know? Surely you'd have a better idea than me.'

I close my eyes and see myself sitting in that tattoo parlour, crushing a photograph of the roses design between my fingers, as the artist pierced my skin, drawing my blood with his thorns and

454

petals. *Did* I understand, as I pretended all was perfect, that Leon was seeking inspiration elsewhere?

When I open my eyes, she is staring at me. I want to be out of here, far away from her chilly scrutiny. 'The phone calls. Were they you?'

She wrinkles her nose. 'Um. Yes. I was grieving too, you know.'

So there was someone who shared my grief, after all. 'OK, Della. If this is not about money, what do you want from me?'

'I read some piece,' she says, frowning, 'some nauseating profile written just before he died, where he talked about how the roses came into his head, a vision. How *you* then made them real by having the tattoo. It was a lie. I want people to know that.'

'Isn't it enough that *I* know? Or do you want to become famous, hanging onto Leon's coat-tails?'

She scowls. 'Earlier on, I said it wasn't *really* about the money. But money helps, doesn't it, to heal pain?'

'I must confess I do not think it will help me, but still . . . how much healing are you hoping for? In cash terms.'

'The cost of a painting.'

I try to think straight. What is it worth to protect Leon's reputation? '*Which* painting?'

'I'd have thought that would be obvious.'

'You want the proceeds of *Muse 7*?'

And then, of course, it hits me. *Muse 7*. The

455

seventh muse. How stupid have I been? Seven muses, seven women who inspired him. And countless others too disposable to merit a mention.

You can know something for decades without ever acknowledging it.

'It seems only fair,' she says smoothly.

My anger at her arrogance dissipates and all that is left is irritation. 'Fair?'

She finishes her wine. 'You will probably need time to think about it. I can give you until Monday.'

I smile at her. 'Actually, that will not be necessary.'

'No?' She reaches into her handbag, pulls out an envelope and hands it to me.

'What's that?'

'My bank details,' she says. 'I'd prefer a same-day transfer, once the funds have been transferred from the auction, though I appreciate there may be a short wait.'

'I think you will find there will be a long wait.'

'Not in my experience. Auction houses are pretty quick off the mark.'

'But widows are not.' I stand up, and put the envelope back on the table. 'There will be no money from me, Della. Do your worst. Flash your tattoo. Pose centrefold in *Playboy* for all I care. People will see you for what you are. Leon was no angel, but he had talent. He will be remembered for the right reasons. Will you?'

And before she thinks of a smart answer. I leave the bar, running up the basement steps and taking great gasping gulps of fresh, dirty, London air.

Dealers cluster around the entrance to the auction house, puffing on longed-for cigarettes. Selina rushes forward to embrace me as I walk up the steps.

'Grazia. Where *were* you? One moment you were the absolute centre of attention, the next you'd disappeared into bloody thin air. Where is your sense of theatre?'

'Cut to the chase, Selina. What did it fetch?'

Her kohled eyelids open wide. '*Double* what we'd hoped for, darling, double! You are one rich woman.'

And so are you. 'But who was the winning bidder of *Muse 7*?'

And then I spot the diminutive Korean collector beaming from ear to ear, and I feel a perverse satisfaction at his success. I imagine Leon's reaction and cannot help smiling.

'So, what are your plans, Grazia, darling? You should have a party. And not at your middle-of-nowhere cottage, either. London's the place to be!'

I am about to make some excuse, to insist that I am not in party mood, that I can not imagine anything more inappropriate. But then I hear him. *Your turn now, Grazia.*

Of course, the voice is not real. I steady myself on the railing, and look down at the street. A portly traffic warden smiles as she tickets a Bentley. A footballer's wife type with blond streaks and caramel skin totters past on killer heels, dragged along by a super-confident Pomeranian dog. Bidders and art dealers chatter in different languages: German, Russian, Korean, and a dozen more I do not recognise. These are people who shared my dreams of the city of Monopoly streets.

This is where I belong. I always did. It is time to come home.

'Maybe you are right, Selina. Perhaps I will have a party. It has been a while since I have seen the old gang.'

'That's my girl,' she says, and it is probably only the euphoria at the profit she has just made, but there is a wry satisfaction in her Botoxed face that seems genuine. 'Welcome back.'

She air kisses me again and leaves me with my thoughts and my memories. *It is my turn now*, I tell Leon in my head. *Goodbye, Mr Smith. It was a pleasure. Most of the time.*

Did I love him? Undoubtedly. Was he worthy of my love? Of course. I made my choices. He was imperfect, yes. But perfection is only found on canvas.

Goodbye too, *Muse 7*. May you make your new owner at least as happy as your value is going to make me. Money cannot buy you happiness, but it can buy you freedom, and now I intend to make the most of mine.

CHAPTER 35

EMILY

'Wakey-wakey, Fredster. It's moving day!' Freddie opens his sleep-crusted eyes, a very grown-up expression of suspicion on his crumpled face. Maybe he can see through my sunny Girl Guide act. I'll admit it's not all that convincing.

I dress him in dungarees and a checked shirt – 'like a proper little removal man!' – and make us both breakfast, using a packing case as a temporary kitchen table. There hasn't been much to pack. My wardrobe back home won't be bursting at the seams with designer purchases from New Bond Street. I won't be filling up the bathroom cabinet with beauty buys from Jo Malone or Amanda Lacey. Most of the stuff in the boxes is the same stuff I hauled up the M4 fifteen months ago. The only glamorous items – a cashmere hot water bottle, a £25 lipstick – are booty from secret-shopping expeditions. They don't really fit my old life, but I will keep them in a box, occasionally taking a peek, to remind myself that this was all real.

At least I have some stories to tell my friends.

Not quite the ones I'd imagined – no Notting Hill lunches with Thandie and Gwyneth, no gate-crèching into the closed circle of West London yummy mummies.

But I wouldn't swap a moment with Sandie and Grazia for a dozen name-dropping encounters. I just wish . . .

'If wishes were horses, then beggars would ride,' I sing-song to Freddie and he cackles a reply.

'Horseee!'

The door bell goes as I am clearing the break-fast things.

'How's it going?' Sandie gives Freddie a big hug, then looks around. 'What can I help with?'

'You know, it's pretty much done. Apart from the few bits of furniture, and the carnival boys are going to take care of that.' Right now, Duncan's dad and a couple of cronies from the Old Devils' Club are travelling from Somerset to transport our rubbish sofa and crap mattress back home.

'Don't they need to leave some furniture, make the place look lived in?' she asks.

I put the kettle on. 'Oh, Duncan's sorted that too. He's employed this company of home-stagers, whatever they are, to bring in funkier furniture. With a "luxe retro vibe", apparently.' However hard I try, I can't seem to keep the bitterness out of my voice.

'He's done well to organise it all at such short notice,' she says carefully.

The kettle boils and switches itself off. 'Mmm.'

The idea that he planned this keeps popping into my head. But it's ridiculous. Even if the Latvians accidentally let the cat out of the bag about the flat renovation. Duncan could never have predicted that I'd mess everything up by sleeping with Will. I couldn't have predicted it myself. 'I don't want to think about it, Sandie. Much more interesting to talk about your future. So, what are you going to do?'

'I'm still going home at the weekend, but . . . well, I reckon it's going to be a fleeting visit. Apart from anything else, I want to be around when Toby finds Luis, to thank him for sticking up for me. And to make sure he gets his job back.'

'Very laudable,' I say, 'but what about *your* job?'

'Well, a back-pay cheque from Garnett's arrived this morning, which means I won't have to be rushing too much to find a new job. I can put down a deposit to rent a new flat, take my time. And I might just do a little consultancy for Toby, keep things ticking over.'

'But you haven't changed your mind? You're definitely not going back?'

'Working for Charlie broadened my horizons, Emily. Who'd have thought it, eh? A shitty secret shopping gig changed my life.' She looks at Freddie. 'Sorry.'

'He'll hear worse when Duncan's dad turns up.' I make tea, wondering how many hundred cups I'll have brewed before the day is out. 'Won't you miss Garnett's?'

'I won't miss the store . . . but I might miss the people,' she says, avoiding my eye.

'The people? Or one person in particular?' I stare at her until she looks up. She giggles, and it makes her look much younger. 'One person like Toby, for example?'

'How did you guess?'

'It wasn't hard. Love makes the world go round, you know, Sandie.'

She frowns. 'I don't think I'd call it *love*. But in the boardroom I did feel, for the first time, that we really were equals. And that there might be more between us. Oh, I don't know why I just told you that. I'm sure it's my imagination.'

'Why?'

'Because he goes for dolly-birds and breast-enhanced bimbos, that's why. Because our backgrounds couldn't be more different. Because he'd be ashamed to introduce me to his parents . . .'

'Whoa. Hang on. Aren't you jumping the gun a bit?'

'I've always been a planner. I introduced SWOT analysis to Garnett's board.'

'SWOT?'

'Strengths, weaknesses, opportunities, threats.'

I shake my head. 'You're something else, Sandie Barrow. I suggest you try ODAAT instead.'

'ODAAT?'

'One day at a time! Get him to take you for lunch. Suss him out. Drop hints about mixing business with pleasure.' I wince as I remember

Will saying the same to me. No danger of that. 'See how he reacts.'

'I couldn't possibly!'

'Sandie, you've had your job stolen, you've gone undercover, you've outsmarted Mad Marsha. Live dangerously for once. There's nothing to stop you.' Like I am one to talk . . .

She sighs. 'We'll see. Oh!' She reaches into her handbag and pulls out a gift-wrapped box. 'A going away present.'

'I wish you hadn't; I'm emotional enough already!' I tear off the glossy paper: it's a palm-sized video recorder. 'Wow! Look, Freddie. This must have been expensive – you really shouldn't have.'

'Think of it as a gift from Garnett's,' she says. 'It's not exactly a *secret* camera, but I thought it was small enough to fit in your changing bag so you can video young Freddie when you're out together. And it's got a wireless link so you can email the footage. A way of keeping us up to date on the Little Londoner's progress!'

'You will come and see me, won't you?' I feel lonely, though that's ridiculous. I'm heading home to friends, family, the people who've known me since I was smaller than Freddie.

'Of course,' Sandie says. But she won't, will she? That's what people always say, but a hundred and fifty miles might as well be a thousand.

I stand up and give her a huge hug.

'Meeeee!' says Freddie, and I hug him too. I

won't ever really be alone, will I? That's something to be thankful for.

Grazia arrives in a cloud of expensive perfume. She wears a floaty emerald dress, and it's clear she has no intention of doing anything practical to help with the move.

'There is a large trailer decorated with blue glittery paint blocking the road,' she says as she steps inside. 'I guessed it might have something to do with you.'

I race to the window. Sure enough, the Old Devils' Poseidon Adventure float is outside, thankfully minus the Shelley Winters lookalike and two-man giant octopus costume. Angry drivers are queuing in both directions, though there's nowhere for the trailer to go. I won't miss the impotent impatience of London life.

Grazia kisses me, Freddie and Sandie, and then flounces around the flat. It's not just the scent and the coloured clothes: here is a completely different presence from the glowering figure I first met in January. I don't know how it happened, but the ghost of Leon has left for good and I would lay bets that this merry widow won't be alone for long.

'So. You are going through with this terrible retreat?'

'Yup,' I say. 'I ought to nip outside and say hello to my father-in-law.'

'One moment, Emily. One question. Would you tell Freddie to give in to bullies?'

'Well, he's not really old enough to be picked on yet, thank goodness.'

'Pah! A minor point. My question stands.'

'No. Of course I wouldn't.'

'Children copy their parents. So how can you offer him such a dreadful example?'

I sigh. 'Look, Grazia, I know you don't approve of what I'm doing, but it's bloody easy to give advice, isn't it? Particularly when you've just made the best part of two million quid from a bunch of paintings.' I move towards the door.

She stands in my way. 'Your husband is a bully, Emily. The reason I can see this so clearly is that my husband was, too. Mine had talent and passion to compensate, of course – something Duncan lacks.'

'He's always been good at mental arithmetic.'

'Pfft! I shall ignore that. Emily, I wish you to learn from my errors. My husband kept me isolated, so I had no friends to point out that though he made the rules, he broke them too.'

Someone must have told her about the other women. 'What rules?' I ask warily.

'The rules of exclusivity. My husband, it seems, required more than one muse.' She stares at me. 'You do not look very surprised.'

Too late, I try to look shocked. 'That's terrible.'

'The woman in Beechford Stores told you; am I right? Everyone knew but me. In fact, I think I knew, too, but would not admit it to anyone, least of all myself. If I had had a friend, a confidante, to challenge me, then maybe—' Grazia stops

465

abruptly. 'Ah, who knows? This is not about me. It is about you.'

'So what would you do in my position, then? Ignore the threats – which I know he's capable of carrying out, by the way; he's got all his dad's ruthlessness – and risk losing Freddie?'

'He would never persuade a judge to grant him custody on the basis of a single night you spent with another man, Emily. And say that single night led to more nights? William Powell is a man who could charm a thousand matrimonial judges. Stable. Kind. Resourceful. A thousand times the father Duncan is.'

I push the thought of more nights with Will out of my head. 'You're missing the point. London was nothing but a fantasy for me. I am a country bumpkin.'

'Charlie would not have allowed a country bumpkin to take over my contract. I would not have suggested you. You cannot allow yourself to be—'

'Well, *hello*, ladies! Not interrupting anything, am I?' Steve Prince, off-licence and carnival baron, steps into the flat. 'This place scrubbed up well, didn't it?'

'Hello Steve,' I say. 'Grazia, Sandie, this is my father-in-law.'

The girls snarl out of loyalty to me.

'Oh, it's like that, is it?' he says. 'Sins of the sons visited on the fathers, eh? And no thanks for dragging our arses to London in the slow lane of the M4 to ferry you home.'

466

I sigh. 'I suppose you want tea, do you? You and the boys?'

'If you're sure it isn't too much trouble.' He disappears again.

'What an obnoxious man,' says Grazia. 'There is still time to tell him to turn around and take his ugly trailer back home. I would be more than happy to do it on your behalf.'

'Stop trying to confuse me, Grazia. If you keep on at me I might have to ask you to leave.' *I just need today to be over, then I'll be OK.*

'Before you throw me out,' she says, 'I have something for you.'

'Not you as well.'

'How gracious.'

'Sorry. I'm emotional, and presents make me feel sad.' I take the small box from Grazia: it's heavy in my hand. I untie the satin ribbon holding the lid in place, and look inside. Multiple edges of a huge diamond sparkle under the new kitchen spotlights and as I pull the tissue paper aside, I realise it's a gold ring. 'Bloody hell.'

'A friendship ring, if you like,' she says. 'Or, to look at it another way, a ticket back to London, any time you need it. It is vintage, so it will keep its value, in case you need to trade it in for a new ring. Or a new life.'

'I can't take this, Grazia. You know I can't.' I try to give it back, but she holds her hands behind her back.

'There is nothing more insulting than rejecting

a gift, Emily. Take it, in the spirit in which it is given.'

'But it must have cost—'

'Money is of no consequence to a woman who, as you said, has just made the best part of two million quid from a bunch of paintings.'

I realise it's time to give in gracefully. 'Thank you, Grazia. And Sandie. I couldn't have survived in London this long without you two, you know that, and . . .'

I realise that my touching speech is being ignored, that the secret shoppers are looking over my shoulder. I turn to see a hairy bloke holding a mallet, with several estate agent signs wedged under his armpit.

'Just checking I got the right place. Duncan Prince's flats, yeah? I've got some For Sale signs to stick up outside.'

What Steve and his cronies lack in finesse, they make up for in brute force. It takes them less than an hour to load my belongings onto the back of the trailer, securing them with tarpaulin and rope.

As they're finishing up, my mother arrives with the car. The Fredster and I get to travel back to Somerset in a little more comfort.

'So, where is my long-lost grandson?'

We go to the downstairs flat, where Sandie and Grazia are entertaining Freddie. My friends are drinking tea and watching *Jeremy Kyle*, looking surprisingly calm for two adults in charge of an irrepressible toddler.

'Freddie!' my mother calls. 'Where are you hiding?'

Sandie stands up. 'Isn't he upstairs with you?' she says, her voice rising in pitch.

'No.'

I hear a strangled cry which I realise is my own. Grazia leaps up from the chair, splashing hot tea all over her green dress, and as the stain spreads down her skirt, we run out of the front door, into the street . . .

It feels as though the world's gone silent, but I think it's because there's only one sound I want to hear and that's my son's voice. The others disperse in different directions, while I jog along the road, past the blue sparkly trailer, past the phone booth, newspaper headlines swimming before my eyes. MISSING! DISAPPEARED! WHERE IS LOST BOY FREDDIE? His photograph on the news, on the front pages.

Your past is meant to flash before your eyes when you die, isn't it, but my *future* is playing out every time I blink. Press conferences, missed birthdays, recriminations and an emptiness that consumes me. 'Freddie, Freddie?'

And then I see them. My lost boy – lost for two minutes or less, though it felt like years – in the arms of my one-night stand.

I sprint towards them. I take Freddie and drink in his scent and squash him in my arms until he begins to giggle, louder and louder. Then I join in, and I'm laughing and crying and laughing some more.

'He was sitting on the wall, six houses down, waving at the cat behind the window,' Will says. 'He looked quite happy but I guessed he was absent without leave.'

Mum and Sandie and Grazia catch up with us.

'I'm so sorry, Emily,' Sandie says. 'It was a misunderstanding. Please forgive us.'

Relief floods my system, making me light-headed. My mother kisses Freddie's cheeks and takes him from me just in time, because I really do feel extremely dizzy. I lean against the gate.

'Who's the rescuer, then?' Mum asks.

'Oh. This is Will. Will, my mother. Will is . . .' My brain's working no better than my legs.

'A friend,' he says.

My mother, ever vigilant, pulls a suspicious face. 'Better get Freddie inside before he tries another great escape.' She throws Sandie and Grazia murderous looks before heading into the flat.

I'm longing to follow my baby indoors, but I'm also longing to talk to Will. My jelly legs make the decision for me: I can't move them. 'What are you doing here, Will?'

He doesn't seem to hear the question. Perhaps I only said it in my head. Instead he says. 'I think we should take a walk, when you're up to it. Can you make it to the park?'

I'm about to say no, when I notice Steve clocking

our conversation. I reach out for Will to pull me up, and try to ignore the familiar tingly feelings this produces.

We don't say anything more until we reach the sorry scrub of land I call Dog Turd Park. We sit down on the bench opposite some empty swings, a gap between us. I daren't look at his face because I might lose my resolve.

'Why have you come?'

Will looks at his knees. 'Because we didn't say goodbye properly, and I'm not sure you meant what you said. Because I think you might be making a mistake and I don't want you to go and I especially don't want you to have to leave because of me—'

'It's not because of you.'

'You're not much of an actress, Farrah Fawcett.'

'No, really, it isn't.'

'Answer me this, then. How come you were all set for a new career as West London's top secret shopping guru, until your husband saw us together?'

'I was living in cloud cuckoo land. Duncan was never going to let me stay here.'

Will looks at me. 'Do I have your permission to be brutal?'

I shut my eyes. 'Why not? Everyone else has had their say lately.'

'Which is exactly my point. You're bright, you're a great mother, you're a coper, you're gorgeous—'

I giggle out of embarrassment. 'Is this the brutal bit?'

'I was getting to that. You really are a fantastic woman, Emily, but you're still acting like a little girl. Now, after spending thirty seconds with her, I'd say your mum seems pretty strong-willed and – if you can bear my thumbnail psychoanalysis – I reckon you went straight from your parents telling you what to do, to Duncan telling you what to do. The difference being that at least your mum and dad had your best interests at heart.'

It's not as though I've never heard the same thing before, from Grazia and Sandie, even back home from my friends. 'Have you finished?'

'For now. Though I might need to keep repeating it if I didn't make it clear enough.'

'I think I got the gist, thank you. *Grow up, Emily.* That was it, wasn't it?'

Will flinches. 'I like to think I put it more elegantly than that.'

'So, despite the fact that I've been on my own for nearly a year, looking after a house and a baby and a job, I'm not a grown-up?'

'That's the thing. You *were* grown-up. Then Mr Evil turns up, throws out a few idle threats, and bang, you're doing what someone else wants yet again. Even though what Duncan wants definitely isn't in your best interests.'

'Right.' I pretend to think it over. But I don't have to, do I? I know he's right. Sandie's right. Grazia's right. The trouble is, I don't have the guts to do the right thing. 'So, what am I supposed to do about it?'

A slow smile appears on his face, triggering a whole series of flashbacks in my head, some so X-rated that I feel my cheeks colouring. But the one that really gets my pulse racing is Will, asleep, wearing the same smile I see right now.

'Emily, if I told you what to do, I'd be just as bad as all the others. Though I do have two suggestions. One, get the beefy blokes to put your furniture back in the flat and sit tight for a while. Days. Weeks. However long it takes to decide what *you* want.'

'And what am I going to live on? Thin air? You saw what Duncan was like. He wouldn't think twice before cutting off the maintenance. The secret shopping earnings help, of course, but they're not enough to pay the bills.'

'You know he can't do that legally.'

'OK, so what do I eat while I'm dragging him through the courts?'

'That's my second suggestion. How would you like to use your hard-won secret-shopping skills to advise a start-up shop? Pick the right product range. Help with the design. Consultancy pays well, too. More than enough to tide you over.'

'Yeah, right. And where do I find a plum job like that?'

Will smiles again, then reaches into his trouser pocket and brings out a large bunch of keys. 'Allow me to introduce you to the new proprietor of Bell's

Emporium, Heartsease Common's one-stop shop for . . . well, I don't quite know yet.'

'You bought the shop?'

'I've taken over the lease for three years.'

'Bloody hell. How did you afford it?'

'A loan from a friend who has come into some money.'

'You are crazy.'

He grins. 'Yup! Life's about taking risks, Emily, but mad leaps in the dark are an awful lot easier to take when you've got someone at your side. Expert advice. I am serious, you know. I need help. And there are no strings attached.'

'Oh, right.' I feel disappointed for a moment, I had let myself believe that Will had bought the shop just to woo me. Beats chocolates any day when it comes to grand romantic gestures.

'Though outside working hours, I'd like to think there might be scope for picking up where we left off.'

That's more like it. 'Have you worked out a system for clocking on and off?'

'I'm open to negotiation.'

'Oh, Will, it's a lovely idea, but it's too late.'

'It's not. Do you *want* to go back to Somerset, Emily? That's the only question that really matters. The rest can be sorted out later.'

I think about the country bumpkin who came to London full of hope that city magic could make all her dreams come true. OK, so I was naive to imagine that a place could do the work for me, but maybe the instinct was right. Somerset isn't the place for me to grow, to change. And perhaps London isn't, either.

Could Heartsease Common be the answer? I close my eyes. Can I picture myself behind the scenes, selling instead of shopping, unpacking boxes of goodies, Will and me in his 'n' hers matching aprons? Working together, living together, loving together.

Suddenly my vivid dreams of Oxford Street seem faded and flat, and I know where I want to be. And who I want to be with. The only other time I've ever felt so certain about anything was the first time I saw Freddie's face.

I stand up. 'Come on.'

He looks hopeful. 'Where?'

'To hover behind me, looking tough. I've got this hunch I might face a bit of resistance when I ask Steve and his cronies to unload my stuff off the van.'

His boyish face lights up. Then he catches my arm and I realise he's looking a lot less boyish. And rather a lot more all-man.

'Just before we go . . .'

'What?'

And then he kisses me. If anything, it's even more show-stopping than the first time.

'I wish you'd done that sooner,' I whisper.

'What, and be accused of trying to influence your decision?'

I answer him with another kiss.

HALLOWEEN

Our cousins across the Pond have embraced this ghostly festival with fervour – but Britons are catching up. Make spookiness your selling point: trick the kids, treat the mums. Halloween profits are nothing to be afraid of.

CHAPTER 36

EMILY

'So who is Mummy's perfect pumpkin, then?'

Poor Freddie. His frown-rumpled face is just visible through the pumpkin head – I've already had to bribe him with carrot sticks to pose for the press pictures. His costume is as round as a Terry's chocolate orange, although the familiar, babyish body underneath is already beginning to lengthen into a boy's slim frame. All the better for running and jumping and getting up to mischief.

Freddie is the star attraction for the official opening photocall at Bell's Emporium, Heartsease Common. Actually, we've been trading since September, but Grazia said we should maximise publicity by staging a special Halloween event. So to accompany the Freddie-pumpkin I am dressed as a witch, with my own Emporium broomstick, and Will . . .

'Miaow! Does this mean I get to curl up in your lap?'

'*Later*, tiger!'

Will is a black cat.

Our Halloween range is the very best in Berkshire. I have been touring suppliers, begging for stock, because as they never tired of telling me, 'You've left it terribly late; we take Halloween orders at Easter.' It's a steep learning curve, but I've discovered a persuasive streak, so the store has become a shrine to all that's homespun and wholesome about phantoms, devils and things that go bump in the night.

Bell's Emporium – named in honour of the original Mr Bell who started his empire right here nearly a century ago – stocks anything that's gorgeous or fun or indispensable for the home. It is, I will admit, a slightly risky concept, one that goes against most of what I learned in my secret shopping months. Except in one crucial respect: Will and I really care about the store, about the products, and most of all, about the customers. We're keeping everything crossed that our passion will attract shoppers who know they're headed for a treasure trove of retail delights.

Grazia's advised on marketing and put up some much-needed investment: a true shopping angel. Sandie's helped with stock, pricing and the all-important window displays: now the clocks have gone back, every tea-time the former Bells & Whistles store can be seen from half a mile away, glowing with demonic fire and fluorescent flying bats.

I love this time of year. At home, it's the carnival season. The theme of this year's Madcap Knights float is *Star Wars*, with the emphasis on wars. The violent theme is no coincidence: relations between the two carnival clubs in our town have taken a nosedive since my kerbside decision to send Steve packing. I suspect he wouldn't have been quite so incandescent if he hadn't landed himself a trailer-sized parking ticket while he was shouting at me.

Duncan was pretty incandescent himself. There were endless phone calls, insinuations, direct threats. But every time he called, I kept two images in my head. One was Emily the Little Mermaid, always waiting . . . for lifts, for life, for other people to make her decisions for her. Everybody's friend. And then there was Emily the Grown-up, grabbing opportunities, making choices. Nobody's fool.

Duncan kept up the pressure for weeks, until he finally realised I was no longer the docile creature he'd married. One day the calls just stopped, and for a while I dreaded the sound of the post dropping onto the doormat in case it was a legal letter about custody of Freddie. But eventually I realised it was over: my husband is a pragmatist and, as much as he'd like to make things difficult for me, he'll only do that if it doesn't involve too much effort. And bringing up Freddie full time involves effort. I should know.

I admit it's been easier since Will's been on the scene, though a boyfriend brings added complications. How serious *is* this, exactly? Grazia has this theory about 'Gateway Lovers', who reintroduce you to the world of dating: she's currently working her way through a few of her own. If Will is *my* gateway, then it's OK for him to behave like a favourite uncle, courting Freddie's affections with treats and tickles. But if there's a chance that the show-stopping snogs are leading to something longer-lasting, then he has to be tougher. Kids need boundaries. My little Londoner is too young for the naughty step, but I can see it's only months, if not weeks away.

I talked the whole issue through with Will, and left it up to him to decide. So I was secretly delighted the first time he told Freddie he had to finish his cherry tomatoes before he'd be allowed to go and play. Will stuck to his guns despite the howls of protest, and every single tomato was consumed.

That's true love.

I agonised over living together too. I spent almost all my waking hours at the Emporium through out August, but I didn't want to confuse Freddie, so we commuted between Lime Village and Heartsease for five exhausting weeks. And then, shortly after the cherry tomato incident, I realised I wasn't really trying to protect Freddie. I was trying to protect myself.

We moved into the cramped but cosy flat above the shop that same weekend.

Pumpkin-related humiliations aside, life for Freddie is pretty idyllic, though strangely not that different from my own childhood in Somerset. Since the Save Our Shop campaign, Heartsease has been turning into a village where everyone knows your name, and your business, but here I can turn that to my advantage, to get customers through the door. Anyway, Grazia says the only difference between networking and nosiness is the former happens in the city, the latter in the country.

Seems she prefers networking. She's sold Rose Cottage to a broody breakfast TV presenter and is moving back to London, to an unbelievably glamorous apartment in South Kensington. Her new neighbour is the rather sweet South Korean man who bought Leon's last painting. She's been to dinner with him a few times – 'nothing serious, but I have remembered how much I *adore* male company,' – and says *Muse 7* looks much better on his wall. She hasn't *said* she's happier – after all, Grazia was never one for confidences – but her clothes get brighter and brighter. She's abandoned secret shopping in favour of the normal kind, spending thousands on kitting out her new place.

It's Sandie who will continue to wield the Secret Shopping Sword of Justice. After a few long consultancy lunches with Toby, she realised that the knowledge she'd gained from Garnett's and Charlie's Shopping Angels could be the passport to a lucrative new career as a retail guru.

'I've learned my lesson, Emily,' she told me when she came to see the Emporium, mid-transformation. 'I gave Garnett's my loyalty for too long. At least if I work for myself, I see the benefits of working all hours. Like you.'

'Yes, but it is frightening. What if we get it wrong?' I said, looking around the dark shop, piled floor to ceiling with unopened boxes of stock.

'We're the shopping angels. We're invincible. And you can do a bit of secret shopping work for me until the shop takes off. There'll be no burger joints or pawn shops, either. I am going for the highest class of clientele.'

And, though she didn't say so, there's another reason why she doesn't want to go back to Garnett's. Sandie tagged along with Toby during the search for Luis: it took them three long nights of detective work to track him down and offer him his job back. I think that as they pounded the London streets, they finally began to see that the toff and the shop girl might just be made for each other.

'Yoo-hoo! Toffee-apple time!'

A vision in black crochet – Jean wearing her homespun spider outfit – appears in the doorway. Freddie's eyes widen in terror.

'Come on in.' I call her over, and the Fredster hides behind my legs until Will swoops him up in his black-cat arms and tickles him beyond terror.

'Oi, what about me?' I call, envious. And Will reaches out one arm to enclose me too.

I look into his eyes, their colour still as much of a mystery to me as the first day we met: some-times green, sometimes blue, right now glowing with a hint of amber. But always one hundred per cent Will.

'You know what, Will? You are the cat's whiskers!'

'And you, Emily, are an utterly bewitching creature.'

So, the country bumpkin turned into a bewitching creature and created her very own happy ending. Shopping can do that – transform your whole life – though not always in the way you expected.

And what of the mysterious Charlie? I never did see the face behind the silhouette on Grazia's computer screen. Somewhere he's still out there, searching for new angels, for women who believe shopping for a living might just change everything. Keep your eyes peeled. Next time, the happy ending might just be yours.

ACKNOWLEDGEMENTS

Like Emily, I find the idea of shopping more fun than shopping itself – maybe I was born without the retail gene. Reading about shops has to be the perfect compromise: cheaper *and* less stressful. If you're interested in the science of shopping, I recommend *Why We Buy*, and *The Call of the Mall*, both by Paco Underhill. For a more eclectic take on this pastime, *The Virago Book of the Joy of Shopping* is a great anthology, with historical and contemporary insight into the world of retail. India Knight's, *The Shops* is terrific fun, and I loved *Still Open: The Guide to Traditional London Shops* by Sally Venables, Steve Williams and Brian Benson, which features wonderful photographs of unique places to spend your money. *Time Out London Shops and Services* is comprehensive, tempting and only to be opened *after* pay day.

I am grateful as always to the many people at Orion who turn a vague notion and a Word document into a real book. Thank you to the reps for sales effort extraordinaire. Thank you to all the people involved in the truly lovely cover, especially Sidonie Beresford-Browne and Ruth Sharvell. I'd also like to thank Angela McMahon for pitching beyond the call of duty, Jade Chandler for keeping everything on track, and Juliet Ewers, Susan Lamb, Lisa Milton and Jon Wood for all their support and belief in the book. I'm so grateful to Kate Mills for helping me to develop the characters and the idea, and to Genevieve Pegg for clear-sighted guidance on how to wrestle it into shape.

Thanks to Araminta Whitley for common sense and inspiration in equal measure, and to Lucy Cowie for making things happen.

The best support network for a writer includes others who know the score. Thank you to fellow members of the Romantic Novelists' Association, the Novel Racers, the Bloggers with Book Deals and everyone on The Board. Special thanks to Linda Buckley-Archer, Matt Dunn, Jacqui Hazell, Jacqui Lofthouse, Sue Mongredien, Meg Sanders, Louise Voss and Stephanie Zia.

Thank you to Andrea, Alison, Caroline, Jean Eden, Lisa, Lucy, Sandro, Shelley, Trudi, and David and Diana Carter. Love to Geri and Jenny, Pat and Pete, Toni, Mum, Dad and Rich . . . and many apologies to anyone I might have forgotten.

Finally, and most importantly, many thanks to you for reading. You can get in touch via my website, www.kate-harrison.com.

Kate Harrison, March 2008